PANTHER IN THE HIVE

PANTHER
IN THE HIVE

OLIVIA A. COLE

CHICAGO HAS FALLEN. SHE WILL NOT.

For Omaun, Hope, and Natasha. My shining muses.

CHAPTER 1

In the silent, shiny world of prepackaged snacks and frozen entrees, the fruit is rotting.

Not all of it: the apples survive, the pears still defiant. But the avocados are caving in on themselves, the peaches developing sinking brown craters like eyes. Above, a solitary fly cruises the wasteland of abandon, enjoying the heat only rotting things can emit. The other side of Jewel-Osco is clean and silent: the deserted aisles are vast stretches of empty fluorescence, Chef Boyardee and Jemima beaming out at no one, motionless on the shelves, dust gathering on their tops. Digital advertisements flash and jerk next to the unmanned cash registers: a pearly smile here, a diagonal slash of a catch line there. No lines at the checkout, no one sampling crackers and cheese from plastic trays, no one standing before the digital tabloids, mesmerized by the rotating spectacle of abs. Silence. And among it all stands Tasha—just Tasha—knife in hand, Prada backpack over her shoulder, dead body at her feet. It's the fourth day.

The dead guy had been a Jewel employee, the only one left in the store, patrolling the aisles like a mindless attack dog. Taking a deep breath, Tasha leans down to poke the wound in his neck with the knife—just to be sure. The flesh makes a sound, sticky and moist like tape ripped from wet paint. But Tasha doesn't vomit, not this time. This is partially because she has stabbed enough necks this week to empty her stomach of bile, and partially because when she withdraws the blade, the Chip is skewered on its point. Her nausea is distracted by relief—he's not getting back up. Nothing else would have killed him, she's learned. Get the Chip, or say goodbye.

Focusing on the guy's face, she realizes she recognizes him from the meat counter before the Change—his name had been Rodney, or Ronald. Robert? His nametag had fallen off at some point, his identity under a shelf someplace collecting dust. Tasha remembers catching him staring at her boobs more times than she had fingers to count, before all this happened. She wishes she had cut him then; when it would've actually made an impression.

Satisfied the R-named butcher is dead, she stands from where she'd been crouching and wipes the knife's blade on her jeans, leaving a messy red stripe. She's done this before, hating to ruin the designer denim but preferring to stain her jeans rather than walk around with the knife dripping a trail of bloody breadcrumbs. The Minkers—psychos like the butcher here—would follow like sharks. Tasha re-shoulders the Prada backpack; special edition green canvas, leather straps, lots of little pockets. She bought it before the Change, and though it's probably not being used the way Miuccia intended, Tasha can't bear to leave it in her closet. It's too cute to wither away in the dark, even if the world has gone crazy.

Backpack on, she glances around. She had thought she would have time to leisurely poke around the store and gather a few supplies, but the butcher had popped up out of the shopping carts like a hellish jack-in-the-box and now taking her time is no longer an option. She has to hurry in case the commotion attracted the attention of any other Minkers in the area. It's one thing to stab a lone butcher's neck but another thing entirely to be confronted with a whole pack of them, drawn by the sound of their kin's call and whining like manic Chihuahuas. With this thought in mind, Tasha quickly gathers a bag of apples—*Organic*, she gloats, remembering the days when she had to pay $8.50 per pound—a few cans of beans, and a couple boxes of crackers. Cheese won't keep, she thinks mournfully, eyeing the still-refrigerated shelves of dairy products with longing, and skips that aisle for the one that contains boxes of granola and protein bars.

The long row of multi-colored boxes of fiber and energy bars stretches out before her and she feels the way Eve must have felt in the Garden—all those snacks to choose from. Tasha already grabbed the apples, so nothing is really forbidden at this point. She enters the aisle and breathes in the smell of unspoiled edibles.

"Preservatives," she says out loud, "praise you."

She puts the first box back—too much sugar—and settles

on Nature Valley. Her dad used to eat these. The green wrapper seems environmentally friendly, but that's unlikely. Regardless, the granola bars go into the Prada backpack with the apples and beans, and Tasha heads for the back door.

Sticking her head around the corner of an Employees Only doorjamb, FBI-style, Tasha pauses, listening and watching. She hears nothing, and there's nothing to see, so she continues through the doorway. The actual door has been torn off its swinging hinges and hangs crazily askew, blocking part of the little corridor. She notices the blood smearing one side of the small round window and tries not to wonder who it belonged to. It could be anyone's. Her friend Scout used to work here; it might be hers. Tasha figures it's probably better not to think about it—it doesn't matter much now anyway.

Exiting the grocery, Tasha finds herself outside in the tiny parking lot, used only for bicycles and masses of electric scooters. Before she ventures out into the open she swivels her head around, an owlish prowler. She had decided the second day—after a risky encounter with a Minker wearing a Walgreens nametag—never to leave a building the same way she came in. This is a good plan, and Tasha is pleased with herself, feeling very SWAT-like for coming up with it and, more impressively, sticking to it. She couldn't stick to anything before the Change, but she guesses that when mutilation and cannibalism are on the line, people become a little more adhesive.

At the corner of the building she peeps again before skittering like a crab to the brick wall that borders the lot, above which the L used to crawl. She doesn't like open territory, and she thinks about this with less smugness than she does about her fancy plot for entering and exiting buildings. Open territory is no joke: indoors, faced with single predators, she is still human. Outside, alone in the vastness of the ruined city, she becomes an antelope. No, that gives her predators too much credit—they're not lions. They're more like noisy, rabid dogs—clumsy in the underbrush with messy tactics. Which makes Tasha what? A raccoon? An opossum? Great.

Berwyn Avenue is deserted like everything else. Under the L, the tiny closet-sized tailor shop—one of the last one-story establishments in Chicago—is dark and broken, its main window shattered. Tasha steps around the crushed glass that litters the sidewalk, forbidding her eyes from wandering into the shop. Above her the L is stopped on the tracks, its doors open. She can see only one body from the ground, the upper half of a balding man in a cheap suit. Gravity has brought the tails of the jacket down by his ears, exposing the pale pink oxford underneath. He's been hanging over the edge of the tracks since the morning of the Change. Tasha hasn't gone up on the tracks to poke around, so who knows what else is strewn across the transparent alloy or who is curled on the floor of the train. Poor bastards, Tasha thinks: most of them were probably on their way to work when the Change happened. She wonders how many were Chipped, how many without Chips were killed. The balding man is one, for sure. She'll have to tell Dinah about the train and its unfortunate inhabitants.

Dinah is the woman in the apartment next door, whose face Tasha hasn't seen since before the Change. Before, they'd passed each other in the hallway every few weeks, arms full of groceries and smiles half-strained, Tasha awkwardly trying to avoid looking at the black eye that blossomed on Dinah's face every week or so. Tasha still doesn't know the boyfriend's name, only that he worked in the financial district and made Dinah quit her job at the youth center. Dinah's boyfriend was the kind of man Tasha's mother had referred to as a sinkhole: the surface looked normal, but he would suck you down if you got near him. He'd installed three deadbolts on the jamb when they moved in, for which there are three separate keys. The keys are still on a lanyard around his neck, Dinah has told Tasha, inside the bathroom where she'd locked him on the morning of the Change. He's still there, keys and all, and so Dinah remains in the apartment, a prisoner.

Continuing down Berwyn, Tasha notices the small dogwoods planted along the sidewalk, their blossoms oblivious to the disaster that has happened right around them: it's May and they're blooming cheerfully, smudged watercolor pools lining the silent street.

"Rude," she says, more about the blossoms than at them, and picks one off a branch as she passes under its branches. She carries it for awhile before letting it fall.

The doorman is dead, as he was when she left an hour before. Tasha stares at him as she heads to the stairway. She hasn't been able to stomach moving him since the Change four days ago, and she clutches the sleeve of her hoodie over her nose and mouth as she passes through the lobby for the stairs. He's slumped in his swivel-chair, his forehead on the surface of the desk. The gaping hole in the side of his neck was courtesy of Tasha herself on the morning of the Change. He was her first.

Upstairs, Tasha closes the apartment door quietly behind her, not quite ready to begin a conversation with Dinah. She puts down the backpack with the groceries so she can move her grandmother's wardrobe in front of the door. It's noisy and blows her cover.

"Tasha? Tasha, is that you? Are you ok?"

The walls are like paper—a quality she has lamented before and after the Change—and she has no trouble hearing Dinah. The voice drifts in from the bedroom and Tasha goes toward it.

"Yes," she says, not loudly, entering the bedroom still carrying her knife, "it's me. I'm fine. Just putting the dresser back in front of the door."

She pauses.

"Is He...still...you know?" Tasha asks hesitantly, knowing the answer.

"I think so," Dinah says. "But He's...quiet."

No name. Only *He. Him.* It would sound reverent if it weren't so unnerving.

"We'll be quiet too," says Tasha. "Hold on, let me go put my groceries away."

She goes back to the front door where she'd left her bags, thinking of Him. Dinah had been attacked on the morning of the Change, woken out of her sleep by her boyfriend's barking. He'd turned and lunged straight for her throat, she'd said. She'd gotten him into the bathroom by accident, she told

Tasha, while trying to lock herself in.

"I'm used to hiding in there," she'd told Tasha, and this was the first time she'd mentioned it. "But He wasn't drunk this time. Just…you know…crazy."

And in the bathroom He'd stayed. Dinah doesn't have much furniture, she's said, but she did move a table in front of the door. However, Tasha has learned this isn't really necessary. The day before, Tasha saw the guy who used to do her laundry bumping into the door of his shop on Kenmore. Over and over, an endless loop. As she passed, knife raised, he'd stopped and gazed in her direction with empty, animal eyes. As soon as she had gone, he was back to his bumping, a dinghy on the rocks with no one at the helm. They're no good with doors, but this doesn't keep Tasha from barring her fortress.

After putting away her groceries, she returns to the bedroom. Sitting on the bed, she settles against the wall, cradling a can of beans in her lap. Next to her is a stuffed tiger, a pilly, tattered leftover from her childhood. She raises the can of beans to the tiger in a silent toast.

Sighing deeply, she closes her eyes.

"I'm back," she says to the air, and hears Dinah shift against the wall behind her.

"What time do you think it is?"

Tasha looks out the window, trying to get a glimpse of the dipping sun from between the newly-built skyscrapers outside. Who am I kidding, she thinks, I wasn't a freaking Girl Scout.

"No idea. Night. Almost night. Six. Seven."

"I'm going to eat soon," says Dinah.

Tasha nods, looking at the can of beans she'd carried in the room.

"It's May," Dinah says. "I hardly remember April."

"I do," says Tasha, looking at her fingernails, their pink polish chipped from various violence over the past four days. "What a month."

They do this—just saying words. Eventually they'll talk about Him, and other hims, and hers, and countless other faces and names that don't matter anymore. Maybe eventually they'll talk about Tasha's parents. It's only day four—who knows what day five will bring. For now they settle into silence, eating their canned foods and straining their ears for shuffling feet, thinking their own private, miserable thoughts.

Tasha reaches for the can opener she now keeps on her nightstand. She sinks its single metal fang into the lid of the beans. She can hear Dinah rustling, reaching for what will pass as dinner.

"Got food?"

"Yes," Dinah says, and her voice sounds hollow.

Tasha know she's probably surveyed the contents of her kitchen at this point, wondering how long she can last before she either starves or gets the courage to kill her Minker boyfriend and take the keys to her freedom. Tasha sighs again before she begins to eat. She thinks about her parents and is glad that they are dead.

CHAPTER 2

Tasha wakes with the can of beans in her lap, leftover bean juice spilled overnight creating a small stain on the sheet. The linens already haven't been washed in weeks: she had been too busy before the Change, and now the electricity is out. She doesn't want to hand-wash them and let them air dry: it seems medieval, and she imagines herself wearing an apron and a bonnet, hands raw with scrubbing. She's grateful, at least, that the water still works to shower with, and pulls herself into a sitting position from where she had slumped over sometime in the night. She stretches, arching her back like a Halloween cat, and thinks of all the dead people beyond her window. The time for waking up and not remembering all that has happened is past.

She listens for Dinah and hears nothing. Over the past several days she has learned to take this as a sign that Dinah is still sleeping, but at first she had knocked on the wall as loudly as she dared just to ensure that her neighbor wasn't dead. Logic tells her that if the boyfriend had escaped in the middle of the night and attacked, the din would have woken Tasha up. But this world defies logic. Ever since the Change, anything has been possible; the worst things are possible.

On the day of the Change, she had huddled in this very spot after moving furniture in front of the doors for the first time. She hadn't moved, sitting on the bed like a wide-eyed gargoyle trembling between life and statue, sometimes hearing the distant screams of neighbors and pedestrians. In the months before, she'd heard cries like that—muggings, domestic disputes, the cops shooting various perps. The morning of the Change, it had all sounded like business as usual until she'd obliviously gone outside and seen firsthand what Chicago had become. Once she'd returned to her apartment, she'd stayed there all day and through the night, staring at the dresser, transfixed, every shadow a new hallucination.

Tasha rises, yawning, and goes into the kitchen, not wanting to wake Dinah yet. She looks around at her scrubbed cabinets and floors. On the counter, arranged from tallest to shortest, are silver canisters that contain wheat flour, white flour, brown sugar, white sugar, yeast, in that order, unused the entire time she's lived here. Next to them stands her Macrowave, the all-in-one nuke, toaster, and oven. In the drawers are neatly arranged silverware and appliances, paisley china that her mother had given Tasha when she left for college three and a half years ago. Then there is the sink, deep and clean and metal, with a knife lying in the bottom of it, the little bit of water around it only slightly red with the blood of yesterday's Minker.

Tasha washes the knife and lets the cold water run over

her wrists. "Wusthof," the handle reads. It's a good knife. She bought the whole set online for her twenty-first birthday a few months before, a set of nine with a polished wooden block, along with a steel and a pair of shears. Her father had owned a set just like it; sold after her parent's deaths.

"I thought I'd be using you on meat," she says to the knife, drying it with a Miracle Cloth, "not the butcher."

Tasha lies on the rug sipping from a bottle of Evian. The rug was a gift from her mother and is made of t-shirt scraps; just the sort of thing her mother would have bought, never wanting to waste anything.

Without Dinah to talk to, the minutes stretch and twist. Tasha wishes that in the days before all this she had possessed even one clock that wasn't digital. All of her clocks—like everyone else's—are on various electronic devices, and now time has no master. It could be going backward on its own accord and Tasha wouldn't know. She stares at the massive digital screen mounted on the wall, a thin square hanging there like a silent black mirror. Before the Change she had hooked it to her Glass and it had served as her clock, her weather forecast, her internet, her reading, her everything. Now both the screen and the Glass sit like a pair of paperweights. When Tasha sits in the middle of the couch with a little light coming through the blinds, she can see her own head floating in the screen, right in the center like a macabre dinner-table centerpiece. Staring at the blackness now reminds her of the night before the Change, when the screen had still been illuminated, its mindless noise washing over her in waves of disembodied breasts, explosions and—of course—Cybranu.

She'd been asleep in front of the screen, waking to find her fingers curled in her hair, a habit she's kept from girlhood. She'd untangled her hand from her mane, remembering how her father used to braid it for her, clumsily, even when she was in college. One of the last times she'd seen her father, before the nameless toxin crept into his and her mother's lungs, Tasha had been home for Christmas and was washing dishes after dinner. Her sister Leona stood nearby, probably proselytizing about one political cause or another. He'd tweaked Leona's tight curls and looped Tasha's ponytail around his fingers.

"Curly and Moe," he'd smiled.

A few months after, the coughing had started. A week later it stopped, and Tasha was on a plane to Kentucky, wondering if people wore black to cremations the way they did to funerals.

That night before the Change, Tasha had awakened and was thinking these thoughts when the tab she'd had up onscreen, still chattering to itself, had gone white, transitioning to commercial. The white lifted Tasha's sleep-blurred eyes, and she watched the materialization of a shimmering woman with skin like the inside of an oyster shell, so perfectly pale it was almost silver. She had beamed at Tasha, staring her in the eyes.

"Is your family safe?" The voice was like clear, warm oil. "Do you think you can protect them? You can't. Not without Cybranu."

Tasha had sat transfixed, as if before a swaying cobra. The woman's glimmer leapt across the room and slithered into Tasha's pupils.

"If you've lost a loved one, you know how difficult illness can be—not just for those lost…but for those they leave behind."

Tasha had risen from the couch and stared at the woman like a sleepwalker.

"With Cybranu, you don't have to lose anyone else. This tiny chip," a beautifully manicured hand gesturing to a smooth, sloping neck, "can protect your family, your parents, your children. There is nothing to fear with the Cybranu health implant."

Tasha had never known how her parents had become sick and thus had never known what to avoid. The information Leona got from the doctors who deigned to see them was speculative: both of her parents' lungs contained traces of the same toxins. There was no explanation. Without MINK, the specialists wouldn't see them. Her parents both withered away like cicada shells. If they'd had MINK policies—and thus the protection of the Chip—then maybe they'd be alive and not vases of ash spread over the goldenrod in Kentucky.

The woman onscreen had faded away, her hands outstretched like an angel.

"Think of your family. Shield them from a dangerous world. Only Cybranu can protect you."

The screen had melted back into white.

Tasha is still on the floor, lying on her mother's rug and remembering. They hadn't been able to afford MINK—not many could without a corporate job—and in the end, it had meant their deaths. Tasha's hands are clenching the rug, an involuntary clinging to the earth. She doesn't like to commit to these memories—sometimes she feels as if she watches them from the ceiling; a ghost of Christmas Past, a voyeur of her own life. To her left she can see the small country of dust bunnies that has colonized the region under the couch. She'd heard somewhere that dust bunnies were the product of humans shedding their skin cells, the cells floating into the air like sparks from a campfire, only to settle into strange lumpy tumbleweeds. Like ash. When she and Leona had sprinkled their parents over the field behind the kennel, she imagined them standing before her, dematerializing, slipping away into smoke. She couldn't have touched them if she tried.

She looks away from the dust. In another time, she might have decided to decimate the bunnies' little town with a vacuum. Not now.

"Tasha?"

Tasha jerks as Dinah's voice drifts into the living room. Tasha's focus on the past had blurred the present, and now it lands on her like a cartoon piano. She scrambles up from where she lies on the floor, suddenly anxious to talk to the voice next door—anything to extract her from the cocoon she's been wrapping herself in all morning.

"Yes," she calls, hurrying into the bedroom, "I'm here."

"There's a group of them on Berwyn. I can see them," says Dinah's muffled voice, sounding thin.

Tasha rushes to the window in the bedroom and, squatting low, peers out.

Dinah's right—there's a pack of the Minkers milling around an alleyway on Berwyn. Among them, there is someone on the ground. On the twentieth floor it's too high for Tasha to really tell, but she thinks she can make out blood on the pavement around the prone form. She clenches her teeth. She can hear Dinah crying softly. Who is that person on the pavement? It could be anyone. It could be Gina, Tasha thinks with a stab of something that might be grief, her sometimes-friend/sometimes-frenemy before the Change, who she had gone to college with, worked retail with, hunted for boys with. It could be Gina, or Scout, or any number of the names that she had known—shopping companions, drinking buddies, spa compatriots. But it couldn't be Gina, Tasha reminds herself bitterly, not that body on the ground surrounded by barking maniacs. It couldn't be Gina, because before the Change, Gina had gotten the Chip. If Gina is down on the sidewalk, she's not dead: she's alive, her mouth coated in blood. There are two kinds of people left, Tasha thinks. Us, and them. In that way, she supposes, not much has changed, just who occupies each category, a shuffling of cards.

Tasha crouches by the window until her legs burn. Next door, Dinah is still crying.

"What a world," Tasha whispers. "What a fucking world."

CHAPTER 3

Like every moron, Tasha wanted the Chip at first. Cybranu was on every e-board, every screen on the L, every ad, sinking into her eyeballs like salt on a slug. Gina had convinced Tasha to take a day off from work (when she still had a job) and go to Cybranu headquarters for the implant. They'd go together, Gina had wheedled, hold each other's hands when the injector came to hover by their necks, whisper clichéd comforts as the pain came—the things friends do. Tasha had agreed. It was a Wednesday. April 27th.

"So she had MINK," Dinah says through the wall. They're talking about the weeks before the Change like the countdown before the shiny dropping ball on New Year's Eve. Everything seems swollen with significance.

"Yeah, she had it. Her dad was rich. She was on Legacy."

Tasha remembers Gina standing in the narrow hallway—Tasha stares at the door, remembering Gina walking through it—applying lipgloss in the hall mirror. Gina had studied her own reflection with her mouth slightly open, either awestruck or appalled by what she saw—as if she wasn't quite sure she believed the glass.

"Figures. Dale was on Legacy too. His parents were loaded. Politicians, I think."

Dale. The beastly bathroom boyfriend. He has a name. "Anyway," Dinah continues, apologetic for interrupting. "Keep going."

Tasha remembers trying on three different outfits the morning she had gone with Gina to Cybranu: it seems so stupid now, but she thinks of the process of putting on and taking off clothes—the fragments of dressedness and undressedness paraded in and out of the mirror—with a sweet, heavy nostalgia. The sweetness is bittered only slightly by the presence of Gina in the memory: smirking Gina. Gina had been dressed already, wearing bright pink, a bird of paradise with cleavage.

Tasha had looked Gina up and down.

"Are you really wearing that?"

Gina looked down at herself, then into the mirror, then back at Tasha.

"What? Yeah, why not?"

"You look like a blonde Kim Kardashian."

Gina paused and raised an eyebrow.

"…who?"

"No one." Tasha had turned back to the bedroom and continued hunting through piles of clothes. Gina followed her.

"What? Jealous? Who knows, there might be some Cybranu

hotties."

Tasha snorted as she tugged on her jeans, doing the time-honored jig of women worldwide to make her butt fit into the denim.

"It's a doctor's appointment, Gina. The doctor's not gonna ask you 'Blood type and cup size, please.'"

"He might!"

"Or she."

Gina paused.

"Maybe if I was drunk."

"Jesus Christ. Get out of the way, we're going to be late."

"Ooh, I like the backpack. Prada?"

"It's new. Let's go."

"We took the L," Tasha says to Dinah. Dinah is silent, no doubt struggling to remember the last time she had ridden the train, what it had been like. Tasha had been staring at people on the train—the collective urban pastime—when an advertisement for Cybranu illuminated the car from above.

"...a new lease on life," Tasha could hear the soothing, vaguely robotic male voice murmuring from hidden speakers, "and a stronger immune system to counteract foreign diseases and bacteria."

Gina was able to move closer to Tasha as a wave of Chicagoans exited the car at New Wilson. Following Tasha's gaze, her eyes reached the ad, which now showcased a young, excruciatingly fit woman with impossibly blonde hair beaming joyfully down at them. Someone was always beaming at you in advertisements. Her voice carried down through the buzz of the car,

"Thanks to Cybranu I lost ten pounds, and I'm stronger and healthier than I've ever been."

"Is it going to hurt?" Tasha turned to Gina.

Gina had been staring at her Glass and checking her messages. The Glass is transparent, like everything that is both stylish and hi-tech, and Tasha could see the words on the screen through the device, even if they were backwards. But that's part of the appeal of a Glass: showing off.

"Is it going to hurt?" Tasha repeated.

"You won't feel a thing," Gina said, not looking up.

Tasha had considered the idea of not feeling a thing as the L rocked soundlessly along the tracks, weighing the advantages and disadvantages. Numbness had its risks: what if they accidentally hacked her throat open while attempting to implant the little chip? She would be laid back on the sterile white table, humming and looking at the ceiling, twiddling her thumbs while she obliviously leaked to death, the doctors scurrying around to stanch the blood. But she supposed this wouldn't be the worst thing in the world. Even if she did die in a puddle of her own fluids, she'd be blissfully ignorant, humming away to her last breath. Above, the ad continued, various beautiful people appearing on the glowing screen to extol the virtues of Cybranu.

"I hope I brought my MINK card," Gina had said, pawing through her purse.

"Rubbing it in your face," Dinah says shrilly.

"I know, right?" It's the first time Tasha has felt like laughing in days. "She totally was. She was that kind of girl." She feels slightly guilty for using the word "was" so freely. But Gina had never been a friend, not a real one. Tasha can't remember having a real friend, not since she and her sister were six and eight, braiding hair and chasing dandelion fluff. But what does that make Dinah, she thinks quickly. Tasha has only known her—really known her—for five days now. But she's certainly something.

The two women on their opposite sides of the wall are silent for a moment.

"You know, I didn't even know what MINK was until I met Dale," Dinah says quietly, almost too quietly for Tasha to hear.

"No?" Tasha tries not to sound shocked. She doesn't know where Dinah was from, but it had to have been in a turtle shell under a rock for her not to have heard of MINK. It was the only provider of health coverage in the country, founded by the great Barton Knox three decades or so back.

"I moved here from Mexico," Dinah says, a little defiantly, "before you guys made it Newest Mexico. We had Universal before we got absorbed. None of this Medical Inoculation Network of Knicks crap."

"Knox," Tasha corrects, laughing a little. "The Medical Inoculation Network of Knox."

"Yeah…him," Dinah says flatly, then laughs. Tasha wishes she could see her face. "Why'd you guys go along with that shit anyway?"

Tasha shrugs despite the fact that no one can see it but her.

"I don't know. My parents would have been too young to vote when it was proposed. I've seen the videos online of the protests. People bombed Barton Knox's house at first. I don't think the States were entirely cool with the whole MINK thing, but Knox was rich. He cannibalized all the smaller health companies and made himself the head honcho." She winces at her use of "cannibalize" and hopes Dinah hadn't noticed.

"What did you even need it for?" Dinah asks. "I mean, besides the Chip." Tasha wonders why Dinah didn't ask Dale this kind of stuff before the Change, but if he was the kind of guy she had to hide in the bathroom from after he'd been drinking, she can imagine that asking certain questions was a no-go.

"Antibiotics, prosthetics, breast implants, new kidneys, everything."

"So if you had the flu…"

"You'd just have the flu unless you had MINK. If you had something as stupid as a yeast infection, you still needed MINK. Most doctors wouldn't even let you in the door unless you had it."

Dinah scoffs.

"At all? What if you just couldn't afford the premiums? You couldn't pay cash?"

"Sometimes they'd let you put it on MCPs—"

"MCPs?"

"Medical credit provider cards." She pauses, thinking of her parents. "But the interest rates were insane."

"How much were the premiums?"

"Put it this way…a year of MINK payments could pay for a seat on the shuttle tour of the Moon they do every three years."

"Oh."

"Yeah."

They're silent for awhile and Tasha feels vaguely annoyed. She'd been hoping to be distracted from thinking about her parents by talking to Dinah, but here she is again. Her parents' condition had worsened, and without MINK the bills charged to MCP cards had mounted rapidly, the lot of them quickly maxed and the credit cut off. That's where the treatment had stopped—any further therapy or medication could only have been paid for by selling the kennel they'd owned since before they were married, which Tasha's parents refused to do. In the end, though, that's exactly what had to be done, as neither Leona, a refugee of sorts, or Tasha, a college student, had any money. Leona had overseen the selling of the kennel in order to pay the stone-faced collector. The two sisters had stood outside the gates after signing the papers, staring through the grim metal at the rows and rows of pens once occupied by keening dogs.

"So you didn't have MINK?" Dinah asks eventually, and Tasha sighs.

"No. But my job would have offered it with discounted rates after I'd worked there for nine months, so I could've had it eventually."

"A discount would have been nice. I should have gotten a

job with you. Where did you work?"

"The Apiary."

"The shopping mall?"

"Yeah."

"Oh. With the blue uniforms?"

Tasha sighs. The uniforms were infamous.

"Yeah. Other companies would've given a discount too, though. Anyone with government contracts. McDonald's. Walmart. The army. Unless you failed the Knox exam."

Dinah shifts in her apartment. The walls are so thin Tasha can feel the movement from where she leans. They must be nearly back-to-back.

"Ohh, I heard about the Knox exam." She's interested now: tabloid stuff. "Like with the Frenches."

Tasha nods, remembering. It was a widely- publicized incident: Maxwell and Sayuri French—philanthropic millionaires, founders of Change for the Socially Estranged— were rejected for MINK coverage because (the Frenches believed) their mission was to build enormous relief centers for the States' homeless, which wasn't too popular with Knox lobbyists. The story burned hot and fast: when pressed for comment, the MINK board released a statement that suggested the Frenches were dangerous radicals and stated that MINK had the sole discretion to reject any applicant whose Knox Exam results were questionable. Furthermore, the statement said, the MINK Corporation believed strongly in "the dignity of the homeless," and the centers the Frenches desired to build violated that dignity. And that was all.

"What happened to them?" Dinah says, no doubt recalling all the crazy rumors. "I heard that Sayuri had some terminal illness that was eating through her internal organs like little *ratones*, and through their money too. After MINK dissed them, they disappeared."

Tasha remembers. Even the *National Enquirer* hadn't been able to sniff them out, though Tasha had seen a headline once: "Frenches Use Final Funds for Last Trip to Space." Tasha imagines them bouncing in slow motion across the surface of the Moon, seeking homeless extra-terrestrials who they could provide some service for. Of course, at that point, they had been more the vagrant ETs themselves. Tasha wonders if Sayuri died from whatever illness she was facing, or if she'd gone down at the jaws of Minkers, who had carried their MINK cards proudly. More like MINK tablets: metal things the size of a business card, thin but solid; not heavy, plated with artificial gold. Gina had shown Tasha hers every chance she got, but never let Tasha hold it.

"What was Cybranu like? Did you see anyone famous getting their Chip? My friend went to get hers and saw the mayor's wife in the waiting room."

Dinah pauses. It's become a mental sequence: one cannot mention someone getting the Chip without then remembering that the person is somewhere in the city now, gnawing on necks.

"No," Tasha says quickly, to pop the heavy balloon that inflates between these thoughts, but also because she has remembered something. "No, I didn't see anyone famous. But I did see this weird lady in the subway."

Downtown, Tasha and Gina had exited the train underground, borne along by swarms of Chicagoans. Tasha remembers the walls and the cracked pavement as damp, a vague dripping sound echoing from someplace down the train's shadowy wormhole. Whenever she was in the subway, Tasha had the half-fearful, half-hopeful expectation that an ancient Teenage Mutant Ninja Turtle would come strolling down one of the tunnels the city had cordoned off when they released the new trains. Tasha had heard about mole people—crazies who withdrew from society, choosing to live in the eternally nocturnal burrows of L's from bygone days. She could imagine one of the loons putting on a half-shell and getting into some throwback crime-fighting. It wouldn't be the strangest thing in the world, or the city. The only uproar would be between the Net hosts battling over interview and reality show rights.

In sharp contrast to the rest of the medieval dankness of the subway tunnel was the Lift, the new-age elevator designed by popular demand. "From point A to point B without the germs or claustrophobia," the dentured commercial models would beam (more beaming). Passengers flocked to the Lift and stood in the silver-illuminated circle, which would close off with some kind of cyber glass like a cylindrical bubble, and lift the passengers to street level in a breath before appearing back below ground in a whoosh, ready for the next group. It was extraordinary to witness for the first time: before you would be twenty-something passengers all standing in the silver circle, then in something like a blink they would all be gone, vanished to the mysterious planet of the street above the subway. The *whoosh* of their disappearance always reminded Tasha of the flush of airplane toilets. She watched the passengers crowding into the Lifts' circles, and imagined her fellow Chicagoans being flushed away, dropped like neat parcels of excrement in an isolated field.

There were still stairways, of course, for those who had adverse reactions to the Lifts—and some people did—which Tasha had taken sometimes if she hadn't gotten in enough cardio that week, or if the Lift was packed. Hardly anyone took the stairs, so you never had to elbow your way up. There was quite a crowd around the Lift now—defeating the tagline about claustrophobia, Tasha thought—so she looked around for stairs.

Her eye settled on the once-red paint of handrails, a rusty stairway that looked more like a fire escape. She took a step in its direction, assuming Gina would follow, but there was something against the wall just before the stairs, in the shadows of a moldy mosaic archway, that caught her attention. It moved. Tasha thought it might be a rat, a beagle-sized subway critter. But it was much bigger than a rat—stepping closer, Tasha saw that it was a shivering form hunched on a mat of cardboard, swathed in a gray blanket, eyes closed.

Mole people, said Tasha's brain. *Ninja Turtles*.

It was a woman. She had muttered and clutched her throat, snuffling. Despite the filthiness of the woman's fingers, Tasha could make out the chipping white crescent of an almost-nonexistent French manicure. Her hair was over her eyes and showed evidence of a dye job that was, at one time, pretty decent.

"Um...ma'am? Ma'am?"

Tasha didn't know why she was talking to the lady. The odds were in favor of her being sloshed. But the woman actually looked up at the second "ma'am" and locked eyes with Tasha. Tasha was shocked by how blue they were.

"Are you alright?" Tasha asked. Of course she wasn't, but these were things one asked in polite society, Tasha told herself.

The woman just stared, looking vaguely angry. Tasha had thought suddenly of every horror movie she'd ever seen and taken a step back to retreat when the woman focused on the person addressing her and seemed to collect herself.

"Me?" she asked

"Yes," said Tasha. "Are you okay?"

"I'm better," the woman said. "I'm better."

Tasha knew that if Gina were with her—where had she gone? to the street already—she'd have been cackling and nudging Tasha's ribs, probably trying to film the woman to put her online. "Viral," she'd say while recording. But Tasha tended to be meaner in her head than she was out loud, and so rather than laugh at the woman—it wasn't funny anyway; it was creepy—she just asked, "Better?"

The woman nodded vigorously, smiling a little, despite the angry look that still lingered around her eyes.

"Better. I'm better."

"Better than what?"

"Than you."

Ahh. A Looney Tune.

"Oh, okay." Tasha thought it best to remain neutral.

The woman's gaze refocused on something a little to the right of Tasha's eyes.

"Those are pretty earrings."

Tasha recognized the look on the woman's face, but couldn't place it exactly. She cupped one of her earrings protectively. Before she could respond, the woman had moved her dirty blonde hair behind her shoulder, exposing her neck, around which hung what appeared to be a string of creamy white pearls. There was something else: a faint etched shape... The hair fell back over what Tasha thought she had seen, and the woman raised a frail hand to the necklace at her throat, delicately, limply, like Scarlett O'Hara.

"I took these pearls from a woman in Arizona," she said, smiling fondly at the memory.

"Took them? You stole them?"

The woman lowered her hand and stared hard at Tasha, her blue eyes two chips of the iceberg that sank *Titanic*.

"I took them."

"What were you doing in Arizona?"

The smile broadened a little.

"I was a rat. I was a rat in Arizona."

There was a flutter in the air, announcing the arrival of the next train, and a scrap of paper tumbleweeded down the platform away from where the two women talked.

"How did you get here? To Chicago, I mean."

"This isn't Chicago."

Tasha just stared at her. Yes, it was best to remain neutral.

"This isn't Chicago," the woman repeated. "It's all the same."

The train slithered up alongside them, moving the woman's hair back over her eyes and shifting Tasha's tight ponytail.

"Give me your earrings," the woman said. The blue eyes seemed very clear suddenly; the rheumy look of a moment ago had evaporated. "Give them to me."

Tasha took a step back, closer to the safe bustle of the commuters.

"Give them to me, you bitch. You little bitch, give them to me." The woman's voice had been calm; even and smooth like a doctor.

"Tasha, what the hell are you doing?" It was Gina, impatient, peevish. "I've been waiting for you on the street. Come on. Let's take the Lift."

"If Gina hadn't come, do you think that lady would've attacked you?" Dinah asks, caught in the tension, her voice tight like a wire.

"I really don't know," Tasha sighs. "Maybe. There were other people around so I feel like she'd have to have been completely batshit to try something for real, but I don't know. It was so weird. She was so…intense."

"I wonder if she was really from Arizona," Dinah says. "I mean, she was probably out of her mind and didn't know what she was saying."

Something about the woman is like an itch Tasha can't scratch.

"She had a manicure," Tasha says.

"A homeless lady with a little class," says Dinah with a small laugh, but Tasha doesn't join her. She thinks about the woman's laughing face, her hair blonde only four or five inches from the ends, the rest dark where the brunette within had reclaimed the scalp. Tasha thought of the pearls she wore and wondered who she'd taken them from. The woman had been like seeing a new coin at the bottom of a murky pond—the shine still visible but slowly rusting over, clouding with algae. Tasha decides to change the subject.

"How much food do you have left, Dinah?"

Against her back, Tasha feels Dinah shift again. She's either looking at her food—does she really have so little that she has it all stacked around her?—or she's uncomfortable. Either way, it's a sensitive subject, one they have avoided. Tasha has gone out to Jewel more than once—her own kitchen pathetically bare, as she often ate at the food court in the Apiary with her discount—but she has been unable to find any food flat enough to slide under the front door to what has become Dinah's prison. Tasha has examined the door when she's ventured out to the grocery store—metal, like Tasha's, impossible to break down. Nothing was wood anymore (too few trees), so Dinah sits inside her metal box, waiting. For what? Courage, Tasha supposes, or inevitability. Perhaps she hopes Dale will die on his own—hide the problem until it resolves itself. Dinah hasn't talked about food, not does she ever bring up the issue of the keys. Had Dinah been Gina, Tasha would have shrugged off her silence, would have thought something unforgiving like, "If she doesn't wanna talk about it, she doesn't wanna talk about it. I can't *make* her talk." But Tasha had known, of course, that friends *do* make friends talk—if they care enough. And Tasha supposes that's the key. Dinah, this woman she barely knows, a voice through the concrete, deserves care. And though her fears are censored, yellow tape wrapping around the subject like a crime scene—*Do Not Enter. Danger Ahead*—Tasha feels drawn to enter anyway.

"Some," says Dinah finally. "Beef jerky. Canned pineapples. Vacuum-sealed green beans. Some stuff."

"Dinah…" Tasha reaches for the caution tape, flexing emotional muscles she hasn't used in years.

"I'm fine," Dinah says.

"Dinah…"

"I'm fine, Tasha! I'm fine!"

Dinah is wrapping up in her fear, pulling the caution tape around her like a shawl. They lapse into silence. Dinah must be sitting very still, because Tasha hears nothing, feels nothing through the wall. She feels stiff. She'd tried, and for what? They have become statues in their dread: despite the days passed in verbal company, they are strangers, separated by a wall. Tasha thinks of all the ways things could be different. Would it be better to be Chipped at this point? A Minker prowling the city? She could have been. She almost had been.

When Tasha and Gina had entered the lobby on the seventy-fifth floor of the Daly Center, the automated voice of a woman had greeted them from somewhere over their heads:

"Welcome to Cybranu. If you have an appointment, please enter the room to your right. If you are here for more information about the Cybranu health implant, please enter the room to your left."

Between the two doors was a gold plaque with the Cybranu address and their motto. Underneath it in small print was the address for headquarters, which Tasha noticed was at the Apiary of all places. Tucked away on one of the upper floors, she guessed, with other super-secret, ultra-rich organizations. Three people, two men and a woman, entered behind Tasha and Gina. They moved in a group to the room on the left. Tasha heard a video begin its loop as the trio set off the motion sensors.

"Are you worried about the constant threat of infection? Do you want a happy, healthy, easy life? At Cybranu, with a simple procedure, you can get a new lease on—"

Tasha entered the room to the right. The fluorescent light, white walls and white furniture gave it a blinding effect and she blinked, looking around to see where Gina had gone. She was already at a white desk, talking in a low voice to a white-clad man seated behind it. They were taking the white thing a little far, Tasha thought. Tasha approached the immaculate desk, but the man leaned to the side to address her around Gina's body.

"Take a seat until you're called to the desk, please."

"Okayy…" She dragged the word out to express her annoyance. The man didn't even notice and resumed speaking to Gina. Tasha sucked her teeth. "Nice guy."

Tasha "took a seat" and turned to the little table that held a stack of Lēf magazines. The one on top was indexed with all the fashion publications, *Cosmo* already opened by a previous patient clicking through the issues. It was the old March issue— she'd already read it—so she picked up a current events Glass instead, clicking into *ChicagoToday* and studying the headlines. The Lincoln Park Zoo's expansion efforts had been completed, one article read. The piece included a picture of a grinning guy wearing the brown safari-esque uniform of a zoo employee. Beside him was a man in what appeared to be an expensive suit, his smile lax and tan. Together they stood outside the cage of a panther slouching on a synthetic rock. The blackness of the cat dominated the photo, its eyes volcanic. Unlike the employee and the executive, who looked into the camera, the animal's gaze was fixated on the men just beyond its reach. Its posture gave the impression of indifference, but Tasha sensed that if the bars separating it from its wardens were removed, the headline for the paper would have been very different: *Captive Cat Mauls Captors*; *Imprisoned Panther Punishes Penitentiary*. You can only cage a hot coal for so long. Tasha was still staring at the picture of the panther when Gina sat down.

"So?" asked Tasha, clicking out of the article.

"He asked my cup size."

"Shut up!"

"Okay, he didn't. But he is kind of hot."

"Oh Christ...."

The man's voice leapt across the lobby,

"Lockett, Natasha?"

Tasha looked up at the voice and blinked. After staring at the panther, the room seemed blindingly white. She'd readjusted her eyes and her purse, then stood to approach the desk.

CHAPTER 4

"Did Gina know you didn't get it? The Chip, I mean?"

Tasha had been half-dozing against the wall and Dinah's voice startles her. She jumps, smacking her head against the wall.

"Um…are you okay?" Dinah's voice is a little clearer; she must have turned her face toward the wall at the sound of the knock.

"Yeah, I'm fine," Tasha says, rubbing her head. "What did you ask me?"

"If Gina knew that you didn't get the Chip. I mean, you guys went together. And I'm assuming she…you know…has it. The way you talk about her."

"Yeah, she got it. And yeah, she knew. The guy in reception turned me away as soon as he found out I didn't have MINK."

"You didn't have cash or an MCP or whatever?"

"I asked to apply for an MCP but he said no. He said some things you had to have MINK for—no MCPs or cash—and the Chip was one."

"Seems like they had a real specific idea of who they wanted to have the implant," Dinah yawns. She must have been napping too.

"What did you say?" Tasha is fully awake now and something about the words draws her.

"What? That the Cybranu people had a pretty good picture of who could have the Chip and who couldn't? I mean, they did, right? No MCPs, no cash. Had to have MINK, and to get MINK, you said you had to either be rich as hell or have a job with a government contract. Did I say something wrong?"

"No," Tasha says, and rubs her eyes. "I just…no. You're right. But yeah, Gina was a dick or whatever when she found out I didn't get it."

"Ha! I knew it," Gina had crowed. "Aww, poor Tasha. Maybe I could've slipped you my card. Or maybe we can, like, steal someone's MINK. People do that all the time, right? Instead of stealing someone's identity, you can just steal their coverage!"

Tasha struggled not to glower.

"I didn't know MINK was a requirement though, really," Gina said airily, adopting the role of a Mother Teresa with fake eyelashes, "but it's probably for the best. I mean, not talking about you, but there's something to be said for a level of exclusivity."

Tasha stayed quiet.

Gina flipped her hair out of her face sharply. She tended to get annoyed when Tasha didn't take her bait.

"Oh, sorry, I should have known," Gina snarled, glancing at Tasha sideways, "you're for equal opportunity healthcare." She used quotey fingers.

Tasha had taken the bait.

"Oh my god, whatever. Who cares about healthcare. I don't need the Chip anyway. It's, like, a flea collar. If it was so necessary, they'd let everybody get it, right? They make it sound like all these millions of foreign bio-bugs are going to be swarming us in the streets."

"They might be," Gina shrugged, gazing out the window. She was serious now and didn't want Tasha to know it. Her germophobic tendencies were overshadowed only by her xenophobic ones. "Korea has been in the webnews a lot lately. And Syria. And so," she shot a look at Tasha before she said it, knowing she was about to turn up the bitch volume, "has the Nation of California. There was that video released of them talking about biological weapons and stuff."

Tasha stiffened but didn't look at Gina. She knew this game, the game of swords used under tablecloths. Women, she had thought then. Women, women, women. The trick was to stab without upsetting the tea; arsenic in the brew, swallowed smooth.

Tasha snorted instead of acknowledging the mention of the Nation. "You watch the news? No wonder you're so worried."

Still looking out the window, Gina shrugged. "The Nation has made a lot of threats. They're terrorists."

"I think they have a lot more to fear from the States," Tasha laughed, trying to sound as if she actually thought it was funny.

They had been quiet then. As the L made its way up the tracks heading North, Tasha gazed at the buildings surrounding their little train. Willis Tower was dwarfed by the new additions—after it was stripped of "Sears" its growth was stunted as the city grew around it. Its closest architectural neighbor, after all, was one hundred and eighty-four stories, one of dozens of swaying pillars in the Chicago sky.

Other than that, not much had changed since Tasha was a child and visiting Chicago for trips to grandma's house—the city continued to get taller and wider, a blob of expanding steel: the vehicles became smaller and quicker, some airborne; the noise quieter and quieter. Neither Tasha nor Gina had been born in the time when the L would still jerk perilously around corners, the nails-on-slate squealing of the brakes as the train rounded each bend adding another layer to the already clamorous cityscape. They were children of the new L—no piercing mechanical wails punctuated the quiet: the L of Tasha's grandmother's Chicago had been replaced car by car with a hushed metal snake of a machine whose doors whispered open at each stop and, when it started into motion, did so with hardly a jerk, continuing like polished oil up the transparent alloy track. The L whose roar had once been the soundtrack of Chicago had been de-barked, its growl phased out as Chicagoans demanded less noise pollution.

They picketed for silence, Tasha thought, but none of them had taken out their earbuds long enough to notice. She looked around at the other passengers in her car: all but one or two bobbed their heads almost imperceptibly, their eyes looking at but not seeing the city beyond the train window. The long wire of the first generations of mobile music devices' headphones had been abandoned for Bugs; wireless Skittle-sized speakers that one inserted into the ear like earplugs. Tasha knew people who never took them out.

"I know you have a thing for the Nation of California," Gina said, refusing to let go of what she saw as her trump card. "So no offense. I'm just saying what I heard."

Tasha knew "No offense" actually translated as "Take that, bitch." But she was tired of playing the game. Gina always had more staying power for the endless circle of stabbing.

"Okay, I don't have a *thing* for the Nation, Gina. I just don't think it's fair to say an entire *country* is populated by terrorists."

"Seems like it. They wanted to secede didn't they? They *did* secede!"

"That doesn't make them terrorists! Nobody got hurt when they seceded, and secession wasn't illegal when they did it."

"Lots of people got hurt!"

"Okay, um, after the States tried to *make* them stay. They offer MINK to a bunch of college kids, and in exchange they send them out there in hovertanks to blow everything up. Including themselves."

Gina had been quiet for a moment, pretending to look out the window again. As much as she liked to goad Tasha about the Nation, she didn't keep up with current events as much as she pretended to. The details of the secession and the following skirmishes weren't her strong suit.

"They ruined what this country used to be," Gina said eventually, echoing some fat-ass Net show host's rantings, most likely. "I heard they were responsible for blowing up the Mall of America. They're terrorists. Period."

Tasha was tired.

"My sister lives there."

"Okay, well not *her*." Gina snapped. "Why'd she leave anyway? We have everything we need here."

Tasha bristled—enough was enough.

"Not everybody can be a Minker like you, Gina."

"Oh shit," Dinah laughs, "you called her a Minker? To her face?"

Tasha laughs a little, but she blushes. She'd thrown the words at Gina and then stood to exit the train, not bothering to look over her shoulder to bask in the effect of her statement. It wasn't a slur exactly, but it was a mean word used impolitely to refer to someone with a MINK policy, legacy or otherwise. It had started before Tasha was born, with protestors picketing Barton Knox when he was still alive, then later, MINK headquarters. The footage was still shown in classrooms—that's where Tasha had seen it—the protestors muted as the YouTube anchorwoman described the scene. Tasha remembers the faces of the rioters as having been multicolored, not just racially but with facepaint, painted up like skeletons and undead monsters. Their signs read "MINK STINKS," "THE MINKIER THE STINKIER," some just "FUCK MINKERS." The word had stuck. It was assumed that anyone using it didn't have a policy, so it wasn't something one uttered in the presence of strangers—not unless you wanted them to know you couldn't pass the Knox Exam, some aspect of your life or beliefs in conflict with the Knoxian standards of worthiness. But it had felt good, Tasha thinks, to say it loud, to someone's face.

"Yeah," Tasha admits, "it was kind of harsh though."

"Psh, she deserved it," Dinah scoffs. "I mean, no disrespect. I know she's, like, out *there* now, but still. She had no right to talk about your sister like that. You don't say stuff like that to your friends."

Tasha agrees, but doesn't say so. It's nice to be comforted; it's been a long time.

"I didn't know all that stuff about the secession though," Dinah adds cautiously. "I was still living in Mexico—when Mexico was Mexico—when California split off. So you know all this stuff she because of your sister? Is she okay?"

"I don't know," Tasha says, feeling tired again. "She writes a lot of letters but I haven't gotten one in awhile. She usually writes every other week. After our parents died we didn't talk as much. She's out there living on a commune or something with her guy and their baby. She loves it. They saw a little fighting when they seceded—the States did some bombing and the typical stuff. But eventually I think the States just kind of stopped caring."

"Seems like they just like having someone to blame."

After Tasha had insulted Gina, she'd gotten off the train at Berwyn and stood for awhile on the platform instead of going straight down to street level. She closed her eyes and felt the train rush by her in a flurry of muffled acceleration. When she opened her eyes again it was already pulling up at the next station down the line, the large illuminated dome that made up the rear and front end of the trains staring back down the track at her like an immense glowing eye.

It had been April 27th and she shuddered in the cool air of early evening. In Kentucky the remaining trees would already be dressing themselves for spring, but Chicago's chill lasted a little longer, with a worse attitude. There would probably be blossoms on the trees next week, but their life cycle wasn't guaranteed. Tasha pulled up her hood and made her way to street level—no Lifts at her stop; they saved those for downtown where rich, important people lived.

"Downtown" had spread, of course—her block had once housed only mid-rises, but had been rapidly built up. As the years passed, Chicagoans could see less and less of the sky as they walked to the L, the moon all but blocked out at night. The newer buildings in Tasha's neighborhood weren't quite Willis-sized—one or two were close—but they were nothing like the monsters that roosted in the sky downtown. Not that the sky was much to look at anymore—the mammatus clouds, a marble-patterned, smoky blanket, had hunkered over the city for years, painting it with a metallic gloom. Not the result of climate change, everyone insisted. And maybe they were right. Either way, the mammatus clouds had staked out the sky above Chicago for good, giving it all the more resemblance to Gotham. Ominous, but kind of pretty, Tasha always thought.

The tenants in her building who had lived in the area for a couple decades were always complaining—"it used to be so beautiful," "you used to see the sky and take a nice morning walk," they said, "you could stroll by the lake and it would all be blue."

Not that those geezers did much strolling, Tasha had thought meanly, still pissed about her conversation with Gina. Hardly anybody strolled, in fact. Everyone used the moving sidewalk—the Volamu—that stretched from the many apartment buildings all the way to the L, one of many miniature superhighways of gliding pedestrians.

Few people drove cars either, though, and the city had usurped the roads on the North Side once reserved for automobile traffic and converted them into the Volamus, lanes of moving sidewalks rushing in each direction. The little roof curving over the top of the Volamu from end to end gave it a tubular feeling, but the sides were open for air, exits, and emergencies. At night the roof gave off a soft radiating light; in the winter, a soft radiating heat. From Tasha's window on the twentieth floor—as low as she could negotiate when she signed her five-year lease—the lighted Volamus looked like the tunnels of a glowing cybertronic ant-farm. When she looked out, she could see the dark moving spots that were people being zipped along on the miles of treadmill. Often she would sit, chin in palm, and observe their quick progress: depending on her mood they looked either like little marbles in a pinball machine, pinging away toward a high score, or like bullets loaded into a slow-motion rifle aimed at something precious.

Tasha never used the Volamu. Even when she was late for work—which was often, as she never set foot out the door until her eyelash extensions were in their proper place—she would click down the long and badly-repaired cement sidewalk at 8:30am and be startled every time someone on the Volamu zipped past her. She would imagine what she might look like to a stranger's eyes twenty stories up: a lone figure moving slowly down a broken path. She would rather be that than one of a hundred other ants in the tube, hurtling along in insect anonymity. It was bad enough she worked at the Apiary.

The Apiary was the enormous shopping center in downtown Chicago. It dwarfed the once-famous Mall of America, which was burned down in a mysterious act of arson when California seceded to become the Nation. President Walker—who had been assassinated a year later while drunkenly pissing on the White House lawn—had, in a fit of drama, pushed through a bill that renamed the country "The States," laying "The United" to rest in a mournful speech that only a few people watched. President Walker was the only one who really seemed to feel the loss—people were more upset about the scorched patch of earth in Minnesota.

Chicago acted quickly. It threw up the obscenely large Apiary in a mere two years and had been bathing in cash ever since. They even donated a huge percentage of their profits to "refining" Chicago's infrastructure. In fact, the Volamus were paid for mostly by the Apiary, another reason Tasha refused to set foot on them. It was her way of protesting. She would have liked to burn it down like the Mall of America, but she needed a job.

Her uniform alone was enough to make her consider explosives: electric blue and made of something between silicone and latex, the knee-length dress she wore to work was straight out of a comic book artist's wet dream. She felt like a hooker from the old movies every time she put it on, and doubly so when she pulled on the knee-high shiny white boots. The hat was too much—a little white nurse-hat thing—and often she "forgot" to put it on, resulting in eye-rolls and write-ups from her superiors. The uniform was a city-wide joke—scratch that: nation-wide. There had even been a flagrantly sexual ad in the Super Bowl about it last year, and a top-selling porno with the actresses dressed as Apiary girls. It was that bad.

"Do you want a job or not, Natasha?" Cara, Tasha's platinum blonde boss who insisted on using Tasha's full name, would ask sweetly when Tasha complained about the uniform. When Tasha dreamed of Cara—and she did; the woman haunted her—she appeared as a lipsticked viper, her fangs extending out of a red and slanting mouth. In reality, Cara had a way of asking questions that was both maternal and sadistically condescending: "Can you be on time for work tomorrow? Or do I need to help you?" This voice was reserved for certain employees. Tasha knew for a fact that Cara's snake voice was never used on employees who looked like Gina. But Tashas? Fair game. Cara was like Nurse Ratched with a nose job. Tasha had been glad to work on level 51 rather than in one of the lower level stores, where Cara spent most of her time.

Tasha's job on level 51—near the top of the retail floors,

the last stop before the corporate offices, which occupied 60-160—had put her in a designer pet shop called Fetch Fetchers. They carried some other species—ermine, miniature cats, rainbow-colored birds of prey—but their specialty was dogs.

The Paris Hiltons of yesteryear—Cara's ancestors, no doubt—had introduced the canine craze, and desperate designers had latched on to the concept and run the forty-year dash with it, resulting in a new breed every few months, offered in a multitude of colors. They hadn't reached the point of splicing yet—it was hard to find scientists who hadn't seen those depressing PETA commercials—so people like Tasha had spent their free time on the clock wearing elbow-length rubber gloves, dying the dogs fuchsia and violet.

Fetch Fetchers was among the busier shops in the Apiary, with the most obnoxious clientele. Tasha had no idea why she was placed there when hired by the Apiary—she guessed that they assumed that since she had been born in Kentucky she knew something about animals. The stereotypes remained, even two decades after horseracing had been illegalized. Although in Tasha's case they had been somewhat accurate—Tasha had never been much of a country girl (her parents, not from Kentucky, had forbidden any hint of a soft "I") but she did know a thing or two about dogs.

Her mother and father had run the kennel in Louisville since they moved there after Tasha's paternal grandparents died. Her parents weren't rich, but they made a decent living from the well-offs who brought their purebreds to be looked after while on vacation or when allergic relatives were in town for a visit. The Love Lockett—it had sounded like a seedy motel to Tasha, but her parents thought it was cute, and so did their clientele. The customers had money, for sure, but even years of afterschool hours spent grooming richies' Rhodesians didn't prepare Tasha for the clientele of the Apiary.

Mostly women. Everything fur. Everything designer. They would come in and ignore Tasha when she asked how she could help them, and then tap impatiently on her desk with fake fingernails when they decided they were ready to address her. They'd always look at her uniform with amused disdain, as if they hadn't noticed that every other Apiary employee was wearing the exact same thing and Tasha had just chosen to play dress-up of her own accord.

Tasha's job had been to ignore the contempt and help the customers select a pet, although the animals in her shop were less pet and more purse. In soothing tones she would explain how each breed was best-suited to what lifestyle: the Shih Tzu with a little pastel dye for the middle-aged divas looking for glamour; the Chihuahua in magenta for the twenty-somethings in search of flash; and the teacup Maltese for primadonnas-in-training. There were larger breeds too—they had a few spotted Great Danes in stock once, their markings tinted with lavender—but they didn't sell as well. The ladies liked small and dainty, the way they imagined themselves. Tasha's role at Fetch Fetchers had been to reinforce that vision, drawing subtle parallels between the sleekness of the animals the women were choosing and the women themselves. Add a little pink to anything and Tasha had a sale.

Tasha had often seen the same women strolling in with their credit cards out. One woman, Mrs. Kerry, would show up every month or so. Tasha had no idea what became of the dogs—and an ermine once—that she had sold Mrs. Kerry in the preceding months, but when she asked her manager about it, she was told to focus on making the sale. What happened to the animals after they left the shop wasn't her concern.

Which wasn't always too hard to accept, since the attitudes of the designer dogs were similar to their eventual owners. The Chihuahuas were the worst: snappy, snooty, bitey—annoying reminders of the girls Tasha went to high school with. Tasha's job description included bathing the stock, and that's when the little rats would get the boldest. Each animal in the store—with the exception of the few birds; try bathing a bird—needed daily bathing (and spritzing with designer perfume) to ensure an animal that didn't smell like an animal. Maybe that's what happened to Mrs. Kerry's purchases, Tasha would theorize while up to her elbows in Chihuahua and suds: they started smelling like what they were, and needed replacing. Tasha had often imagined Mrs. Kerry's perfumes and oils wearing off; her body beginning to smell like what she was. What would that scent be?

When Tasha had no dogs to bathe or customers' egos to stroke, she would sit at the sparkling white counter up front and watch the shoppers in the Apiary meander to various pedways and restaurants. Across from Fetch Fetchers was the entrance to REvolve, the mobile restaurant where the eaters sat at a counter affixed to a pedway that cruised on a circuit of the hundreds of stores. Lazy and/or multi-tasking shoppers could peg out their shopping plan while sitting on their asses eating a sandwich. Next to REvolve was Pemberley, an upscale men's salon where the high rollers would go for shoe-shines before cruising the Apiary for young things to pick up. They weren't the only predators on patrol: there were women too, wrapped in furs with dogs on leashes, on the lookout for a pet of another kind. Then there was Prada, and Gucci, and Hermes, the patronesses of which Tasha had watched with a mixture of envy and condescension. None of them seemed to have jobs, or homes for that matter.

Sometimes Tasha left her desk and walked out into the mall to look down through the immense spiraling atrium of retail below. From where she stood on level 51 she could almost see the massive crystal sculpture of a honeybee that dominated the floor of the ground level, placed royally among the kiosks and sparkling fountains; a gift from the city to commemorate the grand opening of the Apiary. The glass bee was the Queen—a transparent tyrant that oversaw all the happenings in its honeycomb. It seemed to have an enormous radiating power, drawing the people of Chicago into the tunnels of its home where they became squirming larvae, slaves to its bidding.

The Apiary was always swarming, and at the center of it all was the Queen. Sometimes Tasha looked down from level 51 and wanted to squash it.

"Do you hear that?"

Tasha does hear it. She'd been thinking so deeply about her

time at the Apiary that it had taken a moment for the sound to filter through her consciousness, but now she hears it and it can't be ignored: crying.

"It's upstairs..." Dinah says, so softly that Tasha almost doesn't understand her.

Tasha can hear it, right above them. The sound of a person crying, speaking in a language Tasha doesn't understand. Who are they? She's been here almost a week and hasn't heard a single footstep upstairs. They've been quiet—hiding in a closet, crouched in a corner; breathing like a mouse until now.

"Is that Spanish?" Tasha asks, too afraid to worry about sounding ignorant.

"No," says Dinah. "Not Spanish. But I think they're praying."

The crying goes on for a moment and then they hear another sound join it, a sound that raises the hair on Tasha's arms and neck, her skin prickling, her mouth going dry.

Barking. She knows the tone—it's a Minker.

"Oh god, Dale hears it," Dinah moans.

Tasha can hear Dale begin to snuffle in the apartment next door, whining savagely at the bathroom door.

"Dinah, he can't get out, can he? Dinah?"

"N-no....not unless I open the door. Unless he breaks the door. Unless he breaks the door and comes out that way. Are they strong? Is he strong enough to do that?"

"I don't know—I don't know."

Upstairs the crying has gotten louder and Tasha shrinks against the wall. The knife is on the bed next to her and she grabs it, as if whatever is upstairs might come crashing through the ceiling.

"Oh god," Dinah whimpers, "someone is going to die. There's someone up there and they're going to die."

"They might escape. They might kill it. They might kill it and escape." Tasha feels frantic.

There's a scrabbling on the floor above, a door slamming. More crying, more words in a tongue Tasha can't understand. Tasha can feel every footstep in her bones. There's a crash— someone, Dinah or Tasha, screams a small scream. The voice upstairs is wailing. Tasha is gripping the knife so hard her hands have gone pale. She hears the window upstairs open, the familiar grating clank of the shitty old panes. A flurry of screamed prayers.

"The window, Dinah! The window!"

Tasha looks just as the body flies past her vision. She jumps so hard she almost cuts her arm on the knife. She's standing on the bed, not remembering when she stood up. Her whole body is quivering.

She leaps from the bed and is at the window in a few steps, abandoning the knife. She yanks the window open, chipping off more pink nail polish in the process, and looks down. Twenty stories below, she can see the form of the jumper splayed like a splash of paint. She hadn't known if it was a man or a woman. Just 21E, her former neighbor, now dead.

"Tasha, look out!"

Tasha slams her elbow on the window frame as she jerks her body back inside, just before another body falls from the window above. She hears it barking as it blows past her window, so close her hair moves with its wind. A moment later, the distant, dull sound of the body striking the pavement. Now it is silent: no footsteps; no barking; no crying; no prayers.

"Tasha."

Tasha approaches the window again timidly. She looks down—two splashes of paint twenty stories below, decorating Berwyn Avenue with red. The Minker—the moron—had gone straight out after its prey, and ended up right beside its quarry. Up here, Tasha looks to her left, a few yards over, where there is someone: someone living. It's Dinah. She is brown like Tasha but with short, straight hair and a soft face. She has a black eye that is mostly healed, a few burst capillaries in the white of it remaining. She looks afraid, her brows far up on her forehead, still recovering from shock. But her face is relaxing as Tasha meets her gaze, and the woman manages a small smile.

"Holy shit," she says. "Hi."

CHAPTER 5

The morning of the Change was the classic scene of oblivion: the heedless bumbler wandering distractedly out into a world that has gone, overnight, from her comfortable home turf to a wild country; wonderland turned wilderness by meteor, plague, or monster. In this case, of course, it was monster.

Tasha had woken up before her alarm to the sounds of her neighbors fighting. Nothing new. She vaguely remembered them starting earlier, when she had covered her head with her pillow and slept on. By the time 6:22 had rolled around, they had been at it for hours and she considered calling the police. Although the woman had stopped screaming at that point and she could just hear the guttural sounds of the boyfriend, who Tasha had seen before and mentally likened to a Neanderthal anyway. Maybe they were having sex; she couldn't tell from all his grunting. It sounded almost like he was barking but Tasha hadn't thought much of it other than vague revulsion: some people were into roleplaying, she had thought, and then went about her morning routine of hair-straightening and mascara-applying. She thought she could hear the guy across the hall yelling too. He wasn't generally the type to have shouting matches with his wife, but everyone had bad days.

Crisping her hair, she looked out the window at the muted world of Sheridan Road. There appeared to be a person lying in the grass by the Volamu from what she could make out from this high up. Trashed, most likely. Dude...on a Wednesday morning? He was worse than Gina. She'd turned away to brush her teeth.

She put on the Apiary uniform, remembering at once how much she disliked it, the clammy feeling the material lent the skin, like pulling a rubber glove over one's thighs. She snapped the material at the shoulders to cover her bra straps, wriggled to pull it down over her butt, was relieved that it still fit. Cara fired girls for weight gain all the time. These were the things that Tasha worried about on the morning of the Change. She stared at her face in the mirror, a face that, as make-up was added, was like Rorschach's mask; constantly shifting and mutating into new faces, new masks. She imagined it was like Pangaea, masses drifting through the ocean into something only barely recognizable from what it once was. The pieces would fit, a nose lines up with an eye, but it would be jagged, hypothetical. Was it ever really a face? She had a small pimple on her temple.

She flat-ironed her hair. She put on her platform boots, the white monkey hat. She glimpsed her nailbeds and recoiled from the doorknob to retrieve her nail file. She sprayed on perfume. She walked out the door.

In the lobby there had been another mirror, another reflection to check. Down the hall by the supply closet was her doorman, Brian. He stood with his back to her, doing nothing, swaying as if drunk.

"Good morning," Tasha called, a little stiffly. No knowledge of plague, meteor, monster; no suspicion. Brian hadn't answered, of course. He just swayed. She assumed he was drunk on the job.

"Good morning?" she said again.

He ignored her.

Fine. Dick.

Those were her thoughts.

He was just starting to turn around to face her as she headed toward the front of the lobby. He sounded like he was humming, growling. Tasha barely noticed.

Crossing the dim lobby, she heard the dull clicks of her Apiary boots against the bare tile floor. She had stopped at the table in the center of the room where they laid the dailies to pick up a tabloid, but several of the issues were stuck together. Her hand grazed something wet.

"What the hell?"

She peered at her hand in the low light. What the fuck was that? Red. Blood?

"Oh, awesome," she said to no one. "Somebody bleeds all over the papers and doesn't even clean it up. Cool." She used the paper she picked up to wipe her fingers. She had briefly wondered if she might be able to get AIDS from touching someone else's blood. At that moment, it was the worst thing she could imagine.

She had whipped out her hand sanitizer as she headed for the door—*Guaranteed to Destroy All Risk*, the label read. All risk. She had examined her fingers for traces of blood and was reminded of her cuticles. She fished the nail file out of her rubbery uniform pocket. It was silver and pointed.

Outside, the day had felt like May ought to feel. The clear air had lifted her spirits. She forgotten her raucous neighbors; she pushed aside the thoughts of her parents' collapsing lungs; the pimple on her temple. She filed her nails, allowing herself to feel hopeful. Today she'd get her job back. In a few months she'd have MINK. After that, she'd get the Chip. And then everything would be fine. Everything would be just fine.

"So you thought…we were just fighting," Dinah says softly.

They're leaning out the windows now, as they have been on and off since the day before with the jumper. They look out at the sky—anywhere but below, where there are the many shapes of the dead. They'd both felt foolish upon "discovering" that they could talk face to face by leaning out the windows: it had taken them five days to remember that windows could be for more than closing out the world.

"Yeah…" says Tasha. She hadn't wanted to talk about this, but Dinah wanted to hear about the Change. Her experience with it had been limited to the skirmish with Dale that Tasha had overheard. Tasha doesn't say so, but she's sure many other Chicagoans shared the same experience—and she doubts many of them survived.

"Did you hear us fight all the time?" Dinah is looking at Tasha now, but Tasha keeps her eyes on the clouds. Their marble pattern is like a permanent, silent storm, lacking only in rain.

"Yeah," Tasha says after hesitating. "Yeah. I heard him yell at you. And stuff. I heard you go in the bathroom and lock the door. I heard him try to break it down. Then I would hear him leave and lock the door behind him. But I didn't know you didn't have keys."

Now Dinah looks away. She is absent-mindedly fingering the remnants of her black eye.

"Yeah, no keys for Dinah," she says quietly. "He told me if I could go a month without making him mad, then he'd give me one key. Another month, the second key. Another month, the third key."

"But?"

Dinah laughs a short, hard laugh, finally swinging her eyes onto Tasha's face, staring at her frankly.

"But everything makes Dale mad."

They're silent again. A bird whizzes by them and they both jump, afraid that another body has fallen from the sky, a Minker chasing it down to the pavement like a kamikaze Pegasus. Eventually Dinah sighs and said,

"So what happened after you left the building?"

CHAPTER 6:
THE CHANGE

Tasha had been busily shaping her nails with the nail file, head down and eyes on her fingers. Cars mostly extinct, the L debarked, Chicagoans like islands floating along their commutes—the silence wasn't an immediate giveaway. But the dead woman lying across the sidewalk was.

Tasha almost stepped on her. Lost in her cuticles, bracing herself against the stiff wind coming off the lake at her back, she didn't see the woman's body until she was almost on top of it. The red high heels were what brought her attention up from her hands.

"Gucci," she said, before she realized the woman had been murdered. Then, "Jesus Christ." Then louder, "Jesus Christ—!"

The stilettos weren't the only red: the woman's chest and abdomen were a mess of torn cotton and flesh. Tasha stumbled backwards, her back up against one of the dogwoods. It wasn't until then that she screamed. She had only seen bodies in caskets, arranged quietly and politely in the polished wooden frame, their eyes closed in something like serenity. This woman in her red high heels was too broken, too colorful: her eyes, like her mouth, were wide open, the skyscrapers reflected in her irises. Tasha had whipped out her Glass in an instant and called 911. It rang busy.

"Busy?" she said incredulously, then screamed it, "Busy!"

Her voice echoed off the buildings and came back to her sounding small and young. She called 911 again. Busy. When she looked around for help she saw the other bodies. One was a few yards away on the Volamu, sprawled across the moving tread but stuck. His body jerked gently up and down as the track purred underneath him, too softly to budge him and send his body zipping toward the L. His empty face was turned toward Tasha, and she gaped at him. He gaped back.

Suddenly they were everywhere; she just hadn't noticed them before. Looking back the way she came, she saw that she had passed a dead man in the grass between the Volamu and the sidewalk. He was facedown, arms at his sides, his legs straight. Tasha clapped her hands over her mouth. She had never been a screamer, not even in horror movies when Gina would grab her to make her jump. But now she couldn't stop: the sounds rose in her throat like bile; unnatural, hoarse sounds that scrabbled up the esophagus to her mouth. It occurred to her that she sounded like a man mocking a screaming woman, so she stopped and rubbed her throat, leaning more heavily against the tree.

A second or two passed before she realized that what she

rested her head against had more give than the trunk of a tree would typically offer. She took a step forward and glared at the dead woman's red Gucci pumps.

"Fuck," she said. Turning around, she kept her eyes on the ground. She was breathing heavily to keep from hurling. "Fuck."

She looked into the tree. Plaid. A plaid shirt. A hand. An arm. She looked away. That was enough.

"Fuck."

There was a dead man in the tree. Or a woman. She couldn't tell; plaid was in this season, His and Hers. She didn't want to look. He or she had climbed into the tree to get away. Lot of good it did. To get away from what?

A sound from the open window of one of the garden-level apartments caught Tasha's attention. It was a scraping noise, like a manhole being pulled from its socket in the street. She inched over to the nearest apartment building where she thought the sound was coming from. The closer she got, the more she could hear; not just the scraping but a low moaning too.

"Is someone hurt?" she called cautiously. "911 isn't working. Are you okay?"

The moaning stopped abruptly, as did the scraping.

"Are you okay?" Tasha called again. She was almost at the low window. It was open—just the screen between her and whatever was making the sound. She reached the screen and peered in. "Is someone hurt?"

A kid, a boy, probably eight or nine, stared up at her from

the floor of what appeared to be a basement or storage room. The window was well off the ground and he couldn't quite reach.

"Hey," Tasha said, surprised, "are you okay?"

The boy took a step back so he could see her without craning his neck. His eyes were red-rimmed, but his skin had a healthy glowing tan. He didn't answer, just glared at her with something like anger on his face; his eyebrows knitted together, hard lines on either side of his mouth. (She didn't know why he looked so mad, with a tan like that.) His eyes, though, were glazed. He looked at her as if he didn't quite know what she was, what world she came from. He looked high.

"Are your parents here?" Tasha asked, crouching down to see him better. Maybe his parents were with him, also in need of ambulances. "There are some people out here who are hurt."

Hurt.

The boy had opened his mouth. He emitted a short, clipped exclamation: a sound, not a word; somewhere between a bark and a grunt, delivered from the throat. It startled Tasha so much that she cried out.

At her small cry, the boy made the sound again, and seemed to grow excited, though the irate expression remained on his young features. Then began the moaning that had drawn Tasha over in the first place; a pleading animal sound he emitted as he jumped up and down trying to find a hold on the window sill, his feet scrabbling on the wall inside. Each time he got close, his knuckles collided with the screen in the window, bumping the top corner out of its groove. This close, the scraping sound raised gooseflesh on Tasha's arms.

"What the fu—?"

The boy's fingers found a hold. He hung for a moment, still doing his grotesque moaning. After pausing to pant, he scrabbled his way up so that his elbows held him up on the ledge. His face was only a foot or so away from Tasha when he bared his teeth.

They were ordinary human teeth; not all of them were even permanent yet. But the red pieces of some substance between them put a dragon in Tasha's stomach that chewed the lining like bubblegum: something wasn't right. She stared at the child from where she crouched, so near him. His moaning had stopped, replaced by a sweating silence.

Then he snapped his teeth—the sound was terrible—and lunged forward against the screen, his head butting into it. The screen grated again and the metal bent slightly. Tasha thought she screamed, but instead she kicked him in the face through the metal mesh. Her size-seven foot, encased in a platform-boot, connected squarely with his forehead. Teeth still bared but eyebrows momentarily separated in shock, he plummeted backwards out of Tasha's sight. There was a thud as his body hit the floor.

Silence. After a moment, against her better judgment, Tasha approached the screen again and peered down into the dim light. The room was mostly empty: just a few steel crates along the walls and a couple built-in shelves. Who knows what the kid was doing there, or how he got in, but he was now sprawled on his back on the concrete floor, a circle of blood moving outward from his small head. Tasha thought about it—still too terrified to feel remorse—and she figured a five-and-a-half-foot or so drop, with direct connection between skull and concrete, would be more than enough to put a crack the size of a crater down the back of an eight-year-old's head.

Tasha was just trying to convince herself to cry, scream, something, when the kid stirred. He stirred and then sat up. He'd lost an incredible amount of blood: a lot of it stained what Tasha now saw was a Spongebob t-shirt. "Vintage," Tasha thought as the kid stood up.

She had stared at him, disbelieving. He seemed confused, but didn't appear to be in pain or unsteady on his feet. He turned his head to look at the pool of his blood, and it was in that moment that Tasha glimpsed the gaping hole in the back of the kid's skull. More shocking than the wound itself was the fact that it was knitting itself back together, black and red clots moving like animated spiderwebs across the cavity, the blood seeping slower and slower as the hole miraculously ceased to exist. A flashing red light caught Tasha's attention and she tore her gaze away from what was now just blood-soaked hair. Her eyes rested on the side of the boy's neck, where a red light flashed rhythmically through the flesh.

The boy's eyes were on her again. He walked through the blood on the concrete floor and approached the window once more, leaving crimson footprints behind him that were blackish in the weak light. He grunted as he began jumping again, the grating sound resuming as the screen began scraping against its frame.

She had run then, using every curse she knew, screaming the words in a flurry of Tourette's and terror. She leaped over the dead woman in Gucci, ran past the tree with the dead person in plaid, ran without looking at the man bumping softly on the Volamu and the man whose face was buried in grass. The Volamu hummed alongside her in the opposite direction, toward the red high heels and the boy with the flat eyes.

Tasha ran all the way home, tripping every few steps in her mandatory knee-high boots, the stupid white hat she wore to win Cara's understanding flying off her head in the wind. She ran down Sheridan, past the 50-story sex shop, blowing past the Apple dealership—iScoot scooters were all the rage—all the way to her lobby door where she yanked open the entrance and ran straight into Brian, her doorman. He was humming.

No, growling. What she thought was a hum was a low vibrating growl that entered Tasha's eardrums and put in her mind's eye the face of an eight-year-old boy with a hole in his head. She stumbled sideways into the lobby, staring goggle-eyed at Brian, who looked as if he was still trying to figure out what she was and how she got there. He looked dumbly at Tasha, then at the door. The humming sound could still be heard, but he didn't seem to be interested in her, though his face held the same sort of placid, dense balefulness as the kid in the basement. Tasha took a step to her left, wondering if she could make it across the lobby to the elevator. She cursed the Apiary for making her wear these fucking ridiculous platform-heeled boots, cursed herself for leaving her apartment for such a stupid job. She'd trip for sure, or he'd catch her. She took another step. He looked.

Her presence finally seemed to register, and his eyebrows knitted together a little more tightly, his expression one of dull annoyance. He grunted, the same half-bark that the boy had made, and started forward. His gait wasn't overly slow or shambling or animal-like. He did sway a bit, but mostly he walked the way she always remembered him as walking. The slight limp wasn't from some horrible evil mutation, she knew; it was from a baseball injury he'd sustained in college, sliding to home on a very close throw. He was three feet away now. He snapped his very human, very square, very white teeth. A red light in his neck flashed slowly. Tasha fumbled. She didn't know what she was looking for, but her hand found the nail file in her pocket and she grasped it like it was the vine over the precipice. It ripped her pocket on the way out—a momentary flash of regret as the seams tore—and then she buried it in Brian's neck.

She brought her arm back and did it again, stopping Brian in his tracks. His eyebrows were almost touching between his eyes now and he turned his head at an uncomfortable angle trying to see what Tasha had done to him. Tasha stared at her hand. It held a file that, twenty minutes before, had been giving her a manicure. Now it was buried in her doorman's flesh.

The red light alongside the puncture wound pulsed madly now. The flesh began to creep around the file, trying to grow back together with the metal still embedded in the skin. Brian cocked his left arm back and punched Tasha in the face.

The blow hit her like a subway, and she fell back against

the wall behind her. A warm feeling spread across her face. She looked down at the bright red blood gushing onto her stupid blue uniform from her stupid nose.

"Fuck," she said weakly, for the sixth time that morning. She didn't know how she was still clutching the file in her fist. She staggered to her feet, sliding sideways along the wall as she tried to get the platform boots to right themselves underneath her. Brian lunged clumsily at her: his teeth scraped her wrist but didn't draw blood. Tasha swung her arm in a wide arc and the file entered his shoulder. He didn't even flinch this time, just grabbed her powerfully by the arms and stretched his head nearer to her—mouth open, teeth snapping. His grunting was loud and labored. Tasha's panic mounted and she attacked him with both hands, one with the file and the other clenched in a tight fist. The fist caught him in the throat, the file above the eye. Blood spouted from the wound, forming a rivulet that gushed down his face and into his vision. His teeth kept snapping.

"Get the fuck off me!" she screeched, "Get the fuck off me! No!" She knew she sounded ridiculous but she couldn't stop. The file entered his body at various points—his hands, his cheek, his chest—with no visible reaction: just a steady and unhurried groping for her throat as his square white teeth continued their monstrous snapping. And between all the frenzy, she could see every wound she inflicted on him closing up, the skin coming back together indifferently, the red light ever present.

Tasha was getting weak. The adrenaline that had powered

her initial defense was eroding under Brian's steady onslaught. Her stabs were less ferocious. Blood remained on his flesh from the dozen wounds that had rapidly closed themselves, but her attacks were barely breaking the skin now. She felt weary, constantly parrying his seeking teeth. Meanwhile the red light in Brian's neck flashed crazily with a rhythm so fast it matched Tasha's heartbeat.

"I said no!" she cried desperately as she stabbed Brian again in the cheek. To her own ears, she sounded like a person training a stubborn Pomeranian, or a distressed college girl fending off an entitled frat boy.

Brian forced her to the floor. He sprawled on top of her, throwing his weight onto one of her thighs to pin it to the lobby tiles. Tasha writhed like a snake: the hand that wasn't holding the file clutched his neck, squeezing hard enough to close his windpipe but making no difference in his persistence. Brian growled like a mongrel, his face inches from hers. She turned her head to the side, repulsed by his dull expression: she expected his breath to reek but it still smelled of Crest. It was only 9am.

Brian was between her legs. Her wrists were clamped in his robotic grip as he attempted to force them over her head to allow him access to her throat. The red light flashed merrily. She wrenched the hand with the file from Brian's clutches and plunged it into the place on his neck that was illuminated from within by the red light.

There was a spark, and Brian jerked as if he'd been shocked. The steady growl that had filled Tasha's ears since she entered the building faltered and turned into a cough. His grip grew weaker. Tasha let go of the nail file; it stood out from his neck like a maypole, ribbons of blood running freely from the wound and seeping down on to Tasha's neck and cheek. Feeling him becoming heavier, she shoved with the last of her strength and sent the doorman toppling to his side.

Brian died quickly. Tasha lay next to him on the floor panting and still bleeding from her nose, too weak to stand, and she watched his impassive eyes stare intently at a spot on the wall behind her, the eyelids unblinking. His eyebrows were still cinched together. He clutched at his throat as if asphyxiating, his legs spasming like those of a beetle as blood continued to gush from the wound in his neck. Tasha could still see the red light blinking behind the gore, but its rhythm was slowing. Eight seconds or so later the coughing and jerking ceased and Brian lay silent, his eyes still glaring over her shoulder.

Tasha rolled on to her back in exhausted relief, but was forced to flip quickly back to her side as a surge of bile suddenly rushed to her mouth, and she retched on the lobby floor. The viscous fluid crept toward the doorman's corpse. She stared at him. His nametag had been knocked sideways during the scuffle. *Guest Services: Brian*, it read.

Tasha sat up and unzipped the white platform boots that almost cost her life. She kicked them off. Struggling to her feet, she stared down at Brian. Without really knowing why, Tasha went and grabbed him under the arms and dragged him toward the desk where he had spent most of his time. His body had become anvil-heavy and she had to take a few breaks while hauling him, gagging involuntarily once or twice as her grip was made slippery by his blood. When she made it to the desk with Brian in tow, she rested his body against the wall while she pulled out the chair for him. On the desk was a cup of coffee, still lukewarm, and a widescreen computer. Behind the computer was Brian's Glass, a *Playboy* application still pulled up. On the screen a redhead sat with legs spread on the top of a piano, her fingers pulling back the lips of her hairless vagina.

"Real nice, Brian," Tasha said, smearing blood from her nose onto her cheek. "But can she *play* the piano?"

She dumped Brian into his chair with less ceremony than she would have a moment before, roughly arranging him in an upright posture when he slumped to the side like a masterless marionette.

She'd been halfway across the lobby before she had a thought and turned back. She yanked the nail file from Brian's neck, and the tiny, once-flashing mechanism came through the hole too, skewered on the end of the file like a kabob. A chip. The Chip. It was small and square—a little less than an inch in diameter—and a little bulb (a police siren in miniature) stood out from the center. So that's what they looked like. The Chip was sticky with coagulated blood, and she dropped it into Brian's lap. She took a last look at the doorman's slumped figure and then headed back across the lobby. Stepping onto the elevator, she pressed twenty and it hummed upwards, making no stops.

CHAPTER 7

They're learning to pass the time. Tasha can't remember the last time she talked so much; her throat is actually sore. The last time she'd had a sore throat it was from a combination of yelling and whiskey while attending a rave in Wicker Park. This is what fun has become, she tells herself. No more shopping. No more trips to the spa. Over the last few days, she has looked in at her closet of brightly colored clothes more than once, checking on them. You okay in there, guys? She'd considered trying on every single outfit she owned, just because. But if Dinah were to ask what she was doing, Tasha doesn't know if she could lie. If Dinah wasn't confined to her apartment, she could come over and try on clothes too. The thought is absurd, and Tasha shakes her head at herself, but she still thinks it, clinging.

"You know, Dale thought I had the Chip."

Tasha glances over at Dinah. They've pulled chairs up to their windows now and slouch onto the sills. Tasha would kill for a balcony.

"Thought? How could he *think* you have the Chip?"

Dinah smiles thinly and points to her neck. The three yards are just too far to see properly, but Tasha thinks she sees an outline she hadn't noticed before, a faint black square.

"What is that? Is that a tattoo?"

Dinah laughs.

"Yep. You know how people would get tattoos over their Chip to decorate it or highlight it or whatever? Status symbols and all that. Well, I got the tattoo…just not the Chip."

Tasha stares at her, Dinah's smile growing wider and wider. Tasha thinks she might be blushing a little.

"Are you serious? Did anyone know?"

"How could they?" Dinah shrugs. "It looks like a black line around where the Chip would be. Fooled Dale and he saw me all the time."

"But—why'd you do it?"

Dinah shrugs, her smile fading.

"I mean, Dale was from a good family, you know? Rich boy. He was going to introduce me to his mom soon and I wanted them to think I was from a good family too. I mean, my family is great, but we're not rich. I didn't want his mom to get anything in her head about me marrying Dale for money. You know how some older white people are about girls that look like us. Especially when we're dating their sons."

Tasha shrugs, blushing for reasons she's not sure of.

"Were both your parents black, or just one? Or…" Dinah falters. "Something else. Not to be rude."

"Not rude. My dad was mixed. Mom was black."

"Did they care who you dated?"

"No. I mean she married a broke guy from Kentucky, right?" Tasha laughs a little, distracted. Their discussion of the Chip has reminded her of the day she was fired from the Apiary, just two days after Tasha had gone with Gina to Cybranu. Tasha had been behind the desk at Fetch Fetchers, her brain rotting into puppy chow, when the infamous Mrs. Kerry had entered the store like a Versace-clad Cruella de Vil, the usual pair of dark sunglasses covering her eyes.

"Welcome to Fetch Fetchers," Tasha had drawled, trying only a little not to sound robotic. She was tempted to ask Mrs. Kerry "How's that lavender Lhasa Apso working out for you?" but it would probably result in her being fired. She had been warned about staying out of the clientele's business; guilting them about their latest disposable companion wasn't in the job description. So when Mrs. Kerry ignored Tasha's greeting and glided around the store in a cool silence, Tasha went back to reading the *Vogue* app on Fetch Fetcher's Glass.

She only read *Vogue* for the ads; this one was for vodka. The models on the screen were posed like dolls, with X's over their eyes. The one on the right wore a dress like a cake and was pale-skinned with bright lips, her hair teased into a tall pile like meringue. Her frosted mouth was open in an orgasmic expression. The arm of the model she shared the screen with was draped across her thigh, her black skin, nearly naked, a stripe of night across the first one's stark pale flesh.

"I wasn't aware that Fetch Fetchers was in the practice of

employing the *deaf.*"

It was Mrs. Kerry, standing in front of Tasha and tapping her talons on the counter. If the woman had said something, Tasha hadn't heard it.

"I'm so sorry," Tasha said, quelling her belligerence. "What can I help you with?" She shoved the Glass under the counter and clasped her hands in front of her, widening her eyes for an appearance of profound interest.

Mrs. Kerry squinted an eye at the polished brown girl in front of her, gave Tasha a quick up-and-down to ascertain whether she was being made fun of or not. She decided that she wasn't—she was wrong—and lifted her hair behind her shoulder with the back of a limp, laser-tanned hand.

"I want an animal. Something elegant."

Mrs. Kerry turned to survey the store with a disparaging look, a look that implied she was sure that there was nothing of any elegance to be found there. Tasha took that moment as an opportunity to roll her eyes before launching into the speech about pink Pomeranians and such, but Mrs. Kerry halted her with a raised red claw.

"No, no...I said elegant."

Tasha wondered what an elegant animal would look like to someone like Mrs. Kerry. Something resembling the way she thought of herself as looking, no doubt. *Armadillo,* Tasha thought to herself. Out loud, she offered blandly,

"Maybe a micro lynx?"

Mrs. Kerry's first reaction had been disdain—as it was for everything—but after seeming to go through a mental Rolodex of her personal zoological history, she came to the conclusion that perhaps a lynx might be just the thing.

Tasha led her down a brightly lit aisle marked Fetch Felines. Various cats stared balefully out at the two women from the cages that lined the row, their diamond eyes flat with what Tasha always imagined to be malice. It had disturbed her that they never meowed: their starey silence gave Tasha the feeling that she was walking the Green Mile, the long ceramic stroll to Old Sparky. The cats' role in this illusion varied: sometimes they were fellow inmates, regarding her as one would regard one's own reflection in water—a vague recognition with an impression of strangeness. Other times the cats were her keepers, condemning witnesses urging her toward her doom.

Tasha neared the end of the aisle and gestured grandly (as she'd been trained) at the few cages of micro lynxes and the single mini cougar that napped behind the bars. When they first arrived at Fetch Fetchers they would pace the way Tasha had seen big cats do in zoos as a child. But after awhile the pacing stopped and they lay on their beds dully, their mouths partly open like the girls in *Vogue*, gaping.

"What a pretty thing," said Mrs. Kerry, leaning slightly toward the cage, bending at the waist.

"Yes," Tasha replied, laying her hand on the bars, "the micro lynx is a beauty. They are designed not to shed, so their beautiful coats will stay on them, and not on your upholstery." The speech felt like saltine crackers in her mouth, as it always did.

"Oh yes, I can't have the little dear shedding all over my

mink furs, can I? Fur and fur must be kept separate if I…"

Mrs. Kerry had trailed off. Tasha waited for her to continue, and when she did not, she turned to look for the cause of her distraction. Mrs. Kerry's eyes were fixed on Tasha's hand, which still rested on the cage. The woman's customary sharp look had given way to a dull stare. A wrinkle crinkled between her eyes: she would doubtlessly attack it with Botox if she could see it. She stared dumbly at Tasha's hand, as if angered by the sight of it.

"Mrs. Kerry…?" Tasha didn't know what to make of it and considered shaking the woman. Was she drunk? One too many Xanax? Maybe she just needed to sit down. Tasha reached out to touch her shoulder.

Tasha gasped as Mrs. Kerry grabbed her hand. She brought it very close to her face and eyed the ring on Tasha's finger, her mother's ring, an onyx stone set in simple silver.

"Where did you get this ring?"

Mrs. Kerry's voice was slow, thick, like words spoken through a curtain. Tasha had a fleeting impression of a drunken priest, slurring through the confessional screen. She stared at Mrs. Kerry, whose eyes were hooded, the crease between them deepening, giving her a look of idiotic annoyance.

When Tasha didn't answer, the words came again, slower this time.

"Where did you get…this ring?"

There was a lilt to the words—beneath the sleepy drawl, Tasha could still hear the country club emphasis, the "Oh, Victoria, those shoes are simply darling! Where did you *get* those shoes?" Mrs. Kerry seemed to be sleepwalking on a plane that hovered somewhere between inebriation and snobbery.

"It was my mother's."

Mrs. Kerry went on staring, her head swaying a little from side to side, a dizzy duck. She rubbed the ring with her thumb, and Tasha couldn't help but imagine her as Bilbo Baggins, a harmless enough creature turned odd by accessories.

Mrs. Kerry raised her head slowly, taking in Tasha inch by inch. Her eyes traveled up Tasha's slender arm, then wandered up her throat as if memorizing it. Her cloudy blue eyes met Tasha's squinting brown ones, and the voice came again, harsher this time.

"Your mother's dead."

The head had snapped down again, its mouth open.

Tasha had worked with dogs long enough to develop hot reflexes for these situations and she snatched her hand back before the teeth made contact, the ring catching on and chipping Mrs. Kerry's incisor. The older woman went for Tasha's throat with outstretched hands, her face unchanged. Tasha's back slammed against the cage holding a micro lynx, causing the animal to screech in surprise. Or maybe the screech was Tasha's. It was impossible to know which came first, but the air was soon full of screeching: Tasha screaming as she tried to pry the fake-tanned hands from her throat; Mrs. Kerry making a sound halfway between shriek and bark as she scrabbled to get a better hold; the Fetch Felines all raising a racket Tasha had never heard before. In her peripheral vision, their mouths were wide and their teeth were bright.

Marla came sprinting from the back room, a tranquilizer in hand. She had assumed one of the animals was loose and out of control. Tasha saw the dart and managed to gasp, somewhat insanely,

"Shoot her! Shoot her!"

But Marla did not shoot her.

"Tasha, what are you doing!" she yelled. Somehow she had missed the fact that it was Mrs. Kerry's hands that were wrapped around Tasha's throat.

Tasha threw her weight sideways and Mrs. Kerry toppled to the floor and lay still. Marla rushed to her side as Tasha scrambled to her feet, rubbing her neck.

"Mrs. Kerry! Mrs. Kerry, ma'am, are you alright?" Marla felt for a pulse but Mrs. Kerry had just opened her eyes. The blue of them was clear again, but a trace of the furrow between her brows remained.

"I'm fine...I...I..." she stammered, and her eyes wandered before fixing on Tasha, then on Tasha's ring. "That girl! She has my ring!"

Marla turned with surprise to face Tasha, whose jaw had dropped as if broken, touching the ring protectively with her other hand.

"What? This is my mother's ring!"

"You little liar! That is *my* ring! You took it from me!"

"Marla, this is my mother's ring! You've seen me wear it a hundred times!"

Tasha looked into Marla's eyes, but Marla looked at Mrs. Kerry.

"I'll have to call Cara and ask her to come up."

Blonde, strutting Cara lived solely for these moments and had entered Fetch Fetchers accompanied by a security guard, Jason. Mrs. Kerry had collected herself and gave a stunning description of the events that had transpired, beginning with Tasha's initial neglect and disrespect—alluding to previous instances—and leading up to Tasha's aggressive attitude and unwillingness to provide assistance, culminating in her assault of Mrs. Kerry, striking her and prising the ring off her finger. The ring was an heirloom, Mrs. Kerry explained.

Tasha was allowed to give her side of the story, but she heard how ridiculous it sounded. The wife of a millionaire, decked out in Chanel, entering a pet store and attacking the cashier? Robbing her? It was laughable. Tasha recognized the sneer on Cara's pointy face before she had even begun. Tasha pointed to her own neck.

"She choked me! Don't you see the bruises?"

Cara looked at Tasha's throat with a flick of her eyes and exchanged a glance with Mrs. Kerry.

"It's hard to see bruises on someone of your complexion, Tasha, you know that."

Tasha felt the light drain from her body. Cara continued.

"And anyway, look at what you've done to Mrs. Kerry's tooth! It's chipped! You're lucky she's declining to press charges: you would be in a lot of trouble."

"Luckily I have MINK," Mrs. Kerry drawled, examining her blood red manicure.

Tasha's spine was ice. She stared at Cara, who was smiling.

"Give me the ring, Tasha." She turned to Mrs. Kerry. "We'll need to keep the ring in the company safe while we process an incident report, Mrs. Kerry. You can claim your property in about a week, after we wrap up all the loose ends." These last few words she directed at Tasha, who was not crying, but was crumbling like dead leaves.

The ring had crossed her knuckle, entered a cold, pale palm. Tasha went home.

"Whoa," says Dinah. She has her comforting voice on again. "Tasha, whoa."

Tasha stares so hard at the sky that her eyes begin to water. In the apartment building across Berwyn she can just see the bloodied body of a man sprawled across his kitchen table, where it's been since the first day—defused Minker or actual victim, she can't tell. She looks down at her hands, at her empty finger. She had seen Cara slip the ring into her pocket—it probably never even made it to the safe. But *Tasha* was the thief.

"You okay?" Dinah asks. Tasha sees her hand move, as if she had been about to reach out and touch her before she'd remembered how large the gap was.

"Yeah, I just need a couple minutes," Tasha says and pushes off the window frame, returning to the shell of her apartment. She isn't sure if she's currently upset about the firing or if she's reliving the loss of her ring. She looks over at the vanity where there are a few framed pictures. She picks one up. It's of her and her sister with their parents before they died, a cluster of familiar eyes and cheekbones. They're all smiling: her mother with the unselfconscious beam that Tasha inherited but hides; her father with the small offering of teeth that he used only for photographs, and her sister, Leona, standing with her arm around Tasha, her teeth bared in what seems more a joyful snarl than a grin.

"Your mother named you right," their father would say when she smiled. Leona wasn't the type to care.

She and Tasha are different in that way, although they hadn't always been. Looking at the photograph, Tasha examines the face of her eighteen-year-old self. Only three years ago, but the time and distance between that Tasha and the Tasha she is now feels infinite. Her face in the picture is clean of make-up, her hair in complicated braids—Leona's handiwork, if she remembers correctly. When had she started the hair-pressing and the mascara? After the funerals, she knows, with Gina helping her "get over it." Every layer on her face had become another stripe of war paint, another design on the wings of the Polyphemus moth, camouflaging her from the world; a way to disguise herself from grief, as if it were a thing she could hide from. It hadn't worked, she says to herself, thinking of all the death beyond the window.

Beside her in the picture, Leona is wearing a gray sweatshirt and black jeans, her hair a soft brown halo. Their parents are dressed the way Tasha has always remembered them dressing: jeans, t-shirts. The sight of their faces is almost more than she can bear. On her mother's finger is the very ring taken by Cara and Mrs. Kerry—she'd given it to Tasha just a few months after the photo was taken. Tasha rubs her finger like Aladdin's lamp, staring at Leona, wondering if she still has the necklace their mother had given her. She probably does—she doesn't lose things like Tasha.

The only other likeness Tasha has of Leona is one taken a few years later, after California had seceded. It had been Leona's version of nail polish and blush, Tasha knows, moving out there. Tasha, in a rare expression of concern, had asked her sister if she was living in a war zone, and Leona had sent a videograph of her and her partner Morris standing and waving in front of their little house and garden. In the videograph, the house is orange and red and so is Leona's dress, moving gently at the hem in the breeze. Morris, laughing, cups the back of her neck in his hand, his other hand in his pocket. They look happy. Tasha fleetingly wishes she had taken Leona up on her offer to visit—maybe California was blissfully unaware of what was happening here: just tending to their gardens and building new houses.

Tasha returns to the window with the pictures in hand.

"This is them," she says simply, holding up the pictures for Dinah to see. Dinah peers, and Tasha is sure she can't make out the faces, but Dinah says,

"You look just like your mom," and Tasha wants to cry.

They're quiet for a moment, Tasha staring at the pictures in her hands, Leona waving and waving from the frame.

"Tasha," Dinah says gently, "I don't want to sound like a dick. I don't want to sound like your friend—Gina. But...it was just a ring, right? Your mom wouldn't care that the ring is gone. It's not like you pawned it. She'd tell you not to worry.

She wouldn't want you to be so sad."

"I know," Tasha says. And she does. "But it's the only thing of hers that I have."

"You have her smile too," Dinah says, and Tasha wishes she could hug this girl with her fading black eye. The feeling is stiff and unpracticed; she doesn't think Gina has ever hugged her, and it makes her want to cry even more. Feeling the tears coming, Tasha looks out through the buildings, glimpsing the lake between them.

"So your sister," Dinah says. "What made her go out to the Nation? Was she some kind of activist or what?"

Tasha shrugs.

"Yeah, pretty much. She was big into politics and justice and stuff. Conspiracies. I didn't really get why until she got out there and wrote me letters about the stuff the States did when the Nation seceded."

"Stuff? What kinda stuff?"

"Bombings, shootings. Let me get the letters."

Tasha leaves the window again and goes to the bed, using this opportunity to get her tears under control. Kneeling, she pokes her head beneath it and looks around for the long storage container. She drags it out. Lifting the lid, she digs around in the mess of paper: some are warranties, one is her lease, but most are letters, all from Leona, probably the last person on Earth who still writes letters. It's an expensive habit, which is why Tasha had stopped responding to every one: at $4.50 a stamp, letters were a bit out of her budget. Leona generally writes every other week either way, mostly with mundane details and usually with a gentle request for Tasha to come visit. California or not, the Post carries the letters. They drop them at a station just before the border, and someone in Leona's town makes the trip every couple days to retrieve anything that has arrived.

Tasha gathers them up like leaves. Hands full of wrinkled pages, she arranges the letters on the bed like a nest. Some still have the envelopes and she can read the dates in the official red-inked stamps of the Post, but most of them had been lost or thrown away upon receipt, leaving Tasha with nothing but a couple dozen lined pages filled with Leona's scratchy but elegant handwriting. Most are about Morris and the new house, what plants she potted on her porch, what books she was reading. Some talk about the secession, and she takes these to the window to read to Dinah.

"*All the kids from our neighborhood have gone to fight,*" one reads. "*Marina from two doors down just left yesterday. Her father is hysterical, of course, but her mother has some sense and knows Marina can handle herself. Well, she hopes. No one really knows what we're dealing with once we reach the border. A Dallas newspaper that found its way onto my table says that Walker's people have been ordered not to fire on young soldiers, but I think that's bullshit. Johnathon came back with the whole left side of his body burned black, and he's only sixteen. We asked what got him and he had no idea. We've got no clue what they're using out there. If I wasn't pregnant I'd go find out myself.*"

She skims through the next one—it's about the baby, Amani, who was born small but healthy—and skips it for another, which had been sent just before the main skirmishes of secession conflict. A wonder the letters were arriving at all, Tasha thinks, but the States couldn't bump off the Post, which had been struggling for years: if someone wanted to buy a stamp and send a letter, then, by god, the Post would take them up on it. The letter mentions the Mall of America being razed.

"*I heard somebody burned down the Mall! They said some terrorist group did it. Remember when I worked there that one year? (The mall. Not the terrorist group.) What a nightmare. Good riddance to the place, I say. Do you still work at the Apiary? I know you hate it, but keep that job as long as you can. You never know when you'll realize you really need it. But for now, when will you come visit me, Natasha? I know you think it's a wasteland, but it's safer here. I worry about you. Maybe you'd like it. Maybe you'd stay.*"

"Did you ever go visit her?" Dinah asks.

"No, it was too far when I was in college. Too expensive, too risky. And after my parents died and I dropped out of school—"

"You dropped out?"

"Yeah."

"Oh. What did you go for though? Before you dropped out?"

"History of American film."

"Oh. Not what I expected."

"What did you expect?"

"I don't know. Fashion. Merchandising. Something," Dinah laughs.

Tasha laughs and shakes her head.

"No, not even close." She feels embarrassed, although she's not sure if it's because of her major or because of Dinah's imagined one.

"Anyway," Dinah says. "You were saying?"

"Yeah. After I dropped out I just didn't think there was any point to going out there anymore. I don't know. Leona was out there living her life; I was here living mine."

They're interrupted by screaming, and the women both jerk their heads back inside like frightened meerkats. It's not coming from inside. Tasha wonders if the rest of her life is going to be punctuated by bouts of screaming, another death to add to her scrapbook of Change-related memories. Are they really called memories if they continue to happen, every day? This is life now, she tells herself for the tenth time.

"Where's it coming from?" she calls as quietly as she can to Dinah.

"Outside," Dinah answers. "I can see them."

Tasha steps back closer to the window and then she sees too. She wishes she could not.

Two figures, one small and one large, running down Sheridan, almost to Berwyn. The buildings are in the way or Tasha could have seen them sooner. As they get closer, a third and fourth figure appear behind them. Running. The staggering gait tells Tasha all she needs to know about the scenario.

"Is that a—is that a kid?" Dinah gapes.

The one out front; small, stumbling.

"It's a kid," says Tasha. The letters are fluttering out of her hands and floating to the floor. "It's a kid."

The larger figure—presumably the kid's guardian—is limping badly. The child is running ahead, often stopping and running back, trying to help the larger figure, who appears to be waving the kid on. The two shambling figures in the rear—Minkers. They're Minkers.—are gaining. The gap between the hunters and the hunted closes. The Minkers don't tire. Dinah has her hands over her mouth.

It ends quickly. The Minkers gain. They overtake the larger figure and the child is standing still, stricken, screaming. The screams rise from the ground and bounce off the buildings.

"God god god," Dinah is shrieking but it comes to Tasha's ears dull and thick through the pounding in her ears.

"Run, kid, run!" Tasha hears herself screeching, but the kid has already started running on its own. The child doesn't get far. There are more Minkers. They come from down Berwyn, lumbering past the body of yesterday's jumper, barking. In the end, three of them overtake the child.

Dinah is inside her apartment crying. Tasha wants to cry, but her body needs to do something else first. She's not sure what until it becomes immediately obvious. The panic is a balloon that inflates suddenly and then twists itself into the shape of a rubbery animal, a clambering chimpanzee scrambling at the too-small cage of her ribs. She stumbles to her feet and lurches into the bathroom. The little elastic rug that decorates the toilet lid slips off as she yanks open the porcelain bowl, and her string of curse words is lost in the stream of sour vomit. She heaves, the force of it squeezing her eyes shut. When she opens them she is staring at the cloudy continents of bile and spit, an atlas of white and yellow. She blinks hard, realizing that she's still clutching one of Leona's letters: the crumpled paper is torn and half-submerged in toilet water. She can still read its leaking ink:

They're going to blame us. Her sister's handwriting has begun to slant forward at this point, indicating that she's begun writing quickly, either because she was rushing or because she was angry. *Don't let them have you thinking we're a bunch of bloodthirsty nut-jobs. When we asked for a peaceful secession, their mediator laughed at us, Tash. Laughed at us! One said, "But we have so many new toys!" That's what he said. If I'd wanted to reconcile with the States before, that conversation eliminated that option. I've seen clips from the webnews: they're slipping in these little hints about these weapons of biological destruction that we supposedly have. WBDs? They're the ones with the bombs, and other stuff too, from what I hear. Kill-tech. I've heard rumors, Tasha. It's not just us they want to control; they want to get their thumb on people like you too. In case you want to leave for the Nation or something. But who knows. But if you're not going to visit me, just be careful. Anything could happen.*

Tasha stops reading. She laughs, but the feeling isn't quite right in her mouth. Somewhere inside her a lever is thrown and she shifts into deep sobs that vibrate her teeth. The feeling is appropriate and she wallows in it, but after a moment she stops sharply and holds her breath, struggling for control. Out of habit, she uses the heel of her hand to wipe running mascara from under her eyes, but when she looks at her unblackened palm, she remembers that she didn't put any on. Suddenly, this is the worst possible truth.

She scrambles to her feet, hauling on the sink for support. From the cabinet she snatches out her cosmetic bag and rummages through it frantically, her survival dependent on its contents. She draws out the long violet tube and sighs, her heartbeat slowing from its rodent hammering.

She twists open the cap and draws out the wand little by little, watching the tiny velvety bristles catching on the rim and gathering more of the rich black mud. Leaning as close to the mirror as she can across the obstacle of the sink, she steadies her hand. She raises her eyebrows in an expression of surprise and slowly, slowly brings the wand to the base of the lashes on her left eye. With a religiously delicate movement of her wrist, she draws the black-dyed brush up the length of the lashes. Another two or three painstaking swipes and she straightens her back, gazing into the mirror at her handiwork. Both eyes are red from first crying and then throwing up. With the mascara now applied to the left eye, she looks like a comedy/tragedy mask. She experiments with making one side of her mouth droop in a mournful grimace while twisting the other side up in a grin.

"You look ridiculous," she says to her reflection. She decides to do the other eye and inserts the wand back into the tube. Its label is paisley-patterned and reads *Urban Decay.*

"No shit."

CHAPTER 8

Morning. She struggles to remember what day it is. Seven, she thinks. Yes, seven. As for which day of the week…it ends in *y*, that's all she knows. Feeling sore, she slowly realizes she's still in the bathroom, curled up in the tub where she's been all night. Her eyes feel like she'd spent the evening seeking membership to Fight Club—from the sickness or the sobbing she can't say.

She rises. Stretching her body, she feels like an ancient wind-up toy in need of grease. She realizes sleeping in the bathtub probably wasn't the best idea, but it felt safe at the time. She steps out, feeling the damp spot on her ankle where the faucet had dripped on her jeans all night.

"Yay pneumonia," she says with the plastic cheer of a Mouseketeer.

Passing the mirror on her way out of the bathroom, she feels the allure of the mirror and pauses to assess her reflection.

"You need a flat iron," she says to the girl in the glass, fingering her scalp where the hair is coming in coiled. She can't help but think of Leona, who would see the sprouting spirals and smile.

She wanders into the bedroom, feeling guilty. After what she'd seen on the street yesterday she'd gone into the bathroom, first to vomit and then to seek solace. She'd found a version of it in the bathtub and she hadn't budged, even when she thought she heard Dinah calling softly for her later in the night. She couldn't bring herself to crawl out of the porcelain cradle. She had clung to the tube of mascara like a cross against evil, and there she'd slept.

The bedroom is cool. She notices she'd left the window open after she'd fled to the bathroom to hurl but doesn't feel much anxiety. It would be one damned skilled Minker that could trespass that way. She'd reward that beast with a free bite if it could pull that off. She pauses by her closet, peering in before walking to the window. The contents hang like rainbow ghosts, a closet full of witnesses, and she sighs, feeling faintly comforted.

Dinah is already at the window, resting on her elbows, surveying the world.

"Feel better?" she asks. Tasha doesn't hear any judgment in her voice. She wonders how long Dinah has been up, waiting.

Tasha nods.

"I just...I couldn't handle it. Being up here with no way to help. Another day not knowing why this is happening."

"Or what we can do to escape," Dinah adds.

Tasha looks at her, feeling the largeness of the statement, her chest tightening.

"Yes," she whispers.

"We need to know more," Dinah says.

"About what? I mean, we know how to kill them. There's just too many." Tasha feels like she's discussing video game strategy. When did this kind of conversation become real?

"There might be something else, you know? Some secret. Something that will…you know…turn them all off. Or there's got to be some place that's safe. Something. We just need information."

"Okay," says Tasha nodding. "But from who? It's not like we can go to the Daley Center or call 411 and put in an inquiry."

"Your sister," Dinah says quietly.

"Oh," says Tasha. "Yeah. Well, uh, let me just give her a ring. Can I borrow your Glass to make a call?"

"You said she writes you letters all the time," Dinah says, ignoring her. "You said it had been awhile. Maybe she's written you. Maybe there's a letter in your Post box right now and you don't know it."

Tasha considers this. It has been weeks since she's received a letter from her sister. She *is* due. But the chances of Leona having written about the Chip, the Change, or anything of note besides what new thing she planted in her garden are slim to none. On the other hand, if something was going on with the States, Leona usually knew about it, often before Tasha.

"You've given this some thought I see," Tasha jokes in lieu of expressing her doubt.

Dinah shrugs.

"I've been out here for awhile." Then she peers at Tasha.

"Did you…did you put on make-up?"

Tasha remembers her mad scramble to apply the mascara the day before, the immediate sense of calm and control it had offered her, and she guesses it's smeared all over her eyelids at this point. She feels foolish. How can she explain that it makes her feel safe?

"Yeah, I mean…um. Yeah."

"Well, since you're already all prettied up for the world, you could take a little trip to the Post," Dinah smiles wanly.

They're silent for a minute, and Tasha realizes that Dinah is serious.

"I don't know," Tasha says, stalling. "I mean, what if I get there and there's no letter? Then we're back at square one. No game plan…"

She notices Dinah is staring at her keenly, squinting out of the still-healing left eye.

"Tasha," she says in a low voice. "I need to get out of here."

"The keys…"

"I can't kill him, Tasha."

"Dinah…"

"Maybe there's another way. Maybe…maybe you'll meet someone who knows something. Maybe…I don't know. Fuck, you can leave any time you want and I'm stuck in here with a…a werewolf and a can of Pringles."

"A can of Pringles?"

"That's all that I have left."

"Fuck, Dinah! A can of Pringles?"

Tasha shoves off from the window and rushes into the

kitchen. She yanks open the cabinets and pulls out three cans of beans. Her cabinets are thinning—last time she went out was on the fourth day, days ago. She'll need to make another trip outside soon anyway. The Post isn't *so* far. Maybe Dinah's right. Plus, the Post is a government center. Who knows what information they'll have. She handles the cans of beans clumsily and a moment later is back in the window looking at Dinah.

"Can you catch?"

Dinah looks doubtful but nods.

"Okay. I'm gonna throw these, one at a time. I won't throw hard. One…two…three."

Tasha underhands the can of pinto beans and it sails past Dinah's head, knocking against the brick wall just beyond her. Dinah gasps and flinches. They watch the beans fall the twenty stories down, landing a few meters to the left of the two human stains from the apartment above. Tasha swallows.

"Okay, sorry. Let's try again."

Dinah nods.

"One…two…three…."

She underhands the second can and this time it's more on target, just a little short. Dinah's hands shoot out and she grabs it, juggles it, then grips it tightly.

"I got it! I got it!"

Tasha laughs out loud in delight. A can of Pringles. What the fuck.

She tosses the last can—garbanzo beans; she'd gotten those accidentally thinking they were navy—and Dinah catches it easily. They smile at each other.

"You have a can opener, right?"

"Yeah."

"Okay. Eat those. I'm going."

"Be careful," Dinah says. Her face is flat. She knows what's she's asking Tasha to do.

"Duh."

Tasha changes socks in the entrance to the closet and slides on the black and white Nikes she's been wearing since the Change. Before, she'd worn them only to the gym: the shoes are broken in while remaining unscuffed. She feels an unreasonable amount of pride for this accomplishment—she may not have had the best job before the Change, or the best grades in college, or the best future planned out in perfect detail, but at least she could keep her shoes clean. Shoes said a lot about a person. Before the Change, it was the first thing she looked at when she met someone, or sat across from them on the L. Forget the eyes; the shoes are the windows to the soul. Or the sole, she puns silently, smiling a thin smile.

Tasha fetches the knife from the bathroom floor where she'd left it the day before and assesses her readiness. She looks at the blade, sees her mascaraed eyes in its metallic sheen.

"You were a good investment," she says to the knife, and briefly wonders how long she's held conversations with inanimate objects. Has she always been this way, or had things only recently become viable companions? She heads for the door, turning the knob without speaking to it.

CHAPTER 9

Tasha takes the stairs. The elevator has been out since the electricity failed on Day 3, and her quads reaped first the punishment and now the benefits—twenty flights of stairs up and down a couple times will get anybody in Jazzercize condition, and she can feel the difference. "God, I sound like an infomercial," she thinks.

If only her building were connected to the city's massive thirty-day generators; then she would have light in the rooms, and a microwave. Then she could at least heat her beans, or even get a microwave pizza. She's considered making a small fire in her apartment with the windows open for ventilation, but the act points too much to complete societal disintegration. While Tasha sincerely doubts that what is happening in the city, and what must be the country, is just a blip, she doesn't think she's ready to declare herself a citizen of post-Chicago just yet. Plus, if Dinah is right and there's a big red "Abort" button someplace and things go back to normal, she'll have to pay a hefty property damage fee for the scorch marks and smoke damage, and she's broke. Better to just wait it out.

Not that going on a mission to the Post is waiting, Tasha realizes as she passes the twelfth floor. But Dinah's right: they've done enough sitting around since the Change. With the Wusthof knife and her Prada backpack she'll be proactive, get some fresh air and possibly find out more about the Change. She thinks of the city generators and again wishes they weren't just for corporations: if she had power she could turn on her Glass—it's a refurbished model, but at least she has one—and the huge screen it had been paired with. Though there wouldn't be much to see, most likely—a few emergency broadcasts had reported a nationwide crisis on the day of the Change, the anchors appearing cheerful enough at first, still reading the teleprompters. But after a few hours they were looking everywhere but at the cameras, appearing nervous and fidgety, and the next time Tasha checked, the seats were empty, the camera rolling on an anchor-less set, the painted "Good Morning, Chicago" bright and flat behind the desk. Then the power went out on Day 3, and there was nothing to see at all. Who knows why the power failed: maybe somewhere in the city the poor bastard in charge of a massive on/off switch had gotten chewed on by a Minker, and his toppling body had knocked the switch to the off position. Tasha almost laughs.

She reaches the lobby and heads for the side door, partly to avoid seeing Brian's body—which she can smell either way— and partly because she had come in the front door the day before and needs to use a different exit to stick with her SWAT plan.

She leans on the side door with just a fraction of her weight, allowing it to open slowly. Directly across the street is the massive McDonald's. *Their* lights are still on, Tasha notes jealously. She had considered going in on the day after the Change but had decided against it. Now she just envies them their lights, and perhaps their chicken nuggets.

She looks first right and then left, like a first-grader crossing the street, before she leaves the side door. Foster Avenue is deserted. A cluster of pigeons watches her warily from a few yards away, pecking absentmindedly at invisible crumbs on the sidewalk, but other than her silent birdy audience, she sees no one. A flag of Ghana flaps limply from a window of her building, but she hears nothing else. She wishes she were a dog so she could smell the air, but who knows what foul odors she would pick up. She adjusts her grip on the Wusthof and heads west down Foster.

West. It's strange to think that if she continued walking this direction for days and days and weeks that she would eventually arrive in the Nation of California. The thought stirs her a little. She imagines Leona, like at the end of a drama: Leona coming out of her orange and red house, the baby on her hip, one hand shading her eyes from the sun as Tasha approaches the sunsetty horizon. Tasha visualizes herself with a tall walking stick. She would drop it, of course, when she started running to greet her sister with her arms spread like an albatross. Although, Tasha thinks, she'd be walking *toward* the sunset, walking in from the east, so really she'd be the one shading her eyes. Who cares, she thinks. It's my fantasy.

But that's bullshit, Tasha thinks. She'd never make it all that way. Plus she's had a problem with navigation since she was a child: no matter what direction she is facing, she thinks that way is north. "You'd be one lost reindeer," her mother always said. Tasha didn't get the joke until she was sixteen. The organized grid of the city helps overcome her navigational deficiencies: in Chicago, at least, she can follow the Red Line and know for a fact her north is true.

She ignores her shoddy instincts now and continues west down Foster, startling a couple of squirrels feasting on an open bag of Cheetos someone had dropped in the middle of the sidewalk. They take a few hops back from the crinkly plastic, not quite willing to forfeit their find. They look up at her accusingly and chatter quietly to each other. "I thought they were all dead," one is probably saying.

On this side of the building—Foster is smaller and less congested in terms of pedestrian traffic than Berwyn—there are only two Volamus: one running east and one running west. Downtown they go in all four directions, but in this part of the city they only go east and west because it's assumed most people are either going downtown, or home from downtown, and really only need to be taken to and from the L. The Volamus are still humming along—it's only six days since the Change, after all: there are still another twenty-something until the generators fail. At that point Tasha figures not much will change: she hasn't been taking refrigerated food from the grocery since she's been without electricity in her apartment, so once the grocery store is without it she'll just keep doing what she's been doing. When she runs out of canned beans and vegetables, she can move on to canned fruit. There is still Dinah to consider. She can't just throw canned foods through the window forever.

She's been picking through the produce section but it doesn't offer much: most of it has already gone bad. Fresh vegetables that aren't bathed in pesticides have been hard to come by for a few years in Chicago, and everywhere else in the States as well. Following the absorption of Mexico, Dinah's home—now Newest Mexico—embargo after embargo had been placed on the States, other nations expressing their disapproval, but President Willoughby—Walker's vice—was too stubborn, too stupid, and too poorly advised to fix it, so Tasha and her countrymen simply went without while corporations bought up agricultural equipment in an all-out vegetable race. They'd swelled the number of indoor agricultural factories—BioBubbles, they were called—to provide for some of the States, but they hadn't perfected their chemical formula and people kept getting sick from the sprays and other contaminations. Every week or two something was recalled—emergency broadcasts decrying tomatoes, censoring spinach, with shoppers standing near reporters testifying to having caught salmonella, hepatitis, the bubonic plague—so everyone was a little distrustful of the salad bars. Mostly they bought their veggies canned, regarding the fresh stuff as one might regard a strange dog with no leash. Once bitten, twice shy.

Tasha thinks of Leona's letters, some of which mentioned her vegetable garden. She can imagine her sister on her knees in damp earth, weeding out various undesired vines, picking off the odd Japanese beetle and dropping it into a bucket of vinegar. She wonders what kind of vegetables her sister has planted, what the seasons are like in the Nation for someone with a garden. She knows Leona won't have sprayed her tomatoes with any poisons, not with everything that has happened. Maybe it was all a domestic terrorist plot, the contaminated celeries and spinach: wipe out all those annoying vegans.

"And they wanted us to get the Chip to protect us from B-bombs," Tasha scoffs, kicking an empty liquor bottle as she passes under the transparent tracks of the L. "We needed protection from fucking broccoli."

As if the Chip materialized out of her thoughts, she passes a billboard where a woman three shades lighter than Tasha bounces a soccer ball on her knee. Then the image turns and looks at her, the face like her own, one hand holding the soccer ball, the other hand on her digital hip.

"Cybranu's health implant has made all the difference," she beams. "I never get sick and everyone tells me how much healthier my skin looks! I can do everything I want to do outside without worrying about the threat of infection!" She throws back her head and laughs, flashing her brilliantly white teeth. Underneath her cleated feet is lush green grass

"Ha ha ha." Tasha mutters sarcastically. "The grass is probably digital." She stands back to eye the woman in the advertisement, who has gone back to bouncing the soccer ball. Her hair is relaxed and flops easily in its ponytail each time she jerks her knee up to make contact with the ball. Tasha hates

the advertising technology. Each e-board is fitted with MMDs (Microscopic Mirroring Devices) that register the appearance of the consumer in front of the screen and instantaneously alter the appearance of the model in the advertisement. Tasha, with her brown skin and average female height and weight, has been read by the MMDs, which have reflected an (almost) brown-skinned model of a-little-above-average female height and a little-less-than-average weight. Cybranu hoped that by giving passing consumers a representation of themselves with the Chip—themselves, except *better*, because all the people on e-boards are smooth, light, white-toothed Positive Pattys—they would be more likely to run out and get the Chip...but only if they had MINK, she thinks bitterly. Why dangle the carrot, Tasha wonders. Why not state up front that one needed a policy or a legacy to get the Chip? She knows. To make the haves feel even more exclusive, she supposes bitterly; to encourage them to get it as soon as possible so they could lord it over everyone else.

Tasha watches the bouncing ponytail, the bouncing ball. She knows the ploy probably worked...otherwise there wouldn't be a dead body in the alley to her right, and she'd be at work right now, grooming Micro Labradoodles. Or at least asking Cara to let her groom Micro Labradoodles. She might have had a job if it wasn't for the Chip; she might still have everything. The girl bouncing the soccer ball is completely oblivious to what she's done, what Tasha is blaming her for.

Tasha absentmindedly reaches up and feels her own hair. Her fingers wander up the strands to her scalp, and her hand pauses as it meets the curly roots that are reclaiming her head.

She snatches her hand away and glares at the woman in the ad who is still talking about her healthy skin, smiling and smiling. The make-up artist was very clever with the hints of pink on the eyelids and cheekbones, the bronze on the bone under the brow. Some shimmer has been placed along the lines of the bridge of her nose, creating the appearance of a slimmer schnoz. Tasha feels herself snarling.

She looks thoughtfully at the knife in her hand, then makes a decision and jams the point of it into the side of the large screen on which the ad is displayed. There is a flicker—the model is saying "...without worrying about the threat..."—and after Tasha wiggles the blade a little more forcefully into the socket, the resolution wavers and then the screen goes black. She realizes, pulling the knife from the socket, that she probably could have electrocuted herself, but feels only smugness. The screen is shiny and dark now and Tasha stares into the blackness, her face reflected back to her, distorted: the circles under her eyes (genetic half-moons given to her by her father) are deepened by the position of the sun. She turns and gazes up at it. It gazes back. She continues down Foster and turns left on Broadway, passing a lone shoe in the middle of the intersection. Nike.

The encounter with the advertisement had been a little too normal—the advertisement itself, anyway; not the killing of it—and Tasha has to remind herself to exercise caution as she makes her way down Broadway. Thoughts of the jumper from the apartment above her and the child, brought down by a pack of Minkers, slip into her consciousness. She has been out before since the Change, but thinking of those deaths makes things different now. Her stroll smoothes out into a creep, and she holds the knife a little higher as she passes the mega Kindlers store, where there is a lot of broken glass and two bodies, both women. From what she can see through the window, the bookstore looks as if it saw quite a battle: more broken glass litters the inside of the store, with books and tablets strewn about as if they had been used as missiles. Tasha kind of likes this idea, she realizes: Octavia Butler and Charles Dickens being used as ammunition against a swarm of dead-eyed Minkers, Changed over their morning coffee as they browsed through the *Times* best-seller lists, feeling very well-read and cultured. At first Tasha had tried to refrain from envisioning scenarios of the morning of the Change, but it has become unavoidable: every facet of her surroundings can be pieced together to illustrate another Chicagoan's final moments. Even the small things— the bag of Cheetos on the sidewalk, claimed by squirrels. Maybe someone simply got sick of their Cheetos and dropped the bag on the sidewalk. But maybe someone was walking to the train stop, eating Cheetos, when someone else started eating their neck. Everything is a sign of a life ended: Cheetos, broken glass, the shoe in the middle of Broadway. At least there was no foot, Tasha thinks.

Then again, the broken glass in and around the enormous Kindlers could be evidence of looting, not a struggle. Tasha always heard about the role of looters in times of great disaster. But if greedy city-dwellers saw an opportunity to forsake societal codes and smash in store windows to take what they pleased, she doesn't think Kindlers would be the place they would start. Paper books existed there too, having survived decades longer than naysayers had predicted—thanks to a few trendy elitists who brought back the retro cool-factor of carrying around books instead of Glass models, which everyone owned more than one of anyway—but Tasha can't quite imagine hordes of plunderers crushing into the aisles of novels, gluttonously snatching up copies of *The Handmaid's Tale* to add to their piles of booty. More likely, the yuppies who frequented the grotesquely gentrified Kindlers in what used to be Uptown—all swept along in the fashionable necessity of the Chip—had turned on the cashiers and baristas. Maybe her original theory of books being used as missiles wasn't too far off. Tasha can see a number of Bibles at the bottom of the escalators inside; the Kindlers employees would have known exactly where the heaviest projectiles would be in the store and gone straight to the religious texts. Customer service be damned.

"How may I kill you?" says Tasha in her best concierge voice. She turns away from Kindlers and walks straight into a Minker.

She manages to roll her shoulders away in a *Matrix*-worthy move as the man on the sidewalk attempts to bear-hug her with his mouth open. He barks.

"Oh, shut the fuck up!" Tasha cries, swinging the knife at the guy. He is quick for a fat man and mostly dodges the swipe; the blade catches only the tip of his middle finger and the little nub spins off somewhere to Tasha's left. Tasha is impatient to kill him, and a little scared. Not that she's worried about a line at the post office, but the longer she deals with him, the longer it will take to get there and back home again. It could be dark by then. Yes, she's been out several times since the Change, but never in the dark: who knows what it's like. At night she hunkers down in her room and stays away from the windows, eating her canned-whatever, huddled in the corner of her bed. Fatty here is complicating her day.

He heaves his bulk at her, his hands outstretched and flexing like Frankenstein looking for a feel-up. She hacks off one of his hands with one powerful slice. It comes almost easily now, the cutting. Tasha supposes the sharpness of the Wusthof makes it easier: if she were having to chop laboriously through sinew and bone, killing fat guys might not be so undemanding. This particular guy looks like a Driver, one of the many well-paid and black-suited city employees who steer—steered—the trains along their transparent tracks. The uniform and the pay-grade were boosted with the elimination of buses. Despite the copious use of his hands during his former life, the guy doesn't seem to notice the loss of his right hand now: he swipes with the stump, spraying Tasha and the wall behind her. She blows through her mouth like a swimmer coming up for air, determined not to know the taste of Driver blood.

There's a sound across the street, a clatter like tin cans falling into a dumpster. Tasha expects him to look, giving her the moment of distraction she needs to kill the fat bastard, but he doesn't. Great.

"Oh, Christ," she sighs in exasperation and skips nimbly sideways as he lunges again. From this angle she can see the red light blinking, and she resists rolling her eyes. "Blink, blink, blink, of course."

It takes her attacker a few seconds before he realizes his prey has moved out of the way. He looks around dumbly, and then down at the stump of his wrist, the wound mending itself in a sticky-sounding weaving of ultra-rapid skin cells and blood coagulant. No hand grows back, Tasha notes with relief (and also a bit of disappointment—now *that* would have been something to see): the Chip is good, but not *that* good. The Driver seems just as fascinated by the healing of his maimed hand as Tasha was the first time she witnessed it on the skull of an eight-year-old. Tasha is watching the crawling skin spiderwebs too until she realizes she has almost missed her chance.

The Driver falls to his knees with her knife protruding from his neck. The Chip is blinking feebly as its life force drains both from it and from the eyes of the guy, who, as the light ceases to flash, topples onto his side.

Tasha examines his face. The fussy look she's noticed on the features of most of the Minkers remains, but has softened in death. The eyebrows that had, minutes before, been knitted together in a glare of consternation have relaxed slightly and separated: the effect is one of puzzlement. Irritation, astonishment. Astonished by what? That the Chip didn't work? "Safe from the threat of foreign infection..." but still dead. Tasha pulls out the Wusthof and adds another red stripe to the thigh of her jeans. She checks her hair in the reflection of what's left of Kindlers' window and moves on.

The walk isn't as long as she had thought it would be. Constant vigilance makes her surroundings a lot more interesting, so what would have been storefront after storefront becomes a detailed row of scenarios. With the possibility of a new neck needing stabbing at every alley entranceway, Tasha finds herself outside the sterile structure of the Post before she's actually ready. She assesses the loose rubble along the sidewalk—they'd been repaving the walkway in front of the Post: old-school construction machines and large rocks occupy some of the street—and takes stock of her fear. She suddenly becomes conscious of the knot that has formed in her spine, not from sleeping in the tub but from wondering. The possibility of finding a letter from Leona has set loose a net of vampiric butterflies gnawing at her intestines. They hadn't fluttered when she saw the Kindlers or when the Driver fell to the sidewalk. But they'd been wriggling out of their cocoons since Dinah had proposed the trip to the Post.

Tasha had accepted the idea quickly in the fog of smeared mascara and vomitous breath—why not? They'd been sitting in their apartments—Dinah's a tomb—watching the world disintegrate, witnessing children being eaten alive and neighbors leaping to their deaths. They needed movement. Tasha had left the building on Foster with no conscious expectation of finding anything at the Post, but now that she's here, she realizes how much the hope has hardened into a real thing inside her. She needs to find something. Anything. A compass of some kind that will point in any direction except backward. A magic key that will free Dinah. Shit, a welding kit that Tasha can use to open her door. A tool. An answer. But more than that...she needs to know. Like Dinah said, they didn't know enough. Dinah had been referring to the Change as a whole, but now, looking at the doors to the Post, Tasha realizes what she needs to know is more basic than that: she needs to know if her sister is alive. A letter from Leona, waiting in the mailbox like a sleeping lamb, would mean her sister is alive; or had been recently. It would be kindling added to a blaze of hope, which has been flickering lower and lower as the days wore on. The videograph of Leona and Morris outside their orange and red house—Tasha realizes she's been looking at it the way one looks at a photo of someone long dead: with nostalgia and grief, sifting through memories and last conversations, regrets. Tasha needs to know. She holds her hand out to the door of the Post and watches her fingers tremble before dropping her hand to the side. What if the box is empty? She wants to walk away, but then what?

"Oh stop," she snaps at herself and reaches for the door again.

It's locked.

Hours of operation: 9am-6pm

Tasha looks at her wrist—no watch—then rolls her eyes. She reminds herself why she doesn't need a watch—because crazed human beings with maniacal chips in their necks have free reign of the city—and why the hours of operation really don't fucking matter.

"The world is over, idiot," she says, and smashes the glass door with one of the construction site's shovels.

Tasha claps her hands over her ears as an obnoxious alarm

attacks her in a repetitive wail of unfathomably high pitch. She panics…every Minker in a five-block radius will hear the sound and come loping over to check the mail. She needs to hide, but hesitates. Maybe she can get in and find Leona's letter first. Peering inside, Tasha can see at least one body: its pale blue uniform is ripped at the sleeve, which is empty with its lack of arm.

Tasha decides to hide. She looks around, imagining she can hear the rustling of approaching Minkers. Her eye falls on a pair of dumpsters next to a bulldozer, placed there for construction waste, she imagines. She looks down at her pristine Nikes and inwardly apologizes to them, as well as to her Prada backpack.

Tasha gingerly raises the lid of the nearest dumpster and peeps inside. Just some rubble and tin cans: no roaches that she can see, no Port-a-Potty stench rising from the metal; just a vague scent of rotting vegetables. She's halfway in, her torso tilted over the edge, when the backpack swings down from her shoulders and hits her in the face. The added weight almost sends her face-first to the bottom of the dumpster, but she catches herself in a handstand. Wriggling the rest of the way in, she slowly draws in her feet to keep the lid from slamming. It's not entirely dark: various holes allow some light to filter in, not to mention the line of sun around the edge of the lid. She draws herself into a corner and closes her eyes, her knees curled to her chest. She could be playing hide and seek; the seeker could be Leona, ten years old and counting to twenty. Tasha breathes shallowly.

A moment of silence. Two. Three.

Then a sound. A bark. Tasha has worked with dogs all her life—Dobermans, Pekingese, Great Pyrenees, Rat Terriers—and she knows all of their songs. She has only dealt with this new breed for all of six days, but she has gotten to know his tune as well. This bark belongs to a Minker.

Her eyes are open now, as if it will help her hear. There is a hole in the metal beside her head but she doesn't have the courage to look yet. Instead she listens: more barking. It's no horde, but she can hear at least six or seven different pairs of feet; some crunching on gravel, some on concrete, some on the glass of the Post's shattered front door. Tasha clutches the Wusthof, her fingers beginning to feel cold as she squeezes off her own circulation. She finally presses her eye to the hole in the dumpster.

She counts ten of them (more than she thought) swarming around the entrance of the post office. They seem oblivious to one another, and don't seem to know what to do now that they have arrived at this place. Something brought them…a sound? What was it? Now that they have come, they seem to have forgotten why. Tasha has never seen this many of them this close—she feels like Jane Goodall watching a species that wasn't quite as benevolent as her silverbacks. Tasha studies them.

One is a middle-aged woman wearing spandex, a sports bra, and the ridiculous Moonwalk fitness shoes. She is still, staring up at the sky. A guy next to her shifts from foot to foot, moving in a small circle like a wind-up toy: he is—was—a police officer, his gun missing from its holster on his hip, the leather safety strap torn and hanging loose. Against her will, Tasha provides a scenario. The cop could have been writing a ticket for—who knows—jaywalking or something, when he Changed. The civilian freaked (couldn't image how jaywalking could suddenly be death penalty-worthy, and anyway since when is the death penalty carried out on the sidewalk, at the jaws of the boys in blue?) and ended up grabbing the cop's own firearm to protect herself. Maybe she even shot him. If she didn't get them in the Chip, he wasn't going down. Tasha had learned that.

Another Minker is pacing slowly back and forth between the sidewalk and the Post's front door. Pacing isn't really the right word—to Tasha that implies some kind of brain function; pacing while one thinks of a new course of action, pacing while worrying about one's finances. This guy is just walking back and forth, a cycling loop of mechanical humanoid activity. Each time he turns at the sidewalk, his shoulder bumps a teenage girl in her pajamas. She's standing facing the street, looking first to the east, and then west. Back and forth, back and forth: as if she's watching a marathon, ghost runners passing and passing. Her hair is in two ponytails that flop across her face each time she jerks her head in either direction. The others are engaged in other similarly mindless activities. It's as if the Chip has programmed them to seek prey but hasn't provided a command for what to do when there's no prey to be found. They are listless, waiting.

Tasha curses the sweat that she can feel rolling slowly down her back, tiny hot glaciers. How long will she last in this box before they hear her, smell her, track her down? She imagines Dinah waiting in her apartment, watching the sun get lower and lower. The night would come and Tasha wouldn't return. Days would pass, with Dinah withering away, rationing her stack of nutritionless Pringles; eating a bean per hour of the two cans Tasha tossed her. Tasha isn't much of a savior, but if she dies, Dinah will have no chance. Not unless she makes a bedsheet rope that's long enough to carry her down twenty stories. The idea of Dinah, alone, pricks something in her heart.

But then there's a sound: the slapping of sneakers on pavement. At first Tasha thinks it's another Minker coming to join the posse, but the step is a little too fast. The Minkers hear it too, the ten of them gaping around with dull interest. A couple of them wander toward the Post again, but Tasha knows that's not where the sound is coming from. She can hear it getting closer, coming up Broadway.

A man runs into view. Tasha strains her cheek against the dumpster to keep him in her eyesight. She can hear him panting. He slows and looks over his shoulder, then pauses and leans over with his hands on his knees, his back heaving for breath. Tasha scrambles away from the corner to another eyehole that gives her a better view. He's so close. She wishes she could call out to him, give him a signal, or directions to her house. But her fear is a straitjacket—she is bound by it, stuck peeping through the hole in the dumpster like a rabbit from the warren. The man is wearing jeans and a green t-shirt, something with a shamrock on it. She wonders if he put it on actually expecting a bit of luck. What he's found sure as hell aren't leprechauns. He's wearing tennis shoes and she hopes they're good for sprinting. Asics? He looks like the Asics type.

Tasha hears a bark from the peanut gallery. The man's back straightens like a shot, and he stumbles sideways. So intent has he been on getting away from what's behind him that he hasn't noticed what's ten yards to his left. His chest stops heaving—Tasha doubts he has found his breath. He has probably just stopped breathing altogether at this moment. She is sure that what he has found outside the Post is worse than what he was running from a moment before.

One by one the Minkers start to yip; the teenage girl snuffles and is the first to take a step toward Asics, who hasn't yet found the sense to start running again. This time Tasha tries as hard as she can not to make a scenario…what if he thought it was just his wife, or just his boss? He might have gone streaking out onto the street, thinking that if he could just find a cop…

And then he ran into this friendly group. (Well, he *did* find a cop…) It's not just your wife, dude, Tasha thinks.

The guy finally takes off, his shoes pounding on the concrete. He continues running north on Broadway, away from his original pursuer and now also away from the pack. The middle-aged jogger lady ambles gamely after him, the rest of the group in pursuit. None of them run, exactly, but the lady in the sports bra is clipping along and is quickly out of sight of Tasha's dumpster. Tasha leans back and breathes out through her nose. Alone again. Safe. Safe-ish. Her breath is magnified in the metal box she crouches in—it's almost like she has company, the ragged echo indicating that the shadow friend is as scared as she is.

"It's okay," she tells the dark.

She raises the lid a centimeter, ready at any moment to feel the tearing of dull white teeth against her skin. Nothing. Even the alarm of the Post had stopped wailing, though she hadn't noticed when. The sounds of the Minkers had seemed much louder. There's no sign of the pack of them and the Asics guy. She hadn't heard any screams, so she hopes that means the guy got away. Then again, he might have been the strong, silent type.

She raises the lid higher and, straining her triceps, drags herself out of the dumpster with an unattractive grunt that she's glad no one is around to hear. The area outside the Post is deserted—it's as if the whole scene had been a vivid hallucination.

"Jesus Christ…" Tasha says out loud, now that the danger has passed.

"Lord God," says a voice, and Tasha almost screams before she remembers she sounds like a man when she does, and instead clamps her jaws shut, biting her tongue in the process.

She looks around, and sees no one. No one in the Post, no one on the street. The voice had sounded so close, but after spinning around several times Tasha still sees no one.

"Hello…?"

"Hiiii….." says the voice, extending the word before it dissolves into a sigh.

Tasha realizes, feeling stupid, that it's coming from the other dumpster. Readying the Wusthof—although she hasn't yet known a Minker to speak—she creeps over to the hiding place beside her own and cautiously raises the lid. Tasha has cut open a few necks in the past six days, but she isn't prepared for what's in the dumpster.

Sprawled at the bottom is a girl a few years younger than Tasha, her yellow sundress stained almost entirely red with blood. The entire floor of the dumpster is inches deep in it. One hand clutches her throat, the other is draped loosely across her abdomen. She is staring at the metal wall, unfocused and half-smiling. Beside her, dead, is a guy her age. His neck is bloody too, his fluids contributing to the pool they both rest in.

"How long have you been here?" Tasha asks. She doesn't know what else to say.

The girl shifts her head to the side. The angle in which she's slumped won't allow her to look up at Tasha; she twists her neck awkwardly to peer up at her sideways, like a bird or a snake. She has the large plaintive eyes of a Cocker Spaniel.

"Couple hours. Days. I don't know."

They stare at each other in silence. Tasha opens her mouth then closes it. She looks at the body of the man. So does the girl.

"My boyfriend. He bit me. Kept biting me. Not just here," she moves her neck. "On my arms too. My stomach."

Tasha nods.

"He kept biting me."

Tasha bites her lip. The girl sets her jaw, but her eyes well up with tears.

"I ran away. Thought I could get away. But he followed

me outside. When I got here there was a cop standing on the corner. I was afraid he would arrest Ronnie."

She stops and sniffles, tries to move her shoulders up higher on the wall, but she can't.

"I crawled in the dumpster. Ronnie followed me. Started biting my ankle. I crawled all the way in and so did he. I found a piece of glass in here and kept stabbing him. It cut me up too. He bit me a couple more times. When I cut his neck he stopped. He's dead."

She looks at Ronnie.

"He's dead. The cop didn't even turn around. He was just walking in circles. All the cops…they all have it."

"I saw the cop too," Tasha offers. She has nothing else to give.

They stare at each other. After a moment, the girl says,

"You got a gun?"

Tasha doesn't know anyone with a gun. Only policemen are allowed them.

"No. Just this." She shows the knife.

"Something about the neck…"

"I know."

"Ronnie just kept biting me…"

"You're not the only one."

The girl dies, her eyes on Ronnie.

Tasha wants to run away, and she wants to stay. She wants to set the dumpster on fire. She wants to dig a hole for the girl in the yellow dress. She wants to pray; to lie down and sleep; to walk in the rain; to plant a garden. She wants Dinah. She wants her mother, her sister.

At the thought of her sister, she lifts her head from where she had leaned it against the dumpster. She needs to know if there is a letter. She takes one last look at the shell of the girl in yellow and slowly closes the lid.

Turning away, she trudges toward the Post, looking at the ground, the swirls and patterns in the gravel dust where the pack of Minkers had been gathered. She hopes the Asics guy had a plan. Maybe he was leading them toward a trap, she thinks unconvincingly. Maybe everyone had a plan. She sure didn't.

Nearing the door to the Post, she looks up from the gravelly ground and her breath catches in her throat. Not two feet ahead, standing just inside the doorway, is a Minker, its blue Post uniform bloodied all down the front like a trail of unbelievably red spaghetti sauce. Tasha freezes, but the thing just gapes forward, its gaze dull. The breaking glass had drawn it to the door, Tasha thinks, but maybe it's too stupid to realize nothing stands in its way anymore. It doesn't seem to see Tasha at all.

Tasha waves.

"Um…hi," she says, "hello there, hey." She snaps her fingers.

Nothing.

She takes a tentative step forward, her knife ready. The Minker stares off into a nonexistent horizon, the crinkle between its eyebrows softly irritated. Tasha is right on top of it now, despite the warnings in her head of curiosity and the many cats it has killed. But nothing. The Minker is blind to her. It's bizarre.

Tasha darts her eyes down at the ground, not wanting to be taken by surprise. Along with some other debris, there's a fist-sized piece of concrete by her shoe, leftover from the unfinished construction. Taking a slow step back, she bends quickly, snatching it up, then stands ready. Her caution is unnecessary—the Minker doesn't move. Tasha cocks her arm back and throws the rock into the Post. It sails over the head of the Minker and lands with a clatter ten feet beyond the entrance.

It's like a magic word.

The Minker's head snaps to its right and it turns sluggishly to the sound, soft growls emanating from its throat, the crease between the eyebrows deepening into a furious abyss. Tasha watches with her mouth open as the Minker ambles toward the rock Tasha had thrown, leaving Tasha standing in the doorway like a ghost.

"What the…?"

Tasha doesn't know what to make of it, but either way, if there's a letter, it's inside the Post. If the Minker doesn't want to come out—even for easy prey—then Tasha will have to go in with it. She steps inside.

The Minker turns immediately as if Tasha has tripped a wire, its eyes zeroing in on her and narrowing. The barks rise and it starts toward her, arms half-raised.

"Oh, now you're ready," Tasha almost laughs. "What the hell?"

She meets the Post worker halfway, her knife poised to

stab. Farther back in the office she can see the creature's former co-worker, the nearly-dry blood pooled around her forming an almost perfect circle. Poor lady—she didn't know what hit her. Tasha stabs the Minker in the neck but it's not quite on the mark. The grabbing hands snatch at Tasha's chest and shoulder, but the fingers have nails, not claws, and Tasha doesn't feel it. Another stab results in a spark and the Chip is sputtering, the Minker sinking to the ground, its growls growing weaker. A moment later it's dead and Tasha is alone in the Post with two bodies.

She's still confused. Why the hell didn't it come out of the Post? Surely it could see its pack, chasing off the guy in the Asics. She turns back to look at the door. Had someone rigged it to keep Minkers inside? She doesn't see any fancy contraption on the jamb anyplace, yet it had stood there like a statue until Tasha stepped into its realm. Something to tell Dinah, she thinks, but first she needs to get what she came for. Stepping over the body of the Minker, she goes into the enclave to her right, its walls lined with silver doors to the multitude of small boxes.

She goes to 1129. It's her box, and the cannibal moths in her belly begin their chewing. She dreads the white envelope she prays she'll find: she dreads the spidery script of her sister and the stains on the edges of the paper from hands writing after gardening with no soap in between. She dreads mention of the little orange-and-red house, and what has become of it. She dreads news about the Nation, news about the States, news about doctors and germs and Chips. She dreads news. But more than news, she dreads *no* news: to open up the box now, and see no letter...well, it would mean the end. If no letter now, then there will be no more letters written in black ink; no more stacks of paper piling up under the bed; no more loopy L for Leona.

Tasha enters 1004—her mother's birthday—on the little keypad above the number 1129 and waits for the click that comes before the box snaps open.

Nothing.

She does it again, firmly pressing the numbers with her index finger, and waits. Again. And again, nothing. She looks up at the ceiling, realizes the overhead lights aren't what illuminate the room: it's sunlight, coming in through the large windows.

Tasha almost laughs. No electricity.

The knowledge robs her lungs and she sits, her back against the row of steel boxes. The fog of silence that had enveloped her when she closed the dumpster on the girl in yellow envelopes her again, makes its way down her throat. Leona might be above her in the box. Without a letter, how will she know? There's no more Post—she'd have to go to California for confirmation of her sister's existence, and with no planes or lightrail...it's impossible. Why the fuck did the Post have to try and get fancy with the whole keypad entry thing? What was wrong with a key? She remembers asking the manager at the branch when she paid for her box.

"Well, you might lose a key, but you don't generally lose your mind, do you?" He had chuckled a Bel-Air laugh that signaled he told the same joke at least once a day, and never got tired of it. Tasha had snapped back,

"Guess that's not an amnesia-friendly policy, huh? Guess that's not a policy that caters to the numerically challenged?"

He had gotten flustered then. "Ahem, well, in case of... forgetfulness, power failure, or other emergencies, all of our employees' thumbs are fitted with a master print, so, ahem, you will have access whenever you need it."

Bingo.

Tasha looks over at the dead Post worker on the floor. Not the Minker—she doesn't want to go near it again—but the woman who is already missing an arm. Tasha doesn't see it anywhere.

The woman is heavy, but not as heavy as Brian, and Tasha had had to pull him farther, as well as pick him up. This woman, "Janice"—she too wears a nametag—is 130 pounds at most, wearing Chanel perfume, and the slippery tile floor lends itself well to Tasha's mission. As she pulls Janice toward 1129, she tries not to notice the Rorschachian trail of blood left behind. At first Tasha had considered just severing the woman's thumb, carrying it to the box like a bloody key, but something about the nametag, the already-missing arm, and the Chanel changed her mind. She wonders why the woman is dead, Chipless. New, perhaps? Or perhaps some sordid past made her ineligible, government job or not: you could never tell with MINK.

Once at 1129, Tasha pulls Janice's remaining arm upwards toward the box, trying to maneuver the thumb against the little black square beside the dial pad. She aligns them, and waits.

The click.

Tasha sets Janice's arm gingerly down across her chest, hoping it's comfortable, then opens the box.

There are two letters. One is a collection notice from the bank. The other is from Leona.

CHAPTER 10

"Dinah?"

Tasha has made it home and is kneeling outside Dinah's door. She's called her friend's name three or four times and is now crouched with her face against the hallway carpet, trying to see under the door. She hears nothing, sees nothing.

"Dinah?" She doesn't want to knock on the door: the bathroom, Dinah has told her, is close by and Tasha doesn't want to alert Dale. Instead she stands and walks quickly to her own apartment, unlocking her door and entering like a shadow. Maybe Dinah is leaning out the window.

She takes off her backpack, leaving it on the floor inside the front door, and hurries into the bedroom. She opens the window with one quick pull and sticks her head out. No Dinah. She decides to tap on the wall.

"Dinah," she calls softly through the thin barrier, "Dinah, are you okay?"

A rustling sound rewards her efforts.

"Dinah?"

"Hey, I'm here," comes Dinah's voice, soft and dragging. "I'm here."

"Are you okay?"

"I was sleeping."

"But you're okay?"

"I'm…..okay."

"I made it to the Post. I have a letter."

Dinah's voice tightens.

"From your sister?"

"Yes."

"What did she say? Did she know anything?" Dinah says quickly, intensely.

"I haven't read it yet. I wanted to wait 'til I got back here with you."

"Read it!"

"Come to the window, I'll read it to you."

"You can read it here."

"But…why?" Tasha is confused. "I won't have to whisper as much if we go to the window."

"I just, you know, I just woke up."

Her voice is strange. It sounds scooped out, thin.

"Dinah? What's wrong? Are you sick?"

"No, no, not sick."

"Come to the window."

Tasha stands without waiting for a response and goes to the window, leaning out. A moment later, she sees Dinah's head appear, just a piece of it.

"Hey," she says casually.

"Hey…" says Tasha.

They stare at each other.

"Dinah, what the fuck are you doing?"

The sun is setting, and Dinah's forehead has fallen into shadow. Tasha realizes how much she has relied on her friend's eyebrows for her expression. Right now, she can't tell at all.

"Something happened."

"What? What happened?"

Tasha thinks immediately of the child they had seen the day before, whose death has lingered around the edges of Tasha's consciousness since she woke. Had someone else appeared on the street below? Another act of brutality that Dinah, in her cage, had been forced to bear witness to?

"Dinah," says Tasha, when nothing is said, "what happened?"

"I tried to get the keys," says Dinah simply, her voice low enough to make her hard to hear. "I tried to get the keys while you were gone."

"What?" Tasha's heart becomes a sparrow, its wings brushing her lungs and causing her to breathe shallowly. "Did you get them? Why are you still in there? Are you alright?"

"I…I didn't get them," Dinah says, averting her eyes. "I tried. I went in with a knife, like you. But he…he was strong. And I was scared. I've seen him almost like this before, you know. Fists instead of teeth. And I…I was scared."

"Are you alright?"

"I…"

"Are you alright?"

"He bit me. But I'm fine."

Tasha squeezes her eyes shut.

"Where did he bite you? Where?"

"My shoulder. It's not bad."

"Have you cleaned it? They say humans' mouths are dirtier than dogs' and—"

"All the bandages and stuff are in the bathroom with him."

"Christ. Hold on."

Tasha leaves the window and goes into her own bathroom where she yanks open the medicine cabinet. The cosmetics pouch, housing her mascara, sits there on the shelf beckoning her. She half considers putting another coat of mascara on to calm her nerves, give her some steadiness. But instead she grabs the bottle of hydrogen peroxide. It's all she has.

Back at the window, she looks Dinah in her eyes. One of them—the one still healing from the bruise—is shadowed by the setting sun.

"You have to catch this," says Tasha. "It's the only stuff I have and you need to get something on the bite as soon as possible."

"Okay," says Dinah, nodding. "I'm ready."

Tasha had gauged the distance when she had tossed the beans, and she underhands the peroxide now, gritting her teeth. Like anything important, it hangs in space for a moment before landing firmly in Dinah's outstretched palms.

"Whew," says Dinah, and Tasha's not sure if she means it to be funny or if she means it.

"Pour it on your shoulder," says Tasha. "Now."

She hears her mother in her voice and cringes from it, missing her. Tasha wishes she could be in Dinah's apartment. She's dressed enough dog bites in her life to handle a Dale bite. Fucking Dale. She wants to punch him in the face.

When Dinah returns to the window, she's wearing a different shirt.

"Better?" asks Tasha.

Dinah nods, looking off into the dimming sky.

"You okay?"

"I mean, the bite...it hurt. I can't believe I was so weak. He still has the keys," she says, and Tasha can hear the quaver in her voice. Tasha wishes she could put on the comforting voice that Dinah slips on so easily and so well. That cap doesn't fit Tasha as flatteringly. It slides down over her eyes; all she sees is how silly she is, how inept. It's been a long time since she had a friend, she realizes. Gina had been...something else.

"But that's not the worst part," says Dinah, and now she is crying and Tasha is mystified and beginning to panic.

"What? What is, then? What?"

"We broke the lock," Dinah sobs, and Tasha can barely understand her. "We broke the knob when we fought. When I realized I couldn't kill him, and after he bit me, I was trying to just get out of the bathroom without dying. And he had hold of me. And we slammed up against the door and the knob went right into my hip and he was dragging me toward him and I twisted and...and the knob broke off. It broke right off. And I managed to kick him hard enough to push him back. And I got out. And I had my back against the door and he was bumping up against it." Her voice is grating. Tasha sees two tears drop from her face and go spinning down into space, where they would eventually join the corpses on the sidewalk. Tasha is in shock.

"I moved the table in front of the door, but it's small" Dinah finishes, her chest shuddering as she catches her breath. "He's in there. But without the knob, the door doesn't close all the way. Whenever I pass the door he can see me through the crack. I've been in the corner by the window, trying to be quiet."

Tasha lets these words sink into her skin. It's like rubbing in tar and she feels sick. Her stomach feels ornery, as if she might vomit again. She thinks of the girl in the yellow dress, who she had fully intended to tell Dinah all about, a witness to her horror. But she can't now. The girl and her Ronnie are too much like Dinah and her Dale: biting boyfriends, girls locked in boxes, bloodied. Instead she sighs. It's too much. It's all just too much.

"We'll figure something out, Dinah," she says, trying to sound strong since she can't muster sensitive. "Don't worry. We'll figure it out."

"That's why I was hoping you'd get the letter," says Dinah, sniffling. She has another t-shirt in her hands and is wiping her face with it, tears and snot. "Some news. Some plan. Some cure."

She wants a pill, Tasha thinks. A pill she can feed Dale in a hunk of meat—whose meat?—that would transform him back into the man he had been a week ago. A man she'd still have to hide from, Tasha thinks angrily. A cure. An answer. It's ridiculous. She'd seen a policeman—an officer of the law—with blood around his lips go howling down Broadway after a man in a green shirt. This is life now. Isn't it?

But instead of saying these things, Tasha pulls the letter from where she'd folded it into her pocket. She stares at her name on the envelope, written in Leona's hand: Natasha Lockett. That was her. The contents of this letter were for her, from Leona. She wishes she had a bloodhound's nose, so she could hold the paper to her face and inhale the scent of her sister, her niece. Even Morris.

"Read it," says Dinah softly. "Read it to me before it gets dark."

CHAPTER 11

Tasha read it. It took all of thirty seconds.

"Is that all?" Dinah had cried, the tears coming. "Is that all?"

That had been last night. It's morning now and Tasha is awake, waiting for Dinah to come back to the window. She feels like a platonic Romeo in the garden waiting for Juliet to get a clue and hear the pebbles being thrown harder and harder against her windowpane. Except there are no pebbles being thrown—that might disturb Dale.

After Tasha had read the letter Dinah had wept and then dried up almost immediately, saying they needed to "sleep on it." Tasha had interpreted this as Dinah needing to be alone, which Tasha had granted willingly enough. But now it's morning, and Tasha is restless. It's the eighth day. The letter—small as it is—needs to be discussed. Tasha wants to rap on the wall, but with the door to the bathroom broken, she doesn't want to risk riling up Dale. Luckily Tasha had discovered, in her anxious solitude of the night before, that her Glass still had a bit of battery life left, so she sits by the window and clicks through the only thing she had ever stored on it: *Cosmo*. It's last month's issue—the last issue ever, she realizes. Why is this the only thing she has on the Glass? It feels suddenly very stupid.

The woman on the front is Ramona Melón, a newish star, debuting in *Bright Lights*, a poignant tale of the first woman to win such-and-such pumapod race. Tasha wonders if Melón actually rode the airborne motorcycle for the film, or if she had a stunt double. Tasha examines the woman's face: completely symmetrical, the nose straight and slightly upturned, a nose popular in recent years for whatever reason. Tasha liked the actress's previous nose better; it had a little bump in the bridge that gave it some character. The nose before that had been more hawk-like, taken on for a role Melón described as "intense," playing a warrior nun. The actress had sported as many noses as she had roles, which was only slightly unusual: sometimes Hollywoodies had kept one for a sequel, or for personal reasons. Tasha's eyes wander down the front of the woman's shirt. Melón. *Those* had remained unchanged, no matter the role. Tasha vaguely feels as though she's looking at an artifact in a museum.

Tasha opens the *Cosmo* app. Her mother had claimed that they hadn't changed a single word of an issue since the magazine was printed on paper; they only changed the Hollywood interview, she said. Tasha hasn't seen a paper issue since she was eight or nine so she couldn't really agree or disagree, but she figures her mother was probably right. Tasha raises an

eyebrow at the feature article, "201 Ways to Turn Him On."
Two hundred and one seems steep—she suspects a few of the
tips were cleverly duplicated, something like "#74 Lick his left
nipple. #75 Lick his right nipple." She rolls her eyes as she skims
the list, clicking through impatiently. It's the typical hungry-
vagina fodder, written in the same cotton-candy verbiage: "To
really wow your guy pal, wait until he's *almost there*"—this is
written in italics, an editorial nudge-wink—"and then put him
in your mouth for a mind-blowing climax." Tasha is always
annoyed by the use of "him" in place of "penis." What if she
didn't know any better? What if she thought "him" meant *him*?
All of him? She imagines herself an anaconda of a woman,
her jaw unhinged, swallowing her lover like a reptilian black
widow. She skips to the article that interviewed Ramona
Melón. The first question they'd asked Ramona was about
Bright Lights. The second was about Cybranu.

Cosmo: *What do you think of Cybranu?*

Ramona: *Oh, I think it's a fantastic organization, a really great
organization. They really care about people. It's people-centric.*

Cosmo: *Do you have an implant?*

Ramona: *Oh, several!*

Tasha rolls her eyes.

Cosmo:*[laughing] What about a Cybranu health implant?*

Ramona: *Of course! [Ramona swings her long, luxurious hair and
shows us her neck]*

Cosmo: *Did it hurt?*

Ramona: *Oh my god, not at all. They were so nice and gentle. And
now I don't have to worry about anything! I can stay at my ideal weight—*

one-hundred and two—and eat whatever I want, and I never get sick or anything.

Cosmo: Would you recommend the Cybranu health implant to your fans?

Ramona: Oh my god, of course! I would say my fans have to get it. They owe it to themselves. I just wouldn't feel safe in this country without it.

Tasha switches back to the cover of the issue, holding the screen closer to her face to examine the beaming, laughing video portrait of Melón. Tasha can see it now: the faint outline of the Chip nestled just under the styled tendrils of glossy hair. *Cosmo* hadn't bothered to airbrush it out, no: they'd left its vague shape there below her ear to be casually noticed, taken in as part of the whole that was Ramona Melón. Tasha stares at the image, the curly pink font—*100 Ways, Perfect, Abs, Love, Must Have*—and fights the stupid feeling of jealousy. Jealous of what? Ramona Melón is somewhere in Hollywood—relocated to Nevada, big white letters and all, after the secession—chewing on the intestines of her costars. What's to be jealous of?

She wonders what Dinah will say about the prominent placement of Melón's Chip on the cover of *Cosmo*. Tasha thinks she knows. Cybranu had certainly done a good job of shoving it down everyone's throats. MINK couldn't have been blameless either, she thinks suddenly. Partners. She pictures a bunch of fat cats somewhere before the Change, shaking pudgy hands and congratulating themselves.

She shifts her shoulder on the windowpane and looks out at the sky. The clouds are gathering like grey wolves around a carcass. She's glad she's indoors, looking at the circling patterns of the approaching gale. The superstorms have been part of her life for as long as she can remember, but they're just as scary every time. She hopes lightning will strike a Minker or two.

She puts down her dying Glass for Leona's letter, which she's read eight times this morning.

Tasha, it reads.

I told you. Trouble's coming. Not just Chicago. Everywhere. Get to South Side ASAP. It's in the neck. Dr. Rio can help. Find him. Come to LA.

Love, Leona

And that was all. It's written on a torn pieces of paper, as if Leona had snatched the nearest piece of anything and made it her pad.

"Trouble's coming," Tasha whispers, and feels a lump in her throat. No shit, Leona.

The letter is postmarked two weeks before the Change, which disturbs Tasha the most. It must have arrived just before everything went to hell. Tasha might have gotten it on time if she hadn't been moping around about Gina and losing her job at the Apiary.

She strokes the paper, fingers the stains along the border. Leona is alive, or was when she wrote this letter. Tasha wonders for how long.

She jumps as Dinah's head appears out of the window next door. She's combing her hair with her fingers, yawning.

"Hey," she says, squinting at Tasha through puffy eyes. She must have cried more after they said goodnight. "How long have you been up?"

"Couple hours," says Tasha. "The light woke me up." She nods at the strobe-like light coming from the storm clouds.

Dinah looks.

"Oh crap," she yawns. "Glad we're inside. How long do you think?"

"Any minute," says Tasha. "It's been working itself up all morning. Might have to close the windows for awhile."

"Yeah, probably. But before we do," says Dinah. "I've been thinking."

"Yes?"

"About the letter."

Tasha reaches down to the floor where she has set an open can of pears. Plucking one out, she nibbles it while watching the clouds. She wonders if Dinah will start crying again.

"Yeah?"

'Well, what does she mean? I mean, I get the 'get to the South Side' part, even if I don't know why there. And the neck part. Obviously." She sniffs. "But who is Dr. Rio? Do you know somebody named Dr. Rio?"

"No," Tasha says wearily. "Never heard of her. Or him. Leona never mentioned anyone by that name in any of her other letters."

Dinah bites her lip, looking at her hands.

"Not much help, is it?"

"No."

They sit in silence for a moment, the wind whipping their hair around as the storm crawls steadily closer.

"Well," says Dinah, "at least we know what the South Side

means. That part is easy."

Tasha nods, but it's actually almost as mysterious as the mention of this Dr. Rio person. Tasha doesn't know shit about the South Side, and has only been one time since she's lived in Chicago. She worries about going there. Before the Change, the way they told it on webnews, the whole area had been all but quarantined. She wonders if Leona knows shit about it either and if so, why in the blue hell she's telling Tasha to go there. From Tasha's one visit, she remembers it looking much like any other neighborhood, just not as tall as the North Side in terms of architecture. The webnews anchorpeople, however, had one story after another of stabbings, dog attacks, and other ghastly occurrences. She tells Dinah this, who scoffs.

"Psh, that's a bunch of crap. I work—worked—at a youth center on 85th. There are bad areas, sure. But not everywhere. They make it seem like everything past Roosevelt is walnuts."

Tasha considers this. She should know better, really: she remembers there being a stabbing near her own apartment one night around the time she moved in, but when she heard about the incident online they reported it as having occurred on 79th Street. At the time she thought it had been a teleprompter mistake, a coincidence. *There are no coincidences*, she can hear her sister saying.

She remembers her sharp criticism of Gina for believing what was said about the Nation on the news and feels a little guilty. She has seen the kind of people who continue South when she gets off the train downtown: they are sullen and glowering, or chatty and exuberant. They talk loudly on earphones or stare at other passengers. They do the same things as every other passenger, but somehow it is different because they do it. Webnews has told her this, she thinks. She's always felt a bit sour toward anchors anyway: their reporting accents, their clipped syllables, the way they still seem to smile when telling the camera about a noxious gas outbreak in which forty toddlers were asphyxiated. They're being neutral, she argues with herself. But nothing about their stories regarding the South Side is neutral, she knows. She remembers a professor in college—a man in his eighties who had spent twenty-eight years in prison before being released when uncontaminated DNA evidence exonerated him—lecturing about the importance of monitoring one's law enforcement with as much scrutiny as law enforcement scrutinizes you. *Why do you think they continue to pass laws making it illegal to record police officers*, he had asked. *They pretend the South Side is no-man's land. They like it that way. They broadcast it as a warzone, and all force becomes necessary. Do you live past 25th Street, young man? Yes? Then you are living in a police state.*

"They really screw the South Side neighborhoods too," says Dinah, watching the storm. Thunder has begun to growl, the sound of a bruise. "You wouldn't believe the stuff I've heard. The city privatized the trash collection, right? You remember. And they just drew a red line around where they would and wouldn't serve. It was crap. Anything south of the Museum of Science and Industry was cut out. Can you believe that? What are people supposed to do? Where are they supposed to put their trash? Bury it? Burn it? Then they'd arrest them for unlawful fires." She sucks her teeth. "I don't remember what happened though. I think the South Side aldermen or whoever sued the city. They stopped broadcasting after the first riot."

Tasha thinks of the riot and clutches her mental purse. Who she's protecting it from, she's not sure. The protestors? The police? A cop had stared down her shirt once while riding the L. Or is she clutching the purse against the mysterious South Siders, the people who stayed on the train past Chinatown, who were never asked for their stories while mass webnews broadcasts did all the talking? Their eyes are doors within her left swinging open. To close the doors—or to pass through them—requires approach, nearness. Tasha has kept her distance.

She eats another pear.

"Well, that makes me feel a little better," says Tasha, "since Leona thinks the South Side is the safest place to be. For whatever reason."

"We're about as far from there as we could get besides Evanston or the suburbs. It'd be a hell of a walk. I wish she had said more in her letter," she adds.

Tasha hears the bitterness in Dinah's voice and doesn't blame her for it. She wishes the same thing. The letter had been maddeningly short and pointlessly cryptic. *Really, Leona,* Tasha thinks, *you couldn't have spent five minutes telling me who Dr. Rio is? What he knows? What you know?*

"Either way," says Dinah, "we could make it. You know. If we went."

Tasha hears the "we" but ignores it for now. She doesn't want to ask how Dinah plans to get out of her apartment in order to create this "we." It's another subject surrounded by caution tape. Tasha doesn't have an answer either, but she tells herself they will find one. Maybe after the storm she can go break into the offices of their apartment building and see if they have back-up keys on site. One time Tasha had locked herself out of her unit and the building manager had made her call a locksmith, claiming not to have spare keys, but ransacking their desks is worth a shot. The offices are next door, so she'll need to wait for the storm to pass, but once it does, she'll go. She feels a tiny buoy of hope blip inside her. She won't say anything to Dinah just yet—no sense in letting her down. But maybe this could be their solution.

The first drops of rain are beginning to fall, and the first jagged yellow crayon of lightning scrawls across the sky. A moment later is a godly crackle, and Tasha sees a splash of orange in the distance, the fuzzy mist of distant fire.

"Whoa," Dinah says, craning her neck, "it must have hit something. Haven't seen that happen in a long time."

Tasha responds, but thunder drowns out her voice.

"It's starting," she yells to Dinah, "close your window. We'll talk more when it's over."

Dinah nods and her head disappears inside. Tasha hears her window slam shut and then she follows suit. The thunder won't rest for awhile. Like most superstorms, it will be one crack and rumble after another. Watching shows or having a conversation had been pointless during a storm before the Change. She watches the roiling clouds and rain for a moment, but staring out at the churning gray of the sky is like being a sailor staring into the guts of the Bermuda Triangle. She settles down on the bed to read Leona's letter again. Letter. It's just a blurb, really. She wishes she knew Morse code. She could tap messages to Dinah, ask her more about the South Side.

Holding the letter, she stares at her hand and the light beige band on her finger where her ring had been. She sighs. Fucking Cara. To think she'd been heading to the Apiary on the morning of the Change—to get that job back. Temporary insanity, she thinks. The day after she'd been fired she had gone job hunting, heading downtown to see who was hiring. She'd been on the platform waiting for the Purple line, clicking through her Glass for job listings. The Pink Lynx was always hiring, but she hadn't been sure she was ready to greet customers topless just yet. She'd adjusted her coat against the wind, the platform silent except for the chorus of competing voices emanating from various advertising screens. She remembers staring at the moving images, their glossy, persuasive spokesmodels; reminders of things she didn't have. Not just the products themselves but the means to acquire them: a job, money, parents. A guy had passed Tasha on the platform and she'd noted the tattoo he had gotten to embellish the site of his Chip: the ink around the small square was frilly and elaborate, a paisley marker of his status. Tasha's mother had loved paisley, but she would rather have died than get a tattoo. Tasha's father would tease his wife about her vehement resistance against tattoos—"The Vice President has one on her shoulder!" he would say, "and she still looks professional! Beautiful, even!" But Tasha's mother would just sniff, "The

Vice President was not a ballerina."

Before she moved to Kentucky—the roots of Tasha's father's family tree—and opened a kennel, Tasha's mother had danced her way from Chicago to New York, where she had never intended to stay for any great length of time. Her parents would sit in the kitchen together while telling these stories, old songs by CeeLo jangling out from the dock on the counter, the two of them humming along and wondering how they ended up cooking gumbo in Louisville. "Funny what a man can make you do—," she would muse. Tasha remembers the look in her mother's eyes as she said this, sitting at the kitchen table with her chin in her hands, watching her husband slice vegetables. There was more than leaving for Kentucky in this statement, but she never said what else.

What she did say was that she had traveled from her hometown with her dance company to New York, where they were to perform thirty-two shows in Manhattan. Tasha's father had wandered into the empty theater with a Canon XZ9000 in front of his face, photographing the vaulted ceiling of the theater built well over a century ago in 1924. He was so taken with the mahogany pillars he almost missed the twelve mahogany women on stage rehearsing for that night's performance.

Tasha's mother was a vision, he always said: he never understood the likening of ballerinas to swans until that moment. He said she was smiling—he loved to tell this part, stopping what he was doing at the kitchen counter to turn to his audience and gesture—and had just finished a series of pirouettes, finishing in arabesque. She continued smiling as she held her final pose, her leg raised effortlessly as her eyes fell upon him. The serene smile remained—but only for a moment. It was quickly replaced with a scowl, followed by some yelling as she chased him out of the theater, telling him that no show was free, and if he wanted to watch girls dance he could either go to a skin club or come back to the theater that night and pay admission like everyone else.

He did come back that night, carrying an armful of sunflowers from the market on the corner where he'd waited all afternoon. He couldn't afford roses. He watched the performance and at the end tried to clap around his lapful of flowers. He waited in the reception room with the rest of those who hung around to express their admiration.

At this part of the story, Tasha's mother would resume narration. Entering the reception room with the other ballerinas, she was at first overwhelmed by the crush of people: the chattering, the cameras flashing, the clouds of red and white roses being offered to her. But something caught her attention: a spray of yellow at the back of the room, behind the crowd. She looked; saw the young man in his white dress shirt, his camera bag still on his shoulder, his wavy hair combed back from his face, his outrageous bouquet of sunflowers. She knew they were for her.

They saw each other almost every day during the thirty-two performances. At the end of the five-month tour, the dance company traveled back to Chicago, and Tasha's mother stayed in New York. They were married ten months later, sunflowers on the tables at the reception.

On the platform that day, Tasha had allowed her body to be swayed by the rushing air of the arriving Purple line. She'd resisted the urge to touch her empty finger where her mother's ring had nestled every day until Tasha's firing. Tasha was beyond the habit of crying in public—enough time cushioned her from the cremations to give her control over her grief. She boarded the train like a ghost, squeezing between other silent bodies.

Tasha is still looking at her hands, remembering. They are neither her father's nor her mother's hands: long fingers, not slender, not blocky, oval nail beds, square palms. The wrists are small and bony—those are her mother's. Her father's arms, long and leanly muscled. She sees her parents in everything, and every part of her belongs to them. From the time Tasha was walking, her mother staked out her body parts, divvying them up between surnames: Lockett legs, Amaru kneecaps, Lockett hips, Amaru backside. There were some parts that were no man's land: her eyes, her collar bones. "They're just mine," Tasha would say, but her mother would shake her head and cite books she'd read while pregnant: between every piece, between every bone and freckle, a line could be drawn, crossing some genetic bridge, connected to some biological tree root. "The only thing that is yours is your birthmark," her mother would say, pressing the brown blotch above Tasha's eye like a button.

Tasha presses the birthmark now, still staring out the window, but she can't make her hands cool enough to trick the flesh into thinking the touch her mother's. The constant, deafening sound of thunder is almost peaceful compared to the noise in her head. She rests her head against the wall, closing her eyes.

Something slams against the other side of the wall and she screams involuntarily. The walls are so thin that it had felt like a vibration through her skull, a blow. All she can hear is the sky's roar, her room glowing and shadowing in two-second flickering intervals. Then, in the smallest silence between thunder—a scream. From next door.

"Dinah!" She shrieks it, knowing, and the sound ricochets up her throat like it's on fire. She doesn't wait. She tears across the room, flinging the bedroom door open and battering the dresser that she'd slid back in front of the front door to escape. She bruises her finger on the lock, fumbling and fumbling. Then the door is open and she's scrambling down the hallway, darkened by the storm. There could be Minkers roaming, but she doesn't care. She finds Dinah's doors and attacks it with her fists, screaming like a banshee on a cliff. "Dinah Dinah Dinah Dinah!"

Deeper inside the building, farther from the storm, she can still hear the thunder, but the screams filter through it. She hears her name in the screams, Dinah's voice. She hears the horrible, soulless sound of a bark. Vomit is in her throat.

"Dinah!" she yells, indifferent to the raggedness of her voice, "Dinah! Let me in!"

She's pounding the door with both fists, kicking it with her bare feet, wailing. She can hear her friend's cries, she can hear the crashing of dishes and shelves and tables. She hears silverware clatter to the floor. She hears glass break. She hears the brutal coughing snarls of Dale.

"Dinah!" she screams. "Dinah, *kill him*! KILL HIM!"

Her knuckle splits on the door and in the dimness of the hallway she can see her blood on the gray metal that's the same color as the sky.

Something slams against the door inside and Tasha beats harder and harder, her blood a pattern of paisley before her. She's sobbing, her throat a mushroom, clogging.

"Dinah!" It's all she has, it's the last of her voice. "Dinah please…"

Then it's quiet. The screams have died.

She hears nothing but the storm.

CHAPTER 13

Tasha is packing the Prada backpack.

She considers the size of the pack and eyes the assortment of things laid out on her kitchen table that she had deemed important enough to bring along. She has arranged three boxes of granola bars, several bottles of Evian, a can of peaches and a can of pears, the can opener, a fork, lip balm, and her bag of make-up. On her feet are her Nikes, in her hand is the Wusthof. She has also decided to bring a smaller knife from the wooden block—a knife used for paring under normal circumstances—and the nail file she had used to kill Brian the doorman. Last, she has laid out her ID badge from the Apiary. In the picture is a face that has begun to look strange: her hair is styled and her make-up pristine. She touches the face on the badge before zipping it into a side pocket.

She's leaving.

She begins packing the other items into the Prada backpack, putting the bottled water at the bottom; the granola bars next, then the can opener. She has filled up most of the space inside and is down to holding a can of pears in one hand and the bag of make-up in the other. She eyes them. Inside the little purple-and-white striped pouch are her mascara and cream-to-powder shimmering foundation, as well as a tube of light-infused lip-gloss. She had applied all three earlier in the morning, smoothing the foundation on like war paint, coloring her lips carefully. The mascara she always applies last: the act of opening her eyes wide and swiping on the black paste is the chameleon's flesh turning to wood as he freezes on the branch.

Tasha makes her choice and returns the can of pears to the cupboard, stuffing the make-up bag into the backpack. In the outside pocket she has folded in two or three of Leona's letters, including the latest one. She looks around her apartment.

It had started empty, except for the pillow-top bench that her mother had sent with her when she moved out. Now it's full of things. Tasha goes into the bedroom and sits on the bench. It creaks slightly with her weight. It was her grandmother's and needs new varnish and some reupholstering. Tasha has never been one for antiques, but this is the bench her mother had sat on in front of the vanity mirror in the house Tasha grew up in, Tasha watching from the bed.

Tasha pictures her mother's fine toffee skin, the sable powder brush coated in faintly sparkling dust making its way over her cheekbones and nose and down to her throat. Her mouth would open slightly as she used the curler on her lashes, each eye opening and blinking twice after its treatment. Last would come the mascara, the wand dipping into the tube brown and coming out black, making its way toward her widened eyes. After each coat, she would look at Tasha through the reflection of the mirror and smile, and Tasha would smile back. She rubs her palm across its stained surface, stroked smooth by a couple generations of her family's asses.

She has the sudden urge to take it with her, a notion she dismisses as ridiculous as soon as it forms. There are other things she had wanted to take when she first began arranging items to pack: her flat iron, her atom video player, her H-Airless laser-razor. These are all things she would have packed on an ordinary trip, all of them useless now. She'd have felt safer taking them along. She also wanted to bring her favorite green satin Jimmy Choos. She had even tried forcing them into the pack on top of the granola bars, artfully storing bottled water in the shoes themselves, until in the end it became evident that the stilettos would have to be left behind. She's embarrassed by how much it pains her.

She takes a last look at the backpack's contents before buckling it shut. Its green canvas offsets the top she has chosen for the journey, a purple chiffon blouse that falls just over the waistband of her skinny jeans. The Nikes stick out like two size-seven railroad spikes; Tasha makes a face at them.

Tasha carries the rejected Jimmy Choos into the closet, which is almost as large as the bedroom itself and the reason she had chosen the apartment. Inside, she stands among the pants and blouses billowing from padded hangers in a jungle of silk and tweed. She stands among it all and breathes in, taking in the faint scent of laundry detergent and also cedar, which she has stashed throughout the space to keep the moths from munching. There is also a lingering smell of nutmeg, which surprises her. That is Leona's scent, and her sister has never set foot in her apartment. She wishes she could stay here forever. This is a safe place. Outside, everyone is dead. After yesterday, after Dinah, she had scorned the cradle of the bathtub and curled up here in the closet, surrounded by these smells. Now, Tasha trails her fingertips along the lines of garments in the dim light, trying to identify each fabric as her skin comes in contact with it. She succeeds for the most part: twill, cotton, satin, rayon, cotton, silk, cotton. Her careful system of color-coding layers the room in sections of red and violet, strips of yellow and navy blue, a blinding arrangement of white. Separate from the rest of the blue hangs the dejected corpse of her Apiary uniform. She avoids its artificial sheen as she sweeps her gaze over the rest of her wardrobe in a final parting grief.

She looks down at her purple chiffon top and at the Nikes jutting from the legs of her jeans. She can almost hear Gina saying, "Hello, clashy."

She pulls the purple top over her head, cursing as it catches on her earrings. She untangles the gold hoops from the fabric and gently hangs the shirt on its hanger in the purple section, caressing it lovingly before letting it go. She takes a step sideways to the black section and pulls down a cotton tank top, puts it on. She also brings down a vintage Adidas hoodie from the purple section. Gina would abhor the combination of Nike and Adidas, but Tasha needs something to layer if the temperature drops unexpectedly (which it often does), and she likes the hoodie. She looks at herself in the full-length mirror—jeans, black tank top, plain hoops, half-curly hair—and sighs. So much has changed.

She closes her bedroom door behind her without looking back; the rows of designer heels inhabiting the closet floor would beckon to her like children being left behind if she did. Tasha imagines her shoe collection in an infomercial for abandoned accessories, with sad faces drawn on, starving pot bellies and puppy-dog eyes.

The backpack is on her back, the knife in her hand, the hoodie over her shoulder. Almost out the door, she remembers her Guess aviators and gets them from the coffee table. She places them carefully into the back pocket of the backpack and steps into the hall.

She walks the few paces to Dinah's apartment. All morning she has gathered her belongings, said goodbye to others, trying not to think of her friend. Guilt settles heavily into her stomach. It quiets her. It burns her out. She has not even begun the walk South and already she feels tired. But she has to go. There is nothing here now.

The guilt is an onion of tears. She hadn't been able to save Dinah yesterday, but Dinah would not have needed saving yesterday if Tasha had saved her before. All those months of echoing slaps, Dale drunk and roaring every Friday, Tasha curling her pillow around her head, disconnecting the woman she would pass in the hallway from the cries she'd hear through the wall. Tasha had never even known her name before the Change. But Dinah had always been Dinah, and now Dinah is dead.

Now that the storm has passed, the window at the end of the hall illuminates more of the corridor. She stares at her blood drying on Dinah's door in patterns like roses. She wishes she had real roses to place at the entrance, but these blooms will have to do. What else can she give? Her keys are in her hand, and she has an idea. She holds one like a blade and uses it to scratch an epitaph into the metal.

It's time. Returning to her own apartment, she uses the same key to turn the deadbolt, locking in all her precious things, and locking out the world. Behind her, scratched into Dinah's door, are her words, scrawling and ragged:

Here lies Dinah. Day 8. Everyone's to blame.

CHAPTER 14

Tasha exits the building on the side, as she had entered from the front. Outside, the weather has changed again, and she's glad to be wearing a tank top and not the sticky chiffon. The heat makes her back damp after only a few steps; the sweat that is disguised by the black cotton would have been obvious in the purple blouse. She adjusts the straps of the Prada backpack so it rides a little higher; she doesn't like the feeling of it bumping against her ass, and if she needs to run it will interfere with her stride. Across the street is the mega McDonald's, its lights still on, its windows empty.

Tasha has to pass it to get to Lakeshore, but she finds herself striding across Foster toward its doorway. Thinking of the Post, she prepares herself for a locked door, reminding herself about the alarm. But it's open and she enters its wide doorway, sinking into the air conditioning like a grateful fish into a pond. She doesn't know why McDonalds is linked to the city generators—she's sure Leona would have some theory of obesity and corruption—but at the moment she doesn't care.

She moves cautiously into the seating area, knife ready, but the restaurant is deserted. A few tables have remnants of breakfast burritos and enormous cinnamon rolls, an overturned cup of orange juice there by the window. Tasha can see a hand on the ground toward the back, its arm obscured by the elevator leading up to the multiple other floors—McMexico, McThailand, depending on what country of origin you wanted your pre-made, pre-wrapped meal inspired by. Tasha decides she'd rather not to focus on the hand and instead moves to the front by the counters.

Here there is evidence of more activity: a pile of cash strewn about on the floor with some blood staining a few of the bills. A tooth. A Barbie doll. Tasha picks up the doll. There's blood on it too, around its hip, which she avoids, holding it by the neck. The Barbie has flaming red hair and wears a green Lycra jumpsuit, the back cut into a thong, exposing the doll's shiny plastic ass. Tasha sets the doll back down beside the tooth, propping it into a sitting position.

She decides to go behind the counter, where she steps over a dead employee, not looking at her face. The dead girl is by the fry machine—still powered on and roiling hotly—her neck apparently broken. The floor around her shines with grease. Tasha wonders if her death came from falling or something less immediate. She does not investigate.

On the food line are a half-dozen half-made hamburgers. It has been a week since the Change but the food looks undisturbed, unaffected by open air and decomposition. She pokes the top of a bun with the Wusthof. There is a little resistance and a barely-audible crunch. Stale. It's comforting.

The bark behind her brings a scream to her lips—she can't believe how much she screams these days—and she whirls around to face the source, knife at the ready. On the tip of the blade is the hamburger bun she just prodded. She gives the knife a shake; the stale bun doesn't fall off. Ahead of her is a Chipped McDonald's employee, and she turns her attention to him.

There is blood around his mouth, trailing down from the corners of his lips—classic Dracula. The typical frown is frozen on, the crinkle between his eyebrows aimed at Tasha like crosshairs. He is wearing a nametag. She leans a little closer to read it.

"Chip," the tag reads. And beneath it, a sticker: "Employee of the Month."

"No fucking way," she laughs, lowering the knife a half-inch in amusement.

Chip moves forward with startling speed and Tasha has to scramble. She darts around the counter, leaving him with the hamburgers, placing the food prep area between them. He's quick—not like the doorman or the butcher—and moves around the island in an instant. He's on her heels and Tasha darts away again, but now he's between her and the employee exit. She can't leave now anyway: she has to kill him indoors. He's more dangerous out there than he is in here; out there he can get to barking and draw the rest of his kind. He'd really be employee of the month then.

She looks around. She needs more space to get a stab at him, and Chip is looking around too, his head cocking first to the left and then to the right, a pissed-off sparrow. He makes up his mind. Chip lunges and Tasha skips to her left, leaping over the body of the girl with the broken neck—and then the feeling of falling. Tasha's lungs fill with ice as she slips on the spilled grease, her body sinking in slow motion as if through thick water, falling to the floor, the Wusthof spiraling out of her hand and sliding across the slick tile, leaving her unarmed. The dead girl breaks Tasha's fall, but Chip is quick. He has the toe of Tasha's Nike in his mouth, snuffling almost like a puppy as he gnaws.

Tasha twists onto her side and scrambles backward, kicking Chip squarely in the face with her other foot. She hears the crunch and feels the snap as she breaks his nose, which he doesn't notice. She doesn't need to look to know that the red light in his neck is blinking cheerfully as it repairs him.

She can feel the pressure of his teeth through her shoe; he is a famished foot fetishist. She worries for her Nike: she paid $248 for these shoes and the last thing she needs is his flat teeth scuffing them up, let alone severing one of her toes in the process. She gains some leverage by dragging herself up the dead girl's body and hauls herself halfway to her feet, still facing Chip. Her denim-covered shin is in his line of vision now and his glassy eyes almost light up. He goes for it, his mouth wide open like a shark. Tasha hears frantic *Jaws* music in her head as she screams and grabs the closest thing in reach, the handle to the basket of happily bubbling fries that are still in the scalding oil. The fries themselves barely exist anymore—they've been in the oil for days and are a sludge of black mud—but the oil exists very much and it sizzles as she slams the searing oil-coated basket against the side of Chip's head. The remnants of the fries ooze down his cheek and neck, his skin sliding off with it, hissing like lava. The fry sludge is in his eyes and Chip shakes his head, trying to clear his vision as disgusting blisters take over his face. He hadn't felt the left side of his face virtually melt off, but he can't see, and Tasha takes the opportunity to skitter after the Wusthof, which has slid partly under the large machine that toasts the buns.

She snatches up the blade and is back to Chip in a flash, where he still stands blinking fry corpses out of his eyes, not having thought to actually use his hands to wipe off the scalding goo. He crumples after a few stabs in the neck, the Chip failing with sparks flying, his body softening on the oily tile, then laying still.

Tasha breathes heavily and rubs her bare shoulder where some of the oil peppered her skin. She looks at the wound, little white dots interrupting the brown of the rest of her. They aren't really burns. She'll be fine.

She wonders where the rest of the McDonalds crew is. The fry girl has a broken neck and Chip has been taken care of. She creeps around to the office of the restaurant and finds a door with a plaque bearing the word "Manager." It's closed.

"Hello?" she calls. "Anybody in there?"

She wants to put an ear against the door but doesn't in case it flies open. Even so, she hears the quietest hint of a whisper, some rustling. She feels a pang of excitement, and also fear. She taps with the knife.

"Hey, anybody in there? It's okay. Chip is gone."

If anyone living is hiding behind the door, she assumes they will have barricaded themselves in, terrified of what their coworkers became, probably thinking they had gone on a wage-slave rampage. She can smell human waste, and hopes whoever is in there is in there alone. She can't imagine taking a shit in front of anyone she worked with—she thinks bitterly of Cara—let alone having to sit in the same room with them (and it) afterwards.

She tries one more time.

"Hello...?"

Through the door comes a rattlesnake hiss.

"Go...the fuck...away."

The voice startles Tasha so much that she stumbles backward, the knife drooping to her side. The words sound like a wicker chair being strangled by a witch. Tasha thinks the person must be dying. Almost a week without food or water (unless they had had the presence of mind to take some in when they hid) and the stench of their own refuse polluting the air of what Tasha assumes to be a cell of an office...they can't be too well.

"I'm leaving," she says, backing toward the lobby. "Chip's dead. Just so you know."

She thinks about what she's said and adds an afterthought,

"Uh...the employee of the month, I mean. That Chip. Not, uh, *all* the Chips."

She steps over Chip's body and scans the food prep area, deciding whether or not she should take anything. In a cooler by the front counter there are bottles of Dasani water, which she generally scoffs at. She pulls one out. Might as well save the Evian.

Before she leaves she goes into the public bathroom and is surprised by a dead man in the women's room. He's dressed as a woman, his dress stopping below the knee, his hair pulled back. She can see the tracks where the extensions were sewn in. His face is beautiful, uglied only by a gaping bite mark on his neck. Tasha turns to the men's bathroom and uses the mirror to touch up her make-up, using the little comb from her cosmetics bag to perfect her eyelashes. The gray tones of the lights around the mirror paint shadows on her face. She stares at herself a moment longer before turning away.

Outside, the temperature has changed again and she's no longer grateful for the chill McDonald's left on her skin, so she puts on the hoodie that she'd stowed in the backpack. The sky has the purplish tint of smog and storm, and she feels a flicker of concern. Again? If it storms and she's outside it could be bad for her. The color of the sky reminds her of the last conversation she'd had with Dinah before they'd closed their windows against the rain. Dinah had wanted to go South with Tasha. They would've found a way to get her out, Tasha thinks bitterly. Then she wouldn't be alone. Again. Walking across this god-forsaken city like a lonely pioneer. It would be better with someone to watch her back.

Tasha had decided that morning that she would take Lakeshore as far south as she could—she didn't trust the residential streets to be clear of Minkers. The Drive had been reserved for foot traffic, bikes and Segways for the past twelve years, and she had been jogging on it a number of times since she moved up North. It was open enough to enable her to see any approaching Minkers, but sheltered in places by domed gazebos and trees, so she could take cover if necessary. She decides to stick with this plan despite the weather, and continues walking east on Foster.

As she walks, she observes a number of boarded-up windows in the massive building across from McDonald's. It's a government building that housed the black-suited Drivers of the L, a structure normally too classy for wooden boards to be blacking the eyes of its windows. Tasha wonders how many there are like her inside—unChipped and in hiding from a world gone mad. How many Dinahs, locked up with monsters? The Drivers all had MINK as a matter of course, so she thinks there must be only a few exceptions in this particular building: employees new to the company and not yet eligible, cowering with their husbands and children, wondering what's next. The Barbie doll in McDonald's was the only evidence of a child Tasha has seen since the Change, and she shudders thinking of it. One likes to pretend that children simply disappear during catastrophe, vanishing like smoke until the worst is over, when they'll be returned to their homes untouched and unaffected.

The skeleton of a building still being constructed rears up beside her on Foster, a behemoth of a tower with only the spine and ribs in place. It used to be a retirement home, but they were currently renovating it into a mansion of a dance club, complete with attached hotel rooms—bookable by the hour and by the night.

She almost trips over a yellow construction helmet, a swatch of bloody hair stuck to the inside. There's no other sign of carnage around the building site. Tasha wonders where all the people are. Chicago was packed with people before the Change. Even if they're all dead she'd expect at least to see their bodies, but the Volamus are clear in this area—she's almost reached the place where they stop—and except for the helmet with the bloody hair, she sees nothing unusual or alarming. The Drivers' building appeared to be deserted also, but the barricaded windows tell her otherwise. She wonders if the Minkers will notice the difference.

She passes the point where the Volamu ends, its track thrumming into a groove underground which will run endlessly backward toward the L. She wishes she had not wondered at the absence of bodies, because as she reaches Marine Drive there are many, all collected at the entrance of the subway that would have taken them downtown. She peers down the stairs. Only the first five or so steps are illuminated with sunlight and she can't see beyond them. Stretched across the top three steps is a Driver, her suit neatly pressed, the black sunglasses half off her face. Her hair hides her eyes. She must have been new— Chipless. Tasha wonders if she was going up or down when she was attacked: descending the stairs to begin her shift, or fleeing up them as her passengers turned on her, barking.

Scattered around the top of the stairs are at least twenty other dead Chicagoans, coagulated blood like lava around their various wounds. A man and a woman lie very close together, their throats open, their hands almost touching. Tasha imagines the passages under Chicago packed with the bodies of the city's former inhabitants—the Change had taken place during the early hours of the commute when the city was buzzing with people headed to work and school. With so many Chicagoans— almost all—dependent on the trains, many of them must have died early that morning, trapped on various lines while other passengers inexplicably, horrifically, became monsters right before their eyes. All it would have taken was a Minker or two per train car to transform it into a compartment of inescapable terror. Tasha thinks of the train she's seen stopped on the tracks at Berwyn, the man in the cheap suit hanging from the alloy. He had managed to escape the train car, but it didn't matter. If the streets are empty of Chicagoans now, Tasha thinks she would only have to enter the subways to find them.

Her mind goes to the day she rode the L downtown with Gina on their way to Cybranu—even though it hadn't been rush hour, the train had been packed with people. What if Gina had changed right then? The Driver would have been Chipped, leaving the train to career off the tracks or crash into another train. In her compartment, Tasha wouldn't have been able to get away, crowded against other passengers also trying to escape—squalling cattle crammed in the cart, protesting their journey to slaughter. Tasha would have been one of them. No nail file, no Wusthof to save her. She's tired of these scenarios:

what-ifs, what-nows. She looks at the people around the subway entrance. The whole scene has begun to smell—several crows watch Tasha from the rails of the stairwell, no doubt irritated by her interruption—and Tasha finally moves on, the entrance to Lakeshore just ahead.

She can smell the water of Lake Michigan—almost ocean but a tamer scent, mixed with pollution. It reminds her of the year she met Gina, going to the beaches to show off, stretching the legs of their new collegiate independence. Tasha had come a lot farther than her friend—Gina grew up just outside the city in a gated suburb—but the taste of freedom was sweet for both of them. Tasha tastes a vestige of it now, born from her eagerness to wipe the scene at the subway entrance from her thoughts. She finds herself passing the entrance to Lakeshore and crossing under the intricately designed overpass toward Foster Beach. She needs to breathe that air again.

A soccer stadium fills the south field beside the beach, a smallish building that had seated one or two thousand people. It had been built to accommodate the hundred or so players who would congregate there every season. Someone had seen the players' dedication and thought they could make some money by building a stadium, holding events and charging admission. When it was still just grass, Tasha would see the guys racing up the field like herds of wild ponies, brown mustangs glistening with sweat. When the stadium was built they'd mostly wandered off, and the structure became a ghost lodge for drug addicts and people with nowhere to live. A few teams still played, but they were covert about it, some even sneaking in at night to play. Tasha eyes the stadium warily now. It seems quiet enough—it always does. The silver siding has turned gray with neglect; rusty weeds crowd its edges. She listens and hears only the faint lapping of the lake, which she walks toward, picking her way between scattered trash and dog shit.

She nears the shore, passing through the low concrete structure that houses the bathrooms and, once, a concession stand. It's an old building, moss-covered in places; just looking at it makes Tasha feel claustrophobic. The towering architectural goliaths of downtown and the rest of the North Side blot out the sky, but at least they don't create a cramped ceiling of concrete. She feels she can't stretch her neck while underneath it, and she's glad when she passes through it to the beach, where her Nikes sink into the loose sand.

She walks closer to the water, enjoying the squabbling of seagulls peppering the quiet. A few of them stand like pirates on one peg leg, the other webbed appendage stuffed up in their plumage. They chuckle in their throats at one another, little half-threats at their birdy frenemies. Two of the birds are competing over some piece of something they have found in the surf, their voices shrill and irritated. Tasha can't help but laugh a little at their oblivious outrage. They land on the beach with the item between them on the sand. It's a shrimp. Or it could be a finger. At this point the finger seems more likely than the shrimp. The two birds take turns making sudden movements toward their prize, each daring the other to lay claim to it, their smooth white chests pulsating as they complain. Their eyes are fierce and bright.

Suddenly another gull drops out of the sky, a black ring around his beak, either a mark of age or the sign of another breed entirely. He gives one raspy cough of a squall and snatches the finger (or shrimp), winging off toward the deserted pier to enjoy his prize. The other two are left warbling, at a loss, but don't pursue their black-beaked brother. Tasha imagines they are used to it. Now they poke around in the sand, pulling up rubber bands and other rubbish, none of it edible. One unearths a tiny plastic dog, a child's toy, missing one leg. Tasha has the urge to take it from him—it plucks some rusty string in her heart—but she doesn't even know what she'd do with it, so she stops herself. Anyway, the two birds take flight in a hurry, bumping into each other as they struggle to get in the air. Tasha figures the gull with the black beak is back to pester them and looks around for it.

She doesn't know how she didn't hear their feet, dozens of them, at least thirty Minkers making their way over the sand toward her. She can see more behind them farther off, stumbling through the dunes to reach her before the others.

Her throat is suddenly dry. She should be running, should be scrambling, flying, but the fear is like a spine injury—she feels nothing, reacts to nothing, only sees the danger and shrinks from it. Blurs with open barking mouths, their moans and howls enhanced by her panic—every sound is deafening, nearer and nearer. The knife is in her hand but it's slipping— her hands aren't her own. Neither is her throat, or she'd be screaming.

The lake laps against her shoe, the cold water sinking through the nylon and into her sock. Her toes are wet, and she's awake.

Tasha tightens her grip on the Wusthof and runs, staying close to the water where the sand is firmer while the Minkers stumble along in the looser stuff of the open beach. They are not quick, but some of them are in good shape—partly due to the Chip, she knows—and they clip along a hundred meters behind her, their barking thin with exertion. They don't seem to be closing the distance at all; they run at their pace and Tasha runs at hers, her fear a shining silver spur. She thinks of her high school algebra teacher asking questions about two trains traveling on a track at different but consistent speeds. Would they ever meet? Tasha had always gotten it wrong; there was no definite answer, the way she saw it. One of the Drivers could be drunk, could be sleep-deprived. One train could hit a banana peel and go careening out of control. Anything could happen.

Tasha slows a little, feeling a sharp pang in her abdomen from running. Her gym membership and jogging on Lakeshore before the Change had made her fit for distance—turns out the kickboxing hadn't hurt either—but had not prepared her for all-out sprinting. She wishes she had worn a sports bra. Why hadn't she worn a sports bra? The pang is distracting, but she unexpectedly thinks of how many calories she is burning and is momentarily, bizarrely pleased.

One of the Minkers pulls away from the pack and Tasha risks a glance over her shoulder to glimpse his distance, remembering in a flash the people she'd witnessed from her apartment window, the person and their child, being chased and eventually dragged down. With his speed increased, and hers decreased, they are about twenty meters apart. All Tasha can think of is trains and her algebra teacher. She's worried about the rest of the pack—there are more now. The white ones' faces have reddened; she can't tell if it's from exertion, or sunburn from lurking around on the beach. She sees their mob racing along the sand after her and thinks momentarily of Nina Simone and poplar trees.

Tasha sneaks another glance at her closest pursuer, who has closed to a ten-meter distance and maintained it. He's blonde and bulky and she wonders at his ability to race along so easily. On his feet are sanitation boots worn by chefs in high-end restaurants. His stringy hair has fallen into his eyes, swinging back and forth as he lumbers along. Tasha assesses her game plan, little by little cutting across the sand, about to circle around the empty soccer stadium. The chef is gaining.

Tasha lets him gain another yard; he's almost upon her. Timing will be everything—she can hear his moaning, increasing in intensity as he nears his prey. Tasha skids to a stop, whirling around, her arm out like a thorned branch. He slams into the point of the knife, too slow-witted to stop in time, and the flesh of his throat swallows the blade. Tasha yanks the knife free and glances at the rest of the pack, about forty meters back, still on the sand. She draws back the blade and slices across the side of the neck, severing veins and sending sparks flying as she destroys the Chip. He collapses and twitches, but she is jogging again before he is still. The work was quick but the pack has gained; Tasha feels panic rattling her teeth. Her thighs begin to rebel as fear and exhaustion spread through her bones. She thinks of the guy in the Asics running down Broadway. She is him now, the knife cutting the air more slowly as she pumps her arms, struggling for momentum. An Asian woman lopes a little ahead of the rest, barking. Every step Tasha takes has already been taken by someone in the city, someone likely dead. The ground vibrates with the volume of the pack's numbers.

An arm nearly clotheslines Tasha, so quickly does it snap out in front of her. She almost falls on her back with the strength of her recoil, but the arm becomes two arms, two black arms snatching her upright and dragging her into the doorway they appeared from. The door is concealed by the pattern of its material, made to blend in with the rest of the wall, an employee entrance for soccer events. Tasha struggles, her assailant attempting to pin her arms. She slashes out in the dim illumination splashed from the doorway. The door closes, the rectangle of faint light gone, and she is in the dark, spinning, slashing with the knife.

CHAPTER 15

Light. Another door has been opened, a door that meets the sun, and the room is flooded with vision. Tasha is lashing out left and right with the Wusthof but with the room now illuminated, she sees that she is not being attacked; no one is trying to come near her. She stops her frantic windmilling and lets her eyes adjust to seeing.

There are seven people in the little space—no, eight, there's a woman leaning against a wall—watching her. Some look frightened. Some look angry. One or two just look. One of the men who is just looking is tall and dark, a year or two older than Tasha, and bleeding from his left arm. He is holding what looks like a jersey to the wound.

"Are you finished?" he asks her, half-smiling now.

Tasha looks at them all. They're unChipped. They are brown and black—one white man—and dressed in jerseys like the one the tall man is now tying around his forearm. She realizes slowly, stupidly, that they are the soccer players she has seen running the field, footballers.

"I thought you were a Minker."

"What?"

Tasha points at her neck.

"A Minker. Chipped. One of them."

"Oh. No, we're not."

They all stare at one another until the leaning woman pushes off the wall and says,

"What the fuck were you doing on the beach?"

Tasha immediately dislikes her. She is small and toffee-colored, eyebrows arching over round eyes, a wide mouth pursed into a slanted bow. Her body is tight and wiry; her Adidas cleats are orange and match her jersey. Tasha wishes she could see the name on the back. The woman's venom puts Tasha on her guard.

"Sunbathing," Tasha replies.

The woman doesn't respond, just looks at Tasha. The tall man smiles a little more and says,

"Almost got sunburned, ladygirl."

Tasha looks at his arm.

"Did I do that?"

"Yeah, but it was an accident. I shouldn't have grabbed you without warning you, but those...people were right behind you."

"Is the cut bad?"

"No."

They all stare at each other some more. The other players don't seem eager to talk. Some are staring at the floor, some are staring out the door that's letting in the light.

"Where does that door go? Is it safe?" Tasha asks the tall man, who is the only one who seems receptive to conversation.

He nods.

"It leads out into the stadium's field. They can't get in; we blocked the main entrances on the first day. There were a few who," he paused, "changed that were already in the stadium with us. But I...we took care of them."

He turns his head slightly, looking at no one, but those behind him stare at the ground or fidget. Tasha walks through the open door and realizes why.

The field stretches below her, three flight of stairs down. The stadium had been built into the hill, and she had been snatched indoors on the hillside. From where she stands now, the field is a green basin in a shallow stadium-crater below. And across the healthy expanse of artificial grass are bodies, orange-shirted forms dotted across the turf in what eerily resembles a ghost match. There's the striker, lying on his right hip, one arm over his head. Close to him is the right forward, on her back. She could be stretching. They could all be sleeping. There are a few prone forms that are out of position, their jerseys bright and still.

The tall man has followed her outside.

"We were practicing for a match."

"Did you kill them all?" she asks.

"Not all of them were sick," he says. "Some of the ones that were sick had attacked and killed some of the other guys before we even understood what was going on. We didn't know who had lost their minds and who hadn't. One of us, Derek, wasn't sick and he was helping a woman who was being attacked. One of our other guys," he jerks his head behind him, referring to one of their remaining eight, "thought Derek was one of the crazy ones. So Derek died too. It was crazy. Is."

They are silent for a minute. Tasha's heart beats slowly in her ears. Every step she takes has been weighed upon by grief for Dinah, and she had barely known the woman. Here in this stadium, these people have lost friends. Close friends. She doesn't know what to say, so she sticks to logistics.

"And you're sure you have everything locked up?"

The man shrugs.

"We've been here for days now. None of them have gotten in. We've heard them at the two gates we chained up, but the only other entrances are employee entrances like the one you found. They're not too smart; they just knock up against things. Once they focus on something though, like a door, sometimes they stick around."

Tasha nods.

"How many of them are there?" he asks quietly.

How many. Tasha swallows and half looks at him.

Silence.

He asks again. "How many?"

"Everyone."

He balls a fist and presses it against his forehead.

"We tried to get out, we tried to go home." He's talking to himself now, and she lets him. "We took Lakeshore and as soon as we got to Montrose there was a big group of them, at least twenty-five. We were ten when we went out. We had to turn back, and now we're eight."

Quiet between them. Tasha can hear the distant sounds of the lake.

"Are they contagious?"

The question surprises her. For all her mental comparison of the Minkers to zombies, it had not occurred to her that their condition might be something she could catch. Like a reel of film, her brain flips through every horror film she's ever seen: square human teeth tearing at human flesh, the flesh animating; walking dead swarming the streets, rising from their graves. She thinks of Brian, her doorman, the morning of the Change, and the Driver she encountered in Uptown. Their incisors had been so near her, their saliva dripping, fluids waiting to be mixed to transform her into a Prada-wearing flesh-eater. She thinks dully of Dinah. After her death, there had been only one barking voice in that apartment. One pair of shambling feet. No more.

"No," she says, sobering. Even if she hadn't known Dinah, other logic prevails. The girl in the yellow dress flutters through her mind like a ghost butterfly. She had been chewed to bits by her very Chipped boyfriend. Tasha had seen her die. All the bodies she had passed, piled at the top of the subway steps, sprawled out on the streets. Even the paused soccer game on the field right in front of them. No, it's not contagious. The tall man is speaking from fear planted by a decade or two of horror flicks.

"No," she says again. He nods as if he knew this, as if he

had been embarrassed to ask in the first place. It's a question that shouldn't exist.

"What have you been eating?" he asks. "We have hot dogs from the concession stand. They're cold, but they're food."

At this moment one of the other players emerges from the door. They had all stayed inside when Tasha and the tall man ventured out. Tasha gets the feeling no one wants to see the field, and realizes they'd had to kill their own teammates just days ago, had witnessed their goalie gnawing on the throat of their left forward. She figures she wouldn't want to see the field either. The man sidles outside and, as she predicted, works very hard at keeping his gaze on Tasha and the tall man, struggling not to look over their shoulders at the formation of the fallen.

"We need to talk about this," he says. "People want to know where she came from."

Tasha and the tall man exchange a look and follow the other guy inside, where the remnants of the team are clustered together. They break apart when Tasha and the other two enter the room, which Tasha realizes is a storage room, with boxes of equipment and supplies. A few are open—first aid stuff. She tries to be subtle as she looks around for others wearing bandages, wondering who was injured in their scuffles with the Minkers. She doesn't want to think about what human teeth tearing her skin would feel like. She imagines it would require a lot of effort on the biter's part.

"What do you know about all this?" Someone is asking her a question. She turns from her thoughts and sees that it is the one white man. His jersey says #16.

"Not much more than you," she replies.

"You knew it was in the neck."

"So did you, if you killed any of them."

"You knew it was the implant."

"I learned from experience."

"You've killed them?"

At this question Tasha notices the unpleasant woman she had first spoken to change her facial expression. Tasha has either irritated her or surprised her. She answers carefully,

"A few."

They all look at her and at her knife, which she's still grasping. She knows they are probably now noticing the red streaks on her jeans, which have faded and dried into rusty stripes. They are taking her in: her immaculate mascara and her Prada backpack, her breasts, her lipgloss. She feels the way she felt walking to work downtown, eyes moving over her body, assessing, measuring. It irks her. Of course she's killed them—she's still alive.

"How many?" The other woman can't help herself; the question bursts out and she looks surly with herself for asking.

Tasha ticks off the faces in her list. Her doorman, the butcher, the Driver, Chip, the chef. She almost counts the boy on Day 1, but he got up, of course.

"A few. Four or five."

"You did them all at once?"

Tasha laughs at the question in spite of herself. It would have meant something entirely different before the Change.

"No. One at a time, like a good girl."

The woman pauses, her eyebrow raised, then laughs loudly before stopping abruptly. #16 reenters the conversation.

"Why do they change?"

"You know why."

He is silent. Then,

"How do you know?"

Tasha sighs, reluctant to repeat what Leona has told her. It sounds so very stupid, with so little to go on. They don't need to know it all, she decides.

"My sister knew something was going to happen. Because of the Chips, the implants. She said it was something bad. This is what she meant."

"Where's your sister?" one asks. "Here?"

"She lives in the Nation."

At this #16 mutters something and a few of the players shake their heads.

"What is she," he asks, "some kind of revolutionary?"

"She's a mom. And a farmer. She studied law when the States were United."

"Why did she leave?"

"Look, what's with all the fucking questions, okay?" She's impatient now, and tired. "She sent me the letter before all this happened…and then it happened. She doesn't know why, I don't know why."

"Where were you going?" the woman in orange asks. Her voice is soft and Tasha doesn't snap at her.

"Downtown. I have family there."

A lie. Why?

"Your family's probably dead."

It's the tall man that says it. He is staring out the door that leads to the field, his fist on his forehead.

"They might be okay, Ishmael," one of the other players offers. "Your mom is tough, and your brothers are there to help her."

Ishmael gives him a quick, cold look and goes on staring out the door. Everyone is silent for a moment until he says,

"You won't make it all the way there. They show up out of nowhere. We don't even know how they surprised us when we were going down Lakeshore. They just show up."

"I've been outside a few times. I went and got food from Jewel. I went to the Post." She feels like she's trying to prove something and she doesn't know what, or why. "Sometimes you can hear them barking and you can stay away. You just have to be quiet and pay attention."

"Barking?"

Tasha feels uncomfortable. She will not imitate the sound.

"You know...that sound they make. It sounds like...like dogs barking."

They stare at her. She gets annoyed.

"Look, I'll be fine. I packed some food, I'm sneaky. I'm kinda fast. I mean, I *am* fast. It's not that far. If I travel during the day, I can see them coming."

"They can see you too," the woman says.

"Yeah."

"What about at night? What will you do at night?"

"Sleep in soccer stadiums."

Tasha can see the woman wants to smile but stops herself this time.

Tasha looks at the tall man named Ishmael, who is fussing with one of the packs of first aid materials. He's replacing the jersey wrapped around his arm with an actual bandage. #16 goes over to help him, holds the sterile strip ready while Ishmael pours a capsule of hydrogen peroxide over the wound. Tasha can see that he had been right; the cut isn't too bad. He must have been quick: she had made a serious attempt at severing any limbs in a two-foot radius. The others are watching the process too, and she wonders what they're thinking, wonders if they're thinking about war like she is. The Adidas logos on all their sleeves could be military badges. Her shoes are Nike, but her hoodie is Adidas. Maybe that makes her an ally. Or an enemy.

The wound bandaged, Ishmael walks to the corner and comes back with a plastic bag, which, as he comes closer, Tasha sees is filled with hot dogs in buns. She can't help but laugh as he offers her one. He's smiling too.

She accepts a hot dog.

"What, no ketchup?" she jokes.

"Sorry, princess." The woman said it, and Tasha looks at her to see if any malice was intended, but the woman is eating a hot dog and Tasha can't tell. Tasha takes off her backpack for the first time and sits against the door she had been brought in through. She can feel the smallest breeze whisper across her lower back, trickling in through the small crack between the door and the floor. The sensation is almost like breath. She imagines the Minkers from the beach crowding around the doorway, sniffing. She shifts her body to the wall beside the door, dragging her backpack with her.

"How did you guys know I was out there anyway?" she asks between bites.

A short man with a beard—his jersey says #34—shifts the food in his mouth to one cheek and points upward.

"I was in one of the box seats in the stadium and looked out the window and saw you as you got from the sand to the grass and headed this way. I told Ish to get downstairs quick and see if he could give you a signal, call you or something. I didn't think you'd get over here so fast. I for sure thought that one out front was going to get you."

Tasha chews and shrugs, then, finishing her hot dog, uses the clean side of the wrapper to wipe dirt off her Nikes. She can feel them watching her and is self-conscious. She decides to busy her hands and digs in her backpack for a can of peaches, along with the can opener. A minute later she is eating a slice of fruit.

"Can I get a peach?" #34 grins. "It's been nothing but hot dogs and Gatorade for like a week now."

Tasha passes the can, which he leans forward to accept. By the time she gets it back it has been passed to all the other players, who one by one have joined what has become a lopsided circle. Tasha wonders how well they've been washing their hands and considers not eating the few peaches left in the can, but her still-hungry stomach wins the debate, and she munches them, trying not to think about germs.

"So it's everybody?" Tasha isn't sure who says it; it's not

Ishmael and not the woman, who Tasha has heard Ishmael call Vette.

Tasha nods vaguely in answer.

"Man, I wish I could have afforded MINK." It's a player beside #34, a chubby guy with a young face. Tasha has no idea what he means.

#16, sitting a little to the right of Tasha, scoffs across the circle at him.

"What are you talking about? If you had MINK, you'd have the Chip. If you had the Chip, you'd be…crazy. One of them." He looks scornful.

"Yeah, I guess so," the chubby guy says slowly. "But at least I wouldn't have to worry about it."

They ponder this as a group for a moment before #34 says,

"Well, if it's because of the Chip, maybe there's like, a cure. An off switch. There has to be, right? I'm sure the lab knows all about this. I mean, they got to, right? They know. They're trying to fix it. Probably right now. It's not like a plague or some shit. It's an implant. Cybranu just has to figure out how to turn it off."

Tasha glances at him doubtfully but says nothing. Dinah had voiced similar hopes. In the first day or two, Tasha had held off lighting the rug on fire to cook boxed pizza, just in case all of this blew over. But by now, the way she sees it, if the world as she knows it is over…it's over. Although she sheepishly misses her shoe collection, praying for an off switch to what the world has become seems dumb. She would've liked an off switch when her parents died, or a rewind button, and that didn't happen. Get real, dummy, she thinks.

"I don't know, dude." It's the chubby player again. "That seems easy. Real easy."

"Easy?" Tasha asks.

"Too easy. It's neat."

Tasha looks sideways at Ishmael, who is leaning against a cardboard box. He hasn't said anything but his eyes are following the conversation, his fingers knitted.

"Yeah," says #34, rubbing the back of his neck, "but if this was a possibility, Cybranu would have known about it and have like a protocol or some shit. That's what labs have, right? Protocols and shit. They test stuff. They would have had a protocol for this, and maybe it's just taking a while to fix."

Tasha considers this. He's right, on one hand. Labs *do* test stuff. Surely they had to know this was a possibility.

"Some of them act weird," she says suddenly, and they all look at her. "Different than the others. You know, the ones that were chasing me on the beach are the typical ones. But some, like this one Chipped lady I saw at the Post, she acted different. Like she didn't even know I was there. Not until I actually walked into the Post."

"Maybe she was getting fixed by the protocol, see?" #34 insists, nodding enthusiastically.

"She still tried to kill me," Tasha adds neutrally. She feels like she's staring at a mirage inside her head. The lines between her thoughts won't stay still.

"Well, the protocol ain't done yet," says #34, a little glum.

"It is neat, isn't it," Ishmael says suddenly, softly. They all turn to look at him. He's staring at the ceiling.

No one says anything.

"It's neat, like you said, Zayd," he says, nodding at the chubby player. "All the main jobs give you MINK. MINK gives the implant. People without jobs don't get MINK, so they don't get the implant."

Tasha can't help but think of Dinah again, who had said something very similar. Will everything remind her of her dead friend? Is that the way death is? A song stuck in your head?

"Well…yeah," #16 curbs his tone a little for Ishmael, but not by much.

"Just saying," Ishmael says, still staring at the ceiling. Tasha thinks maybe he's looking at a mirage too.

They all sit quietly for awhile, lost in their own thoughts. Tasha watches Ishmael, whose eyebrows still look sewn together. The light coming through the still-open door is fading as the sun sets somewhere opposite the lake. As it grows dimmer and dimmer, he stands and closes the door, asking no one. She hears the dry scuffle of cardboard in the dark as he drags boxes in front of the door. Light comes underneath it, a thin line bright enough to illuminate her backpack, which she drags over to use as a pillow, shifting its contents so the can opener isn't stabbing her skull.

She can hear the others settling too, their breaths deepening not with sleep but with deep thought. With the light of day gone, they are free to be terrified; free to think their darkest thoughts about family members whose whereabouts they're unsure of. They don't say these things aloud; they don't want to be comforted. They wrap up in their despair like cocoons and wait for morning. Tasha knows about cocoons.

Someone shifts close to Tasha.

"Hey."

It's the woman, Vette.

"Yeah?" Tasha says.

"Cute purse."

"Thanks."

And quiet.

CHAPTER 16

Tasha wakes before the others and freaks out on a miniature scale as she becomes aware that she can hear the breathing of other lungs besides her own and that there is a human being very near her. It's Vette, and next to Vette is #34. They both sleep soundly.

Tasha reaches into the outside pocket of the Prada backpack and pulls out one of Leona's letters, pressing the paper to her face and breathing it in like a bouquet. She doesn't actually smell anything, but with her eyes closed she imagines she can smell her sister's hair, the oil she would rub through it. She imagines, too, the warm, comfortable smell of composting vegetables, melon rind. She takes the page away from her face and studies the surface of it for prints, soil, food stains. There isn't much to see. She runs her eyes over the handwriting without actually reading it.

What would her parents have thought of this whole ordeal? Leona had gotten her nose for conspiracies from their father, who Tasha knows would have already had a theory or two ready on the morning of the Change. They would have survived, Tasha's parents. If they hadn't already been dead, unprotected by MINK, they would have survived all this. Or maybe they would have been seduced by the beckoning Cybranu ads that crowded the Net and the world.

Tasha remembers her daily train ride, both sides of her lit up with voices and flashing colors of lips and legs. The man on one of the illuminated panels, modeling for Hanes and talking about the comfort of his crotch, fades as he finishes his half-naked ploy, and the screen lights up with Cybranu. The model in the ad changes as passengers shuffle before it—Microscopic Mirroring Devices at work. An older man, his posture stooped, his hair thin, passes in front of the MMDs and the ad reflects his whiteness, his white hair, his blue oxford. But his Cybranu self has a straighter back, a more defiant hairline, fewer crows' feet. The man gazes at the better version of himself for a moment before getting off the L. Taking advantage of the new space afforded by his absence, a full-hipped girl of no more than 20 finds herself in front of the MMD's, confronted with a slimmer reflection, a straighter nose. Blonder, it seems. The real girl lowers her eyes, changes the song on her Glass, the seed planted.

Another man passes in front of the Cybranu ad, speaking Spanish on his ear-chip. When he looks ahead at the image provided by the MMDs, he has less facial hair and the tattoo on his cheek is gone. His hair is shorter. The real man moves away from the ad. There is no one to replace him—the crowd on the train is thinning—so the image dissolves into what Cybranu programmed as default, an athletic white man in his thirties, smiling. The people on the train nod to their individual soundtracks. The Cybranu ad finishes and then fades into something else shiny.

Tasha sighs. Looking back, she recognizes the carrot dangling from the stick, always jerked out of reach. She folds Leona's letter back into its envelope as people around her in the storage room are starting to stir. She pulls her compact of foundation with its tiny mirror out of the backpack. She glances over at the hair of sleeping Vette. Hair like that doesn't need much fixing, Tasha thinks enviously, but her own does. She peers into the tiny mirror and tilts it this way and that while attempting to tame what's becoming a mane. As for the rest of her, she can only see one eye at a time, her nose disconnected from the rest of her, her mouth on its own. Without her eyes to offset it, her overbite seems dramatic and sharkish.

Vette sits up as Tasha snaps the mirror shut.

"What's that for?" the woman asks, rubbing her eyes.

"My face."

Ishmael is moving the stuff out from in front of the door that leads to the stadium, and now the faint light that had colored the room blazes as he opens it. Vette stands up, rotating the shoulder she slept on. She follows the other players over to the door, where some of them are picking up a couple of the boxes of food and carrying them outside.

"Ish likes to eat up top in the morning," Vette says, motioning to Tasha. She's warmer today.

Outside the weather is cool but pleasant, and on top of the stadium—from where #34 had spotted Tasha the day before—one can look out at the lake in one direction, and in at the city from another. There is no wind at the moment; all is still. The world could be a meadow. The lake is a soft wash.

Someone hands Tasha a hotdog, which she eats without thought. Ishmael stands with #34 and #16, looking out at the beach.

"Check it out," Ishmael says, turning to Tasha.

From his side she can see a swarm of the Minkers wandering around on the beach where she was ambushed yesterday. Their movements are idle, empty of meaning, operating in circuits of activity. Tasha sees them and thinks of the wandering buffalo in an old, old America. She remembers what she learned about pioneers pushing West on trains so long ago, appearing in windows of the freight's cars and clearing the fields of bison with their magical, inaccurate shotguns blasting, not even taking the meat when the train moved on. What she wouldn't give for a long-range rifle here and now.

"There's more today," Ishmael says to no one in particular.

Tasha agrees but doesn't say so out loud; she feels strange beside him. In a bar she would probably be leaning on his shoulder by now, or talking nonstop. Here she feels unarmed, her mascara old and her hair audacious.

"Do you still want to go downtown?" Ishmael asks her, turning his face to her.

She turns slightly away. The less he sees of her smudginess

the better. Besides, she needs to remember her lie and doesn't trust her face not to betray it.

"Yeah," she says. "Gotta check on my family."

Standing so near him, Tasha realizes suddenly that she had not packed underwear. The thought sinks into her stomach like a greased cannonball. More thoughts come, one after another like fire ants: no deodorant, no toothbrush, no H-Airless or even a razor. On Foster, out and about cutting open random necks, she had allowed the existence of her sweaty underarms to shrink in importance. Standing between Ishmael and #16, she feels a lump like a planet expanding in her throat. She needs camouflage. She finds herself flipping through a dusty file cabinet of alibis to be used for escape, untouched since college: she can't use the dead grandma excuse, as everyone's grandma is likely dead at this point.

Ishmael and Vette are discussing the amount of food left in the concession stand boxes. Tasha is imagining what the area between her eyebrows currently looks like. The idea of a forest springs up unbidden; the trees cloud her vision. Ishmael is proposing they ration the remaining hot dogs, and Tasha is imagining each follicle on her glabella extending outward like the legs of massive black spiders. She feels wild, feels in her muscles the desire to pace steel bars in anxious liquid steps. This is why she's better off alone, she thinks. She would leave right now if these people hadn't saved her life. She doesn't know what she owes them, but it's something, so when #34 says, "Someone is going to need to go get food, or we won't be able to hold out," Tasha has to restrain herself from leaping into the air to offer. A store. In its linoleum fluorescence is salvation, things like deodorant and old-school razors that will comfort her. Two birds with one stone, she thinks, stuff for me and food for them. Debt paid. Then I'll move on. She holds her tongue for a moment and then says,

"I'll go. Me and someone else. We can watch each other's backs and carry more food."

Silence greets her offering. Still too painfully aware of her face to raise her eyes, she directs her energy at Ishmael. She isn't aware of the faint feeling of hope until it's replaced with disappointment when the voice who speaks up isn't his. It's Vette's.

"I'll go."

Great, thinks Tasha. This should be fun.

"You sure?" That voice is Ishmael's. He doesn't sound concerned, only diplomatic. The face of #16 is sour but he says nothing. Neither does anyone else.

"I'm sure. We'll be quick. Let's go now while it's still early."

Tasha has offered to empty out her backpack to carry some of the food, and she does so now, stacking the cans of fruit and the bottled water on the floor by the door leading to the field. Some of the team is watching her a little suspiciously, as if expecting her to withdraw some wondrous food or magical weapon that she's been withholding. She removes everything except the letters from Leona, the can opener, and the striped bag of make-up: the can opener so they don't demolish her fruit while she's gone, and the letters because they're private.

The make-up she brings because to leave it would be like a magician leaving his magic top hat on stage alone with a curious audience set on discovering the origins of the pristine white rabbit. Plus, when she and Vette get where they're going, she plans on slipping off to the bathroom to fix her face. She'll feel better when she's covered. Vette can sneer if she wants.

Vette has a duffel bag emptied out of soccer equipment— Nike, unlike the team's uniforms. Tasha resists the urge to say *Just do it!* as they slip out the concealed door of the stadium, the same one she had been hauled through the day before. With #34 at the top of the stadium, promising to give them a signal if the beach herd heads their way, the two women slink across the trash-cluttered lawn of the park. Tasha walks quickly and quietly, saying nothing. She has the Wusthof ready, and has given Vette the paring knife she brought along.

A little way down Foster, Tasha realizes the other woman isn't keeping up and she looks around to check on her progress. Vette is two yards behind, the small knife held in front of her like a miniature Samurai sword. Tasha stops, bewildered.

"Hey, uh, you okay?"

Vette looks at her and licks her lips.

"Yeah, um, I'm good. I'm just, you know, bringing up the rear."

Tasha laughs, in spite of the dead bodies that surround the ground around them.

"Bringing up the rear? The rear of what?"

Vette looks at her helplessly and Tasha realizes the woman is scared. Tasha is genuinely surprised. The scowl that has barely left Vette's mouth since they met has been enough to convince Tasha that she is a warrior, afraid of nothing, tough as nails. Tasha almost asks her why she bothered to come if she was so scared until she realizes no one else on the team volunteered. They would have been just as bad, she knows. Worse, even, on account of their inevitable attempts at dashing shows of bravery. Tasha sighs.

"Look, you don't have to pretend we're in *Predator* or something."

Vette stares.

"*Predator*? Come on. Not even the remake? Okay. Well look, just, like, relax. If they're near us we'll probably see them, or they'll see us and start a riot. You can relax the knife. Right, let it hang down. You don't need it right now anyway."

Nothing said in the circumstances could be reassuring; every positive has a terrifying opposite. But Vette lets the hand holding the knife droop, the creases on her face softening. Vette looks up at Tasha, beginning to smile, then glances over Tasha's shoulder. Her face goes ashen, the knife springing back up to attention.

Tasha pauses, uncomprehending only for a moment before she whirls around and sees them coming, two of them. A couple. An actual couple: the woman wearing a wedding dress; he, a tux. His lapel is torn and her veil hangs crazily off her head and nearly to her shoulder, held on only by bobby pins stuck in her ragged hair. Their hands are outstretched in the typical fashion, but no rings grace their groping fingers. The Change happened early in the morning, Tasha recalls. Who

192 OLIVIA A. COLE

the hell gets married that early in the day? Maybe they were just preparing for a noonish wedding. Bad luck to see the bride before the service. Obviously.

Vette is too terrified to scream. She drops the knife and Tasha curses at her, telling her to pick it up again. The happy couple looms closer and Tasha lets them, standing slightly in front of Vette, who is scrabbling on the ground for her weapon.

The groom yawns toward Tasha's throat and she hacks at his neck, missing and instead lopping off an ear. He doesn't notice, of course, only frowns and barks. Meanwhile his wife— or almost wife—has set her sights on Vette, who has picked up the knife and is standing ready, holding the blade like a gun, pointing straight ahead. Vette's face is grim and she looks as if her mouth might open to scream (or vomit) at any moment. The blushing bride isn't quick—neither is her spouse—but Vette's fear has slowed her down.

"The neck, Vette," Tasha warns, keeping her eyes on the groom, who has finally turned to face her. He lunges, a bit quicker this time, and Tasha sidesteps, jamming the knife into his shoulder. Blood spurts out, as red as the light flashing from his neck. She stabs again in closer quarters and hears the familiar crackle of the Chip. She doesn't wait for him to fall, instead turns to help Vette.

But Vette doesn't need help, not really. She's gotten the woman in the dress onto the ground and is stabbing her in her neck repeatedly. The bride snarls and barks each time the blade misses the mark. Tasha watches for a moment and then realizes the problem.

"Wrong side! Other side!"

Vette pauses and appraises the situation. The bride, who Vette is straddling, struggles upward and snaps at her prey's thigh. The knife plunges into the other side of the neck once, then twice. The second stab yields a pop of what sounds like electricity, and after a moment the bride goes still. Vette remains where she is, bloody from the sprays of her unsuccessful attempts. She's breathing hard, but Tasha can't tell if she's shaking or not. Tasha gives her time, looking around cautiously for more Minkers.

Eventually Vette stands up. Tasha wipes her blade on her jeans, and Vette wipes hers on the wedding dress, leaving a vulgar red stripe across the train. They stare at it for a moment.

"You just said the neck; you didn't say which *side* of the neck."

Tasha shrugs. "I thought they were all on the right side. Mine have all been on the right."

"Okay, well you still didn't say 'The right side of the neck, stab them there.'"

Tasha stares, then laughs a little. Vette looks pissed for a minute, staring crossly at the paring knife.

"How come you get the big knife anyway?" Then Vette is laughing too and Tasha feels something like pleasure. It's a feeling of recognition. It's the feeling of a panther, raised in the zoo and surrounded by tigers, introduced to another panther. Home. Similarity. They laugh until it becomes awkward, and Tasha picks up her mostly-empty pack from where she had dropped it when the wedding party joined them.

"Let's go," she says, still laughing, "before the groomsmen show up."

They pass the L station that Tasha had walked by the previous day. Vette averts her eyes from the crowds of bodies on the steps and in the grass. Tasha sees her swallow hard once or twice. But she doesn't comment. Instead she says,

"What's Predator? Does that have to do with MINK?"

Tasha laughs loudly.

"What? Girl, no. *Predator* is a movie!"

"I've never heard of it."

"Not many people have. I don't even know why I mentioned it."

"Indie film?"

"Ha! No. It's just really, really old." She trips on a briefcase, abandoned, no doubt, when its owner realized there were more important things to be saved. Like his life. "Shit," she says, looking back at its polished leather carcass.

"How do you know about it then? Were you really into movies before all this?"

"Yeah, kinda. My grandmother loved movies. Whenever I would visit her here when I was little we'd just watch movie after movie on a big old player. All stuff from when she was young. She said it was old even when she was young. That's what got me interested in film."

"Did you write scripts and stuff...before?"

"No," Tasha shakes her head. "Film history. Just, like, researching old movies and, like, the impact they had on their time. And vice versa, ya know."

"Oh," says Vette, actually sounded interested. "That sounds really cool. So you got a degree in that? I didn't know they had degrees for that."

"They do. But I didn't get my degree. I…uh, dropped out when my parents died."

Vette shrugs.

"School ain't shit. Sorry about your parents."

Tasha nods.

They're about halfway to the corner store that Ishmael had suggested. Tasha had passed it on the way toward Lakeshore the day before. "It looks like it's just a liquor store," Ishmael had said, "but they have food in there." Tasha can see it now. The store—marked with a large digital sign: "Marvin's"—is just a few yards down from the subway entrance. As they draw nearer, Vette slows her pace a little and gazes around.

"I remember when this was all residential," she says. This is like a handshake, Tasha thinks, but with words. Tasha offers something. Now it's Vette's turn.

They look down Marine Drive, the Volamu a faintly bluish trail disappearing over a slight bump in the terrain. On either side of it are the mini-skyscrapers that had crept up to claim the North Side. Most of them are businesses and restaurants and clubs, still-animated digital signs flashing up and down their edifices. Vette's face is wistful and colored purple from the light of the club on the other side of Marvin's.

"There used to be grass over here, a kind of park. They started building when I was like eight, and we stopped coming here after that. Weird how much it's changed."

Tasha doesn't remember a Marine Drive that was absent of neon. She tries picturing it without the Volamu, without the dancing martini glasses animated on the signs. She can't.

"It looks like New York now," Vette says, still staring. She tosses her hair out of her face prettily, something Tasha has always felt stupid doing. "You know, I would've been moving to New York. If it wasn't for this shit. I got a job offer to handle some media company's advertising campaigns. Came with a good package. I would've gotten MINK. Would've had the Chip."

Tasha opens her mouth to say something, but closes it again.

"Everything happens for a reason, right?" she says. "Well, except this. I can't see a reason for all this."

"Me neither," says Tasha, although somewhere in her mind she can, a coming together of thoughts from Dinah and Ishmael, a suspicion she knows Leona would have some thoughts on. Tasha doesn't say these things. Things are going well—don't start being a cynic and ruining things, she tells herself.

Vette looks at Tasha, and the purple fades from her face as they pass the club.

"Who have you lost?" she asks abruptly and Tasha almost jumps.

"You mean who is dead."

"Yes."

"My mom. My dad. My sister, kind of. Not dead. Just...not here. My friend. My friend is dead."

Friend. Not friends. She'd only had one, and she hadn't even met her until after the Change.

Vette studies her face.

"I'm sorry," she says, and the words are true. "This situation is made for losing. But you can stay with us, with the team. Ishmael likes you, I can tell, and you'll be safer with us than alone."

Tasha hesitates, blushing a little at the mention of Ishmael. Just twenty minutes ago she had decided she needed to get away from the soccer stadium and its jersey-clad inhabitants as soon as possible, insisting that she worked better as a free agent, knowing that she needed to get to the South Side. She can still go, she thinks now. Maybe the team would come with her, or at least Vette and Ishmael. The three of them could watch each other's backs and find this mystery person, Rio, together, once Tasha tells them about him. If she tells them. She doesn't like the idea of planting a seed of hope only to have the tree grow into something ugly and gnarled. Lone wolf versus wolf pack. Which was better?

"Maybe," she says to Vette. "Maybe. I just…I don't know."

Something nags at her, a skulking thing. She thinks of Dinah. Vette had said it herself, this was a situation made for losing. Tasha feels as if she might have lost enough already.

"Think about it," says Vette softly, and Tasha bends a little more inside. "For now, let's get this food and get back to the stadium."

Tasha nods.

They're startled at first by the whining bell that is supposed to let the clerk know someone has entered the store. The second thing they notice is the heat. Outside it had been an even 70 degrees or so, but the store is a good 20 degrees warmer. Tasha wants to remove her hoodie but doesn't. The third thing they notice is the dead cashier.

"Check him out," Vette says. She is pointing at the bullet holes in his chest, two of them. "They don't use guns, do they?"

"No," Tasha says, "they're too stupid to open doors, let alone use a gun. Somebody without a Chip did this. They must have taken the gun off a cop."

"Unless it was a cop."

Tasha finds herself shuddering a little. She nods.

The register is open, the money gone. Pointless, Tasha thinks. Somebody shot this guy thinking, "Hey, the world is over! Time to cash in!" A lot of good money will do him now. A Minker doesn't want your wallet, she thinks, it wants your heart. In its mouth.

The women move on past the counter. Toward the back of the store they find food as Ishmael promised. Mostly canned vegetables and packets of things like ravioli and stew; some boxes of macaroni and cheese; thirty-second microwave pizzas; an endless selection of energy bars.

They start shoveling food into their bags. Tasha feels like she's robbing a bank. When she was alone on her solo missions to Jewel it felt more like regular grocery shopping. Quiet, cautious grocery shopping. But now one of them holds open the backpack and the other slides in can upon can, the scrape and clang of the containers against their shelves seeming too loud; almost rebellious. The Prada backpack fills up quickly and

Tasha tightens its drawstrings, slinging it onto her shoulders. They're more careful about what they put in the Nike bag. It's larger, so a shitload of canned goods will be too difficult to carry, especially if they end up having to run. Tasha chooses a dozen packs of Ramen noodles. She doesn't know if they have a way to boil water in the stadium, but she figures they can find a way. Or, if not, wait until they're desperate and eat the little curls of noodles dry like potato chips. She adds instant oatmeal, the microwave pizzas, and a few loaves of bread with two jars of generic peanut butter. Vette sets the bag on the floor and forces in a box of cereal, then reconsiders and draws it out. She opens the box and removes the plastic bag housing the actual cereal and shoves that into the duffel bag instead. She does this twice more with two more boxes of Cheerios, then adds a bag of pretzels.

"One more thing," Vette says, smiling a small smile as she brandishes a handful of Snickers bars, "my favorite. I used to eat these for dinner when my mom would get home from work late. My first boyfriend in high school gave me six of them on our six-month anniversary. I wasn't even mad. I ate them all on the same day." She laughs to herself, stuffing the chocolate into the bag.

She tests its weight. Tasha looks at her and Vette nods. Tasha nods back. She finds herself with the desire to talk too much and ends up saying too little.

"All set?" Vette is half-picking up the bag.

"One more thing. I've gotta use the bathroom."

"Want me to come?"

Tasha hesitates. On one hand, she does want Vette to come. It reminds her of being with Leona, sisters sharing the bathroom, taking turns. But Tasha thinks of the striped pouch in her backpack, filled with mascara and foundation: her little bag of insecurity. It's a private ritual, and Vette may not understand.

"No, it's okay. Watch the door. I'll be out in a minute."

In the bathroom Tasha balances the Wusthof on the sink and stares in the mirror before unzipping the pouch. She tries to ignore her hair, which has assumed a life of its own, or part of one. Straightened strands are no longer the majority, from what she can tell: the light is dim, filtering in through a high tinted window above the toilet. She fishes her concealer out of the pouch, pauses, then dots it under her eyes over the dark cups of skin. As she goes about the ritual, it's like donning armor. The mascara is last, as usual, and she stares herself in the eyes as she applies it. Finished, she bares her teeth in a pageant smile, convincing herself of something. Does she feel better? Safer? She's not sure. Before the Change, she'd needed the make-up to hide from…what?

With the mascara on, she didn't look like herself, the orphan with a ghost sister. With eyes drawn bigger, perhaps the grief seems smaller. Where are Vette's parents, she wonders. Dead? Maybe they can talk about it. Maybe she can hear about Ishmael's mother and brothers that he'd mentioned. Even if their parents are all alive, Tasha knows they've lost people, their teammates. With something to discuss, this horrible common thing, maybe she can meet them eye-to-eye without hiding her face.

It's then that she remembers the toothbrush that made her want to make this little trip in the first place: the deodorant, the razor. She figures Vette will want these things too, or will when Tasha reminds her of them. She zips the make-up bag, stows it in her backpack with the canned food, then opens the door and follows the narrow hallway back to the storefront.

"Hey, Vette, let's check for a toothbrush or something while we're here. We can get some for the guys too if you think—"

She stops. There is the Nike bag, still zipped, but Vette is not beside it. Tasha looks around, but no Vette. The other woman isn't very tall, but her head would still clear the shelves of the aisles. If she were standing up.

Tasha puts the straps of the backpack on both shoulders and holds the Wusthof ready, walking sideways through the main aisle of the store and peering down each smaller aisle. Nothing in the aisle where she and Vette had found the food. Nothing in the next but liquor. Nothing in the next, or the next. Tasha hears a sound toward the front of the store and skips all the aisles in between, moving quickly and silently, her breath quickening. The very front aisle is marked Toiletries. In it, Vette is on the floor, dead. A man is on top of her. Tasha chokes on air and takes a staggering step forward, her mouth opening and closing like a carp.

The Minker looks up, his mouth bloody. His glasses have stayed on his face, which are low on his nose, his eyes very blue and staring. The wrinkle between his eyes deepens as he sees

Tasha, but he continues chewing.

"Get off her, you *fuck!*" Her voice is loud, too loud, but she can't control it. "Get the fuck away from her!"

He shows no indication of having heard her. He holds himself stiffly above Vette's prone form, like a rabid dog reluctant to give up its find. Tasha recognizes the wide-legged stance from the dogs she raised in Kentucky: territorial, angry. She strides over to where the two sprawl on the floor and kicks him in the chin as hard as she can, sending him arcing backward onto his back. His spectacles tumble to the floor, and she stomps on them spitefully. He barks as he struggles to turn over. She wishes she knew karate, jiu-jitsu, some masterful martial art to punish this creature in a more profound way than her Nike-clad foot can do on its own.

He rises to his feet and Tasha backs quickly away as she realizes how tall he is—at least 6'5". She's going to have trouble reaching his neck, she knows. She glances down at Vette, fighting tears. Vette was at least two inches shorter than Tasha; no wonder she couldn't kill the guy. Why didn't she yell for her help? Maybe she did. Tasha wouldn't have heard her.

The Minker lumbers toward her, another bark rumbling in his throat. He steps on Vette's lifeless hand as he moves toward Tasha, which enrages her. She wants to rush him, tackle him, bring him to the floor that way. She estimates he's around 220 pounds. Her 130 won't do much against that.

She skips backward, trying to keep an eye on him, and slips. She lands hard on her butt, but is back on her feet before he's taken another step. Her ass hurts. But she has an idea.

Turning her back on him, she races past the Nike bag to the back of the store where she and Vette had foraged. From the shelf she snatches a bottle of Crisco vegetable oil.

"This'll put you down, you fuck," she snarls. He's coming her way, still fairly slowly, Godzilla trying to keep up with his small, quick prey. She fumbles with the cap, gets it off. It has a seal. "These fucking things!" she cries.

She's forced to retreat to the other end of the aisle, as Godzilla has gotten a little close for comfort. She pokes the tip of the Wusthof through the waxed aluminum seal. Once broken, she jams two fingers in to widen the hole, plunging her fingers into the oil. Hastily wiping her hand on her jeans, she checks the big guy's progress. He's halfway down the aisle, glaring and growling. The blood around his mouth is an insult.

Tasha upends the vegetable oil, dousing the tile floor like kerosene. *Kerosene*, Tasha thinks as she empties the bottle, *if I had that I'd burn this fucking place to the ground.* Having emptied the bottle, she discards it with a hollow clatter.

"Come here, you big ugly bastard," she yells, trying to amp herself up, hopping from foot to foot, "can't you see without your glasses? Come here!"

He does as he is told, and the plan works well. He hulks right through the puddle of oil, slips, and crashes downward into an unpracticed split, too stupid to try to catch his balance. She thinks she hears a bodily rip of some kind, some ligament tearing audibly. She pictures the red hems inside his body coming apart at the seams as he slides down onto his back and flounders.

Tasha remembers her slip at the McDonald's—just yesterday, it seems as if a lifetime has passed since she'd met Chipped Chip—and bounds nimbly around the spreading pool of vegetable oil to dispatch her Godzilla. She leaps, feet and hands extended like a large ungainly cat, and lands directly on the big guy's stomach. He gasps involuntarily as her sudden weight forces the air out of his body. The knife had stabbed him as she landed, but the red light in his neck is already blinking as it attempts to repair the torn ligaments that are keeping him from standing. She destroys the Chip with two quick slices, leaving him shuddering violently. The shaking is unlike the others she has killed. She scrambles to her feet and backs away, wary that he might explode or something. The wound in his stomach where the Wusthof had stabbed him during her landing hadn't had time to close up before the Chip was put out of commission, and blood seeps through his argyle sweater and onto the oily floor. It's Ralph Lauren, Tasha notices, and she feels half apologetic about ruining it. To her left she sees her little striped make-up bag. It had fallen out of the top of her backpack when she pounced on the Minker. She stares at it. The mascara is poking out, asking to be rescued. It calls to her.

She turns her back on it and returns to Vette at the front of the store. She's hard to look at, her throat open, bite marks marring her chest and neck like overzealous hickeys. Her mouth is almost closed but not quite; Tasha can see her front teeth, the slight gap between them. Tasha is grateful for the blank expression in the eyes as a rock seems to grow in her throat. She has seen movies where the tearful hero must lay a palm against his fallen comrade's eyes to close them, a final romantic gesture of camaraderie and brotherhood. But Tasha can't bring herself to touch her. She feels as empty as Vette looks: the warm, half-smiling Vette from a half-hour ago has become this silent bloody shell. But the orange cleats say it is her, the loose sandy hair. Tasha stares and stares, until her eyes start to burn. Vette is hard to look at, but Tasha stares. Her torn flesh, the blood that has painted the flesh of her neck and chest, is a stain bearing Tasha's name.

Tasha goes to the Nike bag and draws out two Snickers bars. Returning to Vette's side she places them in a cross on the dead woman's chest. Maybe the ferryman will take them in place of the coins, since Tasha has no money. Like with Dinah— another dead girl, another almost-friend who Tasha had not saved—she has nothing to give. She hopes the ferryman likes chocolate. If not, and Vette is forced to wander the Styx for eternity, at least she won't be hungry.

CHAPTER 17

Tasha pauses as she has several times already after leaving Vette and the corner store and readjusts the weight of her backpack and the Nike duffel bag, both packed with nonperishable food items. Tasha welcomes the frequent stops for adjustments—she dreads her return to the stadium, where she will have to explain the loss of Vette to the remaining members of the team. She wonders if they'll even let her back into the storage room without their teammate. She anticipates their accusing stares, their cold silences. Middle school all over again, she thinks. She doesn't know how she'll explain. She can't say it's not her fault. It is.

She can feel a single bead of sweat inching its way down her spine, even though she has taken off the Adidas hoodie and tucked it under her arm. The weather is as moody as ever, a petulant mutant with mutant PMS. It looks like rain, and she decides to hurry. The stadium is in sight now, and now that she is so close to her goal, the duffel bag seems suddenly unbearably heavy, her arms loose and tingly. A mist has risen up around the stadium, a smoggy halo.

She realizes quickly that something is wrong. The camouflaged door that had closed firmly behind her and Vette an hour before is open, ominous. Tasha freezes. She doesn't hear a sound, not even the lake. Creeping forward, she realizes she is still stupidly hefting the duffel bag, and unslings it from her shoulder, lowering it soundlessly to the ground. As an afterthought—and still keeping her eye on the stadium door—she removes one strap of her backpack long enough to stuff the Adidas sweatshirt into it around the canned goods, then re-shoulders the bag. She can feel her internal organs pulsing, not just her heart: her lungs feel like they're vibrating, the shudders snaking through her veins to set her kidneys in motion, her bladder. Why hadn't she peed at the corner store? One more thing she should've been doing instead of standing in the mirror. She tries to push it all—including the possibility of peeing on herself—out of her mind as she approaches the doorway.

It's dark, of course, and her eyes take a second to adjust, a long second in which she feels as helpless as a cavefish set free in noon-lit waters. When she finds her sight again, she sees the bodies.

Well, just one body. She'd expected more. It's #16, sprawled in front of the door that leads to the playing field of the stadium. For a brief moment, Tasha considers the possibility that Ishmael and the others might have killed the guy and taken off, but not only does this not make sense, moving closer

Tasha can see from the chewed state of his flesh that his death was the work of a Minker.

She realizes with a start that there must be more. A single Minker wouldn't have been enough to send Ishmael and the team on the run; there must have been a group. Her mind goes instantly to the herd of them that had tailed her on the beach, hanging around. Of course they had made an attempt on the stadium: why wouldn't they?

She shrieks as something slams against the other side of the door blockaded by #16's body. His lifeless form shifts a little from the force. Knowing it's a bad idea, Tasha goes to the door, puts her ear against it, and listens.

It sounds like a fucking dogpound on the other side.

She can't identify how many there are, but the chorus of barks makes Tasha remind herself to strengthen her PC muscles' hold on her urethra. So they came from *inside* the stadium. Tasha imagines Ishmael and the others sitting in the grass, eating their hot dogs, when the Minkers came through one of the blockaded entrances. Ishmael would have shepherded the others toward their storage room, but #16 had fallen behind. She hadn't pictured him as the heroic type, but it seems he had stayed back to slow up the Minkers by sitting in front of the door. Tasha can't imagine that; knowing she is dying, feeling the life leaking out of her like air from a balloon. She looks at #16, face obscured by his arm. She wishes she had time to arrange a little Snickers bar crucifix for him too. Or maybe something else. Something he would like better. He deserves it, staying behind to lock the door to give his team a fighting chance.

But then she realizes that the door isn't locked at all. The stream of light coming through is widening as the Minkers on the other side bustle patiently forward. #16 is keeping it somewhat closed, plus a box or two he had evidently moved in front of it before his strength gave out. No wonder he wasn't able to lock the door: he died first. A few focused shoves from the creatures and they'd be through.

There's another sudden shove and the gap widens just enough for Tasha to glimpse the Chipped woman at the same moment the woman sees Tasha: she's tall, wearing a stunning silk blouse and slacks. She had worn some patterned pumps, but one shoe is gone and the heel of the other has snapped off. She emits a high-pitched yip as her dull eyes settle on Tasha and the herd rallies around her eagerly.

Tasha turns to run, but the woman is quick and her well-manicured hand shoots through the opening, snatching at Tasha's earring. Tasha's neck arches backward like a horse on a tight rein and she drops the knife, cursing herself immediately. Twisting sharply, she breaks the woman's grip, but now the hand has seized Tasha's tank top and it's not letting go. The Wusthof is out of reach. The Minkers snuffle at the opening, still too stupid to actively rush the door. But it's slowly opening on its own beneath their weight as they struggle to get a look at Tasha, who is wriggling like a fish on a line. An instantaneous thought of Dinah flashes across her mind—is this how Dale got her? Tasha throws her body against the door to hold them off a little while longer, clawing at the woman's hand, trying to free herself.

It's not working. She has no idea how many of the Chipped are on the other side of the door, but she can feel that their lazy pressure is greater than her applied force. Her shirt is tearing. The woman is drawing Tasha toward the herd with her grip on the cotton.

"I loved this shirt, you asshole!" Tasha yells, and tears herself away from the door and the well-dressed woman. Straining against the simple black seams, she feels like a small, curly-haired ox in the yoke. She thought this would be a lot easier.

After another forceful heave against her harness, it happens: the shirt rips and Tasha is free. The black stretchy fabric whips through the straps in the Prada backpack and is left hanging in the pink-painted talons of the Chipped woman, who hasn't yet realized she's lost her fish. Tasha almost falls, but doesn't. She snatches up the Wusthof, takes a last look at her shirt dangling from the hooked fingers coming through the rapidly-widening door, then runs, hearing the fabric of #16's jersey sliding against the floor behind her as he's scooted slowly out of the way.

Tasha rushes out the door through which she entered, pausing momentarily and looking left and then right, as if about to jaywalk. There is a cluster of Minkers to the north, but they're crowding around something and haven't noticed her yet. She hopes it's the entrance the bastards found to get in and not the body of one of the soccer team. Not Ishmael. She can't afford to investigate. Gripping the straps of her backpack, she takes off south, heading downtown.

She remembers what Ishmael said about Lakeshore Drive,

but she takes it anyway. The idea of negotiating the sometimes-confusing streets of Buena Park does not appeal to her—she always got disoriented wandering around there, especially with all the renovations and additions of diagonal roads. Lakeshore takes her directly downtown. That's where she needs to get first. Enough of this bullshit. Downtown she knows her way around, and she can regroup before heading to god knows where on the South Side.

She leaps over the Nike duffel bag, slumped where she'd left it. No time to stop. She can't remember what she'd put into her pack at the corner store, but she knows she has food of some kind, and she knows she kept her can opener.

Either way, she has more immediate problems to contend with. She is currently jogging South on Lakeshore Drive in her bra. She feels like a half-assed version of *Baywatch*. It's not sexy, the slo-mo slink in the sand: she's running flat out, alternating which hand she uses to hold the Wusthof and which hand she uses to hold her breasts as she books. It slows her down. She hadn't thought a tank top was so effective in binding her boobs, but she supposes it was tight enough to impede them from doing all the moving they're doing right now. She thinks about Pamela what's-her-face and wonders how she did it, the sexy jog down the beach, gravity having its way with her with every springy step. Maybe it's different running around with implants. Maybe it's comfortable. She can't imagine.

It's still hot, and Tasha is at least grateful for her absence of shirt with respect to the heat. She can feel the sweat starting to emerge from her scalp, aware also of the small rivulets running from under her arms down to her bra, where the sweat nestles in the fabric. The idea of this pisses her off. Nothing worse than sweat stains around the edge of the cup—you could be wearing $400 lingerie and a sweat stain in the silk will lower you from *Vogue* to *Girls Gone Wild*.

Hot or not, the sky still looks like rain, and Tasha needs to find shelter before that happens. It's hot now, but she knows the fickle nature of Chicago weather well and she doesn't cherish the idea of being outside for a dramatic temperature drop, especially when wearing only a bra to protect her from the elements.

Nearing Diversey, she slows from a dogtrot to a walk. She outran the herd at the stadium with no problem; she was probably out of sight before they even blundered out of the storage room. She's in the clear, at least for now. She evaluates her body, trying to decide how tired she is. Not very, she concludes, which is surprising, considering the added weight of the cans in her backpack. Some of this might be adrenaline, she knows. Running outside is different than running on the treadmills at her gym, but she's paced herself fairly well. Her brain, though, is tired. The loss of Vette seems ages ago; the feeling is dull like a bruise. She gauges by how far she's run that it was about an hour ago, tops, since she left Vette in the corner store with two Snickers bars over her chest. It could have been last year, ten years ago, a story told to her by a grandparent. She wonders where Ishmael ended up, if he got away. She dismisses the idea that the small gathering of Minkers she saw as she fled the stadium had anything to do with him. But she can't think about them right now. She needs to focus.

Ishmael had been wrong so far about Lakeshore Drive. She's jogged at least a mile and a half from the stadium and hasn't seen a soul—not that the Minkers have souls, she corrects herself, and is then surprised by the churchiness of the thought. *You're not in Kentucky anymore, Dorothy.*

But really, souls or not, Lakeshore is deserted. She doesn't even see any nervous pigeons or pilfering squirrels, no irritable seagulls drifting overhead. She finds herself gripping the Wusthof a little tighter, wondering if her dulled human instincts are failing to warn her of the nearness of danger. Tasha remembers the dogs of her youth, their hackles rising inexplicably at times, cautioning them about the nearness of something threatening. Thinking of it now, gooseflesh rises on her body. If she had hackles—and thank god she doesn't, she thinks; just another thing she'd have to have waxed or lasered off—they'd be rising now. The heat settles around her like it's making a nest. She realizes she's thirsty, but doesn't like the idea of digging around in the backpack, wasting time and making noise. Instead she keeps walking, pausing only at the place where Lakeshore Drive rises above Diversey to observe the casualties below, dozens of bodies clustered around the crisscrossing Volamus. The carnage looks like a mosh pit in a freeze frame, or a silent game of Ring Around the Rosie. *Ashes, ashes, we all fall down,* she thinks before moving on.

She walks with the knife raised, imaginary hackles still standing, her heart still double-dutching. Ishmael's words about Lakeshore hang over her like an omen. But Ishmael might have been a false prophet. Tasha feels the way she felt when she watched *The Village* in her living room as a kid, the antique player making a clicking sound. Her grandmother had told her it was a scary movie, and she'd watched it with her nerves on edge. When it turned out the only things to be afraid of were some spiky armadillos wearing red capes—and not even *real* spiky armadillos—she'd felt a sense of both relief and disappointment. She'd written a paper on it in college. Now Tasha has seen her world's armadillos, and they're certainly real, but Lakeshore Drive isn't swarming with them, and she feels her adrenaline slipping, sapping her. No Minkers? Nothing to stab? She feels almost let down. But a little proud. She'd had a feeling that this route might be clearer. The Minkers would be sticking to the more populated streets, where there was food. She would have run into a lot more of her bitey friends if she had taken Broadway. She'd seen the activity in Uptown on the way to the Post; she doesn't even want to know what Boystown is like. She knows she'll be passing near the Gold Coast, and she'll need to be careful over there. A lot of people with MINK and money to burn on extravagances like the Chip lived around there before the Change. She wonders if they've flown the coop or if they've stayed close to home, patrolling their upscale beats.

She's shivering a little, and assumes it's from fear or nerves, but she realizes she's actually cold. The temperature has dropped, as she knew it would. She cups her hands over her breasts, annoyed that her nipples are hard in the chill.

"Stop it," she scolds them.

Then she remembers the hoodie.

"Idiot." She rolls her eyes at herself and unslings the backpack, still walking as she extracts the purple pullover. Now she stops to put it on, setting the Prada backpack between her feet and resting the Wusthof on top of it. She snakes her arms through the sleeves but hesitates before pulling it over her head. She looks around. It would be just her luck to get attacked by a pack of them while she's struggling to get her big-ass hair through the neckhole. The coast seems to be clear, and she sweeps the hoodie down over her, wriggling her fluffy head through the hole. Once it's on, she swivels around again, prepared to see hundreds of Minkers bearing down on her. There's no one. Nothing. But something else catches her attention: a drop on her head. Then another.

Rain.

"Fuck," she groans.

She pulls the hood quickly up over her hair out of habit, forgetting briefly that she has no perm to protect now. Either way, she doesn't want to be caught in the rain. She remembers her last day with Dinah and the superstorm that had swept in. She and Dinah had witnessed the first surge of lightning, and Tasha doesn't want to see it now, not when the object being struck could be her. Before the Change when it would storm, the subways would be packed with the homeless, and CTA officials weren't legally allowed to make them leave. It was that bad.

Overhead, a little east, Tasha hears the first sound of thunder. As if on cue. As if it had been eavesdropping on her thoughts. As if it had held a pair of binoculars to its eye, spotted

Tasha, and rubbed its hands together in anticipation.

"Fuuuuck," Tasha moans and looks around. She's just passed Fullerton. The nearest houses are three blocks away, and she doesn't fancy the idea of breaking into a home only to be received by a Brady Bunch of Minkers. Ahead she sees the sign for the Lincoln Park Zoo, and runs for it, still holding her breasts down at intervals. The thunder grumbles at her back as she reaches the sign. The zoo is huge now, renovated and expanded to the point where some of its exhibits actually incorporate Lake Michigan. All that's between her and the zoo is the lagoon where yuppies parked their yachts, a handy aluminum bridge arching over it. She races across the bridge, hearing the thunder gaining volume. She nears the zoo. They really did a fantastic job renovating it, she notices. They planted a lot of trees. But she doesn't have time to admire the shrubbery; the rain is falling faster now, the temperature dropping. Her eye falls on the Visitors' Center, and she sprints to it, almost pulling her arm out of its socket as she yanks on a door that's locked. She looks around desperately. No boulders to throw through the glass, and she's wary of security alarms now anyway. The first flash of lightning comes, illuminating the darkening sky. She sees another sign, carved in wood: Cat House. It's about twenty meters away and she goes for it, the sky threatening her every step. She pulls on the door. Mercifully it's unlocked, and she ducks in.

She closes the door softly behind her instead of letting it slam, and leans back against it, exhaling long and slow. Outside, the rain is loud against the glass of the door. Inside, it's eerily quiet, and dim. The Cat House feels big: she can feel how much room there is in the air. As the lightning flashes again, she sees the cats, all lit up in white.

They're all in cages, crouching in corners or against their walls. The faces of the cages are tall, reaching the ceiling from where they begin close to the floor. The cages line the walls of the long hall that is the House, each pen elevated slightly. The visitor of the zoo must climb two or three steps to stand directly in the animal's presence. Closest to Tasha, on her left, is an ocelot, a lithe, smallish creature with spots that Mrs. Kerry would have killed to have on a leash.

Tasha walks down the center of the Cat House, looking left and right at the captive beasts. They look at her too, and with great interest. Two lions stand and move closer to the bars, crouching as she walks past. Their eyes are savage, staring planets. Tasha waves at them. The lioness twitches an ear. Tasha thinks of her sister.

Like the other inmates of the Cat House, she seeks a corner where she can curl up, lick her wounds. At the other end of the hall she sees the emergency exit sign, a door that doesn't open from the outside. That's where she needs to be, somewhere hidden and dark.

The exit sign casts a faint greenish glow over her hands, and she tucks them into the pouch on the front of the hoodie. She sits, bringing her knees to her chest, and watches a jaguar whose chin rests on its paws, watching her. Together they wait out the storm.

CHAPTER 18

Tasha wakes slowly, the light growing brighter and clearer a little at a time, as if she's rising to the surface of a deep pool. When her eyes are fully open, she focuses on the jaguar behind its bars several feet away and jumps. She'd had strange dreams. In one she was looking in a mirror, and a girl in yellow had stared back before beating her fist against the glass over and over until her hand broke through and grabbed Tasha by the throat. Tasha was paralyzed as the girl continued coming through the mirror, her dress transforming into a jersey as she stepped through the rest of the way. The girl had a black eye and a soft face. Then Tasha was wearing the jersey and looked into the mirror to see her face painted brightly like a horrifying china doll, her teeth falling into the sink as she grinned madly.

Tasha shudders. Across from her, the jaguar licks its paws.

"What's new, pussycat?" she asks it. It blinks.

Tasha looks about her, and realizes it's early morning, maybe even dawn. She must have slept for 12 hours. Less. More. It's hard to say: without a watch she has no idea—the marbled mammatus clouds (storm or not) have always made it difficult to see the position of the sun in Chicago. Her ass is asleep, as she's spent the entire night propped up against the exit door, her blood flow confused by the angles. She stretches, and her back protests, but she stands and peers out the window of the door she made her bed. The storm had left many of the trees of the zoo looking as if they'd spent a long night out drinking: their branches hang crazily in various levels of destruction. One entire tree has fallen, partially blocking the door of what Tasha can make out as the Bird House.

She raises her arms above her head, elongating her spine, and looks about her at the Cat House. The cats are languid, their tails twitch. Tasha's stomach growls and she bends to pick up the Prada backpack. She digs inside and pulls out the can opener and a can of Spaghetti-O's. She wishes she were able to warm it up, but she imagines that wouldn't help the taste much anyway. She doesn't have a spoon, she notes irritably, and sticks two fingers and a thumb into the can, trying to avoid the sharp edges of the lip, scooping out pinches of the room-temperature red pasta. Her mother never let her have this stuff as a kid, but it's not half bad.

Eating her Spaghetti-O's by the fingerful, she walks down the wide corridor of the Cat House, able now to see its many prisoners. The ocelot, the jaguar, and the lions she had seen, but there is a panther, a caracal, a tiger, a lynx—full-sized; not like the miniature cats at Fetch Fetchers—and several others that the gloom of the storm the night before had hidden from her. They all stretch out quietly in their various imitation-habitats, their eyes following Tasha intently, but not raising their heads. Tasha's stomach gives a rumble; it has not yet gotten the message that the cheap, salty pasta is on its way. The lynx's nose twitches.

Tasha realizes suddenly that the animals are at various stages of starvation. She doesn't know much about cats, as dogs had been her specialty, but she imagines that captive animals don't go about storing fat the way their wild cousins do throughout the season. It has been nearly a week since they were fed, trapped behind the bars with no one to look after them. Their keeper, on the morning of the Change, had likely gone off to feed himself on the blood of Chipless Chicagoans, neglecting his captive charges. No wonder they're so languid. Tasha observes their intense stares in a new light. She had seen animals like them stalk toddlers from their cages even when they were well fed. Tasha can only imagine how badly they want to eat her now.

"Sorry, guys, I don't think you'd like Spaghetti-O's," she says to them.

But she feels foolish saying this. This isn't the "Sorry, Spot" one tells one's groveling Jack Russell from the dinner table. These animals are starving. Their fate will be found where they lie now unless Tasha decides to call it quits and climb into one of their cages, which would still only delay the inevitable. The cats would die, one by one. The lions, caged together, might kill one another, but the others would deflate, become still, each alone in their 20x20, fading. The thought makes Tasha almost unbearably sad. She'd heard college philosophers spouting their crap when she was in college—"every man dies alone." What about women? What about cats? She hates to think of the lynx, the panther, starving in their prisons. She thinks sharply of Dinah, and herself too. She looks at the tiger, who stares back with blazing eyes. Its cage has small trees planted along the back wall, clouds painted on the bricks with an orange blazing sun. Pretty, Tasha thinks, but a placeholder. She thinks of her closet of shoes and clothes. Pretty, she thinks. Pretty cage. She looks back at the tiger. It would tear her to pieces if given only a fraction of a chance, but while it remains on the other side of the bars she feels no fear: only sympathy and a heavy sense of sameness.

She finishes her food and licks her fingers, averting her eyes from the many fiery stares around her. Tasha goes to the door she came through the night before. Outside, the sky is as mottled as ever, but the light coming through in persistent dapples tells her that the storms have indeed passed. So what now?

She considers the situation. She's wearing her Adidas hoodie with nothing but her bra underneath. Her socks probably stink. After the fiasco of the corner store with Vette she had been unable to get the razor, toothbrush, and deodorant for which she was so desperate. She smacks her tongue against the roof of her mouth, tasting the staleness. She can't believe she even dared to have a conversation with Ishmael yesterday at the top of the stadium. She can't remember the last time she had gone a day without showering, without brushing her teeth.

Even after the Change her water still worked, and for some reason she thought she would have been able to make it to the South Side in a few hours. Not two days. Never this long. She needs to get downtown.

She charts her running path from her days of exercise before the Change. She'd jogged on Lakeshore from Foster to the Magnificent Miles (long pluralized to suit the waves of new shops) before, and she imagines she's only a few miles from what used to be her home away from home, the dense streets of department stores and boutiques. Somewhere on the Miles she could get underwear, socks, a new shirt, maybe even a toothbrush. She isn't sure what time it is, but it's early: she could be on Michigan Avenue by noon.

But first she has to pee.

The Cat House, she has found, does not have a bathroom, and she is loath to pop a squat in the corner on the tile. She'd only peed on the ground once before, after a long night carousing with Gina and her friends, and even then it had been in a darkened alley with Gina and the others laughing and cursing, possibly peeing also, a few meters away. Peeing on polished tile in broad daylight beneath the judgmental eyes of a jaguar seems low. Even now.

She peeps out the front door of the Cat House and across the tree-strewn grounds of the zoo, looking for Minkers. None in sight. She cracks the door—it is mercifully well-oiled—and sticks her head around the edge, looking left and right. She hears nothing but the distant shuffling of elephants. The main office is only twenty or thirty meters away, next to a huge wooden likeness of a bear and her cubs. Birds land on the bears' backs, looking around imperiously.

Tasha runs. She tries to run softly, on the tips of her Nikes, and is proud of how quiet she's being until she trips. After that she just jogs, every step jolting her whining bladder. She picks her way quickly across the concrete, hopping over branches and rubbish. The grounds were so orderly yesterday, she thinks— chaos descends suddenly, like a black-feathered bird.

She sighs with deep relief to find the door to the office building unlocked, and she slips in, closing it quietly behind her. She locks it as a precaution, though she knows the Minkers aren't handy with doors. Inside the office—which has windows on three sides—is a dead girl dressed all in khaki like a safari hunter, her Pocahontas braids bloodied. Tasha steps over her and peers around the office.

The space is a bit like an announcer's booth, with computers and microphones and blinking machines. Blinking. So there's power. Is the zoo hooked up to the city's grid too, or is it solar powered like the museums?

She turns away from the microphones and walks through another Employees Only door, finding herself in what is labeled as the Control Room. One entire wall of the room is taken up with rows of flat, shining screens, each one showing different angles of the wide expanse of the zoo. From the Control Room she can see the giraffes extending their necks across their bars to nibble at neighboring trees, as well as the meerkats sitting on their mounds of mud, gazing skyward.

But Tasha's not interested in controls; she's interested in a toilet. Luckily there's a bathroom in the Control Room as well, where she pees gratefully. She tries to wash her hands, but the dispenser is out of soap, which shocks her. Next to a football stadium or a train station, a zoo seems like the dirtiest place in the world, a place *most* in need of soap. Only in a zoo is there a possibility of both zebra urine and your own urine being on your hands. Soap should exist. She supposes it's because of the zebra urine that they go through soap so fast. Luckily she's already eaten, especially since she had no spoon.

She tries to avoid the mirror before leaving, but can't, of course. It calls her like a topless siren sitting on a rock. And like a siren, it dashes her careful little ship on the crags with what it shows her. Hair wild, mascara smudged, foundation sweated off—

A sudden, persistent beeping distracts her from her mutant reflection and she freezes. In another time she would have thought it was her Glass, but this world has departed from the one that had Glass devices in it. She moves quietly to the door of the bathroom and stands flat beside it. Any sound could be a dog whistle for the Minkers—before she goes back into the Control Room she has to be sure she isn't tottering blindly into a massacre. She pulls the door open a millimeter, pressing her eye against the crack and trying not to think about germs as she scans the Control Room. Nothing. No swaggering shadows with bloody breath, no half-eaten zoo employees clinging to life. Tasha opens the door a little wider.

She almost slams it again when she sees the flashing light, thinking only of the many illuminated necks of the past week.

But it's a light on the panel of monitors in the Control Room, a yellow bulb that beeps shrilly in rhythm with its flashes. She darts out into the room and over to the source of the beeping, eager to quiet it. It hasn't drawn a predatory audience yet, but it could. She quickly scans the panels, looking for what she hopes is a simple "Shut the Hell Up" button, but instead her eye falls upon a box of text on a smaller screen below the flashing light. *East Motion Sensor Trigger* the small, blinking words read, and underneath it a touch-screen option: "Acknowledge." Pretty simple after all. Tasha's finger acknowledges the motion sensor trigger, and the flashing and beeping halt abruptly. Well, there's that, she thinks, and moves back toward the front office. She has almost reached the doorway when something on one of the many shining security screens catches her eye. Movement.

She crosses quickly back to the rows of monitors and stares numbly at the glaring screens. Minkers: at least a dozen of them wandering between the main office and the Cat House. Some dawdle by the Visitors' Center, the first building she'd seen when she arrived at the zoo yesterday. Others drift loosely across the area like ants swarming a picnic. On some of the cameras Tasha can see their mouths moving. In another world, someone watching the screen might believe that they're witnessing a pack of drunks who had come to hassle the flamingos. But Tasha knows without hearing them that the sound their mouths are making is nothing so human as drunken babble. They are short clipped syllables, more Schnauzer than Chicagoan. Her guts knotting, Tasha reaches for her knife.

She doesn't have it.

Or the backpack. Everything important in her life at this moment is in the Cat House. She wants to vomit but doesn't want to get it on her shoes and she has no time for regurgitated Spaghetti-Os: the crowds of Minkers are moving through the zoo, closer to the office, closer to the Cat House, closer to her.

She flies to the front of the office, staying low. She peers over the edge of the counter with all the microphones. She can't see the Visitors' Center from this angle, but she can easily see the Cat House and the crowd gathering outside it. She curses under her breath and curses, from a distance, the Prada backpack and all its precious contents.

The pack of Minkers hasn't shown any interest in the office building where she huddles yet, and for that she's thankful, but their focus on the Cat House concerns her. Where did they come from? Did they follow her scent? Do they even use their noses in that way? She remembers reading about Harriet Tubman, her treks through creek-beds to throw off the hounds on her trail. The storm last night should have washed away her scent. But here they are. Maybe it was chance. She can tell by the khaki uniforms of some that they were zoo employees before the morning of the Change. Now they gather with three or four high school girls in the plaid skirts of prestigious St. Xavier's. She can also see a few men in suits, a woman in a stylish navy-blue dress. Tasha struggles to catch a glimpse of the shoes. She's always had trouble matching shoes to navy blue.

Tasha looks around the office for something that might be used as a weapon if one of the barkers happens to wander over. She thinks she's relatively safe in the office as long as

her presence is undetected, but even if they don't breach it…
she's stuck. Her food, her backpack, Leona's letters, her can
opener—all in the Cat House. Her knife. She can't leave the
zoo without the Wusthof.

Nothing in the office looks like it would serve well as a tool
of Chip-destruction. There is a stapler on the desk behind her,
which would be amusing but wouldn't actually work. What
else? Paperclips. Those won't do.

Checking to make sure the door is still locked, Tasha
crabwalks back to the Control Room with its dozens of
illuminated screens. She looks frantically at them, trying to
find the one that shows the building she's in. She finds it in the
third row, and breathes a miniature sigh of relief to see that the
Minkers haven't moved around behind the office, or multiplied
their numbers. There are, however, still quite a few she will
have to deal with. She counts thirteen.

"Fuck," she rasps.

Another scan of the control room again shows nothing
that might be used as a weapon. The illuminated screens hum
lightly. She curses again and almost turns away when one
screen catches her eye.

"Cat House," she says aloud.

She steps closer and examines the screen marked Cat
House. On it is a layout of the hall she slept in the night before,
the digital rectangles running along the edges clearly marked
"Ocelot," "Jaguar," "Caracal." Tasha looks more closely at
the screen and the menu at the bottom: "Change House,"
"Temperature Control," "Assistance," "Emergency Menu." She

touches her finger to "Change House."

The screen now displays a layout of the entire zoo, various rectangles labeled with the different creatures: "Bird House," "Reptile House," and others. The elephants have a crib to themselves, she sees, with a yard attached. High rollers. When she presses the Elephant House rectangle, she's shown the elephants themselves, viewed through the cameras installed in their building. The elephants lounge in the yard, except one who stands alone inside, swinging his trunk back and forth. Agoraphobic, perhaps.

She switches to the Primate House, which also shows her the inside of the building and its inhabitants. Some of them appear to be dead. On the Primate House screen, Tasha looks again at the menu at the bottom, and "Emergency Menu" catches her eye. This *is* an emergency, after all: there are carnivorous, sadistic former-people wandering the zoo grounds. Maybe the menu will tell her where to find a fire axe or something.

Tasha presses her finger against Emergency Menu.

The list that pops up has a number of options. One is Sprinkler System. Wrong kind of emergency. One is Seal, which Tasha assumes will lock all the doors to the Primate House. Another option says Release. This she presses. Another menu pops up: "Release 1-6," "Release 7-12," "Release 13-18." Tasha presses the first option.

Nothing happens. At least nothing loud or flashing or jarring or emergency-appropriate. But Tasha sees something on one of the other monitors. A flash of activity on one of the screens. What was it? Had the Minkers wandered over to admire the baboons, or had they begun to swarm the office? She checks the screens. She doesn't have company. She exits the Emergency Menu, returning to the view inside the Primate House, and jumps.

The monkeys are loose.

Not all of them; only a few. They are creeping out onto the floor of the large hall like cautious cavemen, looking about them, picking at each other as they're joined by their brothers. Tasha laughs, shocked. She's freed the monkeys. And why not?

Again she opens the emergency menu. This time she presses Release 7-12, then returns quickly to the camera view. More freed monkeys wander out of their tall prisons. She's amazed by how easy it is, this emancipating. A simple touch of the screen and monkeys are out of their cages, loose in the halls of the House. Gorillas too. She sees them lumbering like sumo wrestlers out of their pens, supporting themselves on fists like hams. She opens the Emergency Menu once more and opens the final six cages with Release 13-18. On the camera she sees the caution first exhibited by the primates melting with their fantastic realization of freedom. They beckon to their shyer brethren, inviting them past the pens. The dead remain where they are, and if the living are starving, they forget their condition long enough to bask in liberty.

Tasha is still laughing. It's fabulous! It's what every child longs to do: throw wide the cages of the zoo and release the admired creatures within. She wishes Dinah was here to see this.

She switches to the Bird House menu. It, too, has a cage

layout, with many more rectangles than in the Primate House, bearing the names of exotic avian types she's never heard of. No matter. She opens the Emergency Menu, bypasses the sprinklers, and goes straight to Release. There are six sections of six cages, and she opens them all, pausing a moment between presses. When she flips back to the camera view, only a few birds have flown the coop so far. She can see a brilliantly blue macaw roosting close to the camera, nearly blocking it, its dazzling plumage ruffled in confusion. A little beyond him, a gyrfalcon edges out of its cage, shuffling strangely on the floor instead of flying. Tasha realizes that once he's acclimated, he'll probably eat some of the smaller birds that have found themselves uncaged. She hopes they're not endangered species or anything.

House by house, she presses Release. The elephants amble out gratefully, and one overturns a recycling station in his haste. A small elephant calf tiptoes briskly behind its mother. The hippos stay stubbornly submerged. The giraffes skate out slowly, stripping leaves from overhead trees with their black, eel-like tongues. Tasha releases a panda bear and it sits staring blankly at its freedom. The monkeys have embraced their independence with open arms and can be seen on many of the monitors, swinging from welcome signs, opening the doors of the Bird House, and forcing open recycling stations to pick through their contents.

Meanwhile, in her zoological orchestration, Tasha has almost forgotten about the Minkers and the problem they pose. She remembers quickly as she sees them on the screens, tottering a little closer to the office building. Bonobos freed or not, the Minkers are between her and the Cat House, between her and her Prada backpack, her can opener, her knife. A couple of the Minkers have seen the monkeys and are gaping at them. Tasha isn't sure if they recognize the primates as food yet; they just observe them as if in awe. Perhaps the monkeys will hightail it and the Minkers will follow in hungry pursuit.

Tasha looks at the zoo layout on the screen. All of the Houses glow red, indicating Emergency Release has been activated. All except one. The Cat House. She stares at it, debating, a seed sprouting. She opens the Emergency Menu and presses Release before she has a chance to talk herself out of it.

The rectangle highlights red when she has released 1-6 and 7-12. She waits, afraid. She has just released two lions, a jaguar, a tiger, a panther, an ocelot, a caracal and other soft-furred killing machines from their cages. The ocelot she thinks she could take if she had her knife and maybe a broom or something. But the tiger? The panther? The jaguar, which only that morning had eyed her through the bars like she was a turkey dinner basted in Adidas? She returns to the camera view and, of course, the cats are out of the bag, more eager than the giraffes, more eager, even, than the monkeys. They prowl around, bellies low to the tile, eyeing one another and growling raspy threats. Tasha changes the camera angle for a different view. The only animal still in its cage is the ocelot. It crouches cautiously near the edge of its pen where the bars used to be before they withdrew into the ceiling as a result of Tasha's button-pressing. She wonders why such a button even exists. She doesn't care.

Now there is movement by the door of the Cat House and Tasha hastily switches the camera angle again. The Minkers have seen the movement in the Cat House and cluster dumbly in vicious curiosity. From Tasha's remote view from inside the Cat House, she can see the woman in the navy-blue dress gaping in through the entrance door, pawing at it. Tasha still can't see her shoes.

But now the cats have seen the Minkers too. Tasha watches, unconsciously holding her breath, as their ears prick up. Their bellies rise from the floor in a momentary forgetfulness of fear as their hunting instincts take over. They are wary of one another and snarl, but they edge closer to the window, their savage amber eyes widening and becoming bare with desire. Tasha has seen Discovery Channel hunt footage a thousand times, but this is something else.

Tasha watches the two breeds of predators watching one another. The cats, in their House, are velvet stones. She can see their muscles tightening like coiled springs as they look through the glass, only an occasional tail or ear twitch betraying the fact that they are alive. Tasha doubts they're even breathing. On the other side, the Minkers sway and paw and, Tasha assumes, bark. They are game of an oblivious sort. Tasha knows the lions must wonder at their prey's stupidity.

The stalemate ends quickly. The jaguar eagerly springs at the crowd of Minkers. If he had leapt a foot to the right, he would have smashed against the glass, nursing a bruised nose. But he doesn't hit the glass. He hits the door, and it opens.

In an instant he is upon the woman in the navy-blue dress. Tasha claps both hands over her mouth, stifling a scream. Somewhere behind her knowledge of Chipped behavior, she'd thought the Minkers would run; that the sight of uncaged wild animals would infiltrate the haze of Chip-induced mania and clear their minds long enough to send them fleeing for safety. As it is, there is no flight. Or fight. The Minkers snarl and Tasha sees their arms open as the cats fall upon them, as if embracing their children, long lost and only just returning.

The screens provide enough angles to observe the melee, missing nothing. Tasha is surprised by the tears that her fingers find when she touches her face. She's cut many a neck in the last week, but this feels like murder, or at least its cruel cousin. There is joy in this bloody work: the lions seem to rejoice as they, together, bring down a man in an Armani suit. Tasha is so captivated by the carnage that it doesn't occur to her to regret the ruin of the suit's fine silk stitching as the man is mangled in their jaws. She only stares at his face in the high-definition picture of the security screen. He looks as puzzled as Brian did on the morning of the Change, her nail file protruding from his neck. The female lion has her jaws around the man's throat. His face is blank, the Chip already destroyed. Tasha wonders if the lioness swallowed it, and what that might mean.

Now she has to move. The Minkers are down: nowhere does she see them pacing in their monotonous, mechanical circles. The screens show only feasting beasts and loitering monkeys. Tasha did her work, now the cats are doing theirs. Staying low, she trots to the front of the office and peers over the countertop again.

Clear.

The closest cats are the lions, snarling lackadaisically at one another as they share their prey. They've dragged their kill to the bear statues where they crouch, half-alert in their gluttony. Tasha briefly wonders how close to death they had been when she opened the cages. Maybe they could have survived for weeks, or maybe this would have been their last day. She tells herself she might have saved some lives, at least, even if the lives weren't human. She'd rather a tiger get a meal than a Minker.

Tasha scuttles to the door and unlocks it. The lock seems to make a horrible grating sound, its brazenness amplified by her fear. She opens the door a few inches and pauses, watching the lioness. She read somewhere that the female is the more deadly, so Tasha keeps her eye on her. She opens the door another few inches. The lioness cocks an ear but doesn't stop eating. The door opens another inch and Tasha squeezes through.

Now she's out. She feels giddy, stoned. Here she is in Lincoln Park, creeping around behind lions eating guys in Armani suits. She gives the lions as wide a berth as she can without putting herself too much in the open. It's surprisingly easy, getting to the Cat House. The cats have spread out across the area, each munching its kill. The lions are the only ones who eat together. Some of the cats have disappeared. She spies the leopard drawing its tail up into a tree where it has dragged its prey, the woman in the navy-blue dress. The woman's shapely leg hangs down, its shoe fallen to the ground beneath. A beige platform pump.

At the door of the Cat House Tasha jumps as she steps over a body she had thought was dead. It's one of the high school girls, her teeth snapping at Tasha's ankle. Both of her arms are gone, the stumps soldered handily by the Chip. One leg is also missing; Tasha sees it a few yards away. She wonders which cat worked the girl over. She waits for the feeling of hate and haughtiness as she looks down at the plaid-clad form on the ground, but it doesn't come, even as the girl wriggles closer, trying to get a bite. The Chip glows merrily in her neck, repairing wounds Tasha can't see. Tasha blames the girl's parents, wherever they are. The kid can't be more than fifteen; her parents had put the Chip in her. Now look at her. Her skirt has risen in her attempts to bite Tasha; she can see the crotch of her blue underwear. Tasha leans forward and tugs down the hem of the girl's skirt, covering her single tan thigh. At this the girl barks, and Tasha moves away quickly.

The door to the Cat House is slightly ajar, and Tasha slips in sideways so as not to push it open farther. Inside, it's quiet. The smell, a combination of cedar and blood, tingles in her nose. She stands for a moment at the front of the hall, gazing outside at the carnage she orchestrated. Some of the Minkers leftover from the pack simply lie dead, de-Chipped and deflated. Others are in pieces, still twitching, the Chip unable to sprout them new limbs or connect the head back to the neck. Others are gone, dragged away, dangling from trees, or being digested. Farther off, Tasha sees the cougar stalking a gnu, also recently emancipated. She'd seen the same cougar devouring a schoolgirl. Maybe the gnu is just for fun.

The big cat has never seen a gnu before, she is sure; they had grazed and hunted on different continents in the times before their captivity. Now they are thrown together by the push of a button, an easy connection of finger to screen. It's like splicing, in a way: bringing together strangers, putting them side-by-side. Wildlife Deathmatch. Noah's Ark.

Tasha turns from the window and walks down the now-empty hall. Her steps echo the way they had the night before, but louder somehow. The cats' breath had been quiet enough, but they had filled the space. Their hunger had taken up much of the air, or maybe it was her fear. She isn't afraid now. Not even when the rippling growl enters her ear from the right side of the hall, a sound without rhythm but deep enough to remind her of all the ominous *Jaws* soundtracks in history. She stops. Turns.

It's the panther. Her blackness is like a glittering hole in space, the center of a collapsing rainbow. She's so alive it's thrilling, so black and so beautiful Tasha doesn't care to tremble at the blood in the whiskers. She has her paws around the limp body of another man in a suit even finer than the ruined Armani; the man's pale hair is stained red. Tasha doesn't need to see his face: the Chip is no more. Cats go for the throat.

Tasha and the panther stare at one another. Neither one moves, not even the impatient tail. Tasha remembers only minutes ago, the cats and the Minkers staring one another down through the glass: the Chipped swaying and moaning and barking. She stands as motionless as the phantom cat, trying to mirror the gaze of savage indifference.

The panther studies her, the amber eyes two blazes of old knowledge. Tasha thinks of Aslan and his biblical preachiness. This is not Aslan. This is Aslan's grandmother, a creature whose coat has been blackened by depth. This cat was pacing jungles when Aslan was still a kitten chasing yarn. Tasha has the urge to salute. She doesn't, imagining the mouth closing around her impertinent wrist. Of course, the cat wouldn't go for the wrist. She'd go for the neck. Tasha has no Chip that would need to be crushed before stilling her struggles. The animal would absorb her blood like a black velvet sponge.

The panther seems to make up her mind. She breaks their gaze and resumes gnawing on the man in the suit, whose body rocks limply and without protest. When the great black head drops, it has the effect of a nod. The glowing eyes no longer pin Tasha to the floor. Tasha accepts her permission and moves sideways down the remaining length of the hall to the door where she'd left her few possessions. She quickly puts the can opener back into the backpack and grips the Wusthof firmly after cinching the bag. She swings the pack onto her back, adjusts the straps. She puts one hand on the bar that will open the back door of the House. She looks over her shoulder once, at the panther. The eyes are watching again, knowing.

She slips out the door. The panther lets her go.

CHAPTER 19

Tasha wipes blood off her shoes.

She'd made it to the Magnificent Miles without encountering a single Minker, but the zoo had been tricky to escape—she'd woven between the feasting grounds of various large cats, most of which had been too gorged to offer more than a growl and a flickering whisker, and she'd run into an ostrich that had made an unpleasant sound in its long hairy throat and chased her like an over-sized goose—but she'd crossed another bridge over the lagoon, hit Lakeshore Drive, and jogged until she saw Gucci. Now, creeping down the wide, still street—silent except for the hum of the Volamu—she breathes in the familiar and comforting smell of retail.

Downtown has more cars than the North Side, and she sees them now, dotting the side streets like beached whales. Some of their windows are broken; some of their glass is stained red; some of their doors hang open like the lopsided wings of condors. She trails her fingers along the body of a Mercedes, the sexy red paint camouflaging the blood smeared on its side. It's very small, as most cars are, and parked to the side of the promenade that Michigan Avenue has become.

Michigan is much like a boardwalk. Each side, of course, is lined with towering stores and shops, but Michigan itself is no longer a place for cars: what used to be the street is now divided into four lanes of Volamus, two running south and two running north. In between, dotting what used to be the traffic median but is now much larger, are smaller shops (some mobile), fountains, art installments, and small, vertical, multi-level parks. Cars and electric scooters—and the rare pumapod, modified for citizen use—are not allowed on the promenade: one southbound lane for motor traffic edges one side of the promenade; the northbound lane edges the other. Shopping on the Miles before the Change had always felt as if she were walking on an island: an oasis of retail framed by the buzzing of automobiles that seemed to pace the painted barriers like hungry predators.

Ahead, Tasha can see a pink Benz that had crashed through the barrier. Its nose is buried in a mobile scarf shop. She approaches, admiring the car. She's never owned a car, and has only driven one a few times since she has lived in Chicago. In Kentucky there were lots of them, almost all electric, but she left for college when she was seventeen, only a month after getting her license. Once in the city, she'd devoted herself to the subway and had glanced at automobiles only with appreciation, never desire. With the Benz she feels the twinge of want. Its soft pink paint actually causes saliva to gather at the root of her tongue, as if she were looking hungrily at a car-sized wad of cotton candy. She approaches it curiously, hand outstretched to stroke it.

She almost falls backwards when the woman inside throws herself against the window. Around her neck is a handsome necklace of heavy shining stones. Above the necklace is her gaping, gnashing mouth. Tasha admires her teeth: implants, surely, but well done.

The woman claws at the window and Tasha can hear the dull *click, click* of her nails against the glass. The woman's throat convulses, so Tasha assumes she's barking, but either the glass is thick or the barks are hoarse, because she doesn't hear a thing.

Tasha peers into the car. The seats are smooth white leather, the steering column a polished ivory. A Barbie car.

"Where's Ken?" Tasha asks. She glances into the backseat. "Oh."

The white leather is a mess of red. The rear window looks like it was on a stage set for *Carrie*, water-ballooned with blood. Tasha turns away, feeling sick.

She picks her way down Michigan, averting her eyes from the prone bodies she finds there. There are many. She wonders how long it will take to get used to the sight of the torn clothes and mauled flesh, the empty eyes yellowed by death. Part of her hopes soon, and part of her hopes never.

Ahead, between a street kiosk that sold Gucci pet accessories and a crashed pumapod, a body catches her eye. It is a man wearing a pinstriped suit that likely cost four months of Tasha's rent. One pant leg is pushed up, revealing its satiny lining. Its redness, exposed and curled over the gray exterior, reminds Tasha of a gutted fish, its rainbow of entrails alongside the silver scales. Tasha gets closer. The man has a neat wound across the side of the neck and nothing else—not the work of anyone Chipped. Rather, he is—was—a Minker. Tasha kneels to examine the wound, staying alert for any sounds of approach. The man's eyes had been oddly blue in life, like a bird's egg. He stares vacantly now, past Tasha, appearing to be gazing at the Louis Vuitton store behind her. The familiar crinkle is between his brows—angry at Tasha, pissed that she separates him from leather Louis. His lips are slightly parted. Tasha can see the red matter in his teeth.

His neck wound is a clean slice. Tasha looks around, wondering who had done it, if they're dead nearby or if they escaped. A lucky break, she knows. Maybe the suited guy grabbed the wrong Chicagoan on the morning of the Change. Out came a switchblade, the quick chop across the neck.

A glimmer of something catches Tasha's eye, and her stare travels down to the man's waist. On the ground beside him is something gold, shiny. She reaches for it—it's slightly under his body. Her fingers close around the thin gold metal and she holds it up to examine it: a MINK card.

Gina had never let Tasha hold hers for very long. Now she holds this one with both hands, rubbing her thumbs across its smudged surface, feeling the texture of the inscription.

MINK, in large letters across the top. Under it, in smaller letters, *Medical Inoculation Network of Knox*. And in still smaller letters beneath that, *The Few*. On the back of the card is the man's name, Citizen Security number, MINK account number—all that made him matter in the world. The card now feels warm in Tasha's hands.

"The Few," she says out loud.

She looks at the dead man, at the red in his teeth. Yes, he's safe. One of the "few." His MINK had given him the Chip, armor against infection and assault, and now against the Chip itself. Tasha's mind wanders to the weeks before the Change. Gina, Cara, Mrs. Kerry, Tasha's neighbors. The Drivers of the L. Her doorman. Policemen. They were the few. Who were the many? Tasha looks around Michigan Avenue, the Promenade littered with corpses. Some of them might be Chipped—laid low after a lucky strike from their would-be victim. But most of these bodies, Tasha knows, are the unChipped. Regulars. The many. She wonders if any of them realized—too late—that if they could just destroy the blinking red light… Too late.

Suddenly the MINK card feels like an anchor in Tasha's hand. She lets it drop. She imagines it quakes the street as it hits the ground.

She continues down Michigan. The hum of the Volamu has become something like tinnitus. It being the only sound, she finds herself sticking her finger in her ear and wiggling it, thinking her ears are ringing. The silent Magnificent Miles are not as she remembers them from just over a week ago: brimming, buzzing with the sound of credit cards being swiped. A week ago she was squinting at the purses of swaying women; she was curling her lip at passing men and their lewd remarks; she was ringing Gina on her cell and demanding that they meet for drinks. Now the silence is a shroud around her shoulders. It blends in with the heavy sky and the musky smell hanging in the air.

What is that smell? Tasha sniffs a few times in quick succession, reminding herself keenly of a Basset hound. Where's that smell coming from? It smells like a barn; a vague hint of vanilla; sweat.

She pauses, points her nose down. Sniff, sniff. She pokes her nose into the corner of her armpit. It's her.

The reality that she's been wearing the same sweatshirt for days, the same socks, the same jeans, the same—god— underwear, reenters her consciousness in a flurry like birds' wings. She takes comfort from the fact that Ishmael—or any attractive man—isn't anywhere near her. She'll probably never see a man again, let alone be close enough to one for him to smell her sweat—or her underwear, which makes her despair even more—but the sheer knowledge that she is walking alone down Michigan Avenue in Chicago and can smell herself inspires her to issue an ultimatum, the conditions of which include soap, a toothbrush, and a change of clothes.

She surveys her location. Michigan and Ohio—only a block from the Web, the Apiary's biggest shopping competitor. Harmony's Beauty Bar and Spa in the lower level, where she could find soap. Clothes in the rest of the mall. It's a plan.

Walking toward the Web, Tasha nearly steps on a small machine lying among some debris on the pavement. It's an iPod. An old generation, one of the models her grandparents might have had. Some people her age had taken to buying them off eBay before the Change; retro items such as this always had a certain amount of appeal. She picks up the iPod, a white one with a large display, and clicks the little scrolling wheel. After a moment a faded apple appears on the dim screen. It loads, and Tasha takes the earbud that isn't bloodied and puts it to her ear. The shrill, nasally voice of an artist whose name she vaguely recognizes sings a few bars before the battery of the iPod dies:

"*Some boys try and some boys lie, but I don't let them play. Only boys who save their pennies make my rainy days.*"

Tasha drops the extinct iPod back onto the pavement, noting with a new satisfaction that the screen cracked a little on impact.

The Web is empty, emptier than she's ever seen it. She had expected to encounter at least a few Minkers, but she sees nothing but the endless polished tile floor, and entrances to stores thrown wide—at least on this floor. She feels the way Oprah must have felt when she went shopping; the owners closing the stores, barring all shoppers except the one who matters most: Tasha.

This is ridiculous, of course—she is essentially going to be shoplifting during her visit today—and doubts that Oprah would approve, but then again, Oprah has been dead for decades, long since given her own national holiday. Maybe she wants a bit of excitement from where she sits, bored to death, in Heaven. Tasha imagines Ms. Winfrey pumping her fist in angelic fandom and smiles to herself as she heads down the escalator to Harmony's.

The lobby of the spa is as deserted as the upper-floor of the mall, and the music is quieter here. Probably Enya or something. She looks around, fearful of finding the aestheticians' bodies stretched out, still wearing their pink spa gloves. But there is nothing, and no one: only the chanty yoga voice coming through the speakers, and the smell of chamomile washing over her in waves of artificially-scented nostalgia.

From one of the glass shelves that line the walls she takes down a few bottles: facial scrub, body wash, shampoo, lotion, toner; bottles of potions that had filled the shelves in her apartment so far away on Foster, each one a promise. Arms full, she picks up a pink spa towel between her elbow and hip and wanders off to the baths, the Wusthof clenched unsafely in her teeth. She's sure she looks like a pirate. A pirate with a soft spot for Deep Sea Facial Scrub and Apricot Masque. Pirates gotta stay pretty too.

She's visited the spa enough times to run the bath herself, and she's soon up to her chin in hot water. She hadn't thought to grab any bubble bath, so she sits glaring through the clear water at the shifting mirage of her naked body. It reminds her of going to the public pool when she was a kid. She had sat with Leona on the edge of the deep end, gazing at her shimmery legs. They were almost like fins.

In her past visits, she'd had cucumber slices over her eyes, which doesn't lend itself well to awareness of one's surroundings. So instead she sits studying herself, surprised by how dirty her ankles are. She's curious about her body. When was the last time she's really looked at her ankles other than to make sure

246 OLIVIA A. COLE

they weren't turning into cankles? Does she sweat from her ankles and has never known, the truth hidden by daily showers? Her skin is a mystery. She doesn't even know its name.

She washes under her arms and is annoyed by the hair she finds there, but also a little fascinated. She hasn't gone more than two days without lasering the fuzzy parts of herself since she was thirteen. Now her inquisitive fingers pet the tiny patch in her armpit as if it's a small, foreign animal, strange but strangely welcome. Eventually she leaves her armpits alone to wash her neck and behind her ears and, finally, now that she has worked shampoo through it, her hair. As she submerges, she knows there will be not one straight strand left on her skull when she comes up for air. The water will undo the last of the flat iron's labor.

Underwater, she keeps her eyes wide open, afraid that any minute a gaping, barking face will appear above the surface and plunge its hands into the tub to grab her throat. She hears the alien clicking one inexplicably hears under water as she holds her breath, a sound she has always equated to the whisper of a seashell pressed against the ear. She knows it's not the sound of the ocean, here in this pink bathtub; it must be the voice of the ear itself, a tiny creature of a mermaid sitting inside the canal, tapping the drum.

She can't hold her breath any longer and breaks the surface, her hair plastered to her cheeks like octopus tentacles. She paws it back impatiently before stepping out of the water. It's murky with everything she's washed off. She stares at the draining tub as she dries herself with the huge pink towel, and is only half-disgusted by the gray water. It could be worse—it could be red. She ties the towel tightly around her and picks up the Wusthof to carry with her. She's going shopping.

She only has to go up one floor from the spa. At the top of the escalator she goes into Guess. The mannequins stare accusingly at her and she gives them all, each one of them, the finger. None of them react.

Fitting rooms have always been her nemesis, so she tries to make it quick, discarding the first two pairs of jeans she's gathered for their tightness. As good as they make her ass look, she won't be able to run in them. She briefly mourns the idea that all future clothing will be worn for its functionality.

As she's pulling her feet from the legs of the denim she pauses. Behind the auto-tuned voice of the singer wafting through the speakers of the fitting room, she can hear a sound. In another time, she would have thought it was someone in one of the other fitting rooms, singing along, tapping out the beat. She focuses on the sound. Breath, and an almost rhythmic bumping noise. It's coming from inside the fitting room. Tasha jerks her second leg out of the jeans and snatches up the pink towel. She ties it tightly around her body, grabs the knife, and sticks her head out of her little fluorescent stall, looking left and right. She doesn't see anyone, but with her head out in the small hallway she can hear the sound more clearly. It's at the end of the hall, in the fitting room reserved for the differently abled. She wonders for a moment if it's someone in a wheelchair, their little steering stick stuck in the forward position, wedged in their dead fingers.

She creeps down the hallway, grateful for the silence her bare feet allow her. She holds the knife ready, one hand outstretched, prepared to yank open the curtain of the stall at the end. In her hand the knife is trembling.

She rips open the curtain with a yell. She doesn't know why she yells; perhaps the anticipation had bubbled up as she held her breath. Either way it is unnecessary, as the Minker she sees before her barely acknowledges her presence.

It's a girl. No more than fourteen years old. She's naked except for a pair of bright blue underwear, cut to show the bottom of each buttcheek. Across the ass is printed the word "Smart." Tasha wonders if the girl—or her parents—was aware of the joke, or if she just thought the best way to advertise her intelligence was to wear panties that attested to it. The girl's back is slender and crossed with the tan lines of a one-piece bathing suit. A swimmer perhaps. Tasha imagines the girl's parents getting the Chip for her, thinking it would protect her from muscle deterioration, bursitis, chlorine poisoning or whatever dangers lurked in pools, just waiting to contaminate unsuspecting youthful dog-paddlers. So much for that. But what's she doing here? And alone? Perhaps her parents had left her when she'd come out of the fitting room snapping her teeth. Tasha tells herself that she would have at least tried to muzzle her own kid had it come out acting like a rabid coyote. Or maybe not.

Tasha stares at the girl, who stares at herself in the mirror. She is bumping her forehead against it every eight seconds or so, resulting in the rhythmic sound Tasha had heard. The girl must have been at it for awhile; her forehead sports a light-colored bruise. The Chip has probably been keeping up with the damage, preventing her from spilling her brains all over the glass. Although she's not hitting her head very hard, Tasha imagines the skull to be very much like an egg; if you tap and tap, eventually the shell will split and release its contents. This particular egg is just difficult to crack.

Tasha feels strange watching the nearly naked girl. Surely the girl has noticed her in the mirror: Tasha's surprised she's not turning, barking, biting. She just bangs and bangs, her brow furrowed and her eyes glazed. Tasha considers the possibility that the girl hasn't yet noticed Tasha's presence. She decides to announce herself, just to be polite. She coughs.

Bang, bang, bang.

Tasha coughs again.

"Um…excuse me?"

The girl is deaf to Tasha's gentle pronouncement, and goes on butting her forehead against the glass. At a loss as to what to do next, Tasha half-heartedly raises the knife and feels her leg twitch, as if it had decided to take a step forward and then changed its mind. She knows it would be easy to dispatch the girl—she can see the Chip's square nesting ground on the bare neck—but the idea feels strange. The girl's face is lineless and clean of make-up, the eyelashes unblackened. Her naked body seems too soft, too exposed. She's like a mole, blind and unfurred.

"I'll just leave you to that then," Tasha says. She takes a step backward and slowly, quietly slides the curtain closed again, like a hospital sheet up to a patient's chin. She takes the jeans from her fitting room and leaves. As she exits the store, she can still hear the faint rhythm of the girl's skull against the glass.

Tasha leaves Guess and crosses the hall to Victoria's Secret, which has become less and less secretive. Inside the store aren't the faceless, motionless mannequins Tasha had flipped off in Guess. Instead, Victoria—whoever she is—has upgraded to six-foot holographic women, their iridescent asses wearing brightly-colored panties, sparkling. They strut up and down the tops of the long platforms, which house drawers of drawers. Tasha gazes at the ghost-women only for a moment. Passing one of them, she slashes at its calf with the Wusthof, the blade slicing through the air, not even interrupting the hologram.

She goes straight to the demi section, and opens the drawer with her size. This she doesn't need to try on; she's been wearing the same bra since she started college: black demi-cup, lace back. She has it in beige too, but the black is sexier. She pulls two out of the drawer. Does this new world have a place for black lace? Black lace is like the Great Auk—impressive, but dead. The women who the holographic thong models imitate are dead. Sexy is dead. The thought is both heavy and weightless, and Tasha feels the shifting pressure and the void. Without sexy, who will she be? She supposes alive is the only *who*, the only *what* that matters at this point. She hasn't yet decided if this is enough. Oh, look, underwear is on sale.

She stops in a few more stores, picking up two black tank

tops, a pack of socks, a Nike hoodie, and a toothbrush that's self-foaming when you add water, the toothpaste stored in the handle, discharged with a twist. She's also collected a recycled cotton shopping bag to carry her bounty back to the spa.

Heading spa-ward, she passes the gleaming entrance to Macy's, the entire floor of which is dominated by cosmetics. Tasha stands undecidedly in the entranceway, shopping bag in one hand, Wusthof in the other. The thought of the endless, pristine surfaces of the beauty counters beckons to her. She thinks of the teetering towers of eyeshadow clams, their exotic and interesting colors. From where she stands, she can see the fluffy brushes used for applying the shimmering powder that will conceal all her flaws. They will have lavender face lotion. She takes a step forward.

The loudspeakers in the mall switch on with a crackle, and a voice echoes through the empty Web.

"They're coming."

Tasha freezes like a doe caught in a backyard floodlight, her heart a mouse playing a rickety tambourine. She tries to move her eyes and search for the mouth the voice comes from without moving her body. It had sounded like a woman—where is she? Tasha remembers she's still in a towel and scrambles to tighten its knot as surreptitiously as possible. She hopes it would stay on in a fight, but if she has to kick ass butt naked, she will.

"Didn't you hear me?" says the voice, "I said they're coming. Get to the second floor *now*."

There is only one "they" in this new world. Tasha hesitates a second longer. If she's a doe, this could be a decoy fawn, a snare using her fear as bait.

Then she hears the first bark.

She's off like a shot, bare feet slapping against the marble, her shopping bag rustling as she makes a beeline for the escalator ahead that will take her to the second floor. The cringing homunculus in her brain whispers that there might be more of them one level up, two levels up—the whole place could be swarmed. She can't afford to listen.

She trips up the escalator, fully prepared to be torn to pieces when she gets to the top, packs of rabid shoppers who'd been up early for a sale dying to get a piece of her. In a place like this she might as well have a red "seventy-five percent off" sticker slapped on her forehead; she'd be gone like Black Friday clearance.

But when she gets to the top, panting, the only person waiting for her is a pretty Asian-ish woman with a black backpack over her shoulder and a box cutter in her hand. She smiles, looks down at Tasha's towel, then over the rails at the barking crowd gathering outside Macy's on level one and says,

"You'd better get dressed."

Tasha does get dressed, banishing any shyness as she dons the pilfered underclothes, jeans and tank top. She hadn't gotten any shoes; she'd assumed she'd be going right back down to the lower level spa for her Nikes. She starts to put on socks but changes her mind: if they have to run she doesn't want to slip. She remembers a brief image from an old film she'd seen freshman year: a young man sliding in his underwear. Better to stay barefoot. Once Tasha is dressed, the Asian woman extends

Tasha's knife, which she'd been holding for her.

"Ready?"

Tasha takes the knife.

"Ready for?"

The woman nods down at the Minkers. Tasha sees there are four, not as many as her fear-crazed brain had imagined.

"We've gotta get rid of them."

"Wait, what? Us?"

The woman laughs.

"If not us, then who?"

Tasha goes on staring, so the woman expounds.

"I've gotta sleep here tonight. I really don't want to worry about those four making it upstairs and sniffing me out."

The idea of hunting Minkers is a new one—so far Tasha has mostly just cowered and lashed out when necessary, a poison dart frog hopping around trying to stay out of reach then releasing toxins when caught. This is different. She thinks of the lions in the zoo, their hungry gaze through the glass of the Cat House. She looks down at the Minkers outside Macys, trying to look at them that same way. She could be a panther, she thinks. She tightens her grip on the Wusthof.

"Let's do it."

They ride down the escalator in silence. It feels a little anticlimactic; not the thundering hooves and war cries that Tasha would expect from what really boils down to a charge on the enemy. Nearing the bottom, the Asian woman says,

"You go right, I'll go left."

Although Tasha would appreciate more specific direction, she doesn't ask. Instead she just follows suit when the woman breaks into a trot as they reach the first floor. The Minkers see them, and turn toward the two of them snarling. Tasha's comrade lets her black backpack slide down her arm to the floor as they get nearer. Tasha wonders if this woman is just a hundred-and-ten-pound Rambo or if her heart is pounding as hard as Tasha's.

Then they're upon them and Tasha is hacking at the neck of what used to be the Web concierge, keeping the pantsuited body between her and another Minker, a young guy in cargo shorts and a graphic tee. The concierge goes down with a spark and Tasha turns to the guy. Out of the corner of her eye she can see the Asian woman stepping over the corpse of one of the others, about to start on her second as well. Her box cutter drips blood. It's not very big, but then again neither is the Chip.

The guy in the cargo shorts isn't as easy as the concierge. He's bigger and Tasha can't get at his neck as easily without her arm being high and vulnerable to his grabby hands. She scuttles behind him, looking for an opening. He keeps turning and turning. They could do this for hours.

"Need some help?" The Asian woman has put down her second target and approaches Tasha with her box cutter half-raised. Tasha feels flustered—it's like being the last kid to finish her quiz in school.

"No," she says, and lunges in at the guy's neck, her arm passing by his cheek for a stab.

It happens very quickly. His hands spring up and snatch her

forearm, his cloudy-eyed face snapping sideways in a flash, his teeth burying themselves in her bicep.

The pain is like a dog bite, simultaneously sharp and dull. The pressure of the flat front teeth through her flesh is intense, the stupid bearded jaws squeezing and grinding. She can feel the warm air from his nostrils flaring against her skin. Bright white flashes of pain burst in her vision. He's tearing her arm off. Her throat is next.

And then it's over. His jaws loosen, his teeth slip out of her flesh, and he tumbles to the floor, his neck sparking.

Tasha stares at her arm, the circle of punctures, the pulse of blood rising from them. She slaps her hand over the wound, feeling queasy. She wants her mom.

"No, no, no, don't touch it yet. Your hands are dirty."

Her head swimming, Tasha looks up. There's a woman with her, dark-haired and light-skinned, her eyes concerned. She's holding a box cutter, standing over the body of the man who, a moment before, had latched onto Tasha's arm like *Jaws*.

"Hey, you should sit down," the woman says.

Tasha does as she's told, nearly crumpling to the floor where she stands. Her arm is throbbing. It's the only thing she can feel: her fear is gone and all she feels is teeth, teeth, teeth.

Then the Asian woman is there with the backpack she'd dropped and is fussing over Tasha's arm, ripping open a pouch of peroxide and pouring it on the wound. Tasha can hear her skin fizzing. Through the curtain of nausea that's drawn around her, she thinks the liquid stings. The woman is wrapping Tasha's arm now, a long white bandage tightening around the red maw in her bicep. It feels better. It feels secure.

"I'd give you a shot of Tranquilix, but the security office was out of syringes."

Tasha gazes dreamily at the woman crouching next to her. The fog of shock has lifted slightly, but she doesn't think she remembers how to speak just yet. The woman studies Tasha's face.

"You need a sandwich," she says finally.

After helping Tasha collect her things from Harmony's spa, Tasha's new friend leads her up a few floors to what used to be the food court.

"Welcome to my kingdom," the woman makes a grand sweeping gesture, giggling. "I swear to god I spend more time here than the guard room."

"What are you even doing here?" They're the first words Tasha has spoken since she was bitten. She had been shocked. She's killed many of them since the Change, and she'd always worried about being bitten, killed, eaten. But actually being bitten never seemed like a real possibility. It was like playing Grand Theft Auto, then actually stealing a car and getting your brains blown out. No restart button. Thank god they're not contagious.

"Well, I was mall security before everything got weird. Now I'm just a chick with a Taser."

Tasha looks at her belt for the Taser. The woman sees the glance and shakes her head, smiling.

"Well, I *had* a Taser. I used it on the first day and realized it doesn't really work on these guys."

"How many have you..." Tasha pauses. "Gotten rid of?" *Kill* sounds so...something.

"Prob'ly close to thirty. There were a ton of 'em here on the morning of. It's easy with the cameras in the guardroom. I can see the isolated ones and just go after them."

Tasha is impressed. Her own numbers seem pitiful. Not so bad if she counts the massacre of the group at the zoo, though. She decides she'll hold off on that story for now. Maybe she'll tell it later.

"Have you been downtown this whole time? Why'd you come here? Just felt like doing some shopping?"

Tasha shakes her head.

"No, I lived up North. But I needed to leave. So now...I'm here."

The woman shrugs.

"I had just gotten to work when it happened. Obviously. My supervisor was my first one."

"My doorman was my first."

"How was it?"

"It was...bloody. Scary."

"Yeah. Me too. What's your name, anyway?"

"Tasha."

"My cousin's name is Tasha. My name's Z."

"That's a letter."

Z glances at Tasha as they cross the huge, empty food court, raising her eyebrow.

"Short for Azalea."

"Yeah, Z is way better."

"See? My sister's name is way worse though: Viburnum. My brother? Snapdragon."

"You're a liar."

"I wish I was. My dad had a thing for flowers. Viburnum… can you imagine? Guess what we call her?"

"V?" Tasha guessed.

"Yes!" The woman laughs. "At least my brother can get called Dragon. That's actually kinda cool."

They approach a counter emblazoned with shining red cursive letters: Big Mama's Subs. Tasha's stomach gives a little clench, whether of hunger or anticipation she can't tell. She's been eating canned peaches and Spaghetti-O-esque meals for a week: the idea of a submarine sandwich makes her more excited than she can remember being for quite some time.

"Bon appetit," Z says as she sits up on the countertop and scoots across behind it.

They raid Big Mama's while Z explains why it's the only place she's been eating. She ate Spumoni's on the first and second days, she says, because the pizza was first fresh and then just stale. But after that it was either inedible or unmade, and she doesn't know how to work the ovens. All the other food joints—Mexican, Chinese, burger places: the food floor has it all—require some kind of cooking, and she hasn't figured out their various technologies. Big Mama's, on the other hand, is pretty self-explanatory: the massive refrigerators store seemingly endless quantities of meats, cheeses, and vegetables; the breads are stored in air-tight containers; the condiments are chilled;

the chips individually packaged. The Web—like the Apiary, and McDonald's, and most other big businesses—is connected to the city's power grid, and will be for thirty days.

Tasha makes herself the most obscene foot-long sandwich known to woman: turkey, ham, cheese, spinach, tomatoes, and olives with oil and vinegar. Z eats a salad—apparently she'd already had a sub for breakfast. They eat at one of the dozens of tables in a sea of blue and green plastic, sitting at the edge in case they need to bolt. Tasha keeps the half of the sandwich she's not yet eating wrapped and ready: if they have to run, she's sure as hell not leaving it behind. It is her new most precious thing.

"So why are you…you know…alive?" Tasha asks through a mouthful of turkey.

"Rude!" Z laughs, crunching on a cucumber. "I guess you mean *how* am I alive. I mean, I dunno. The first day was the hardest, with Mari, my supervisor. After that there were shoppers that I had to take out. The first ones I took care of had wandered into the Employees Only area. Then the first time I ate at Big Mama's, there was a kid behind the counter who used to work there. He got a little bitey. As you can see, I'm still clearing the rest of the mall."

"So you're just going to stay here?"

Z looks uncomfortable but stares resolutely at her salad.

"I mean, yeah. I can at least see what I'm up against in here, with all the cameras and stuff. It makes it easy to hunt 'em down. Out there, I mean, who knows. Plus, I figure it's just a matter of time until the Army comes in and gets everything straightened out. Just gotta hold down the fort."

Tasha's sandwich is halfway into her mouth, but she pauses. She hasn't considered the Army. She's given the President some reflection and imagined the fate of the White House, but as far as jets and hovertanks swarming in, vanquishing the biting masses and waving red, white and blue flags with the missing California star—not a thought. She feels a brief stir of a hopeful spider in her stomach, but it's squashed quickly. This feels like Santa Claus. She's seen enough in the past ten days to know— to think she knows—that there is no fat man in a camouflage suit squeezing down the rotting American chimney. This is not a world for that anymore: she's seen lions tearing flesh from bodies still clothed in Armani suits. The Army? Nah. But she remembers Dinah's frail hope that had urged Tasha to go to the Post, desperate for some bit of news, and remembers Dinah's bitter disappointment when all Leona's letter contained was a warning. She doesn't know Z at all, but the woman had saved Tasha from what might have been an ambush, had dressed her bitten arm, brought her up into her food palace. Tasha doesn't want to dash her hopes so casually. So she takes a bite of her sandwich and says,

"The Army, huh?"

Now it's Z's turn to stop eating. She looks carefully at Tasha's face, and Tasha feels something like a blush in her chest. She had tried not to be a dick about it.

"The Army," Z says flatly.

"Mmk," Tasha says, and her ears tell her she sounds like her father. But Z hadn't known him; she can't know this is a gentle sound. To Z Tasha sounds like Tasha, and Z doesn't know Tasha either. She tells herself not to be such a jerk. Z hadn't known Dinah and her pointless hope. Tasha changes the subject.

"So what's it been like, cooped up in here?"

Z shrugs.

"I mean, it definitely hasn't been boring. Not at first, anyway. There aren't tons of 'em in here since it all happened so early, but there was enough to keep me busy. I see them on the security cameras and if they look manageable I go take care of 'em."

"So what we just did by the escalators was no biggie for you, huh? Old hat?"

"Eh, kinda. I went through security training so I can kick some ass. The boxcutter to the neck though," Z makes a violent, descriptive gesture, "that's a little different."

"Wow," Tasha sighs. The feeling of being outdone returns. All the running and hiding she's been doing, the cowering. "You're...I don't know. You're a beast."

Z throws back her head and laughs, unabashedly showing Tasha the half-chewed contents of her mouth. Tasha smiles in spite of her insecurity. She's been holding back a little—she had just begun to open up to the idea of Vette, and look where that got her—but she feels a little piece of herself unfold.

"Oh please," Z chortles, chewing. "Don't tell me you've had an easy time since you left the North Side. You've done your share of neck-hacking, I bet. Come on. Dish."

Tasha dishes. She tells Z about Brian and the others she'd

killed. She tells her about Chip, employee of the month at McDonald's. Z laughs ruefully.

"Ha. See! Anyway, that's what you get for eating at McDonald's!"

"Oh, like Big Mama's is a lot better!" Tasha cries, brandishing her sandwich.

"Have you seen anyone else alive? Besides me."

Tasha tells her about the running man on Broadway, about Ishmael, and #16 and #34. She tells her about the girl in yellow. She doesn't tell her about Dinah, but she does find herself telling Z about Vette.

"Christ," Z says quietly.

They're silent for awhile after that and finish their food without further conversation. Tasha begins on the second half of her enormous sub, even though she's sure she won't be able to finish it. The gluttony feels normal. Sitting in this blue plastic chair feels normal. Talking to Z is beginning to feel normal.

"So you'd think there'd be a ton more of...*them* downtown," says Tasha, taking a sip from the bottle of water she'd also taken from Big Mama's.

"Yeah, I thought the same thing. I remember when things were normal I'd see tons of people with the implant. Even a couple of my coworkers had it, and they'd brag about it."

"Same here. But Michigan Avenue was a ghost town today."

"Maybe they have, like, a mother ship," Z jokes. "I wish the ones in here would get beamed up or whatever."

She pauses, abandoning her salad for the moment.

"It was just me and Mari that morning. She'd worked the

nightshift and I'd come to relieve her. I got here at five and she was already...gone. It must have just happened, though: nothing in the mall was too weird or messed up yet. But she was the only one I saw that morning. It took me awhile to... shut her down, you know? I didn't know what to do."

They've wandered back into uncomfortable territory again and the silence has them in its grip once more. In her discomfort, Tasha has finished her entire sandwich without really paying attention. Now she looks down at her stomach. Z notices and laughs.

"Do you have a food baby?"

"A what?"

"A food baby!" Z pushes her stomach out and pats it. Tasha laughs.

"Yeah, I think I do. Oh my god, that sub was amazing."

"I told you. That's one thing I liked about working here: this is the only Big Mama's in the city. I'd come here every day even when things were normal. We can come again tomorrow. You are going to sleep here, right?"

"Yeah, probably. I hadn't really thought that far ahead," says Tasha, feeling bashful, although she's lying.

"You should sleep in the security room with me. It locks. They're not great with doors."

They journey up to the twelfth floor of Macy's—Z says she hasn't been up much higher than that and doesn't want to—and procure a sleeping bag for Tasha from the Outdoor section, and a pillow from Home. They brush their teeth in the women's bathroom. Z tells Tasha a story about a male co-worker who had stumbled in drunk one morning when Z was putting on mascara in the mirror. He'd asked to borrow the tube of mascara, which she, mystified, had given to him. He'd put it down his throat, used it to trigger his gag reflex, and puked in the toilet five feet away from her. He'd even tried to give the tube of Maybelline back. Z had told him to keep it. The florescent lights are bright; the tile walls blindingly green.

In the guardroom, Tasha has trouble sleeping at first, a problem Z does not seem to share. The many screens that are such a comfort to Z are bright with their countless views of the Web. Tasha imagines waking to see them filling up, one by one; all the Minkers in Chicago storming the mall to come pound down the door of the guardroom like the gates of Troy. But the cameras are still and empty. All except one. It's the camera that looks in on the fitting rooms at Guess. It doesn't view the stalls directly, but through the curtain Tasha can see the shadow of the young girl, naked, banging her head against the mirror over and over and over.

CHAPTER 20

"What are you going to do when you run out of chicken?" Tasha asks.

They're eating again—Tasha a salad, Z a toasted sub with nuked chicken pieces. They've spent the morning walking around the Web. Had there been music and other people besides those who popped up now and again trying to eat them, it would have felt like any day: two girlfriends in the mall making small talk, aimlessly circling the vastness of retail. The Minkers they'd encountered they'd put down—only two so far. Having someone with Tasha made it easier, both the actual killing and the thinking about it. As Z had said when they met by the escalators, it was just something that had to be done. It seems obvious now.

"Eat turkey."

"And when you run out of turkey?"

Z makes a face.

"Eat ham, I guess."

"What's wrong with ham?"

"I never used to eat ham before all this shit happened," she shrugs.

"Why not?"

"Pork on your fork will make you speak Pig Latin."

"What?" Tasha laughs.

"I don't know, it's something my dad used to say. We never ate pork. Well, Dragon did. But he did everything we weren't supposed to do." Z smiles faintly, looking down at her food.

Tasha swallows her bite of salad. It seems they can't talk about anything without these moments emerging from the thickets of their recent pasts. It's like a damp glass set down on tissue paper: the ring of moisture spreading outward and outward, a darkly expanding radius.

"Do you know where your brother is? Or...any of them?"

"My mom died giving birth to V, so I don't remember her much. My dad lived in Humboldt Park. Dragon is in jail in Arizona. V lives in New York with her girl."

"Did any of them have the Chip? The implant?"

"Dad did. He was a cop. Maybe V. I don't know."

"Oh."

There's not much Tasha can say besides "Oh." Z's not a stupid girl. She doesn't think her father in his apartment in Humboldt Park is some miraculous exception. She knows he can't be rescued. Yet Z thinks—with however much conviction—that the Army is going to swoop in and save them all, a topic they haven't broached since its first gloomy emergence. Even so, she has wisely stayed holed up in the Web;

has made no grand heroic journey to save the people she loves. They are leaves now, drained of chlorophyll, scattered by the wind. Her sister in New York might as well be in California with Leona. Unreachable. Tasha wonders how long it will take her new friend to realize that the Army and everyone else is similarly withered.

As if she were reading Tasha's mind—or at least a piece of it—Z murmurs,

"Do you think New York is...like this?"

Tasha is prepared to walk alongside Z as she wanders through the cycles of wondering that Tasha has already roamed through. In the nights since the Change, she has imagined the miles of city around her first as they once were and then as they are now. It had seemed impossible to believe at first, the magnitude of it. Living in Chicago these past few years, she could scarcely believe the way the city went on and on. She tended to wander in small circles, not trusting her knowledge of public transportation to get her home safely. She thinks of the miles of life she has passed on West Lawrence alone. Lawrence goes on forever, with no Volamu, no L; just a couple of the old-timey CTA buses trundling people up and down it. She can barely comprehend the size and length of Lawrence Avenue, let alone the entire span of the States. She imagines it as if flying like a bird, the miles disappearing underneath her, the landscape blurring as she zooms overhead, all the way to California, where there are no Chips. She imagines the miles to the Nation passing below, crowded with the faces of flesh-eaters. Thousands. Millions. How many people really have the

Chip? She thinks of the inscription on the coveted gold cards—"the few." How few? How many? The Driver, the doorman, the grocer, the groom, and so many more…they condense into a single drop of oil dripping slowly into an immense black bucket.

"Yes," she answers Z. "Yes."

Z sighs deeply, and Tasha thinks she might have already been preparing for this knowledge, despite her hopeful clinging to the idea of a military insurgency. It reminds Tasha of Ishmael, his yearning for his brother and mother. He'd wanted facts, but in a desperate way, desperate to be contradicted. Z wants to be wrong—she hides in the Web, waiting for good news. She wants Tasha to laugh in her face and say, "The whole country? What are you, crazy? No, it's just this small thing, this small time. Take an aspirin and go to bed. They'll be here with guns and a cure tomorrow. It will all be better in the morning."

Z finishes her sandwich and Tasha her salad. Tasha has opened a bag of barbeque chips today and eats those too. The damp ring has spread through the metaphorical paper, and it settles around the women like a noose. Tasha almost wishes a great lumbering Minker would come and pounce between them, overturn their table, spill their drinks. It would give them something to think about besides the dark scattered pieces of their lives.

"What about you?" says Z. "I've been yammering about my people. What about you? Are you alone up here?"

"Yeah. Kinda. My parents died three years ago. I only have one sister and she lives in the Nation with her guy and my niece."

"Oh. Did she…?"

"No, none of them got the Chip. California wouldn't let it in, so pretty much everyone is safe over there." She pauses. "At least from that."

"How did your parents die?"

"Some kind of lung infection. The doctors never really figured out what caused it."

"I'm sorry. There wasn't a cure or anything?"

Tasha swallows.

"The only medicine they would give them wasn't enough. If they'd had MINK they might have had more of a shot. Could've gotten more aggressive treatment or whatever."

Z nods.

"Yeah, same thing happened to my grandmother. Not the lung stuff, but the MINK thing. She was at the same job for twenty years—they never gave her MINK. Dug up that she got an abortion when she was in college and said she wasn't eligible. She petitioned and everything, especially when she got sick. They didn't care. She died five years ago."

Tasha crushes the empty chip bag.

"Man…"

Z nods again.

"I know, right?"

They are silent. The chip bag makes quiet crinkling noises as it gradually uncurls itself. Tasha watches the ball come undone—it won't stay put. Z brushes it onto the floor.

"Let's walk some more."

They walk up a few floors to one of the huge spherical windows that look out at the city. The glass has been crafted with large circular designs inside it, webs for the Web. The landscape outside is only slightly warped because of it. Outside, below, is Michigan Avenue, its promenade as still as it was her first day at the Web. Tasha looks north, looking for the pink Benz with its clawing inhabitant. She can't see it from here.

"I hated working here," says Z, gazing out the window, "but what a view. It's even better on the high floors, but there's lotsa offices and some residences up there too. I have a feeling they're probably pretty, you know…swarmed."

Tasha nods.

"Yeah, probably the same thing at the Apiary."

"Ha! Wait, you worked at the Apiary?"

"Mhmm. I hated my job too."

Tasha rubs her ring finger, thinking of Mrs. Kerry. And Cara, of course: she thinks of Cara. Dinah would have said something kind, some sensitive thing that Tasha needed to hear to override the sour feelings that arise when she thinks of Cara. Z watches her carefully—it's a shrewd look, one that misses little. Tasha wonders how Z would've handled Cara. Maybe the way she handled her own supervisor, with a knife to the neck. Tasha wishes she'd had the same opportunity.

"I'm surprised there weren't more looters," Z says. She's turned to look at the stores now but Tasha gets the feeling that she's still regarding Tasha closely. "You know, breaking in and stealing stuff. There's supposed to be looters during this kind of stuff, right?"

"Hey, I'm a looter!" Tasha cries. "Give me some credit!"

They laugh. Another sound, almost like laughter, joins them. Minkers. Tasha's knife is already in her hand—lately she's starting to wish she had a scabbard of something so she didn't have to carry it around all the time. It would make pulling out the blade a lot cooler too.

Z points.

"There they are."

The two women ride the escalator up one floor, the three Minkers waiting almost patiently around the top. Tasha isn't sure if the creatures had spotted her and Z where they had been standing by the circular window, or if they had just began barking on their own for the hell of it. Either way, the Minkers see them now.

"I'll take the redhead," Z says as they near the top. "He used to work in the building. I never liked him."

It's business as usual. Tasha sidesteps the lunge of a woman in Versace—she's gotten good at that move—and then slashes at the neck. Blood surges down the green satin material—the emerald sheen reminds Tasha of a pair of shoes she used to have. Jimmy Choo? She can't remember just now. Z has handled her former co-worker. Tasha takes a step toward the third one, an older man who looks like he might've walked with a cane before the Change but whose limp the Chip repaired. His shirt is embroidered Gucci.

"Oh, I was going to get him," says Z, gesturing to the oldie.

Tasha gives a half-bow.

"Oh, by all means…"

"No, after you."

"Paper rock scissors?"

They shoot for it, keeping out of reach of the third Minker, who follows after them squalling. Tasha wins, and the straggler hits the floor a minute later. They use his pant leg as a rag for their blades.

Finished, they look at each other.

"Want to go try on clothes?" Z shrugs.

There's little to do besides eat sub sandwiches and walk around window-shopping, clearing the occasional encountered Minker. A few times they do go in and try on clothes, but the activity lacks meaning. In Betsey Johnson Tasha tries on a red flouncy dress, parading out in front of Z, who, wearing pink satin, claps and wolf-whistles. They look in the endless panels of mirrors at their reflections. At one time Tasha would have turned this way and that, admiring, assessing, adjusting. Now she just stares, arms limp. This is her body. This is a dress. This is her body in a dress. The red fabric burns the glass as she stares; she could be on fire, but she feels cold. A cute dress is only as useful as a napkin when there are no clubs to go to wearing it. Tasha doesn't miss clubs yet. She wonders if she eventually will.

Later, they're lying on benches by the fountain on the floor they had just finished clearing, half-dozing. Tasha has been at the Web for two days. Between them, they've cleared nine floors. Once a floor is cleared, they can hang out, nap, relax. There's not much else to do, and the Minkers on the higher floors aren't exactly calmly boarding escalators to come hunt them down. Tasha has seen them on the cameras in Z's security room, yawning at the mannequins through the store windows, bumping against the glass like blind puppies. The creatures monitor their own floors but don't attempt to get to other levels. Z stirs and asks,

"Where were you going anyway? Like, where were you on your way to when you stopped here?"

"The South Side," Tasha answers, half-opening her eyes.

"The South Side? Why?"

"It's safer there," says Tasha slowly, wondering if she'll tell Z everything.

"Were you going to walk the whole way?"

"I walked this far, didn't I?"

"Yeah, but you could have, I don't know…"

"Taken the L? I'd have liked to if all the people who drove them weren't dead. Would've saved me a couple blisters."

"Touché. Okay, what about a scooter? You could steal one. Well, take. Borrow. Whatever. It's not really stealing anymore."

Tasha tilts her head toward Z.

"That's actually a good idea. I hadn't thought about that. I didn't even see any scooters until I got downtown. I'd just need one that's charged."

Z waves her hand dismissively.

"There's tons. I'll show you where some are if you still want to go. There's a lot full of them behind the mall that they used to let employees use to make deliveries. Do you still want to go?"

Something about the way she says it makes Tasha hesitate.

"I mean, kinda. My arm is healing up—thanks to you—so I figured I'd get going soon."

A shifting silence stretches between them before Z responds. "Why the South Side though?"

"Well…" Tasha pauses. She still hasn't told anyone about the mysterious Dr. Rio, not since Dinah. She doesn't fully know why. In one way it's like the feeling of picking the restaurant for a group outing. If the food is good, the person who picked is a hero. But if the food sucks, if the silverware is dirty, if the waiter is rude, the person who picked is a leper, bearing the guilt of a false prophet. Only the prophecy that Tasha carries is more important than recommending a steakhouse; there is more to lose than one's appetite. People can die. Two people *have* died, two people that Tasha could have protected.

She swallows. Then she opens her mouth and tells Z about Dr. Rio. She tells her about Leona's dire letter and the warning of the bad thing that was coming, her urgency about Tasha getting to the South Side. Telling it, Tasha wishes she had divulged the story of Dr. Rio to Ishmael. He was more familiar with the area. He could've helped her. She had been too concerned about needing deodorant and a razor. Make-up. Stupid things. Stupid, dangerous things.

When she has finished telling the story, including the part about Ishmael, she looks at Z, who is sitting up on her bench, looking excited.

"See?" she says.

Tasha is confused.

"See what?"

"This Dr. Rio guy! He's a doctor! She wouldn't send you to him if it wasn't important, right? He must know something." She pauses. "Maybe even something to fix this."

Tasha sighs inwardly. Ishmael's soccer team had said similar things: cures, rescues, off-switches. Dinah too, and Vette. Tasha supposes it's human. But then what does that make her? Maybe they're just naïve, but Tasha's sister had always described *Tasha* as exactly that. How things change.

"I don't know, Z," Tasha says evenly. "I mean, how do you *cure* an implant? This stuff is pretty much kill-tech, and the only way you turn that off is the way we've been doing it—by putting them down. It's not like an infection, you know. And even if it was…the Minkers won't exactly line up for a shot."

"I mean, maybe it's like a ray gun—"

Tasha snorts.

"Seriously!" Z protests, waving her hands. "Like, a magnetic wave or something that can be put out city by city—or maybe even nationally: we're in the Midwest, in the middle. Maybe it could reach the coast and stuff—to get everything back to normal. Maybe they hid it in the South Side somewhere, you know? Somewhere not obvious?"

Tasha sits up and looks earnestly at her friend.

"A ray gun, Z? A giant microwave strong enough to 'turn off' millions of Chips?"

Z laughs, shrugging and blushing a little.

"Okay, okay. Yeah. You're right. That's outrageous. Just throwing out some options here."

"Anyway," Tasha laughs, "my sister isn't some radical with secret doctor contacts. She's a mom. And a malcontent. If anything she wanted me to go find Dr. Rio because he's, like, a guy with a bomb shelter and a basement full of canned goods. She'd call that safe. But given the circumstances, I figured I might as well check it out. Nothing to lose."

"I guess not. I wonder what he's like."

"Who knows. My sister hung out with a bunch of political scholars when she still lived in the States. She probably knows him from college. He's probably a big nerd."

"Big nerd or not, I hope he's alive at least. Otherwise you'll be going down there all by yourself. It's dangerous down there."

"Dinah said it wasn't as bad as they made it seem online," says Tasha quickly.

"Who's Dinah?" asks Z, looking puzzled.

"Dinah is….Dinah was my friend."

"Oh," says Z, and nothing more. Tasha feels torn. Saying Dinah's name out loud makes her eyes sting slightly, and the sting makes her want to get away from Z, and quickly. But she also—

"I'm sorry, Tasha," Z says, interrupting Tasha's focus on her feelings. "I'm sorry you've lost so many friends. That's all the more reason I kinda worry about you going down there alone. You'd be…well, alone."

Tasha looks at her, evaluating her feelings: balancing her chameleon armor against the softness in Z's eyes. Is it worth it? Tasha takes a deep breath.

"You could come with me," she ventures.

The tinkle of water striking water in the fountain fills the silence. Z says nothing. The quiet is heavy.

"Or not," Tasha says quickly.

Z stirs.

"It's not that I don't want to. I mean, I know Big Mama's Subs aren't going to last forever."

"No, they won't."

"But they would last for awhile."

"Yes, they would."

This is a courting dance of a different kind—minus the plumage, a game between peahens: the feeling out of new friends, the risks and rewards. But—a familiar stirring on Tasha's shoulder, a wooden something daring someone to knock it off—if Z doesn't want to come, she doesn't want to come. If she wants to stay in the Web hiding from the world, that's her decision. Tasha won't beg her. *She saved your life*, the lonely part of Tasha says, the part of her that knows she needs an ally. *But*, the fear whispers, *she could die, and then what would you do?*

"What if there is no Dr. Rio?" Z asks and Tasha feels grim. It's the thing she is afraid of; one of the things: what if, what if, what if.

"I don't know," Tasha says slowly. "Something would be next. I'd do...something. Go to California," she laughs wanly, "and cuss out my sister for making me come so far."

"You could just wait here with me," Z says, and Tasha can tell she's trying not to beg either. "There will be soldiers eventually, seriously. They're probably just handling D.C. first, you know? Getting the President safe."

The laugh in Tasha's mouth is not right. She doesn't want to be an asshole. She doesn't want to crush the frail bird bones of Z's hope. Tasha feels a little sick.

"I'm going to head out in the morning," she says finally, looking away from Z and back at the ceiling. As much as the idea of staying here with this new friend beckons to her, Tasha knows she needs to go South. She's followed nothing but the letter and her gut so far, the only things she has to go on. Leona had said go to the South Side, so that's where she's going. She just hadn't wanted to go alone.

Z looks like she wants to speak, but doesn't. Instead she just nods. Her hair, pulled from her ponytail, is a shining black fan around her head. They hadn't talked much about the Change today until now—it's easier just wandering through the Web, taking out the occasional Minker. Besides those encounters, the Change is easy to ignore in here, with the endlessly playing music and the constant thrumming of escalators. It's a different sound than the Volamus outside, Tasha thinks. It's a friendlier sound, absorbed by the stores and tables and mannequins. Outside, the hum of the Volamu dissolves into space. The sound climbs to the skyscrapers, with nothing to bind it to the earth. Tasha feels as if she's on a merry-go-round, passing the world by on the back of some beautiful and artificial animal, the music replacing all other sound. She sits up on her bench and looks at the fountain. Its bottom is covered in coins—dimes and nickels and quarters like a long-stretching layer of aluminum foil. A bronze spot among it all catches her eye. A penny. Pennies have been out of circulation for a decade. Leona had collected them for awhile until she realized how pointless it was. Tasha stares at the penny.

"Do you think people really expect to get the things they wish for when they throw money in?"

Z turns her head to look at the water, her face still troubled.

"Maybe. Probably. People wish for stupid things, so it makes sense that they'd be stupid enough to expect them to come true."

Tasha considers this, wonders if Z knows that she is describing her own Santa Claus wish of the Army. It's not stupid, Tasha decides—that's mean. It's just futile. But, she supposes that's why it's a wish to begin with.

"I mean, I don't know every wish everyone has ever made, but I've watched the kind of people who toss coins in there. Mostly kids. What are they wishing for? A puppy. A doll. Oh, and teenage girls threw money in too. They want to be popular, right? Or skinnier. Those are stupid wishes."

Tasha thinks she remembers wishing she were skinnier, and she wasn't a teenager either. She didn't wish in a fountain though; just in the mirror. Some girls wished in the toilet bowl.

"I mean, people want what they want," Z goes on, still looking at the water, and Tasha wonders what her friend sees. "I guess I can't say it's stupid. I just wish they would wish for something, like...I don't know...smarter."

"And there's your wish," Tasha smiles, pushing their discussion about Dr. Rio out of the conversation. "Throw in a coin."

Z pats her pockets, smiling sadly.

"Out of luck. I'm broke."

It's Tasha's last night sleeping in the guardroom. Z has taped a piece of paper over the screen showing the girl in the Guess fitting room. Tasha is grateful for it. With the girl's headbanging hidden, she sleeps more easily. Z's breathing fills the small room like a smoky chant. That night Tasha dreams she's in California, being held by Amani, who is a woman with long, strong arms. Her fingernails are perfect unpainted ovals, the skin without lines. Somewhere nearby Leona is singing, her voice echoing like coins dropping in a well.

CHAPTER 21

Tasha has packed three sub sandwiches from Big Mama's. She wants to bring a bag of chips too, but knows they will only be dust by the time she gets where she's going. Whenever and wherever that is. She has laid the subs gently on top of her clothes in the backpack, double-wrapped. The self-foaming toothbrush and a stick of deodorant are wedged into a side pocket now to accommodate the sandwiches. The Wusthof is in her hand, as always. She feels like an action figure carrying it around all the time, a Ninja Turtle that comes with its weapon already attached, fixed and unremoveable; or a stuffed dog with his stuffed bone stitched permanently into his mouth.

Z is quiet in the morning as Tasha packs. She's fiddling with her box cutter, pushing and pulling the lever so the blade slides first in and then out again. It makes a clicking noise as the lever ticks over the notches.

"Got everything?" She sounds like Tasha's mother.

"Mhmm." Tasha sounds like Tasha.

They had discussed where Tasha would be able to find a scooter. There are several of them in an employee lot behind the Web, where Z will take her. Z has warned her that she doesn't know what kind of charge they carry, but if they don't get her all the way South, they'll get her close.

Z walks her to the employee exit at the back of the building. They come across more bodies here—mostly victims, not Minkers—more than they've encountered in the rest of the Web. The mall hadn't been open yet when the Change went down, so most of the skirmishes inside would have been between Chipped and unChipped employees, the Minkers and the MINKless.

Z is silent as they pass the bodies on the floor. Tasha knows she probably recognizes more than a few of them, but she keeps her eyes bravely ahead, even as they fill with tears. They don't speak. Tasha doesn't relish the idea of leaving her here alone in the Web, munching pilfered subs and watching the motionless monitors in the guardroom. Besides the roving former employees and the odd shopper, there is nothing here to monitor. Nothing left to guard.

They reach the back door and Tasha pretends to adjust the straps of her backpack, switching the Wusthof to her left hand in case Z wants to shake her right. It would feel too final and very Old West, and Tasha hopes she doesn't.

"Well…"

They don't look at each other. Z peers through the little window out at the scooter lot.

"Looks like the coast is clear."

"Okay. Good." Tasha can't think of much else to say.

"I hope you find Dr. Rio," Z says lamely.

"Yeah, thanks. Me too. I hope you...um...stay safe."

"Yeah, I will."

"Okay, well, I guess I'll...okay. Bye, Z."

"Bye."

Tasha slips out the door, making sure it closes firmly behind her, hearing the click as it locks automatically. The lot is a dry, square patch of asphalt with twelve or thirteen electric scooters, their various colors of paint gleaming like candies. She has never ridden a scooter, but it has a seat and a gas pedal and handlebars. How hard can it be?

She picks out a little silver model and walks over. It doesn't have a key, only a keypad for the ignition code. Z has told her the code for the employee scooters—700—and she enters it. A light next to the keypad illuminates. There is no sound, no engine stirring to life, but the scooter is now vibrating slightly, so she assumes that means it's on. She looks over her shoulder at the door where she left Z, but doesn't see her in the window: she must have gone back upstairs. Tasha feels her heart sink a little—these past few days had been peaceful. Enjoyable. It was like summer camp—an oasis of leisure. She wonders if she and Z would have been friends before the Change, if they had ever met. Maybe—Z liked shopping as much as Tasha had, and knew a thing or two about mascara. She had a sense of humor. As a security guard, she never would have registered on Tasha's radar as friend material. Then again, who did? Dinah lived right next door and she'd only ever avoided her.

Tasha, with the exception of Gina, had never had too many female friends. And most of the women she knew—through work, or when she was in college—didn't have many female friends either. Tasha always supposed it was because they didn't want to compete over men, clothes, whatever. But maybe it was something more. When summer camp is over, there is always the keen sting of friendships parted. Perhaps you'd pricked each other's fingers and rubbed the cuts together; blood sisters. Highly inadvisable, sanitationally speaking, but bonds are made out in the wilderness; the end of the summer was unavoidably painful. Better to skip the summer part altogether to avoid the pain at the end. Tasha looks back for Z in the window one more time. No one. It's probably for the best, she consoles herself. Besides, she doesn't want anyone watching when she attempts to ride the scooter.

She straddles it hesitantly, leaving her backpack on her back. She continues holding the Wusthof as she grips the handlebars, flexing her fingers around them experimentally. Her foot rests lightly on the accelerator.

She gives the throttle the tiniest bit of pressure. The scooter lurches forward with the quietest of purrs, and she brakes. She resettles her butt on the seat and notices the fluttering of her heart. It's a little different than a bicycle, but not much. She looks around, preparing to ride the scooter out of the lot, and sees she must open a gate first, a formidable-looking sliding metal barrier with a keypad like the ones on the scooters. She unslings her leg from the scooter, annoyed.

She approaches the gate. Z hadn't mentioned it, but she

assumes that's because its code is the same. She enters 700. Yep. The keypad illuminates green and she hears the grumbling of gears as the gate prepares itself to open. Good.

She turns her back on the gate and walks back over to her still-vibrating silver scooter. She adjusts the Wusthof in her hand against the handlebar and rearranges her butt on the seat once more. She exhales sharply, readying herself. "Okay."

She looks up to make sure the gate has opened as the green light promised, and is greeted by the sight of five Minkers, standing dizzily in the open space the gate had created. In her shock, Tasha jumps, and her foot slams against the accelerator. The scooter gives a shrill electronic whine and hurtles ahead, eating up the dozen feet to the gate and throwing her right into the midst of the Minkers. She falls off the back of the scooter, nearly stabbing herself in the thigh with the knife she still clutches, landing hard on her tailbone. The scooter had knocked over two of the Minkers and it takes the others a second or two to realize the scooter isn't food. Another few seconds for them to realize that Tasha *is*.

She slashes at the first one to reach her, a teenager with a green Mohawk—Mohawks hadn't been cool for at decades. Her slice cuts the front of his throat, misting her arm with an initial spray of blood, but the wound is healing quickly, although his bark is cut short by the damage to his larynx. Another approaches her from the side, a girl of seven or eight in a basketball uniform. Tasha punts her, sending the kid flying three or four feet. The kick feels good. She wants to kick someone else. Who's next?

She turns and almost freezes. It's a hot dog. A six-foot-tall hot dog. The hot dog wears a sign around its neck—bun?—that says "Jerry's Wieners." She stabs at it, but the costume is foamy and her knife isn't much good against it, so she kicks him in the knee, or where his knee ought to be. A little low. She kicks again, so hard that it likely breaks the kneecap. He topples over. The Chip will heal the fracture easily, but with his arms pinioned to his sides by the hot dog costume, he'll have trouble getting up.

The little girl is ready for another try, and so is the Mohawked kid. Their cronies, who had initially been bowled over by the scooter, have joined them: they're all groaning toward her and she regards them with fear. One of them wears a douchey weightlifting shirt with the sleeves cut off to reveal unreasonably mountainous biceps; the chest reads "FBI: Female Body Inspector."

"You can try," she threatens the musclehead, trying to rekindle the bravado she'd built with Z as they cleared the Web's floors, trying to feel like a hunter. But the past few days seem very far away now that she's alone. She looks around. Nowhere to run. The Minkers block the only exit to the lot, and the door to the Web had locked behind her. She's trapped.

She decides to rush them. She shoulders the little girl with an NFL-worthy move that sends the kid flying again. The Mohawk teen grabs one of Tasha's arms and she struggles to keep him from towing her bicep into his snapping jaws. It's the same bicep that had been bitten her first day at the Web, and she can feel the bandaged area tingling, remembering the sensation of teeth. It puts panic in her heart, the memory of recent trauma. The musclehead has her other arm and is also pulling. His weight is an anchor on her arm and Tasha feels her joints stretching as Mohawk yanks and whines. She feels as though they will rip her apart. The fifth Minker, a supermodel-type wearing a fabulous gold knit-sweater, has been slow out of the gate, but she's ambling over now, her perfectly white teeth bared and coming for Tasha's throat.

Tasha wriggles as hard as she can, feeling her lungs taking in less and less air in her fear. She's begun to pant. The knife is in her hand but useless with Mohawk's weight clinging to her. She can't pull away from the gym-rat without putting herself nearer to the green-haired teenager, and vice versa. The little girl is getting up from where Tasha tossed her. The supermodel is bearing down on her, her reed-straight hair framing her face attractively as she moves in for the kill.

The supermodel's head explodes.

Tasha blinks. Even her assailants pause for a moment at the sound, a deafening noise, followed by the unpleasant, muted splatter of brain matter falling onto concrete. Tasha might have been able to pull her arms free at that moment, but she's too shocked by the decapitated body of the supermodel, which sways before her: tall, slim, and tanned, perfect except for its lack of head. The body finally succumbs to lifelessness, and it collapses onto a nearby red scooter.

There's a clatter as Z drops the gun and whips out her box cutter. The little girl has made a move, and Z cuts out the Chip with a deft flick of her wrist, her face screwed up in disgust. She looks at Tasha and smiles a little.

"Need some help?"

Tasha laughs with relief and feels her eyes sting with tears. She kicks out at the Mohawk kid, but he doesn't budge. Z steps up and grabs the musclehead in what looks like a wrestling hold, breaking his grip on Tasha's forearm. He turns to bite Z, but she jerks his body and Tasha hears something snap.

Tasha turns her attention to Mohawk and lets Z handle the musclehead. The teenager is pretty strong and Tasha grapples with him for a minute before she breaks his hold. Her arm free, she plunges the knife into his neck where she'd seen the red light flickering. She's an inch off. She pulls out and tries again. A spark. Bingo was his name-o.

The musclehead is already dead when Mohawk hits the ground. Z is barely out of breath. Tasha regards the guy's stupid FBI shirt and gives his body the bird. Tasha looks around at the damage, her eyes settling on the supermodel. The woman's neck is sealed over as if with flesh-colored grout, her head gone but her body losing no blood. Her fingers and feet twitch continuously, but she doesn't rise. The Chip in her stump of a neck flashes ceaselessly.

"How does *that* work?" Z is eyeing the supermodel too.

"I'm sure there's an acronym. Very scientific. Or something. So…um…gun?"

Z looks embarrassed.

"I took it off a cop in the hallway after you came out here. His name was Desmond. Nice guy until he got the Chip. Looks like somebody took care of him on that first morning."

"Damn. That was a nice shot though."

Z looks pleased.

"Thanks. Never shot a gun before. It's not like I could really miss, though, as close as I was."

"You totally could have missed. And you put in work on the big guy! What did you do to him?"

"I dislocated his shoulder. They taught us a couple things like that in training."

"Nice," Tasha says admiringly. "Do you know, like, karate and stuff too?"

"What, because I'm Asian I know karate?"

"No," Tasha says, unflustered. She's so happy to see the girl she could cry. "You're just so fast."

"Well thanks. But no, no karate. Just what they taught us here. You're the one who must know karate, with those kicks!" she laughs, imitating Tasha kicking the giant hot dog, making kung-fu-ish sound effects. "You were kicking everybody! I got up to the guardroom and saw you kick that kid across the lot and I about died laughing until I saw there were more of them. Then I, like, hauled ass getting back down here."

Tasha smiles at her. The smile is too big, but at this moment she can't make it smaller.

"Yeah, and picked up a gun on the way."

"Hey, it was just…there. So I grabbed it and kept running. I didn't even know what I was gonna do with it."

"Glad you could make it. If it had just been the hot dog then I might have been okay…" Tasha remembers the hot dog.

"Oh, crap. He's still alive."

They walk over to where the hot dog flops on the ground. They can't see any part of him except his shins and sneakers. They stare down at him and Z giggles.

"You kicked him right in the wiener. Get it?"

"He deserved it. What should we do with him?"

Z shrugs and nudges the hot dog's shoe with her foot, which results in muffled growling from inside the costume.

"Let's leave him. By the time he gets up we'll be long gone."

"We?"

Z shrugs her shoulder, jostling the bag she has slung over it.

"Yeah, I brought my shit. I'm coming too. I figure if the troops come, they'll come. I'll be around. Besides, I can't exactly let you go off on your own—I've had to save your ass twice now."

Tasha looks at her, wondering if the relief shows on her face. She looks down at the Wusthof and stoops to wipe the blade off on the hot dog's pant leg, not wishing to stain her new jeans. At this angle, a tear slides down to the tip of her nose, which she wipes off busily with her sleeve. If Z notices, she says nothing, also cleaning her box cutter on the hot dog's other leg. Inside, he growls impotently.

Weapons wiped, they look to the still-open metal gate.

"Shall we?"

"We shall."

They're halfway out of the lot when Tasha stops.

"Wait, we need scooters. I think I might have broken the first one; let's try different ones. I think I want a green one anyway."

"I actually had something better in mind."

Five minutes later they're opening another gate—the password is different: Z types it in while looking at a strip of paper she's fished from her pocket—that bars a lot two stories above the one housing the employee scooters. Tasha keeps watch as the gates rumble open, and together they slink in. Sunlight streams in through the cloudy glass sides of the structure, illuminating the glorious machines waiting there like painted thoroughbreds.

Tasha had considered the Barbie Benz on Michigan sexy. If the pink Benz was Kelly Rowland, these cars are Beyoncé. Tasha doesn't know cars—she knows clothes, she knows shoes, and she knows dogs—but she doesn't need to know cars to know she's witnessing Grace in machine form. They're still small—electric versions of their big-body predecessors—but their class is unmistakable. Lamborghinis, Paganis, Bugattis, lined up like shining museum exhibits behind invisible velvet rope.

"Who drives *these*?" Tasha gasps.

Z strolls among them, her voice echoing slightly in the lofty trove.

"No one, really. The CEOs that lived on the top floors of the Web own them—including the guy who owned the whole place, my boss—but those guys never really had to leave their little palace, so the cars just ended up sitting here. They still paid people heavy clams to come up and wash them though.

So dumb."

"How are we going to get one out of here?"

"I assumed you knew how to hotwire."

"What, because I'm black I know how to hotwire?" Tasha mocks.

They laugh, and Z reaches into her pocket, withdrawing something small wrapped in tissue.

"No, you don't need to hotwire anything," she says. "We have this."

"What's that?"

Z dangles it teasingly like catnip. Tasha steps closer to examine it. It's a finger. Well, a thumb: a severed human thumb, pale and slightly hairy around the chopped knuckle.

"The fuck! Why do you have a finger?"

"It's a thumb," Z corrects her. "It was my boss's. He was the second person I met with the implant on the morning everything happened. I had just gotten rid of Mari and I'd run out of the guardroom, and there he was. He was pretty easy, the fat bastard."

"You've just been carting his thumb around all week?"

"No," Z laughs, "I had put him and Mari and some others in the employee break room after things settled down. I was still, like, debating last night if I was going to come with you or not, so while you were packing I went in and cut it off."

"Um…okay. Like, a souvenir?"

"Ha! No, you freak. To start his car."

Z walks over to a sleek red Ferrari—of course the guy drove a Ferrari, Tasha thinks—and presses the lone thumb against the driver's-side door handle. There's a chirp, and Tasha hears the click of the locks as the Ferrari grants Z access. Tasha stares. Z tosses her bag into the tiny backseat.

"Coming?"

The inside of the car smells like cigars and leather. They adjust their seats, and Z adjusts the mirror and steering column.

"I haven't driven in forever!" she crows, buckling her seatbelt.

Tasha hurriedly does the same.

Z presses the severed thumb against a pad on the dashboard and the car comes to life. The electric engine—fitted with unique technology simulating the coveted roar of a twelve-cylinder—growls convincingly, and Tasha looks across the car at Z, who throws back her head and cackles.

"Let's gooo!"

She steps on the gas and the car rockets out through the gate and squeals onto the downward curving path of the lot. Tasha grabs her seatbelt to keep her head from banging against the window. Z steers the car down another level and they whip out onto Ontario. There's a side-street ahead that will take them onto one of the roads running alongside Michigan Avenue, but Z jerks the steering wheel to the right, urging the Ferrari through the space between two painted barriers, the side of the car knocking one over. They break through onto the promenade where no car (except the crashed Barbie Benz) has driven for almost ten years.

"What are you doing?" Tasha squeals, half-giddy and half-terrified.

294 OLIVIA A. COLE

"Driving!"

"We're not on the road!"

"So what! It's not like we're gonna get a ticket! Put your window down: it smells like old rich guy in here."

Tasha presses the button that lowers the window and the wind comes into the car like the hands of a titan. She knows she should stay alert, keep her eyes open in case a Minker leaps in front of the car. But she has Z to worry about that, and the wind through her curls is like a prayer. She thinks that until this moment, she has spent her life in a flat-ironed up-do, inside the confines of a silent train-car and its nodding prisoners. This roaring engine—artificial or not—this rush of air sending her curls to chaos, this booming of wind in her ears…it closes her eyes and draws her hand out the window, floating it through the air rushing by as the Ferrari speeds south down Michigan Avenue.

"What the fuck?"

The car is slowing. Tasha's eyes snap open. She expects to see a swarm of Chipped Chicagoans crawling up over the hood, gnawing their way through the windshield like demonic hamsters.

"What? What is it?"

Z is incredulous.

"There's a fucking kangaroo on Michigan Avenue."

Tasha sits up straight and peers ahead. Sure enough, a kangaroo has paused on the promenade ahead of the car, its small front legs clutched in front of its body like a little furry T-Rex. It looks at the car, which Z has brought to a stop several feet away, and twitches a large ear in their direction.

"How the fuck did a kangaroo get out here?"

Tasha coughs into her hand and twirls a curl of her hair around her finger. Z glances at her, then glances again, harder.

"Wait, you said you spent the night at the zoo, but did you…?"

"Oh look, he's eating a carrot!"

The kangaroo is indeed eating a carrot, munching it like an enormous brown rabbit.

Z steers the car carefully around him and Tasha waves at him as they pass.

"Hope you washed that carrot first, buddy!"

Her eyes are closed again, her hair a cyclone. She can relax, at least in this moment. Z turns on the owner of the car's music, an old song she knows well from her parents' kitchen— CeeLo— blaring through the speakers as the Magnificent Miles blur past them.

"No one is ever gonna love you more than I do," Tasha sings, running her bare fingers through her curls. The world is a clear place. "No one's gonna love you more than I do…"

CHAPTER 22

"Why do you think some of them stay inside?"

They're continuing to drive down Michigan Avenue, slowly now. Tasha had expected the area to be swarming with Minkers, and in some ways it is, but they're not on the streets. Store windows are smashed here and there, debris and bodies clotting the sidewalks and still-humming Volamus, but the Minkers watch from their retail caves. Like the worker at the Post when Tasha had gone to retrieve her sister's letter, they stay inside the confines of their various places of employment, guarding their wares like humanoid watchdogs. There are others that roam the streets, of course. Z had hit one—quite purposefully—as they passed Wacker. It had barred their way and gnashed its teeth as if the Ferrari was just a large red object of prey. Z had smashed right into him, rolled over him, and kept going, not even looking in the rearview.

"I dunno," says Z. "It is weird. It's like they're on house arrest. Not one toe out."

They cruise past a Jamba Juice. The cashier in her white apron stands right at the smashed doorway like an expectant Chihuahua, her jaws slowly opening and closing. She doesn't react to the car passing just a few meters away. She just waits.

"Yeah," says Tasha. She shudders. "It's so creepy though. Seeing them, you know. Knowing if they came out...how fucked we'd be."

"They're not coming out," Z says. But she looks nervous too. She'd allowed herself to be pried out of the Web, her safe haven, but she's unsure of what's next. So's Tasha. What's the plan? South. That's first. She'll worry about finding Rio when she gets there.

"Hey, what the hell is that?"

Tasha snaps her neck, noting the urgency in Z's voice. She sees what Z means immediately. Cloud Gate is on their left, where it has sat for nearly seventy-five years, only now it is completely covered in red paint.

"...what the hell?"

Z brings the car slowly to a stop on the promenade. The Bean is still a ways off what used to be the road, but from where they sit in the Ferrari they can see that the iconic sculpture has been painted almost entirely red, only the upper parts still silver and shining.

They sit in silence for a moment, staring at it. It's as if a massive bloody organ has been dropped from space, the kidney of a giant ripped from her belly and left for the birds.

"Who do you think did it?"

A who hadn't occurred to Tasha. Yes, someone must have

done it. It is not, in fact, an enormous bleeding body part. It's a metal sculpture, one she's seen a thousand times since she moved to this city. Seeing it this way is like being in a strange dream, a cruel wonderland.

"I don't know," she says. "Someone, I guess. One of us."

She unbuckles her seatbelt with a click and reaches for the lever that will open the car door. Z's hand whips out and rests on Tasha's shoulder.

"What are you doing?"

"I'm going to go look."

"Why?"

"What do you mean why? Somebody painted the Bean red. I want to see it up close."

"Why?"

"Z, what the fuck?"

Z removes her hand from Tasha's shoulder and licks her lips, peering out at what used to be one of the major tourist attractions in the city. It's a small thing now, compared to some of the newer, flashier, Chicago-built traffic-magnets, but a city staple nevertheless. It's a little shocking, Tasha knows, seeing it this way. Like walking in on a family member in the bathroom and finding them there with their wrists slashed. Terrible, yes. But you check the body. "Z, I'm going to go check it out. Do you want to stay here?"

A long pause, Z looking out at the window, unblinking.

"Fine," she says finally. "I'll come. To watch your back."

She unbuckles her seatbelt grumpily, Tasha hiding a smile. She can hear her mumbling as she opens the driver's side door:

"I can't believe I left the Web for this shit…"

They pick their way across the grass of Millennium Park, stepping over bodies clutching cameras and backpacks. Tourists. Some of the cameras are small—the tiny, Post-it note sized contraptions that efficient tourists carry when seeing the world, the photos sent directly to a remote tablet; not even stored on the camera itself. Others are huge to Tasha's eyes, the size of a shoe, like the one her father had kept, even after his hobby waned. "Big," he used to say, "but you get a better picture. A bigger lens will always get you a better picture. You can't capture the world from the eye of a needle."

He wouldn't want to capture this world anyway, Tasha thinks, and she wonders if she were to pick up any of the larger cameras, what the memory chip would reveal. Photos of the Change, when the first wave of hell swept across the city: carnage documented entirely by accident, the finger on the shutter a spastic, useless trigger.

"On your right," Z says, crossing in front of Tasha. A Minker has appeared from the end of the park, staggering at first and then trotting toward them with excitement. It's a cop, or was. Tasha half expects him to yell "Keep off the grass!" But he doesn't. He only barks and snarls as he gets within earshot. Z walks out to meet him, her box cutter held ready.

Somehow she misses her first strike and the two of them are suddenly a jumble of limbs on the ground, thrashing about, one trying to get on top of the other. Tasha sprints over, her knife slicing through the air.

"I'm coming," she calls, trying not to be too loud. The Minker could have a squad nearby. If they're not coming already, she doesn't want to attract them.

"I've got him," Z calls back. She's managed to break his arm, which hangs limply while the Chip repairs it, and she's stabbing his neck over and over, each strike missing as he flails in her grasp. He's like a salmon out of water: flopping and flopping. Tasha approaches and grabs his good arm, giving it a yank and pulling him off balance from where he'd been struggling to stay upright. He flails again, but she grabs the other arm and holds him by both, holding him as still as she can while Z rights herself. She flips her hair out of her face, focuses on his neck, and gives the Chip a solid stab with her box cutter. A burst of flailing amid the electric sound of the kill, then Tasha releases his arms and pushes him to the ground where he falls, twitching, before lying still.

"He still has a gun," Z says, nodding at his belt while she catches her breath. "Should we take it?"

"I don't know," Tasha says, panting a little. "I mean, it's not good for getting the Chip. I mean unless you're like an expert marksmen. I'm not."

"Yeah, but what about for...other people. Not Minkers."

"Like who?" says Tasha, puzzled.

Z's eyes widen suddenly and she's pointing.

"Like her." Her finger is aimed at the Bean.

Tasha turns. Under the arch of Cloud Gate is a woman in ragged clothes waving at them enthusiastically, her filthy blonde hair flopping over her face. She doesn't make a sound, just waves and waves, as if signaling a passing fleet from her shipwreck. She certainly looks a wreck, Tasha thinks, although they're not close enough to really see her face. But something about her erratic movements, her silent gesticulation, is profoundly creepy.

"Do you think she's dangerous?" Tasha murmurs, not taking her eyes off the pale figure.

"Maybe," says Z. "She's a mess. Minkers don't wave, but that doesn't mean she can't do some damage."

They stare a moment longer, not moving any closer. Neither does the waving woman. She just goes on signaling her silent signal. From where they stand, Tasha doesn't think her face has changed at all.

"Let's go see," Tasha says finally. "There's two of us and one of her. If she gets crazy…well, we'll see."

Z nods, looking reluctant. She stoops and takes the gun from the belt of the Minker cop they'd just killed. She doesn't put it in her waistband, the way Tasha thinks people carry guns. She keeps it in her hand.

They make their way slowly over to the woman, stepping over bodies and cameras. Her whiteness is stark against the violent red of the Bean, against which she stands like a small pale doll, her arms flapping. When they get closer, she stops, her arms flopping abruptly to her sides. She squints her eyes at them, smiling a little. Her hair, Tasha sees, isn't blonde from root to tip. The inches closest to the scalp are brown, the color of a mouse. The hair itself is dirty and hangs around her face like a dingy curtain, stringy with oil and some dried blood.

It comes down past her shoulders, a mop. She moves the hair away from her face, and that's when Tasha sees the pearls.

"Shit," she says, grabbing Z's arm and jumping back. Z raises the gun like a shot, ready to shoot something, anything. "I know her."

"You know her?" Z is incredulous. "What the hell do you mean you *know* her?"

Mole people. Ninja Turtles.

"I mean, I don't know her. But I've seen her before. I've seen you before," she says to the woman, a little loudly. "Do you remember?"

The woman grins at them, playing with her disgusting hair.

"This used to be my crown," she says.

"Fuck," Z whispers. "She's a walnut."

"Yeah, she's off her rocker. I saw her in the subway once. Before the Change."

"Well, who the hell is she?"

"I have no idea."

"Who the hell are you?" Z demands, poking the gun in the woman's direction.

The woman closes her mouth, covering her mossy teeth. Then she turns her back on them, walks toward the Bean, and disappears around the corner of it into its archway.

Tasha and Z look at each other, making a silent agreement.

"Stay close," says Z. Tasha nods.

They move slowly along the side of the Bean, cringing away from its bloodiness, the paint still dripping in places. Had the blonde woman done this? This spectacle? Tasha doesn't see any ladders. It would take a whole day with a crew, let alone a single person.

"She's sitting on the ground," says Z, who is slightly ahead of Tasha. "I think it's okay."

There she is. A huddled form on a cardboard mat, the same as the day Tasha had first seen her in the subway. She's wrapped in her rags like they're a stinking cocoon, and she peers out at her watchers from its folds, the smile returned to her lips.

"Did you paint the Bean?" Tasha asks.

A pause. A smile.

"The Bean painted me."

Tasha looks at Z, who rolls her eyes hard and slow. She holds her finger to her temple and revolves it in three quick circles.

"Okay," says Tasha. "What are you doing here?"

"Sitting."

"Okay. How did you get here?"

"I walked. And I flew. And I rolled. My feet will always hurt."

"Why?"

"So far. It was very far."

Z puts a hand on Tasha's shoulder and arches her eyebrows.

"Hey," Z says. "Look. Look at me. What are you going here? Why did you paint the Bean red?"

The woman hums, chewing on a strand of her filthy hair.

"Let's go," says Z. "I mean, she's fine. She's crazy, but she's made it this long without getting chewed up. Let's leave before things get weird."

Tasha hesitates, but is inclined to agree. The woman can't tell them anything. Tasha feels wrong leaving her behind, but Z is right: she's stayed alive this long alone.

"Are you okay?" Tasha says. She knows the woman is crazy but she still feels like she needs to ask.

"Okay?"

"Yes. Are *you* okay?"

"I'm better."

"Someone's coming," whispers Z urgently.

Tasha catches her breath. She hears the sound that must have alerted Z: footsteps. Slow, heavy footsteps coming from the other side of the Bean. A chorus of whining groans. The scrape of many shoes.

"Fuck," Tasha rasps.

Tasha grabs Z and pulls her around the corner from where they came. They can run, but the pack is close: they'll hear. Depending on how fast the group is Tasha and Z may not make it to the car. The blonde woman is rising from her rags like a ghost and Tasha wonders if she'll run with them. She can barely speak, let alone run. She'd have to. Tasha wonders if she'd stop and help her, this strange specter of a person, or if she'd leave her behind to satisfy the pack. The idea makes her sweat, and she tightens her grip on the Wusthof, the feel of its smooth handle against her palm something to concentrate on. A moment passes and the blonde woman has not joined them. Tasha can hear the pack's footsteps. One pair echoes. It's under the Bean. My god, Tasha thinks, have they seen the woman yet? She hasn't heard any barks. Tasha peeps around the corner.

The pack of eight is led by a large Minker in a suit, one pant leg torn up to the thigh and flapping with each step like loose skin. He takes a step or two under the archway and sways, looking about him. The blonde woman is standing on her cardboard as if on a pedestal.

"Oh fuck," Tasha hisses. It's too late to call the woman over. They'll hear her. They'll all die. Eight is too many for Z and Tasha alone. "Oh fuck."

"Oh my god, look," whispers Z.

Tasha doesn't want to. She hasn't heard any barking but she doesn't want to see what she knows she will see: the blonde of the hair disappearing, drowned in red. The cardboard soggy with blood. The throat open and reflecting in the parts of the Bean where the paint has slid and dripped away.

She looks.

The blonde woman is standing beside the leader of the pack, rocking slowly side-to-side on the outsides of her feet. They don't look at one another. They sway mechanically, two alien violinists with unseen instruments, moving to the same vile rhythm.

"Holy shit," Z whispers.

They stand like this for awhile. The pack leader moving in a half circle, his eyes empty and traveling slowly. The blonde woman swaying from foot to foot. Eventually, snuffling, he wanders away, finding no prey under the Bean, and she follows him for a few steps to the edge of the archway as if to see him off. The pack moves away, the leader's suit still flapping. Ten minutes have passed, Tasha and Z frozen at the edge of the bizarre scene, only their eyes visible around the corner, watching.

When the blonde woman leaves the edge of the Bean, the pack disappearing over the hill toward the lakefront, she returns immediately to her cardboard square. She sinks down on it as if her legs suddenly lost their bones, her skin whiter than ever.

Tasha goes to her immediately, ignoring Z's hisses for caution.

"Who are you?" Tasha demands. It stinks. All of it stinks. She's been smelling it since the day she spoke of it through the wall with Dinah, since the day she left Cybranu Chipless; indeed since the day she sold her parents' kennel to pay their posthumous medical costs.

"I am a rat."

"You said that before. What does that mean?"

"I was a rat in Arizona."

"What do you mean a rat? What kind of rat?"

"I was the first," she says with something like sadness.

"The first."

"I was the first rat."

She sweeps her grimy hair away from her neck. There are the pearls. And above the pearls there is the unmistakable shape of the Chip. Not a tattoo, but a raised square area under the skin, only the faintest red light visible through her flesh.

"Chipped. Holy shit." Z has come up behind Tasha and together they stand staring at the woman, who has dropped her hair again and sits curling her fingers through it.

"Why aren't you...one of them?" Tasha asks.

No answer.

"How did this happen?"

"There were men."

"Men?"

"Doctors. A man with four eyes."

"...Tasha..." Z whispers, annoyed.

"Shh," says Tasha. "Ma'am, what did the doctors do?"

The woman looks up at Tasha from her spot on the ground, her eyes large. She turns a little to face the wet red wall of the Bean and touches it with her index finger. She moves it, making symbols, drawing shapes, the silver of the sculpture shining through the red. When she's finished, her finger still and dripping, Z squints.

"What does that say?"

"*CYBRANU*," Tash reads. "*CYBRAKNEW.*"

"Cybraknows," the woman says, smiling, and closes her eyes.

308 OLIVIA A. COLE

CHAPTER 23

They've reached 59th Street when they notice the little bar showing the life of the car's battery has gone from dark green to light yellow.

"Our little Energizer bunny isn't so energized," Tasha says, tapping the dial.

"Yeah, he could use a drink. But I don't think anything down here is on the city's power grid or whatever, so I don't know where we'd plug him in."

They'd left the blonde woman by the Bean. She'd closed her eyes and refused to open them again, even after Tasha checked her pulse to ensure that she was in fact alive. She'd simply shut down. So they'd left her two sub sandwiches nestled against her body and returned to the Ferrari where they'd left it on Michigan. From there they'd veered over to State and made their way through the Loop and the South Loop—past Chinatown, which houses the tallest high-rises in the city next to the ones downtown—and continued south. Now Tasha looks around. Past 45th Street there has been a noticeable change in architecture: a downward slope as the newer high-rises gave way, first, to older high-rises, then to mid-rises, then to rows of one- to three-story buildings, both residential and commercial. Tasha has never been this far south except once for a concert, and had struggled to find a direct route— the train stations after Roosevelt had been thinned from nine stops to four after a summer renovation decades earlier. The bus routes were phased out little by little. Eventually the only way to get out of the South Side was the Red Line, with seven miles between stations. If people wanted to get to work...they did a lot of walking. Unemployment skyrocketed in the winter. So did exposure-related deaths.

As they cruise down State, Tasha observes that this part of the city looks like it has a few miles on it, a palette of grays and browns. It reminds Tasha, a little nostalgically, of Louisville in the late fall: sleety and slatey, rust running together, the occasional pink smudge of street trees. Compared to the slick, metallic texture of downtown, the neighborhood she finds herself in now is more like brushed velvet. The transparent alloy of the L tracks is the only glittery thing she sees; a shiny artificial bone implanted in an ancient skeleton, a stainless steel rod inserted into worn flesh. The buildings are shades of charcoal around the shocking silver of the L's cradle. Early models of electric cars dot the streets like carcasses. There are real carcasses, too.

"There's not as many down here," Tasha says out loud.

"As many what?"

310 OLIVIA A. COLE

"Dead people."

"Nope. The farther south we go the fewer there are. I don't see any Minkers either though."

"Yeah, I know."

They cruise along in silence, observing the landscape. Tasha thinks of what Dinah said about the city's efforts a few years before to cut the South Side out of waste pick-up. Tasha thinks she remembers something about excluding the area from the annual planting of tulips that they did up and down State. The thought vaguely pisses Tasha off. It's almost blatant assholery, she thinks. *No tulips for you, South Side*, as if Chicago was blowing a giant raspberry at half the city. As for the trash collection, though, they must have worked something out, Tasha thinks, seeing no overabundance of garbage crowding the sidewalks. There's rubbish, certainly, but that could have been from the Change. The North Side had looked like a hurricane hit it too.

As they pass 69th Street, the battery life display on the dashboard turns a deeper shade of yellow, threatening to become orange. Z has curbed the lead foot that had rocketed them down Michigan—probably what drained so much of the battery to begin with—and they cruise at an even twenty-five, driving as hesitantly as they feel. Tasha examines the buildings from her window: hair salons, restaurants, shops, accountants. This aspect doesn't look much different than her neighborhood except there's no blue glow of the Volamu, and there seems to be more air. The shorter buildings block out less of the sky, and though it's still marbled with pockets of clouds, at least she can see it. She puts her window down a little farther.

"See anything?" Z asks her.

"No, just regular stuff. It's so quiet."

They pass a brightly painted restaurant, Harold's Chicken. She ate at the South Loop location regularly when she was in college. Harold's served bad chicken, but bad in the best possible way.

"Did you ever eat Harold's?"

"Of course," says Z. "Me and my boyfriend would take the train to the one on Wabash on Friday nights."

"You have a boyfriend?"

"Well, had a boyfriend."

"Oh."

Tasha doesn't push the issue. Z looks at her, then, as if reading her mind, laughs.

"No, no, not because of this. We broke up before all this crap happened."

"What happened?"

"He didn't like my job. I don't think he was cool with the fact that I could kick his ass. He'd rather I worked at, like, The Pink Lynx or something? Jesus."

"Oh my god!"

"I know, right?"

"No, look!"

Z brakes and looks where Tasha points. It's a playground, an old-fashioned outdoor one, with a slide and monkey bars and a jungle gym. On top of the slide is perched a kid, a boy, probably eleven or twelve years old. He's wearing a red-and-blue plaid shirt—Tasha's stomach clenches a little at the memory of the last plaid shirt she saw, bloody and lodged in the branches of a tree—and brandishing a shovel. Halfway up the ladder is a Minker, a woman. On the ground below, looking up and barking, a Chipped kid around the same age as the kid with the shovel. The woman hasn't climbed another step of the ladder; rather, she stays where she is, growling up at him. Whenever she stretches out a hand, he swipes at her with the shovel. Tasha can hear his voice, but can't make out the words.

"Damn! He's just a kid!" Z breathes. She's afraid, Tasha can tell. Probably wishing she had stayed at the Web instead of coming out here with Tasha. She could cut and run at any second. Tasha makes a move.

"Hey, kid!" she shouts out the window. "Kid! Over here!"

The kid's head snaps their way, and so does the Chipped woman's. The Minker kid doesn't seem to notice; he's too eager for his turn to climb the slide. The kid with the shovel points at himself, a gesture asking "Me?" Tasha laughs. Is he serious?

"Who else? Come on!"

The kid takes another swipe at the Minker with his shovel, then turns and sits at the edge of the slide. With a little push, holding the shovel in front of him like handlebars, he slides down the polished metal path. The Minker climbs more steps slowly—Tasha is impressed; she didn't know they could do that—but is stuck at the top: the actual act of sliding is a little beyond her capacity. The other Minker, the kid, is attracted by the motion of its quarry reaching the bottom of the slide and begins tottering over to claim him. But the kid in plaid is ready and swings his shovel impressively, a resounding crack as it connects with the Minker's skull. The Chipped kid topples, blood arcing, and although Tasha knows he won't stay down for long with his Chip still intact, it buys enough time for the boy with the shovel to reach the Ferrari.

"Get in back," Z calls past Tasha as he approaches the car.

He does, taking care not to slam the door once he's in the backseat.

"Nice car," he marvels, running his palm admiringly over the interior.

"Thanks," says Z, her fear seemingly gone. "We found it."

Tasha chuckles, then turns in the seat to look at the kid.

"Who are you? What were you doing out here by yourself?"

"I'm Malakai. I was taking a walk."

Tasha looks disbelievingly at Z, who has begun driving again—in no rush, as the Minker woman is still stuck confusedly on the slide, and the Minker kid is still repairing his skull.

"He was taking a walk," says Tasha.

"A walk? Oh. Well, that's nice. A walk."

Tasha turns back to Malakai.

"Do you often take walks when there's flesh-eating freaks wandering around?"

He shrugs.

"There's not really that many. Not around here. I mean, there's some, but we take care of everyone we come across. There was one in my neighbor's garden yesterday," he says without emotion. "My brother killed it though." Tasha imagines he probably played more than a few hours of Halo 20.0 before the Change.

They drive on for a little while, the boy enjoying the ride. Tasha can see his mouth turned up gently at the corners, his demeanor calm and almost peaceful. Who does he remind her of?

"Make a right," he directs Z as they approach 79th Street.

Z turns the car obediently, and Tasha looks interestedly out the window at the change of scenery. It's more residential here, fewer shops and restaurants. The road needs repairing: she wonders if the Mayor redlined this area for street work too. She thinks of the footage she had seen of the area before the Change—it had looked like a warzone. Maybe other parts are, but this isn't so bad. It's gray—no city-funded flower-service here like downtown—but homey. Why didn't they ever show this part on the webnews apps? She continues looking. The buildings she sees now, however homey, have boarded-up windows, chains around the gates. The fences, she sees, are lined with strings of aluminum cans and glass bottles.

"Nice decorations," she says out loud.

Malakai regards her through the rearview mirror.

"They're there to make noise so we hear it if any sick people come in the yard."

"Oh."

"We're in the red," Z interjects, pointing at the battery level. "We'll be stopping pretty soon."

Tasha notices the nervous edge in her voice; she's feeling panicky again. She was so comfortable at the Web, and she seems to be okay when they're in motion, but the great outdoors dulls her spunky edge a bit. The wide world outside the shopping mall is unpredictable without the cameras showing her all angles of her kingdom, reporting any movement. At the Web, she was in charge. Outside, they don't know what's around the corner until they turn it; no one is the boss. Every Chicagoan for herself.

"It's okay if we stop," Malakai says brightly. "We're almost there."

Tasha wonders where "there" is. Home? A safehouse? A trap? There was a trend in horror movies a few decades back, Tasha remembers from school, in which even kids like Malakai were suspect: kids were cheese in the mousetrap. Tasha considers the idea, sneaking a look at the boy in the backseat through the rearview. He looks serenely out the window. Whatever, she thinks. She has enough to worry about without agonizing over the possibility of an eleven-year-old stabbing her in the back. Plus, he seems to know his way around. Maybe he can help her track down a trace of Dr. Rio when they get where they're going.

A block later the Ferrari runs out of juice. It makes a pale dinging sound, as if making a last plea to be given a power source. There isn't a socket for miles, though, to answer its prayers, and it whines to a slow stop in the middle of 79th Street.

"Should someone say a few words?" Tasha says as they get out of the car.

Z is too nervous to reply, and Malakai is too busy mournfully admiring the dead Ferrari as they prepare to leave it behind. Tasha supposes his admiration is prayer enough, and she shoulders her backpack. Z has done the same; she's looking all around, her neck swiveling like an owl. She has rescued the Ferrari owner's iPod from the console and clutches it like rosary beads.

"You okay?" Tasha asks. Malakai is leading them up a street marked Perry Avenue, spinning his shovel like a drum major. It twirls artfully in his fingers. He must have been in the marching band in school, Tasha hypothesizes. No one is just that good at twirling things.

"Yeah, I think so." Z's neck is still swiveling. "It's just, like, different. It's so open."

Tasha nods. She thinks back to the first few days after the Change; skittering along walls and hiding behind dumpsters, bobbing and weaving through a parking lot warzone. Her fear of open spaces has not disappeared—indeed, she feels the hungry moths of it fluttering in her stomach under layers of sub sandwich—but she's quelled it out of necessity. Fear only adds more lead to the legs: running down Lakeshore Drive had been taxing enough with a backpack full of canned goods and no sports bra (or shirt). Fear is like love: it complicates things. Tasha doesn't know how to say these things to Z, so instead she pinches Z's arm awkwardly and says,

"It'll be fine. This kid doesn't seem too worried, right? I mean, look at him: he's like twelve, if that. And he's not even scared! He's, like, chilling. I'm sure wherever he's taking us is safer than the Web. I mean if you think about it, we're safer just by, like, geographical location." She babbles in her effort to be positive. "We're on the South Side, right? This is where we were trying to get. Plus Malakai said himself that there aren't even that many Minkers down here."

Malakai looks over his shoulder.

"There's not," he says.

"See?"

Z looks reassured. Her face has relaxed and her shoulders fall a little. Tasha remembers reassuring Vette, just before their encounter with the bride and groom. It had been so true coming out of her mouth, then transformed into a lie seconds later. It all seems like a lifetime ago. Z looks at Malakai, who is still twirling the shovel artfully.

"Geez," she says, watching its arc, "was this kid a drum major or what?"

Malakai leads them up a walkway to a two-story building with old-school concrete molding around the doorway and windows. Tasha can't tell if it's a house or an apartment building. It's gated, and Malakai walks rights up, uncoiling the heavy chain from around the posts.

"No lock?" Z asks.

"Nah," he says, standing aside to let them pass through first, "they're not too good with opening stuff. The chain is enough."

After he succeeds in re-wrapping the chain around the posts, which he does carefully and studiously, he leads them up the path to the porch, which is wide and decorated with various potted and hanging plants. It reminds Tasha distinctly of Louisville. In front of the door is a welcome mat, with an image of a smiling cat stitched beside the Welcome. Beside it is a pair of muddy soccer cleats, the laces orange.

"Oh good," Malakai says, seeing the shoes, "my brother's home."

He reaches for the doorknob, but the door is already swinging inward, a tall figure standing to the side of the entrance to allow them in. It's Ishmael.

CHAPTER 24

Twenty minutes later Ishmael is ladling soup into bowls for them, telling them what happened at the stadium while Tasha and Vette were gone to gather food.

"We were out on the field," he says, "moving the bodies into a locker room. We'd been meaning to do it for awhile, but no one was really up for it. Anyway, we were out there moving them when Jeremy—Number Sixteen—comes running, screaming that they found a way in. Sure enough, they had. I don't know how. They're not good with doors and stuff like that. You know. But they were in the stadium, about sixteen or seventeen of them. Way too many for us. I knew there were probably even more where they came from, so me and Jeremy starting telling everybody to go back to the storage room. Everyone was running. The...people with the implant were running too. Some of them are faster than you'd think.

"One caught up with Jeremy and got him on the ground, but I didn't realize it right away. By the time I looked back and got to him, there was one on his leg and one on his neck."

At this point he looks at Malakai.

"Malakai, go put the ladies' bags in the guest room."

Malakai hesitates. Tasha doesn't see Ishmael bat an eye, but she knows some unspoken signal has passed between them, and Malakai takes Tasha and Z's bags, carrying them upstairs without a word. Ishmael sets the two bowls of soup in front of them on the table with salt and pepper shakers. The shakers are in the shape of sheep, one black and one white. Tasha reaches for the pepper. The sheep's eyes are painted on round. She stares into them as Ishmael resumes his story. *Baa*, she bleats silently at the pepper.

"I got them off of Jeremy, but I didn't have anything to kill them with. So I just grabbed him and we kept running. It was hard as hell getting him up those stairs.

"When we got to the storage room the rest of the team was gone. The door was open. They just…left. I guess I can't blame them. Maybe they thought we were right behind them."

Tasha says to herself that the only thing the team was probably worried about was whether the Minkers were right behind them.

"In the storage room I guess one of our guys must have slammed up against the door on the way out. Broke the handle. Jeremy was on the floor. There was a lot of blood. He told me to leave him. It felt…really bad. It felt bad. But he told me to go. I think he was dead before I even left the room. When I got outside, I didn't see anyone, none of the team. There was a crowd of sick people to the north but they didn't see me. I ran."

"Where?" Tasha thinks they must have barely missed each other.

"South. Took Lakeshore to Montrose, then over to Broadway. I ran into a bunch of them there. I broke into a lot and took a scooter, rode that on Broadway until it turned into Clark, then Clark to Roosevelt and over to State. I charged it in the train station. Had a nasty little incident with a Driver while I was waiting," he adds, shaking his head.

"Then I came here. Malakai thought I was dead." He pauses, gathering his thoughts, before finally, slowly, turning his eyes to Tasha.

"Where's Vette?"

Tasha tells him. It's more difficult than when she told Z—Ishmael had known Vette, had run alongside her in the sun, had high-fived her, had known her last name. Tasha watches his face crumple as she tells the story of his friend's death. She doesn't go into detail, hoping she doesn't sound cold, monstrous. A monstress. She doesn't tell him that she left a chocolate crucifix on his teammate's chest. He might not understand—might mistake the gesture for mockery and not tenderness. Besides, Vette's memories of her grade school flame and his bouquets of Snickers bars might have been a secret only for Tasha. Tasha will keep her secret.

"It's so fucked up," Ishmael says, his fist against his forehead. He turns back to the stove. Tasha knows this kind of speechless grief from her father, the dam built hastily before tears. Conversation over.

Tasha and Z eat their soup, and Tasha stares at Ishmael's

322 OLIVIA A. COLE

back. If he had just waited a little longer at the stadium, she wouldn't have had to travel alone. They could have mourned Vette together. Tasha also wishes she had thought of stealing a scooter—or a car—sooner. Her calves would be a lot less sore, her Nikes less scuffed, and she would have gotten South a lot quicker. But then she might not have met Z. Or run into Malakai. Or have been able to eat this soup, which is tasty. She looks into the broth, which is the color of honey but tastes like chicken. It's thick with barley and carrots and pieces of celery, punctuated with flecks of black pepper. Tasha looks up at Ishmael, hoping to extract him from his misery.

"How are you cooking this? The electricity is out, right?"

She looks around. What's left of the daylight illuminates the kitchen, but the many unlit candles perched on various surfaces tell her that when the sun goes down, the house sees by candlelight. She takes in the kitchen while she can. The floor is graying white linoleum squares with pale green diamonds at the vertices. It needs to be washed, but it's not filthy. The table where she's sitting is small and square with neat wooden chairs; an empty bowl is the centerpiece. There's a vase on the windowsill with dead flowers sprouting out of murky water. They might have been roses; it's hard to tell in their browned and withered state. The refrigerator is tall and silent, covered with magnets and notes and a calendar with a picture of cats wearing hats. It's turned to April, various pre-Change dates circled: dentist appointments, lunch dates, anniversaries.

"It's an old gas stove. As long as I have matches I can light the pilot. How's the soup?"

"It's really good," says Z, wiping her mouth with the cloth napkin he'd given her. "Tastes like something my grandmother would have made."

Ishmael laughs, and bows slightly.

"My mother's recipe," he says. "Malakai helped."

Malakai appears in the kitchen, grinning. Tasha thinks he must have been listening at the door. He looks at Tasha and Z expectantly, reminding Tasha very much of a Border Collie waiting to be told what a good boy he is.

"It's good soup," Tasha offers.

"Great soup," Z adds.

This seems to satisfy him and he sits at the table with them, watching as Ishmael fills two more bowls.

"Is it just you two here?" Tasha asks. She knows Ishmael had worried about the safety of his mother. He mentioned her only a moment ago in regard to the soup—calmly; not with the heavy grief she would expect from someone who had only recently found out that his mother had been eaten by crazed, roaming fiends. He seems content, or close.

Ishmael sits at the table with them, scooting one of the bowls he's brought with him toward Malakai.

"Just me and Malakai now. We sent our mom West yesterday with our older brother Marcus."

"West?" Z says with interest. "Like, the West Side?" Tasha knows she's probably thinking of her father.

Ishmael shakes his head.

"No, farther than that."

"...Downers Grove?"

He laughs.

"No, even farther. California."

"California? As in, the Nation? Of California?" Tasha feels a little dizzy. Are they flying? She hasn't heard a jet in weeks. Driving? They couldn't possibly be walking.

Ishmael nods.

"Lots of people have gone," Malakai pipes up. "The whole block is pretty much empty at this point."

"Just gone?" says Tasha. "How?"

"They go in groups. It's a long trip, obviously. The group that went yesterday—with our mom—was about forty people."

"Wait, they're *walking*?" Z has been wondering the same thing as Tasha.

"Yeah," says Malakai. "Crazy, right? They start off in cars, but those don't get them all the way there. Cuz the batteries die. So eventually everybody walks. We haven't heard from anyone after they've left. The first group left the day after everything happened, so Ishmael says they're probably only in Iowa. If that."

"So people are walking. To California." Tasha almost laughs.

"Manifest destiny, baby," Ishmael grins. Tasha smiles back, without really knowing why. It's not funny; it's insane. But she's seen enough insanity in the past week to be unsurprised by the idea of groups of people walking all the way from Chicago, Illinois to the Nation of California. She imagines them in long strings, pulling cargo—a new incarnation of the Oregon Trail. What are they seeking? Gold? Opportunity? Freedom? The story has changed with every generation—eventually it melted down to fame, plastic surgery. California's secession meant an interruption of the great American journey, but now it has begun again. Tasha wonders how many other cities have had the same idea, how many survivors have packed their bags and struck out West, inspired by a rumor?

"What do they think they're going to find when they get there?" Z asks. "If they get there. I mean, seriously, how many miles of walking is that? Hundreds. Thousands."

Tasha doesn't contribute, but she looks to Ishmael for his answer. Z's right. It's more than just a long walk. How long would something like that even take? She hopes the people from Ishmael's block have packed extra pairs of shoes. And good shoes. Payless brand wouldn't cut it.

"We heard there's no sick people in California," says Malakai.

"We heard that too," Z says after draining her bowl of broth. "But there have to be a bunch of them between here and there. I bet Denver's crawling with them."

"The Shepherd says the big cities are the worst," Malakai says. "He says if we can stay away from the big cities, we can make it there in a few months."

"The who? The *shepherd*?" Tasha raises her eyebrow, ready to be scornful.

"Who's the shepherd?" Z is equally judgmental, but slightly more curious.

Malakai is pleased that he's said something that interests them both.

326 OLIVIA A. COLE

"Yeah, sure. He lives a few blocks from here. He's the one who's been organizing the groups going West. The cops were after him before the Change. His cousin hid him in the basement of a church for awhile. No one really knows how long."

"Okay, well who is he?"

"He's a hero," Malakai gushes. "He could have left when this whole thing happened but instead he stayed and helped people. He's been giving people food and showing them how to kill the sick people. The Chipped people. And stuff."

Outside there's a sound, which Tasha at first interprets as the peaceful tinkling of a wind chime on the front porch, the gentle clink of glass against metal. Malakai stops talking and Ishmael is up from the table and at the window before Tasha can begin to comment. Ishmael parts the blinds with two fingers, peering through the glass into the evening that has darkened, his body only inches from Tasha's face where she still sits at the table. He smells like earth turned with a spade and the soup he'd spent the evening stirring.

"What's going on?" she says to muffle her impulse to ask what cologne he wears.

Malakai has backed over to the stove and has made no move to join his brother at the window. His back is pressed against the kitchen counter, Tasha notices, and pushing. If he could melt in with the ceramic and disappear, he would.

"How many?" The kid's voice trembles only a little, but he's scared. He'd seemed so fearless on the playground, the way Z had seemed so fearless in the Web. There are conditions to bravery, Tasha thinks. The playground is a kid's kingdom, Malakai's; the Web was Z's. Where would Tasha need to be to become a lionheart?

"Just two." Ishmael backs away from the window. "Excuse me," he says to Z, and takes a hoodie from the back of the chair she sits in. He puts it on. It's gray and says University of Chicago on the front. Tasha wonders what he majored in.

"Do you want me to come?" Malakai says.

"No."

"Do you want me to come?" Tasha says.

"Everybody stay here."

He goes to the front door. Tasha, Z and Malakai follow him to the foyer and stare from the entrance of the kitchen like wide-eyed puppies. On the table just inside the front door is a flashlight. Ishmael takes it in hand and, moving the blinds aside, shines it onto the street out front, clicking it on and off three times. He pauses and Tasha sees an answering three flashes from one of the gated houses across the road.

"Mr. Jackson," Ishmael says to nobody.

He puts down the flashlight and takes up something Tasha hasn't noticed until now, leaning in the corner behind the door. An axe.

He opens the door and leaves without saying a word. As soon as it clicks shut behind him, Tasha, Z and Malakai move quickly back into the kitchen where the view is better, peering out onto the dim street.

Ishmael is just closing the front gate, rewrapping it dutifully with the chain before walking out onto the street. Sure enough, two Minkers stagger around nearby. Across the way, Tasha sees a figure leave another yard and walk in a straight line toward Ishmael and the Minkers—Mr. Jackson.

Ishmael carries the axe easily but lets it hang almost straight toward the ground, his body relaxed. He makes a wide circle around the two Minkers, who are just beginning to notice him. Tasha hears the muted bark of one, her flesh prickling as if the creature called her name. Ishmael walks over to Mr. Jackson, who carries what appears to be a knife about the size of Tasha's Wusthof. Mr. Jackson is forty-something as far as she can tell, wearing what might be a raincoat. Tasha's nearly-healed bicep wound gives a phantom throb. A raincoat would be good protection from seeking teeth.

The two men stand close together and confer, taking a few steps away from the now-approaching Minkers. Tasha realizes Malakai is gripping her wrist. She lets him. Z just stares, her hands knitted together as if praying.

Ishmael and Mr. Jackson separate quickly, a plan made, much like Z and Tasha did in the Web when they first met. Instead of following suit, the Minkers both follow Mr. Jackson. Mr. Jackson jogs away and arcs back toward Ishmael. It's a game of tag. The Minkers both follow gamely, speeding up their stumbling pace. Tasha feels like her brain is commentating a football game. *He goes wide! He's bringing it home!*

The Minkers are both barking as they close in on Mr. Jackson, celebrating what they think will be an easy kill. Ishmael raises the axe once and delivers a vicious, sidelong slice that takes one of the heads clean off.

Tasha can imagine the sound the head makes hitting the ground—a solid wet thunk like a watermelon. Mr. Jackson hasn't dealt with the other Minker yet. He circles it, waving his hands, until Ishmael approaches again and swings the axe one more time. Another watermelon hits the pavement.

Ishmael stands with the axe gripped in his right hand, breathing heavily from the looks of his rising and falling chest. He and Mr. Jackson exchange a few words before Mr. Jackson goes to kneel by the bodies, crouching down with his knife held like a pencil. Tasha assumes he's fiddling with the Chip: she had done the same thing early in the Change, wanting to be sure they were dead and perhaps exact some petty posthumous revenge. She sees a spark in the dusk as Mr. Jackson pops out the implant—Ishmael's axe must not have hit it in the chop. Then he puts the Chips into the pocket of his raincoat.

The two men put down their weapons and squat by the bodies, hoisting them up and carrying them one by one to a house two doors down from Mr. Jackson, entering the front yard. There's no chain on its front gate. Tasha assumes this means there's no one there left to protect. From Ishmael's kitchen window, she can just hear the gate swing open with a rusty yelp.

"That's where they put the bodies," Malakai says, unblinking.

Neither Z nor Tasha respond.

The two men return to the kill site and talk a second longer. Mr. Jackson is pointing at his chest and then putting one hand on top of his head. Ishmael shrugs and hands over the axe he had retrieved. He bends over one more time and then makes another trip to the house two doors down. He's carrying the heads.

When Ishmael enters his own house again, he's carrying the axe as if it's dragged downward by some alien gravity. Tasha, Malakai and Z stand wordlessly in the kitchen door as he returns the axe to the corner behind the door and strips off the hoodie. There's only a little blood on the sleeve. A moment passes before Tasha realizes he's crying.

"Who were they?" says Malakai, his voice sounding like what it is: a small boy's.

"Mrs. Lockhart from two blocks over. The other I didn't recognize. His nametag said Gary. He worked at White Castle."

"Oh darn," Z says with a weak smile. "I could've asked for some chicken rings."

Ishmael stares at her as if she's willfully thrown a baseball through a church window.

"Why does Mr. Jackson take the Chips?" Tasha wants to diffuse the sudden tension, but she also wants to know.

Ishmael rubs his face with his arm and sniffs, turning away from Z.

"He keeps them as evidence for when all this is over. He's a lawyer. Says he's going to sue Cybranu on behalf of Chicago, and the police too for not protecting us."

Tasha feels a laugh bubble up in her throat. Or it could be vomit. Either way, she swallows it and coughs slightly.

"He knows the cops have Chips too, right?"

"I've told him."

"So he thinks this will pass."

"Yes."

Tasha's eyes burn a little; she's not sure why. Hearing her own buried hopes—Dinah's hopes, Z's hopes—out loud and knowing they're absurd is like a headbutt to the gut. She wonders what Z is feeling; Z who hopes even harder, and out loud.

"Do you?" she asks.

Ishmael rubs his stubble, the patchy beard of a man who's younger than he seems. He walks over to Malakai, who is standing motionless between Tasha and Z. Ishmael puts his hands on the kid's shoulders, two pairs of brown eyes staring into one another. Ishmael touches his brother's cheek before he answers.

"No."

CHAPTER 25

Tasha wakes in a yellow room on a bed she shares with Z, who is still sleeping. After the events of the night before, there had been a quiet agreement to go to bed early. Ishmael had led Tasha and Z up the narrow staircase, lit by the same flashlight he had used to signal Mr. Jackson. Ishmael and Malakai slept together down the hall. Some blurred part of her was glad that none of them were sleeping alone. Tasha and Z's room was small and warm. They hadn't even crawled under the covers.

Tasha looks around the room. The paint is fairly new, a cheerful sunshiny color whose full effect is muted by the drawn drapes. A bedside table on Z's side bears a straight lamp with a green shade. The body of the lamp, with leaves growing out of its sides, was made to resemble a vine. Or a flower, she thinks, if the shade is seen as a blossom. Besides the bed and the table, the room contains a dresser and two doors, one leading to the hall and one opening to a closet. The dresser is crowded with picture frames. Tasha rises as softly as she can and pads over to it. She doesn't remember taking her shoes off the night before, but they're off.

The pictures are family photos. One is of Malakai, several years younger, wearing the tasseled uniform of the marching band, smiling a small smile like the one she has seen him offer to Ishmael. *Ha*, she thinks, *I knew he was in the band.*

Another is of Malakai, Ishmael, and another man, a year or two older than Ishmael. This must be Marcus. He looks more like Malakai than Ishmael, but with Ishmael's straight back and wide shoulders. Those will come to Malakai when he's a little older, she knows.

A third picture catches her eye, of Ishmael and a smallish, smiling woman. Her hair is soft and only a little gray. She wears a black suit. Not a Driver's suit; just a suit. Her smile is Malakai's, and Ishmael's, and Marcus's. Tasha wonders what it would be like, being a woman surrounded by sons who share her face.

"Hey, snoopy."

Tasha almost drops the picture frame, which she's been holding to get a closer look. She sets it down carefully and turns to Z, who is propped up on an elbow.

"Good morning to you too. You scared the shit out of me."

"I do what I can." Z cranes her neck. "What were you looking at?"

"Pictures of the guys and their mom."

"Let me see."

Tasha brings the frame with the three brothers together and the one with Ishmael and his mother.

334 OLIVIA A. COLE

"Oh, she's so pretty," Z says, studying the picture. "They all look so much alike. Especially Malakai and…what's the older one's name?"

"Marcus."

"Marcus."

She studies them a moment longer, then hands them back to Tasha, who returns them to the shelf.

"So what do you think?"

Tasha returns to the bed, leaning against the headboard.

"I don't know," she says. "I mean, we're here. There's so much I didn't know."

Z nods.

"People walking to California! It's crazy. I mean, it would take forever. If I was them I'd take a scooter or two just in case. You know, maybe they could find a hook-up somewhere along the way."

"Would you really want to ride a scooter across the country?" Tasha laughs. "Your ass would be so sore."

"That's true. But it's either that or your feet."

"Yeah."

"Good thing I wore Nikes and not my uniform shoes."

"Planning on going with them?"

"Hey, I'm keeping my options open. The cavalry may not come."

Tasha thinks she hears a touch of shadow in Z's voice. The events of last night—the conversation about Mr. Jackson—it must have sunken in through the hope like rain into soil. It dampens everything.

Tasha changes her underwear and puts on deodorant. There's a mirror on the back of the closet door and Tasha avoids it purposefully. She fluffs her hair. She can feel its wildness. Okay, maybe just a glance. She approaches the mirror like a shrinking cur.

There she is. Brown and somewhat elongated by the mirror's warp, her hair an explosion around her skull. She fluffs it again, works out a tangle or two with her fingers. There's not really much that can be done without a big comb and a hair-tie. She finds herself smiling. The circles under her eyes are present as they always are, but she's more interested in the eyes themselves. Whatever mascara had been left on her lashes is now a thin line of smudge under her eyes, the lashes bare. Without the mascara, her eyes seem softer. She uses the insides of her index fingers to wipe away the last traces of it. She runs a finger over her lips, which need Chapstick. Her skin is a little dry.

"I have Vaseline," says Z, holding up the little jar. "Want some?"

"That'd be great, thanks."

Z tosses the jar and Tasha catches it, turning back to the mirror. She rubs some over her mouth and a little more onto her face. Her skin is shiny now. She holds the jar, the lid off, staring at her reflection. Is this her real face? She looks for a mask in this reflection but can't find it.

"He's cute, right?" says Z, grinning a little.

Tasha isn't sure she's heard the whole sentence and darts

her eyes at Z in the mirror.

"Who?"

"Ishmael, duh. I'm not talking about Malakai. He's a *child*. What kind of perv do you think I am?"

Tasha puts the lid back on the Vaseline and tosses it back to Z.

"Yeah. He's cute."

"I'd even call him a hottie. I see why you were worried about him, a fine specimen like that."

Tasha laughs. Z sounds so much like Gina—the best parts of Gina.

"I would agree with that."

She's glad when there's a knock on the door.

"Come in," Z calls.

It's Malakai. He peeps around the doorjamb and his eyes sweep over the room before settling on Tasha. He's probably seeing if there are bras or anything lying around, she thinks. Ahh, puberty.

"Hey," he says.

"Hey...," Z replies, laughing when he doesn't say anything else.

"Ish is making food if you guys want some."

"Yeah, sure. We'll be right down."

He closes the door as slowly as humanly possible and Tasha laughs quietly.

"Boys," she says, and Z nods.

Downstairs, Ishmael is stirring around cubed potatoes in a

skillet on the stove. There are peppers in the mixture as well, and onions.

"What's up," he says as Z and Tasha wander into the kitchen. "How was your night? I hope Malakai didn't wake you up with his snoring."

He's cheerful. Smoothing over last night, Tasha assumes. She wonders if he's embarrassed at all that they had seen him crying. He hadn't seemed ashamed at the time. It makes her like him.

"I don't snore!" Malakai calls from the next room.

"It was fine," Tasha says, "very quiet."

"It's an old house," he says, dishing the potatoes out onto plates. "Built in 1980, I think."

"Whoa. That's old as hell," Z says, looking around at the walls and ceiling with new interest, like she's looking for priceless antiques or the Holy Grail.

"Still standing," he says, making another plate. "My dad made a lot of improvements to it before he died."

Tasha chews the potatoes, nodding. "It's beautiful."

He gestures to the food.

"Sorry it's so weak. It's hard to make breakfast just using canned food and all that. No eggs, no cheese, no meat. We've been eating a lot of potatoes."

"No, it's good, don't worry. Thanks for cooking."

"No doubt. Malakai, come eat!"

After breakfast, Tasha and Z convince Ishmael to let them wash the dishes. As the sink fills with filmy white suds, the strangeness of the world settles around her like the fog when waking up from a dream. She scrubs the last sticking potato from a plate. At the Web she and Z had cleared the floors one by one; here, Ishmael clears his block. Then they eat. They sleep. They wash hands and make conversation, they smile at each other. Then, if necessary, they kill again. She hands the last clean plate to Z to dry, turning off the water and flicking her wet fingers into the sink. Anything could be next. She feels as if she's lived a thousand years. Ishmael reenters the kitchen with Malakai on his heels.

"We're going on an errand in a few minutes. Do you want to come?"

"An errand?" Z laughs. "Meaning? Going to pick up a movie? Go shopping? If you could grab me some Doritos while you're out, that would be great."

Ishmael half-smiles. Tasha briefly, almost defensively, wonders if he's annoyed by Z's sass.

"Actually we're going a couple blocks down," he says. "Remember last night we told you about the guy who is organizing people for the walk to California?"

"The Shepherd," Malakai inserts.

The term "shepherd" doesn't sit right with Tasha. It's a little too blatantly messianic. She wonders if this mystery herder dubbed himself as the Shepherd, or if it was bestowed on him by his flocking followers. Surely he knows that one can't give oneself a nickname, she thinks. It's deeply lame.

"Yes, him," Ishmael says patiently. Tasha hopes his tone means he thinks the moniker is lame too. "We're going over to help him with a caravan that's leaving tomorrow—preparing provisions, thinking about logistics, all that." He pauses. "You can come if you want."

Tasha looks at Z, who nods.

"Yeah, sure. Let me get my backpack."

"It's not far, right?" she hears Z ask as she heads for the stairs.

"Only a couple blocks. We're going to walk. Don't worry, we probably won't see any action."

Upstairs, Tasha picks up her backpack from where she left it on the bed. She doesn't really need it, just the knife, but she doesn't feel comfortable leaving it behind. There are things in it she has come to depend on, namely the can opener, and if she's separated from these people too—it's possible—she doesn't want to be without her stuff.

She wonders if Z needs her bag, and goes to where it sits on the floor. It's a black nylon thing that Tasha imagines the FBI carted drugs around in. She picks it up, and something flutters to the floor. Stooping to retrieve it, she sees it's a photograph. She's almost afraid to look—her own photographs are people she has lost. But she looks anyway. It's a handsome young man, his hair black and shaggy, a mole on his cheek. His smile is even and broad. He looks remarkably like Z. He wears a uniform, all white, a Navy man. His arm is around a girl's shoulders, her hair styled high, her slight figure wrapped in a pink dress. It's Z. She's a little younger, but it's her. Tasha flips it over, but there's no date. The picture was taken with a high-end camera like Tasha's father's: the image is crisp and bright, their smiles glowing. The photograph itself has been taken care of: its edges are neat and unwrinkled. Tasha puts it back in the bag, from where she supposes it fell.

Downstairs, Ishmael receives her with a nod.

"Ready? We're going out the back door."

Ishmael's mother's house has a backyard as well as a front one, and a snug back porch screened in to keep out bugs. The backyard doesn't have a garden like the neighbor's; instead there's a birdbath at the center with a narrow concrete path leading to it and lots of flowers. The flowers take Tasha by surprise. She's lost track of the days and suddenly it's spring. It's May, she knows. Sometime in May. Even with the strange weather, and even in Chicago, there are flowers in May. Tasha has the urge to stop and smell them as the group passes through the yard, but she knows this is stupid. Instead she trails her fingers along a row of tulips, their heads bobbing in her wake.

The back gate is tall and wooden, a privacy fence. Tasha thinks it's more likely that the Minkers would mistake it for a wall, but it has a chain wrapped around its posts too. As they approach it, Ishmael kneels, knitting his fingers together. Malakai steps into the web of his brother's hands and Ishmael hoists him up until Malakai's fingers curl over the top of the fence. He peers over the top, looking around, then says "Okay" and Ishmael brings him down. They open the gates, and the group moves into the alley.

The alley behind Perry Avenue is less pleasant than Perry Avenue itself, which had been neat and cute. The alley is narrow and cluttered with trash bins and the rusty skeletons of old bicycles. There are bodies here, too, always bodies. They pass a young man around Tasha's age, staring blankly up at the sky.

Malakai looks at the body, then away.

"He used to sell break," he says, referring to the hybrid drug developed in the '20s, an amalgamation of crack and household chemicals. "We weren't too upset when we saw that the Minkers got him."

They continue down the alley until it opens onto another street, 78th Place. It's a short lane that lacks the charm of Perry Avenue, but there are more trees: old trees, not like the dogwood saplings on Berwyn in Tasha's neighborhood. She doesn't know what kind they are—she vaguely recognizes some of the leaves as oak or maple. She wonders if the giraffes she let loose in Lincoln Park are somewhere happily munching on similar flora. You're welcome, she thinks.

Ishmael turns again, and they follow him onto Lafayette, a broader street from which they can see the L. Like at Berwyn, a train is stopped on one of the four sets of tracks, its doors open. There's another train too, not the L: the Metralux, a high-speed bullet of a machine that had carried Chicagoans as far as Florida. Somehow it's come off the tracks entirely, and has crossed over multiple lanes where other trains would have been had traffic conditions been less fortunate. Malakai sees her looking and says,

"It was really loud when that happened. Mom thought something exploded. It kind of did. It burned for awhile."

Tasha can't imagine a train burning fifty yards from her

house. She thinks of the intense silence of the first few days of the Change, how she'd holed up inside her apartment like a mole, cleaning her burrow as if it really mattered. What a joke.

They come to a corner on Lafayette with two garages facing the street. Tasha gets the feeling that nothing has changed on this block in decades. Close to the garages is a bus stop, after all. There are zero buses in her neighborhood; the Volamus and trains take people where they need to go. But the city neglected this part of town in most ways, and public transportation was no exception.

Ishmael approaches the garage on the right and stoops to raise its door a foot or so. Malakai rolls under and Ishmael uses his head to beckon to Z and Tasha, who do the same. When they're under, Malakai holds the door while Ishmael rolls in, and together they lower it quietly.

The garage is dim and smells vaguely of an old smell it takes Tasha a moment to recognize: gasoline. Her parents' house had a shed that smelled like this: gasoline and wood, and the sharp odor of metal. She also, inexplicably, smells peanuts. What else? She sniffs. Tar. Cabbage. Sweat. In all, very unpleasant.

Ishmael leads them through the low light to a small staircase, at the top of which is a white door. He raps on it, and it opens almost immediately.

At the top of the stairs, peering out from his kitchen where Tasha smells tea or perhaps coffee, is an average-sized man of sixty-five or so. He's the color of an almond and wears almond-shaped glasses sitting on the bridge of a nose that might have been broken when he was a younger man. He looks serene.

Probably because of his fine curly hair, Tasha thinks. At his age she would think it'd be thinning by now, but it's not. He wears a black cardigan sweater with pockets and three buttons holding it closed over the slightest of potbellies. At first glance, he is a great-uncle. A piano teacher. But Tasha looks into his eyes, which are sweeping over the little crowd in his garage, eyeing them like a sparrowhawk. He is sharp, fierce. His spectacles could be X-ray vision goggles, disguised on his neat, studious face.

"Guys," Ishmael says, standing to the side to allow Tasha and Z first entrance, "this is Dr. Rio."

CHAPTER 26

"The Shepherd," Malakai says from behind them. "Oh, Malakai, I wish you wouldn't call me that," Dr. Rio says, standing to one side to allow the small party entrance.

"Why not?" the kid says, looking gloomy. "That's what everybody else calls you."

"Everybody else," Dr. Rio bustles into the kitchen and takes a pot off the stove—tea—, "does not know me as well as you know me. So Dr. Rio will suffice."

"Okay," says Malakai. He's cheered. He's in a secret club.

Tasha remains close to the garage door, attempting to keep her face as flat as an ironed shirt and hoping Z—whose eyes are darting to and from Tasha's face—has the sense to do the same. She's standing in the kitchen of Dr. Rio, watching him pour tea. For some reason it's like meeting the mayor, or a local celebrity: she feels like she should be asking for his autograph, rushing up and fawning over him. *I've heard all about you*, she could say, *I love your work*. But she hasn't, and she doesn't. She knows nothing about him other than her sister wrote his name in slanting, urgent letters on a torn piece of paper, telling her to find him. Well, she found him. And although his kitchen smells nice and he doesn't appear to be dangerous, Tasha thinks she'll play her cards slowly and quietly for now.

Dr. Rio turns from pouring tea into a mug. Not one of those mugs that releases sugar and whatever else into the drink from the base of the cup—just a mug. He looks at Tasha and Z appraisingly—a hint of the sparrowhawk gaze from a moment before—over the top of his spectacles. Tasha notices that he holds his left hand in an almost-ball: the fingers bent as if ready to become a fist at any moment, or to grasp a tool which might become a weapon.

"Who are your guests, boys?" he says.

"These are some friends I reconnected with, Tasha and Z," says Ishmael from the other side of the kitchen, where he leans against the counter. "They gave Malakai a ride home."

"A ride?"

"We had a car," says Z, "but it didn't last very long."

"Ahh, like most machines, my dear," the doctor laughs.

Tasha studies his spectacles, which have slid a little lower on his nose. They add to his doctorly appearance, but they're elegant. She wonders if a wife helped pick them out.

"Does anyone want tea?" he asks, turning back to the stove, the almost-fist opening to reach for another mug.

No one wants any, so they all move into the living room, which is carpeted with low beige shag and is filled with chairs. There's a couch too, but where a coffee table and end tables might have been are several recliners, a cluster of kitchen chairs, three barstools, and five or six folding chairs. The walls are covered with maps and charts, some of them dotted with lines and the curving paths of red pens.

"Come, sit with me," he says. Tasha chooses a green corduroy recliner that's about as old as Ishmael's house, her backpack on her knees. The chair envelops her. It's not quite comfortable—she feels too sunken in—but she doesn't want to be awkward and move to another spot, so she stays put, flexing her legs a little to keep the armchair from swallowing her.

"Do these girls want to leave with the penultimate group the day after tomorrow?" Dr. Rio asks Ishmael, sipping his tea.

"Oh," Ishmael looks at Z and Tasha, who look back. "No. I mean, I don't think so. We haven't really talked about it. I think we'd all rather stay together, at least for awhile?" He says it as a question, directing it at Tasha.

"I think we'd all rather stay together, at least for awhile," she repeats.

Z nods. Tasha wonders how much thought she's given it, if she's made any decisions, if she still wishes she were in the Web.

"I still want to go with you," Malakai says to Dr. Rio. He's sitting closest to the older man.

"I would like that. You and your brother have been a lot of help with this project of mine. I'm sure the neighborhoods are grateful too. But as you know, there are more things that need taking care of before we go West ourselves on Sunday."

Sunday. So soon.

"What's today?" Tasha interjects.

"Today is Thursday," says Dr. Rio. He says it calmly. "We're sending a group on Saturday, and I plan to leave with the last group on Sunday. I imagine Ishmael and Malakai have told you both about the chosen course of action most citizens around here have taken?"

Tasha nods.

"West," she says. Every time she says it she feels like a cowboy, or a gold miner. She feels like that kid in the *True Grit* remake, gone West to avenge her father. It was one of her grandmother's favorites. Maybe this Dr. Rio is her Rooster Cogburn.

"Yes, West," Rio replies, looking up at the map behind him on the wall. "We laid out the route all together in this room. We haven't put away all the chairs yet, forgive me." He sweeps his hand at the clutter.

"What's the route?" Z asks him. Tasha knows she's concerned about the distance, but Tasha herself is not. How hard could it be, really? As long as you have a compass, and water, and shoes, you just walk due West and eventually you end up in California. Eventually. Leona glows like a beacon at the end of the red lines snaking across the map.

Dr. Rio rises, still clutching his mug. He drags his finger along the map, following a previously drawn line.

"Due West from Illinois into Iowa, on into Nebraska, a little south into Colorado, avoiding Denver, across into Utah, staying south of Salt Lake City, all the way across Nevada, and into California."

"That easy, huh," laughs Z.

Dr. Rio smiles placidly back.

"Not easily done, but able to be done," he says. "It is able to be done."

Tasha thinks of him marching from god knows where all the way to Illinois to warn his hometown of the impending doom. He's already walked halfway across the country, she thinks, assuming he walked. Why not walk all the way back? He's an older man, but he's in excellent shape: all his hair, all his teeth, all his brain cells. And all that without the Chip. Take that, Cybranu.

Dr. Rio takes his seat again.

"Ishmael and Malakai will be coming with me Sunday. We'll be just under two weeks behind the very first group. We've been keeping a good schedule."

"Has everyone down here gone?" Tasha asks him.

"No, not everyone. Some believe the trip is too long, or that they are too old or their children too young to make it. I understand. But I am not a young man either," he laughs, "and I think I can make it."

"How many have gone so far?"

"Oh," he rubs his temple, very much the harmless piano teacher. "Quite a few of us, as you might have gathered from the emptiness around here. Of course, many are simply hiding. I've heard of other neighborhoods packing up and walking, too, although I don't know what their aim is. On our part, another thirty on Saturday, then the last group Sunday. So you do the math. Quite a few of us."

"How many have stayed?"

Dr. Rio sighs.

"Everyone else. Everyone without the Chip, of course, and everyone who's not dead. They see what has happened but don't want to leave what they have here: their homes, their property, their possessions." He sighs again.

"You think they're naïve."

"I think they believe they have more than they do," he replies, leaning forward in the chair so it creaks. Tasha glances at his left hand, still in its claw-like almost-fist. "And I don't blame them. We were raised in a world that convinced us to trick ourselves into believing that the more things we owned, the safer we would be, the happier we would be. We have come to believe we have more than there is to be gained by abandoning what we have. This is a lie. We have nothing."

Tasha thinks, as she often has, of the emptiness of the city since the Change. Ghostly, as if the enemy were aliens instead, zapping Chicagoans up into hulking spaceships, leaving no trace of their former human existences. Tasha wonders if there will be a study of all this one day, if anyone survives. Will they have data on how many suicides affected the population after the Change? There have probably been a lot. As for death by actual attacks, she thinks the number of Minkers is modest, based on the amount of people who could afford MINK in the time Before, the number of people that were rejected—then again there were the worker types who got it through their corporate jobs and didn't necessarily qualify on income alone. However large the actual Minker multitude, they seem to be eating their way through the unChipped population pretty adroitly. She imagines the average citizen simply didn't know how to defend herself. Tasha sure as hell didn't. Luckily she's a fast learner.

Dr. Rio has continued speaking, and Tasha emerges from her thoughts.

"And what's more, what we had and have now lost due to this catastrophe, we will not get back. Look around," he waves the left hand, which is tightening into a stone. "If it wasn't for that gas stove, I'd be eating canned fruit. And only if I have a can opener in that kitchen. Is a can opener worth staying in Chicago for?"

Tasha's brain says *Amen*, but she's reluctant to become a disciple so easily. Besides, while she thinks she agrees with most of Dr. Rio's speech, his hand distracts her from the sermon. The almost-fist has evolved into a tightly clenched rock, the veins under the light brown skin beginning to pulse. The hand has a life of its own. He goes on.

"This isn't Chicago." He's shaking his head and looking at the empty chairs that crowd his living room, a ghost audience, and she feels as if she's heard this before. "This isn't the city we built by the lake, then burned, then built. This isn't our city. Chicago is extinct. This is the city of the dodo."

The dodo. Who is the dodo? Is the girl in the yellow dress the flightless bird of history—dead, gone? Is it Dinah, a fossil in a cage? Or is it Tasha, walking through a world of tall bones, pretending there's still life in them? She thinks of walking toward the Web on Michigan Avenue, the carcasses of cars and Chicagoans surrounding her. It had felt like being in the museum; walking down a wide corridor lined with exhibits of extinction. The storefronts, once brightly lit and buzzing, were dodos. Tasha, looking in with longing, was a dodo too. She looks at Dr. Rio, who is gazing at his audience of empty chairs, the animated fist clenching and clenching, and wonders if he considers himself part of the extinct, or if he has already moved on to whatever comes next.

"Mrs. Randall is outside." Malakai is standing at the window in the living room, looking out at the street.

Ishmael stands quickly and goes to the window. Tasha stays where she is, in the belly of the armchair. How many times will this same scene replay, she wonders, watching him go. Will this be an eternal routine, she wonders: bacon, eggs, and killing in the morning; slaughter with the soup at night. Here they are at tea, necks needing cutting between crumpets.

"She's alone," says Ishmael over his shoulder. "I'll take care of it."

He moves across the room toward his axe where it leans in the kitchen by the door.

"Stop," says Dr. Rio. "This is my street, Ishmael. You take care of yours, I'll take care of mine."

Ishmael hesitates.

"I can do it, Dr. Rio. Or at least let someone else on the street come out and help."

"Sit down, Ishmael," the doctor orders. His voice is not unkind, but Tasha hears the glint of metal in it. "I have done enough waiting for others to do the right thing."

He stands up. So does Malakai.

"Do you want me to come?"

Dr. Rio ignores him and crosses into the kitchen, placing his mug on the counter before disappearing through the garage door. It shuts with a muted thud behind him.

Z looks at Ishmael, whose brows are low.

"He's going out through the garage," Ishmael says.

"He didn't take your axe."

Ishmael doesn't respond.

Tasha extracts herself from the chair, like a heifer escaping quicksand. She goes slowly to the window, not wanting to watch, but drawn to the spectacle. The daylight glows through the window, giving it the effect of a large silent screen. Outside in the yard, close to the street, is a stocky woman wearing an apron. Tasha doesn't think she's ever seen anyone wear an apron in real life. The woman's hair is light gray, still half-pinned at the crown of her head, the rest of it falling down around her ears and forehead like a feathery hat. Rio appears in the picture. Tasha wants to change the channel.

"Is he going to be okay?" Malakai is asking. He and the others have joined Tasha at the window.

"He knows what he's doing," Z says. Tasha wonders how she can be so sure.

Rio is walking slowly across the yard. He looks older from a distance when she can't see the hawk eye and she's distracted by his slight stoop. The old man's going to throw his back out, she thinks, out there playing soldier. She opens her mouth to tell Ishmael to help him when Dr. Rio attacks.

At first she thinks he has a sword, a scimitar. It wouldn't

have surprised her. But it's smaller than a scimitar, its curve more dramatic. It's a sickle. She can't imagine why he even owns one as he charges the now-barking Minker with the tool raised over his head.

The first swing of it catches the aproned woman at the shoulder, a splash of red rewarding his efforts. The arm goes limp before what Tasha knows are tarry fingers begin to plaster the wound, the arm regaining its strength. The arm reaches for Rio.

The sickle is like a half-moon curving from his hand. What does he remind her of: his black, buttoned shirt, the slight stoop, his barely visible bony wrist? Tasha wonders how long he hid in the basement of the church, peeping up through the floorboards at the bootsoles of his seekers. Months maybe. Longer. Did the congregation sneak him food? Had he fed on churchmice?

The woman in the apron sees Rio as a churchmouse. He might be. Tasha wonders if she's about to watch him be torn apart. Some remote part of her reminds herself that she'd need to turn Malakai away. A kid his age doesn't need to see that.

Rio's winding up—Tasha is commentating again—and the sickle is a bright slice of metal against the sky for a frozen moment before he brings it down on the body of the woman in the apron. Again. Again. His arm is a whetted windmill, a shining blur. Tasha had seen the spark of the Chip failing after the second blow, but the sickle comes down and down like a rod, a whip. Even when the body falls, the sickle continues its work. The hand holding it is relaxed. The other hand, the left one, is in the pocket of the black cardigan, at rest.

She could look away—they all could. But it's the pistons churning toward a brick wall, the steam engine becoming a ram, the crumpling of steel like paper. When it stops, the yard is red, the apron nothing, the face nothing—obliterated. The thing that is Dr. Rio turns and looks toward the window, right at Tasha and the others. His gaze is bald and white, blood spattering his spectacles. He raises his arm one more time, and when it falls, what's left of the head of the woman on the lawn lolls away from its home, separating. Dr. Rio removes his glasses and cleans the lenses on his sweater, staring deep into the window from which they watch. His eyes are depthless. Only then does Tasha, unblinking, slide her hand slowly over Malakai's eyes.

That night they're back at Ishmael's mother's house, to which they had returned in silence.

"If he's so smart, why hasn't he gone to California himself?" asks Z. She's the only one willing to blatantly criticize Dr. Rio. "Why just help a bunch of other people get there and not help yourself?"

"He wants to make sure as many people as possible go. Says he'll go with the last group." Ishmael seems neutral, but he hasn't smiled since they returned from Dr. Rio's house.

"You said the first group went the day after the Change?" Tasha asks. She wants to contribute something, anything.

"Yeah," says Malakai. "He sent them off right away. He'd been saying something was gonna happen for awhile, so people were mostly ready."

"So wait," says Z, leaning back in her chair, "he predicted this or what?"

"He had privileged information," says Ishmael. "From what we know, he was one of the scientists who developed the implant. He told me that when he saw it wasn't being tested properly, he ditched the company. Apparently it was originally supposed to be military technology, which makes sense if you think about it. The Chip repairs the body. It would be a good thing for soldiers to have in battle. But the lab tried to hunt him down and everything. Remember I said he hid in a church? His cousin was a pastor on 73rd and hid him in the basement for two months while people in uniforms came looking for him. They knocked on our door too."

"My mom wouldn't let them in," boasts Malakai, some broth left on his upper lip. They're eating soup again. "They didn't have a warrant so she wouldn't let them. They said they'd come back with one, but they never did."

Tasha takes it all in, imagining Dr. Rio as a Denzel Washington character in a thrilling action movie with explosions and dramatic monologues: Dr. Rio/Denzel striding all the way to Chicago from a sinister hidden lab; Dr. Rio/Denzel hiding under the floor of a musty church cellar; Dr. Rio/Denzel rallying survivors and sending them West to start anew and escape the murderous enemy. It would seem cooler if she hadn't met him already. She can't picture him doing any of these things. She only pictures his stoop and his steely detachment as he swung the sickle into the flesh of the aproned woman.

"Wow," Z says again.

"Why didn't you go with your mom?" Tasha asks. It's been nagging at her since she saw the pictures in the guest room that morning. They all seemed so close. Why split up when you didn't have to?

"When I didn't come back from the soccer stadium after everything happened, they assumed the worst. I don't blame them," he says, looking pointedly at Malakai, who smiles a small smile. "So they made plans with Dr. Rio to go West. I came back the day before they were set to go, and that changed things a little. Marcus took Mom. He's the oldest. We knew she'd be safe with him and I wanted her out of the city. I wanted to stay here and help Dr. Rio, and Malakai and me are kind of a package deal." He grins at his brother. "So we decided to stay for a little longer. We promised her we'd come with Dr. Rio in the last group."

"Ish says he owes Dr. Rio," Malakai adds.

"You owe him? How?"

Ishmael looks out the window that overlooks the neighbor's garden, probably the same garden Ishmael rooted the Minker out of.

"I didn't believe him," Ishmael is saying. "Dr. Rio had warned everybody and told us all that something real bad was going to happen. He didn't know how many, or when, or how bad it would be, but he knew it would be something. He even tried to get everyone to go to California before the Change even happened. I ignored him. I was playing soccer like any other day," he says, now looking at Tasha. She's forgotten that he'd been wearing the jersey when she'd met him. He wears a clean white t-shirt now. He still has a bandage on his arm where she'd tried to cut it off the day they met. The almost-gone bite on her bicep throbs empathetically.

"What if something had happened to my mom while I was off playing soccer? Dr. Rio took care of her and my brothers and planned for them to go to California and be safe. I can at least help him now. If I had believed him, I would have been more prepared. I could've...you know, been ready."

Tasha doesn't know if anyone could have been ready. She doubts Dr. Rio himself had been ready. She remembers Ishmael asking her in the stadium, "How many?" She'd had to tell him, "Everyone." But she hadn't been giving him new information, she sees now; she had been confirming his worst fears. At least his family is safe. She bites back the familiar taste of bitterness.

He stands, collecting their bowls, and carries them to the sink. The kitchen is dimming as the day exhausts itself, and Ishmael asks Malakai to light a few candles. He talks to Tasha and Z over his shoulder as he washes the dishes.

"So with the people in the street last night, I never got to hear how you two linked up."

Z leans forward eagerly so Tasha lets her tell the story. She needs to talk, Tasha knows. She'd been okay today, even with the incident at Dr. Rio's house, but Tasha still senses the buzzing restlessness that has exuded from her since they left her safe little bubble at the Web. Tasha's glad she came. Z is social: she moves her hands like butterflies when she talks, her hair swishing when she gets to animated parts of the story. Ishmael listens, and laughs when she talks about Tasha kicking everyone in a five-foot radius in the scooter lot.

Tasha slowly becomes aware that Z is bragging about her, talking her up. Wing-woman. The way she tells it, Tasha could be Jet Li, a curly-haired kung-fu master who tore apart every Minker in downtown Chicago while balancing a baby on her head and wearing ballet slippers. Tasha returns the favor, fast-forwarding to the part of the story where Z rescued her by blowing off the supermodel's head with one shot. Malakai has come back into the room at this part of the story, bearing two lit candles, and he raises his eyebrows at Z.

"You shot her head off? For real?"

Ishmael groans, taking a candle from Malakai and handing it to Tasha.

"Don't even get this guy started. He watched so many gory movies before all this stuff happened, I don't think anything he's seen so far has surprised him. Marcus told me Malakai used a shovel on the Postman on the first morning, right on the front porch. He's carried the damn thing around ever since."

Tasha thinks of Malakai perched on top of the slide. She and Z had thought they were rescuing him. Ha.

Ishmael leads them into what might have been called a parlor two centuries before. There is a low couch and some other furniture —bookshelves filled with more picture frames—and an impressive stone fireplace, which is glowing. It's definitely an old house. "Is that a real fireplace? A real fire?" Tasha feels the tugging of bluegrass. Her parents' home had a fireplace, though they'd only used it around Christmas. Her mother would put dried apple slices and sticks of cinnamon in with the wood, and the house would fill with the smell of it. Tasha can almost smell it now; it's curling out of her memories like fog.

"Yes, and yes," Ishmael says, kneeling next to it with a heavy black poker, teasing the flames. They rise up to meet him, as if they'd been waiting to be asked to dance.

Malakai takes the cushions from the couch, along with several more from a large wicker basket shaped like a boat in the corner. He arranges them around the hearth and they all sit. The fire is warm, but not hot. Outside, night has fallen and she thinks she hears the far off thunder of another stom. She wonders if they're safe—she'd been too tired yesterday to think about it. On their way back from Dr. Rio's, she had seen Malakai wrap the chain around the gate, but what other entrances are there? What about the windows? She's used to being high above the ground—at home, at work, at the Web with Z. She can see the street out the window from where she sits—it's like sitting on the floor of the jungle, exposed. Ishmael is watching her and says,

"Relax," he says quietly. "You can relax."

Later, Malakai and Z have fallen asleep, and Tasha and Ishmael sit in silence watching the fire, which is low and makes whispering sounds every now and then. Ishmael whispers too. "So you knew about Dr. Rio before today."

Tasha looks at him sideways, half startled, then back at the fire.

360 OLIVIA A. COLE

"Yeah."

"Yeah, I thought so. Family on the South Side, huh?"

She doesn't know what he means at first, then remembers her lie at the stadium; why she was headed south. Yes, she should've told him about her sister's letter then. Things might have been simpler.

"Oh. Yeah. Well, I didn't know what to say. It sounded so crazy, you know. I knew your team was freaking out: I didn't want to tell them about something and have it turn out not to be real. If I had known you already knew the guy—everything he said would happen—I would have told you."

Ishmael nods.

"I understand. So your sister is in California, right? Or was that a lie too?"

Tasha grimaces, smiling. "No, that's true. She's outside of what used to be Los Angeles."

"So?"

"She wrote me a letter, right before the Change. It didn't say much other than looking for Rio. Here."

She pulls the letter from her backpack and hands it to him.

He leans close to the fire, studying the paper, Tasha studying him. He reads it quickly.

"Damn," he says, "not much to go on."

"Yeah, tell me about it."

"Do you think Rio is right about California being safe?"

"My sister is right, I know that. She wouldn't tell me to come if she wasn't sure."

"Are you going?"

"It's really far."

Silence.

"I can't believe they just lost control of everything," he says.

"Lost it, or gave it up?"

"What? What do you mean?"

"I don't know," she sighs.

She stares at the grate of the fireplace, a cage keeping the fire in, it seems. Really, it's just keeping her out. The burning wood crackles. She could be in Kentucky. She could be anywhere. She could be in France. Does the rest of the world know what's happening here? Do they give a shit?

"Your hair is different than it was at the stadium," he says, bringing her back to Chicago.

She freezes. She hasn't seen a mirror in hours. She knows she can't be wearing mascara—she'd left the make-up pouch in the store where Vette's body lay. She struggles to imagine her eyelashes, her skin. He's too close, the room too quiet. Her hair must be a viper's nest. She imagines her Medusan curls leaping from her scalp to strike him, the venom of her eyes stiffening his body into rock...

But he's on to the next subject.

"Did you really karate kick a Minker in a banana suit?" Z had spared no details.

She laughs quietly in the dying light of the fire, and Z stirs a little, breathing peacefully.

"He was wearing a hot dog suit," she says, "and yes, yes I did."

CHAPTER 27

Tasha wonders where he got all the knives.

When she'd returned to Rio's house this morning, the kitchen and living room had been transformed from the quiet den of an aging doctor into a war room: maps laid out; backpacks arranged; piles of lethal-looking hunting knives with serrated edges; packages of vitamins and rolls of bandages; canteens.

"Some of this stuff is really high-tech," Z says quietly to Tasha.

They are in the living room, charged with the task of making sure all the knives are sheathed, distributing one per lightweight black backpack. Each pack also gets a vitamin roll, a canteen, a solar-powered GPS map, and a package of energy bars and other small food items. The canteens, in particular, are of interest to Z. The side of each has a small display near the top. As one fills the vessel with water, some genius mechanism at the neck tests the liquid for toxins, bacteria, and general drinkability, then purifies it, releasing the bacteria from the neck in a vapor that one can't see, but hear. It's a short, piercing sound: like the first sharp exclamation of a teakettle before it's snatched from the heat. Malakai had tried to trick it, he'd told them before being carted upstairs with Dr. Rio, Ishmael following reluctantly behind. Malakai had opened a beaker of Pepsi, he said, and poured the fizzing liquid into a canteen, waiting to read the sensor. The little panel had flashed red and read, "Undrinkable." Malakai had poured it out.

"Yeah, I know," says Tasha, fingering a map before folding it into a backpack. The map isn't paper, but it folds and rolls easily. It's a thin synthetic material that feels uncomfortably like skin: a digital, solar-powered map of the States. The world too, Rio had said, but Tasha can't figure out how to scale it back to the larger picture. The route for the walk to California has already been programmed in; the vein of it glows in red. The map is constantly moving and changing, loaded with a weather sensor that picks up changes in temperature and detects approaching storms. The fronts travel across the surface of the map in differently-colored smudges. Tasha likes looking at it. It's the closest thing to the Net that she's seen since the Change, and she feels a little nostalgic.

"Where do you think he got all this stuff?" This time Z is holding one of the knives. She looks at it like it might bite her.

"I don't know, but it must have taken awhile," Tasha says, looking around. They're seated in the living room—the crowds of chairs have been spirited away—surrounded by backpacks sorted into two piles: packed and unpacked. They've done about twenty so far. It feels like office work, putting together pamphlets in an assembly line: one, two, three, staple, one, two, three, staple. She supposes anything can become dull if one does it enough times, even if it does involve lethal objects.

"Malakai and Ish said that Rio had known this was going to happen before it did." Z lowers her voice a little, even though they can hear footsteps upstairs where Dr. Rio and the boys are doing whatever it is they're doing.

"Yeah, he had to have. How else would he have all of this stuff?"

"Think he stole it?"

"He had to have stolen it."

Z glances around at the piles of supplies.

"It's so much. How the fuck did they not notice?"

Tasha shrugs.

"He's an old dude with glasses and a paunch. They probably thought he was a sweet old man."

"My ass," Z snorts.

"You feel it too, then," says Tasha.

"He's a fuckin' creep. Something about his eyes. And that hand." Z fake-shudders.

Tasha rubs her thumbs over the peculiar texture of the tech map. He's creepy, alright. But despite the chill factor, Rio does seem to have good intentions. Stealing all these supplies, creating plans to get people away from the Minkers, mobilizing entire neighborhoods for a journey to safety, albeit a long one.

"I think I want to go," Z says suddenly.

"Go? Now? But we're not done yet. Ishmael—"

"No, I don't mean from *here*. I mean, go to California.

Sunday. With Dr. Rio."

"Oh. But you said he's a creep."

"He is. But…you know. Why not?"

Tasha thinks about this answer, wondering when her friend's fantasy about a military rescue fully evaporated. It makes sense for her to want to go west: Z's father is certainly a goner, her mother is dead. Her sister may or may not have the Chip, and Z hasn't spoken to her in years. Her brother is in jail, very likely dead from starvation—Tasha thinks of the pacing lions in the zoo—or violence. Z's boyfriend hadn't been her boyfriend for many months. Tasha thinks of what Dr. Rio had said the day before: Z certainly has more to gain by leaving than to lose. She hasn't even mentioned her apartment or any belongings she might have left behind. Chicago is nothing but bones for her. To the West lies meat.

"Think about it," Z continues, leaning forward. "He's right, right? *You* were right. I don't see the National Guard. It's been two weeks. The President is probably dead—worse, he's probably, like, eating his Cabinet—and the House is probably a pile of rocks. Everybody who was anybody got the implant. You know how many people lived in the city. Where are they? Have you seen them? They're all dead. Or hiding. Or walking around trying to eat people like us. I didn't really understand how big this shit was until we left the Web, but Chicago is, like, done."

Tasha nods. Z is convincing her of what she thought she'd need to convince Z of.

"Malakai was telling me about a woman who left for

California already," Z goes on, her voice lowering. "Her name is Laila. She was in the Army and apparently they make you get the Chip when you enlist, to keep you from getting sick overseas and stuff. Well, apparently they can track the soldiers' Chips, so they don't go AWOL. Well, Laila, she got pregnant in January and had to bounce or they'd lock her up. So she had to dig her Chip out of her *own neck* with a knife to escape. So they couldn't track her down, you know? Malakai said the scar is really gross looking, but she's a survivor. If it hadn't been for her cutting the Chip out, she'd be a Minker right now. Think about how many people were in the Army, Tasha. All Minkers. Holy shit. They can't come to rescue us. They're…them."

"All the troops," Z continues, looking at the map on the wall with its drawn-on veins and arteries. "And all the workers, right? Think about the Minkers we've seen. McDonalds employees. Post workers. Public transportation drivers. Government jobs. Your job at the Apiary. All these big corps. Wal-Mart. The more wage-slaves, the more Chips. Can you fucking imagine what New York must be like?" She pauses. Tasha knows what's next. "I almost hope V got the Chip," she says bitterly, "so she doesn't have to deal with this shit."

Tasha is reeling between processing everything Z is saying and trying to decide if Z needs a shoulder. This is the part Tasha is no good at, the part Dinah had mastered: the comforting. The muscle in her that consoles has been too rarely flexed; it is weak, a numb limb. She fancies herself a realistic person, and her realism agrees with what Z has said, however brutal: if V were her sister, living in New York, Tasha too would hope she was Chipped. It's better to think of loved ones doing harm than coming to harm. Isn't it? She imagines the streets of New York, gray and crowded, packed with Minkers barking in Brooklyn accents. If not Chipped, she doesn't think anyone wandering the streets would stand a chance. If Chicago is the city of the dodo, what is New York? The mammoth perhaps, with all its rotting bulk.

"Maybe there's someone like Dr. Rio in New York," Tasha offers weakly, knowing Z needs something. At some point they have switched roles: Tasha the naïve hoper, Z the streetwise knower. "You know, someone to give people information and keep them safe. Before all this happened, New York wasn't on the best of terms with the rest of the States, remember? They were threatening to do like California did. Leona said get the South Side and find Rio because she knew it was safe. Maybe New York has a part like that, or someone like him."

"Did you say Leona?"

Dr. Rio is leaning in the doorway of the kitchen, mug in hand. He might have been there for awhile. He looks comfortable.

Tasha feels her face grow hot. Had he heard them discussing him, calling him a creep? She feels both defiant and embarrassed. He could have announced himself.

"Yes," she answers, trying to sound firm.

"Leona who?"

"Leona Lockett. My sister."

"I wasn't aware that you had a sister," he says, his eyes narrowed behind the almond spectacles.

"Well I do."

"Alive?"

Ishmael enters the room, followed by Malakai. The boy looks from Rio to Tasha, his eyes vaguely concerned.

"What?" she says.

"Is your sister alive?"

Tasha stiffens.

"Yes. Leona is alive."

"Where is she? Not here."

"She lives in California."

"Oh? For how long?"

"Three years. She went during the secession."

"Of course. She must be a brave girl."

"Yes."

"Do you know how your sister knew my name?"

"What?"

"I heard you say that Ms. Leona Lockett told you to come here. To find me. Do you know why?"

"No. A lot of refugees come through her town. I assumed someone like that told her. Or something."

"Ah."

They stare at each other. He studies her, and although she fights the cold feeling in her spine, she is afraid. His glasses have slid a little farther down his nose, adding to his doctorly appearance but reminding her of yesterday, the sickle. She passed it in the garage on her way inside this morning: he hadn't even bothered to wash it off. His eyes are a lighter brown than she'd thought at first: he was probably thought to be very handsome in his younger years. His eyes are taking her apart now, dissecting what she's told him.

"Do you love your sister, Natasha?"

The urge to run away from him is strong. It's the feeling of knowing the animal before you is fanged, even while wrapped in its lamb-like cloak, courtesy masking violence. Snarls pretending to be smiles.

"Of course."

"Do you want to see her again?"

She can feel the threat in it. He might as well have slapped her.

"Fuck you, Rio." She spits the words out like bullets. Malakai cringes.

He doesn't speak, but his lips tighten into a cement smile. She doesn't look at the hand not holding the mug, but she knows it's either a fist or becoming one. A moment more of silence and then,

"Well?"

"Of course I fucking do."

His eyes glint like a rattlesnake.

"Your sister wrote you a letter, yes? Let me see it."

She stares at him for a moment, feeling mulish. She hates him. The realization of it is disorienting: the good doctor, the good shepherd. She hates him. His black cardigan. His fist. His sickle, somewhere in the garage still wet from the woman in the apron's butchered blood. But the mule fears the snake. She uproots herself and goes to the table where her backpack rests, opening the outside pocket. She pulls out her sunglasses, which she's forgotten she'd packed and are miraculously unbroken; her Apiary ID badge with its perfect portrait; and the letter. It's been through a few pairs of hands now and is now even more tattered than it had been when it had arrived. She wishes she'd kept the envelope. She hands Rio the letter sullenly.

He glances at it, as if merely confirming its existence.

"Leona Lockett. Why did she never come visit you here?"

Tasha is surprised by the question, so much so that she answers it honestly.

"Chicago isn't for her; it's for me. She has California to make her happy. I have Chicago."

"Had."

"What?"

"You had Chicago."

More plugging for the long walk. Tasha feels like Little Foot, a silly little dinosaur with a pod of others that set out to find the Great Valley. Was there a family waiting for the longneck when he found it, after they'd destroyed the Sharptooth? She thinks there was.

"Why didn't you visit her?" he asks.

Enough of this shit, she thinks.

"Do you know my sister?" Tasha demands. "She knew your name. You seem like you know hers. How?"

The pause is long and heavy. Behind his eyes, something is pacing.

"We worked together." The stupid mystical smile.

"My sister isn't a doctor. She's a lawyer. Where did you work with her?"

"Why didn't you visit your sister in California?"

Tasha just scowls at him.

"Alright then. Anyhow. I'll need your help," he says mildly. "As we prepare to go West, I'll need your help."

"I *am* helping," she says, more petulantly than she intended, and gestures at the backpacks.

"Yes, yes. But there is more to be done."

"About what? About leaving? Or about the Minkers?"

Something in his face opens like a crack in the earth, the hot red center glaring through at her like a glimpse into the pit. It scares her. But then it's closing up again, the crack stitching together, the hot thing buried under cool doctor exterior.

"About Cybranu," he says coldly. If they were on the phone he would have hung up without saying goodbye. She gets the feeling the conversation is over.

Shaking her head, Tasha folds the letter and tucks it back into the front pocket of her backpack, along with the sunglasses. Then she picks up her Apiary badge and starts to slip it back into the pocket too.

She gasps as Dr. Rio snatches it from her hand before she's able to tuck it away. Even Ishmael is a little startled at the suddenness of the motion and watches, puzzled. Rio holds the badge close to his face, looking over the top of his glasses.

"Is this yours?" he demands, his eyes still fixed on the ID.

"What?" she stammers, even though she'd heard him. "Yes, it's mine. What the hell?"

"You were an employee at the Apiary."

"Yes, I did, but I quit," Tasha lies. She's less worried about him having the badge than she is about Ishmael or someone seeing her picture on the front of it, her tight ponytail, her lipsticked mouth.

"For what purpose did you use this badge when you were employed by the Apiary?" He's staring intently at the badge, at the face in his hand. She's annoyed.

"Employee doors, the employee elevator, conference rooms. The trash room. The stores." She could go on but doesn't—what's the point?

"But you didn't turn in your badge."

She considers snatching the ID back. Who gives a shit if he's a doctor, she thinks; it doesn't make him a saint. Jesus was a carpenter, not a neurosurgeon, so Dr. Rio can piss off.

"No, I didn't give the badge back. I got fired and kept it. Okay?"

He's not angry, as she thought he might be. Instead, he smiles at her and picks up his mug of tea from where he'd set it on the arm of one of the chairs, holding the badge out to her like an olive branch.

"Fired?" he asks.

She wants to punch him.

"Yes."

"You're a lucky girl."

Z enters the conversation mercifully, seeing how uncomfortable things are becoming. Tasha wonders at her silence throughout the exchange with Rio. Malakai's too. And Ishmael's. Each probably thought there was something to learn.

"I said the same thing," says Z, laughing her merry laugh.

"I mean, who wants to work at the Apiary? That uniform—Jesus!"

Ishmael scoops up the rolling ball.

"Oh yeah, that uniform was the worst! They had you guys in there looking like Martians' wet dreams."

"That's what I always said!" Tasha laughs, relieved.

They talk a little longer, Rio in the background listening to their chatter and smiling and nodding. But his mind is elsewhere, and every once in awhile Tasha glances at him, still angry, and sometimes she catches the crack in his face opening, or looks at him just as it's closing up. She wonders what magma is inside him that keeps him so close to breaking open. She wonders if Ishmael knows that Dr. Rio is on the edge, that he is at the lip of a deep canyon.

Dr. Rio sees them off that evening, sending them home with cornbread he baked in his gas oven. As they pass through the garage, she notices the distinct smells again: the almonds, the tar, the cabbage. In the corner is the shadow of the unwashed sickle. She's grateful to gain the open air of Lafayette, its clean, silent smell. Dr. Rio waves at them from the door of the garage as they head back to Perry Avenue, reminding them to be back tomorrow at eight in the morning to see off the next group bound for California. Tasha doesn't look back as she walks, her Wusthof held at the ready in case they should attract the attention of any Minkers in the area; but the only eyes she feels upon her are Dr. Rio's, burning into her back.

CHAPTER 28

It's Saturday. The people who gather at Dr. Rio's in the morning are multi-colored—men, women, kids, pressing together in the rooms of the big old house, their voices filling the space. Tasha blends in.

At one point, the kind of people who went to California looking for dreams were young, idealistic; wearing tie-dyed shirts and carrying headshots and scripts. This group lacks that spark. Their optimism is small and hunched, peering out of shuttered windows. Geese know no joy in their flight from north to south—they migrate because they must, and the Chicagoans are no different. To the West lies a new life, one they have little choice but to begin. Tasha figures they liked their old lives just fine, thank you very much. Or did they? She thinks of her closet full of shoes, how leaving them behind had felt like an act of unspeakable treachery. She wonders if the shoes would still even fit. She feels as if it's been years since she's worn them—surely she has grown?

Tasha, Z and the guys are helping the caravan make final preparations before the journey, and Tasha watches the group packing final objects, imagining them folding up their memories, sticking their pressed dreams in between the yellowed pages of books. She sees their turmoil as they decide what to leave behind, and she remembers trying desperately to make the green Jimmy Choos fit in the Prada backpack. Some of the people in the group carry an extra small bag or have an item tied to the back of the backpack—things they can't part with. These objects might become burdensome on the journey, but some burdens can't be put down.

Tasha is helping an old woman, Bianca, who tells Tasha that she was born in the year 2000. She has fine copper skin and says that one side of her family was Sioux. Tasha helps her repack a backpack after Dr. Rio tells her that the things she has packed—picture frames and jewelry—will become too heavy for her on the long walk ahead. Tasha sits in the living room of the doctor's home—crowded again with the appearing and reappearing chairs—once more, helping Bianca remove the photos from the frames and tuck them between the pages of a diary, which Bianca insists she is taking with her, even if it does take up space that could be used for food. She is tall for a woman her age, but delicately boned, her wrists as slender as Tasha's.

"Telling me I can't take my picture frames," Bianca whispers conspiratorially as they slip the photos gently into the pages of the diary, which is bound in worn velvet and yellowed at the pages' edges. It's the kind of thing Tasha would like to read, leafing through the dates for significant days in history and seeing what Bianca had to say about them. She's a little younger than Tasha's grandmother would have been if she were living—they might have had similar movie tastes in the old days. Tasha has to stop herself from asking to read the diary.

"It's alright," Tasha tells her as they stack the now-empty frames. "The pictures are what really matter."

Bianca hums at this, stroking the edge of one frame, which is metal and decorated with butterflies. It's commercially made, generic. There are millions like it, Tasha is sure.

"Yes, I suppose they are. But this was such a pretty frame. I got it at Target, I think. Years ago. It's only ever held the one photo, the one of my son, there." She points. The young man in the picture is beautiful, his skin almost black, with slanting, smiling eyes. Tasha wonders where he is. Is he dead? By the Chip or by other circumstances? It's strange for Tasha to think that she classifies all deaths in this way now: death, and death by Minker. She is glad her parents are not just dead, but dead. Not killed, not eaten, not torn apart. Safe.

Around them are other people packing last-minute nonperishables and testing the weight of their backpacks. There is a steady hum of conversation, colored with excitement but also tension, the stiff anxiety of a platoon being deployed.

Dr. Rio has a system, which Ishmael explained to Tasha and Z the night before. The group as a whole—around thirty people, as Dr. Rio had said—is headed by six captains, each leading a small group of their peers which, including themselves, consists of five people. Each quintet gets a can opener, a compass, and a first aid kit. In addition, each person in the pod carries the backpacks that Tasha and Z packed, stocked with canteens, hunting knives and solar-powered maps, along with any personal objects. Some people take tampons and shoe inserts, sunglasses and tech toothbrushes like Tasha's, combs and sunblock, nail files and muscle rub. Some people have been assigned to carry the tiny packaged inflatable tents that she's seen sold at Columbia. Tasha wonders what will be the item that is most often forgotten, most desired after the journey begins. She imagines many things they need might be acquired along the way. The walk West is not as it was in the time of oxen, covered wagons and cholera: there will be Walmarts every twenty miles, especially in states like Nebraska. There will be the hordes of Minkers to watch for, of course, and avoid, but things they lack will be found. Tasha assumes this is why the backpacks' food stores are so unsubstantial. The packs of Ramen noodles and bread and dried fruit are not meant to last the entire journey— only until the next town or pit stop they might come across, where they can stop and forage. It's a little daring, but without the actual oxen to which Tasha has been mentally likening the travelers, the food packed must weigh as little as possible. She wishes they had NASA food: powdered nutrients that take up very little space but nourish the body. But she figures the "food" of astronauts isn't very comforting, and the people walking to California will be in need of comfort. She imagines the long-stretching expanse of land between where she currently stands and where her sister, far away, sleeps to be much like Mars: vast, empty, strange, and possibly populated with hostile life forms. She has never been to Iowa, or Utah, or Nebraska. Or Nevada. Or California. They might as well be alien planets, sixteenth and seventeenth rocks from foreign suns.

Bianca, finished repacking her diary, is looking around at the others making final preparations for the trip. Tasha finds herself wondering if Bianca, in her late seventies, is too old to make such a journey. She seems spry, and the people in her assigned pod seem smart and strong. The pod's captain is Elmo, a youngish Puerto Rican guy with long shiny hair. He addresses Bianca as "mother." The group also includes a woman with a heavy Nigerian accent named Kimberley, a nineteen-year-old boy with braids called Juno, and a quiet balding man named John. None of them knew one another until they'd been grouped together by Dr. Rio.

Tasha wonders at Rio's selection process. He can't have randomly paired these people—Rio doesn't strike her as the type of man who leaves things to chance. Elmo isn't very buff or massive, yet he's been put in charge of Bianca and the others. Perhaps he is deadly with the pool cue he carries as a walking stick. Or perhaps he's merely navigationally gifted, and making him responsible for the group's compass was logical. Tasha wants to ask, but she's been avoiding Dr. Rio since their bizarre conversation the day before. Ishmael has skirted the subject carefully, venturing onto the topic only to ask about her former employment at the Apiary. He's both interested and amused by the fact that she had been one of the blue-clad drones in the platform boots.

"You just seem too...smart for the Apiary," he'd said the night before when they'd arrived back at his mother's house. "Let me see your ID again; I don't believe it." She had refused, not willing to allow him a prolonged examination of the badge and her permed, make-upped features. He hadn't really seemed surprised.

Dr. Rio comes near to exchange a few words with Elmo, and Tasha drifts away, trying to make her retreat seem casual. She spots Z in the kitchen, leaning against the counter and watching the proceedings. Z had spent the morning by the atlas on the wall, double-checking the route drawn on the maps each captain carries. By now she must know the route by heart, Tasha thinks.

"So many of them," Z says as Tasha leans beside her. "How many do you think will make it?"

Tasha laughs.

"I don't think they have a choice once they leave Chicago."

"You don't think any of them will die?" Z asks quietly.

Tasha isn't prepared for this question; she hasn't even considered it. The challenge she's been weighing in her mind has been whether they will make it to California with their shoes intact, not whether they will make it there alive.

"I mean..." She doesn't know how to finish.

"There's Minkers, illness, injury, starvation, dehydration..." Z makes circles with her wrist, indicating that there are dozens of other ways one of them could die that she just doesn't care to expound upon at the moment. Tasha continues the list mentally: snake bites, meteor showers, dart frogs, packs of vicious roving hamsters recently emancipated from domestication…

"Rio said if they avoid cities, they can avoid big groups of Minkers," Tasha says, keeping her vision of rampaging gerbils to herself. "And illness? It's not like it's the nineteenth century. Nobody'll die of pneumonia or anything, and Dr. Rio is giving every group pouches of medical supplies. He's even putting in those X-packs, the super antibiotic cocktails that cost like $600. It knocks out any virus. Even, like, rabies."

Z nods.

"Yeah, that's true. He must have spent a ton of time stealing all that shit from the research center. I really wonder how long he'd been planning on deserting."

Tasha shrugs, watching Rio move about the room, putting a reassuring hand on an arm here, smiling encouraging words there. He's like Captain Kirk, minus the spandex, preparing his crew for a galaxy they've never seen before. He walks past Tasha and Z with a pod captain, a woman named Yani, into the garage, which has been lit with large battery-powered lanterns, the garage door cracked to let in more light. It doesn't smell of cabbage and tar anymore, Tasha had noticed when she arrived. Rio must have taken the trash out. Somewhere.

"Such a weirdo. People really seem to trust him," Z says after Yani and the doctor have passed.

"People always trust doctors."

"Yeah, except when they're suing them."

Tasha laughs.

"Yeah, except when they're suing them. Hey, there's Malakai. Where's he been? Hey, Malakai!"

Malakai hears his name and looks over. Seeing them, he picks his way through the crowd and comes into the kitchen.

"Hey," he says. "Good thing Dr. Rio has a big house, right? There's more people in this group than the last two. He says a few more people showed up this morning asking to come. He doesn't say no." Malakai clearly admires the man, and Tasha can see him look around for Rio.

"He's in the garage with that really small lady," she tells him.

"Yani?"

"Yeah, I think so."

"I like her. She's cute."

Tasha rolls her eyes.

"Where have you been?"

Malakai tilts his head toward the garage.

"I was in the other garage putting some stuff in Dr. Rio's car. He's got some project he wants to do before we all leave on Sunday."

"What stuff were you putting in the car?"

"Just a couple backpacks. Nothing big."

Bianca comes wandering over to them. She's wearing the backpack Tasha helped her pack.

"Well, I think I'm all set." She tugs on the straps. "It doesn't feel too bad. But we'll see how I feel after a thousand miles or so. I may just decide to resettle in Utah if I can't make the whole trip. There's towns in Utah," she says, more to herself, "that wouldn't mind an old lady renting a room. Although the rent would have to be free." She cackles before moving into the garage, still talking to herself about Utah.

"Think she'll make it?" Z murmurs to Tasha. "She's pretty old."

"She'll make it," Tasha says.

She sees Ishmael across the room in the doorway that leads from the living room to a foyer inside the front door, through which Tasha has yet to enter. He's looking around, moving his head slightly back and forth as milling people interrupt his view. He's looking for her, she thinks. His eyes drift farther than the living room and search their way into the kitchen, and he sees her. His eyebrows relax and his head moves to one side, then back to center.

"What's up?" she says when she reaches him. It took a few moments, picking her way through the crowd. They let her pass when they notice her, but most are too concerned with finding their captain, staying with their captain, eyeing their pod, counting their bags of dried fruit. It feels like a strange, strained summer camp. When Tasha had left the kitchen, Z had started to come with her, but had stopped. She must have seen Ishmael. Wing-woman.

"There's something I want you to see," he says, turning and walking down the hall to the foyer. She follows him.

"What is it? Is everything okay?"

He's silent as he pulls open the front door, and they slip out onto the front porch together. He shuts the door behind them and it closes with a soft click. It's quiet here, the bustle of summer camp shut out by the brick of the big old house Dr. Rio has set up shop in. She doesn't look at Ishmael; she thinks he might kiss her. But instead, he points.

She follows his long dark arm, her eyes stopping to admire his fingers. They are smooth and well-made. A sculptor's hands, she thinks. Beyond the hand is the yard, and the street, and a row of ancient clipped hedges growing beyond their neat boxes with no one to tame their ambition, and beyond the hedge is a humming line of Minkers.

She starts, and feels Ishmael's hand on her back to steady her. She wonders if he knows he has chosen his palm's placement perfectly: low enough to differ from the hand-on-shoulder friend zone, and high enough to differ from the I'm-only-touching-this-part-of-your-back-because-it's-as-close-as-I-could-get-to-your-ass-without-you-realizing-I'm-a-creep zone.

"Don't worry," he says softly, "I don't think they're interested in us."

He's right; they're not. Tasha can't tell what they're interested in: she's never seen Minkers behave this way. They seem to be swaying in a long line, one behind the other. This effect is partially because of her vantage point, which views them from the side, so they appear to be almost militaristically aligned. If she were standing directly in front of them—and thank god she isn't—she's sure there would be some irregularity, but from the porch, it's like watching a long row of many strange ducklings, swimming in a line ordained by Nature. They sway a little. Penguins, not ducklings.

"What are they doing?" Tasha whispers. She realized the moment she saw the Minkers that she'd left her constant companion, the Wusthof , on the counter in the kitchen. She hopes Z has picked it up for her. She hates to think of someone taking it to California without her.

"I don't know." He's taken his hand from her back, and her skin feels cool under her tank top where his palm had been. "They're just...walking."

"All one direction? In a line?"

The line moves like a centipede. How many are there? Twenty? Thirty? More. She can't even see the back of the line from where it comes around the corner, back around Dr. Rio's garages.

"Right. Walking north. Like somebody blew a dog whistle. Where do you think they're going?"

Her mind flashes to the conversation she'd had with Z in the Web—Z's stupid hypothesis of a giant ray that could fry all the Chips. It sounded ridiculous at the time, and still does, a little. But seeing the Minkers behave like this raises her inner eyebrow. If something can call them, something can kill them. How's that for scientific logic, she thinks.

"They're headed downtown. Who fucking knows after that."

They're still whispering. If the long line spots them, they'll be in trouble.

"Shouldn't we tell Dr. Rio?"

"I already told him." Ishmael doesn't take his eyes off the slow-moving line. It's like a chain-gang. "He closed the garage doors, don't worry. He didn't seem worried. Or surprised, actually."

Tasha glances at him.

"Not even surprised? I don't know why he wouldn't be. I've never seen them act like this."

Ishmael shrugs.

"He knows a lot more about the implant than we do. Maybe this is what they all do before they die or something," he says. "Wouldn't that be something? Then we could all just stay here."

"Stay? I thought you wanted to go. I thought you were all gung-ho about going."

"Kinda. I mean, I am now. My mom is gone. But I grew up here. I've only ever lived here. This is my city."

"Weren't you listening to the good doctor?" she mocks. "*Had*. You *had* this city. This isn't your city anymore. It's the dodo's."

"The dodo's," he repeats, shaking his head and watching the Minkers. "Maybe we're the dodos. Or the dodo's kids, at least. It's a wasteland, but maybe we have to make do with what we inherit."

They're quiet. She feels strangely calm, even with several dozen of the Minkers walking so near. It feels more the way she felt in the zoo as a child: the danger present and observable, but dulled by thick glass.

"Why are you always rubbing your finger?"

She looks at him, and he's looking at her hands. She looks too and realizes that her left hand is caressing the fourth finger of her right, rubbing the empty skin.

"Just a nervous habit, I guess. I used to twist my ring when I had it. It was my mom's."

"What happened to it?"

She stares grimly at the swaying Minkers, wondering what she would do if she glimpsed Cara's face among them.

"This rich lady at my job said I stole it from her, and my boss took it from me. It's locked up in a safe in the Apiary. That ring was my mom's, and they took it."

"Is your mom…?"

"Dead, but not Chipped. Just dead. About three years ago."

"I'm sorry. About your mom. And the ring too."

"It's just a ring," Tasha sniffs.

"It is. But do *you* know that?"

She doesn't answer. She can see the end of the line now; the last few Minkers sway up the block, heading northward behind their brethren.

"Had to have been at least fifty," she says, more to herself.

"Fifty-four."

"You were counting?"

"Yeah."

The last Minker in line is a kid wearing jeans and a Blackhawks jersey. Tasha can't tell if it's a boy or a girl; the swaying gait of the Minkers reveals nothing. Soon she can't see the kid anymore; the bodies sway in their penguin line, obeying some silent call. She vaguely hears the tread of the herd's feet, shuffling away toward downtown.

CHAPTER 29

Dr. Rio's caravan is in the yard now Tasha imagines the people gathered to leave as a herd of multi-colored mustangs. They paw at the earth impatiently, their anxiety tangible. Some of them look pissed off. Tasha imagines that they, like her, want someone to blame. She thinks of Dr. Rio and his panel of smug doctor buddies in immaculate white lab coats that he almost certainly spent time with, their heads bobbing like marionettes as shadow-faced government operatives laid out the plan of action. She snarls inwardly. What a bunch of bastards, she thinks. They thought they'd prance in and make a quick gajillion bucks, playing off a divided nation's fear, driving the haves and the have-nots further and further apart. "Just give it to the MINK carriers," she imagines some suited asshole sniggering. "Make everyone want it. Make them fight for it."

Look who's laughing now, Tasha thinks. But she supposes grimly that it's still *them* who get the last cackle. The people lucky enough to have money to pay for MINK or corp jobs that would provide it were turned into cannibalistic maniacs, but who were the people getting eaten?

"The rest of us," Tasha says out loud. But then she thinks of the kids signing up for the military—most of them barely out of high school—and it takes the venom out of her. They were being used by the same white-coated jack-offs. But used for what?

No one hears her, because they're going. They're climbing into cars and loading backpacks in trunks. This part might feel normal, the preparation for a road trip, the embarking. Even when the cars die, and they all go on foot—that might feel normal at first. After a mile, minds might change. After ten, the feet will complain. Only two thousand more to go! Tasha imagines herself in pink Lycra and a headband, an overly-peppy aerobic instructor, walking at the head of the caravan. "And one and two! That's right! One more mile! No, two! You can do it! Get those knees high!"

She exhausts herself.

They leave quietly, a caravan spreading West. As Dr. Rio suggested, they leave in cars, all electric, good only for a few hours. When the first car dies, all cars will be left behind; each pod will carry on as a unit. One on foot, all on foot. They will be on foot for a long time after that. That's the plan.

Dr. Rio has seen to it that everyone has worn practical shoes and packed an extra pair. What will the Chicagoans' feet resemble when they arrive? If they arrive? Will the Nike checks be eroded from their soles? What about their skin? Will freckles reveal themselves in the long bath of sun, like invisible handwriting exposed by lemon juice? What does Iowa have in store for them? And Colorado? And Utah? Tasha sees the silver Ford carrying Bianca and her pod, driven by Elmo, receding down the road where it will travel West, and West, and West, until it dies. They will leave its body like a dinosaur's bones left to bleach by the side of the road, probably still in Illinois, probably still in sight of the city and its swaying towers of Willis and Trump. If the city burned, they would probably still be close enough to feel its warmth, so near will they be even after the feeling of traveling so far.

Tasha and Z watch the caravan of cars go. Others watch too, Ishmael and Malakai and their neighbors, some of whom will leave Sunday with Dr. Rio, some of whom will change their minds and hand back their compasses, too afraid to leave behind the mortgages they've spent their lives paying and were so close to paying off; the living room whose walls they'd just painted; the yard they spent last summer landscaping; the tax-refund check they'd spent months looking forward to; the green Jimmy Choos shimmering in the closet. They'll hand back the compass and say, "I'm sorry, I'm so sorry, but that place is too far and who knows what's out there. I have all this here, all this is mine; this is my place, here." They will stay, and Dr. Rio will go, and so will Ishmael, and so will Malakai, and so will Azalea, who has no one and has never looked over her shoulder at the apartment she might have left, the earrings she'll never get to wear again, the mother's ring she left behind. Z hasn't looked back at the purse she might have brought if she had known she'd never go home again, the bottle of perfume given to her by a boyfriend when he was still a boyfriend. Z looks forward, never back. Now that's she's shaken off the military fantasy, she grips the compass so tightly it tattoos her palm, and Dr. Rio hasn't even given her the damn thing yet.

They go. The cars are gone quickly, and none of the passengers wave. They'd hardly known each other, after all. Tasha wonders if Bianca will remember her name: Tasha, the nice brown-skinned, curly-headed girl who helped her fold up her memories and stow them in a bag. Or maybe she'll look back on her as the girl who could have talked her out of a fool's errand and didn't; the girl who'd allowed an old woman to take up a cross-country journey on foot. Maybe she'll remember Tasha's name just to curse it.

Dr. Rio looks on a bit sadly, like a father bird seeing another flock take wing, never to return. He's the only one who waves, limply, as if waving a handkerchief. When the caravan is out of sight, he turns away and says to the small gathering who remain,

"They have gone on to a better life, and soon we'll follow. In two days' time you will leave for California. Remember everything we've discussed."

He opens his mouth as if to say more but stops and goes back into his house. The rest of the crowd doesn't hang around: they're worried that Minkers might shamble upon the gathering and no one really feels like dealing with the hassle. Besides, there are homes to say good-bye to, precious things to lock up. Tasha has heard some of the people discussing this: putting their jewelry in safes and burying valuables in backyards.

They'll never return to reclaim these things: once buried, they will remain buried, skeletal leftovers to be found by probing archaeologists, aliens, a century or two ahead. Hoarding these things seems silly, thinks Tasha. Yet she remembers locking her door when she left her apartment, so far away on Foster. She'd had the fantasy then of returning, coming back to embrace her closetful of abandoned treasure. When Dinah had died, the parting from Tasha's closet seemed even harder to bear; her cave of comfort. Now, looking West, standing beside Z and Ishmael—Malakai had followed Dr. Rio inside—Foster seems to drift further and further outside the realm of reality. It's almost hard to remember ever having lived there at all. She doesn't even have her keys. Lost along the way.

Leona feels nearer than Tasha's bedroom and her closet of suede children. Tasha will walk to her. She has a brief vision of introducing Z to Leona, and Ishmael too. She thinks of Leona's garden. There would be no Minkers to clear from the pumpkin patch there, no fences wreathed in clanging aluminum cans. What is Leona's kitchen like? She sees Ishmael standing in it, making soup.

"I think I'm going to go," she says randomly and it's Z's turn for confusion.

"Now? By yourself? Where?" Her voice is colored pink with concern, and the mild orange of panic. Tasha wonders if Z would still be in the Web if Tasha hadn't wandered in for a bath.

"No, I mean Sunday. With Dr. Rio. With you."

"Oh," says Z. "Oh. Well...*yeah.*"

CHAPTER 30

Inside, Tasha retrieves her knife from where Z had told her she stowed it, between the cushions of a sagging green couch.

"People were eyeing it," Z had said with a shrug when Tasha asked her why the hell she put it there.

Ishmael is sweeping the kitchen, the dust and debris billowing out into the garage. Malakai sits on the counter, watching wordlessly. They're all thinking. They leave tomorrow. At dawn they'll get up, say goodbye to Ishmael's mother's house—it will be a more difficult parting for the brothers, of course—climb into a car with Rio, and strike out toward the part of the world where the compass claims California to be. Riding even a tenth of that distance with Rio seems like torture, Tasha thinks: he's become more and more strange, the bizarre clenching fist resembling a claw when he's off in his head and unaware of eyes upon him. Tasha looks around for him now but doesn't see him. Upstairs again, she thinks. Doing god knows what. Plotting, no doubt. He's a plotter.

Z is flopped in the armchair that had swallowed Tasha during her first visit to Rio's house days ago. Her eyes are fixed on the wall and all its maps. Tasha wonders if she's thinking of her father, her sister, her brother. She wants to ask her about the photograph she'd come across in Z's bag, but isn't sure how to broach the subject. Was the young man in the picture her brother Dragon? Or maybe a boyfriend? Suddenly the thought of a photograph stops Tasha's breath.

She hadn't brought the photo of her parents.

The one she had shown Dinah, the one with Tasha and Leona and their parents, when they'd been happy, when they'd all been a family. It's locked in her tomb of an apartment on Foster, an artifact among artifacts, dust collecting on their faces. She can't breathe, nor can she speak. The absence of the photo sits on her chest. She stares at the floor, her hands hanging limply before her, robbed of strength. How could she have been so stupid? To pack her make-up but not the only photograph of her family? Ishmael is still sweeping, Z and Malakai staring off into their own private worlds, and Tasha clenches her fists to keep from sobbing right there.

Her empty finger. Her fists in front of her eyes, she sees the light path of skin where her mother's ring had rested. Her mother had been wearing the ring in the photograph, and now Tasha doesn't even have the thing itself to remember her by. Dinah and Ishmael had said the same thing—"It's just a ring"—and they were right, but it's also not *just* a ring. It was her mother's ring; she has clutched it like a talisman. She remembers her mother's smooth dark skin, the ring glowing on it like a bit of star...

Two black shoes appear in front of Tasha, just beyond her still-clenched fists. She doesn't look at them, or up at who they belong to. She stares at her empty hands.

"Ms. Lockett," says a voice above the shoes. "I need you."

Slowly she looks up. Dr. Rio is above her, gazing down over his glasses in the way that he does. The red crack in his stare is closed up, she notes impassively through her haze of sudden grief, no crazy peeking out today. Not right now.

"Ms. Lockett?" he says.

"You need me. For what." She can't quite manage courtesy at the moment.

"Well, not *you*," he says. He removes his spectacles and wipes at them with a corner of his cardigan sweater. It's not the reaper-black one he'd been wearing when she'd met him; it's heather gray. "A part of you."

Ishmael has stopped sweeping.

"What...like my arm?"

She's being a smartass, but a small bit of her is afraid that's exactly what he means, that he'll whip the sickle out of empty space and take her apart the way he had the woman in the apron.

"Not exactly," he says evenly. "Your badge."

"My what?"

"Your badge. Your employee badge for the Apiary."

Malakai has hopped down from the kitchen counter and come into the living room to listen. He hovers in the doorway like a small ghost. Z, too, is listening; she's swiveled the bottomless chair toward the green couch where Tasha slouches, watching Dr. Rio with alert eyes.

"Why do you need my Apiary badge?"

"To get into the Apiary, naturally."

"But why?"

"I have business to attend to."

"Business."

Rio puts his glasses back on and looks at Tasha with the sparrowhawk gaze. He's deciding whether or not he wants to reply.

"Business regarding the…*situation* of Chicago," he says quietly.

Z has stood up silently, floating toward the couch almost imperceptibly. Suddenly she is beside Tasha and sits down lightly.

"The situation of Chicago?" Z says. "What does that mean exactly?"

Rio turns away from the two of them on the couch and faces Ishmael, who has joined Malakai in the kitchen doorway.

"I would like you to come with me, Ishmael. And you too, Malakai, if you're willing."

Malakai's eyes light up and he nods eagerly. Ishmael looks troubled.

"What exactly do you need us to do, Dr. Rio?" he asks. "Is this dangerous?"

"It would be a short operation. With Ms. Lockett's badge, we could easily admit ourselves to the upper floors of the Apiary and complete the task at hand. It is very uncomplicated.

Regardless, there is only one way to help Chicago, and that method lies in the Apiary."

Which means yes, it is dangerous, Tasha thinks. So dangerous I don't want to tell you. But what the hell does he mean about helping Chicago?

"I'll go," says Malakai, his eyes wide. "I want to—"

Ishmael's hand is on his brother's shoulder and Tasha thinks she sees his bicep flex, squeezing hard. Malakai falls silent immediately.

"What do you need us to do?" Ishmael asks again. He is struggling, Tasha can see that. Still feeling that he *owes* Dr. Rio, she guesses.

"Carry my equipment. That's all. Once we get to the upper floors, you may leave."

"Leave?" says Z.

"If Ishmael so chooses," Rio says, not taking his eyes off Ishmael.

Everyone is silent. Behind Ishmael's eyes is a factory of turning wheels, scales and balances. He is studying Dr. Rio hard, his hand still gripping Malakai's shoulder. Rio stares back, and Tasha thinks she can sense his lava starting to swim.

"Unless you'd rather not help me," Rio says airily, his hand a claw. "Unless you'd rather get on the road to meet your mother. Tell her hello for me. She'll want to know I'm well, after I stayed behind with you and Malakai..."

It's the most transparent guilt tactic Tasha has ever seen—she'd expected more from a doctor, a bit more tact. She leans forward and opens her mouth in outrage, ready to call foul, but

Z puts her hand on Tasha's arm, stopping her.

Ishmael widens his eyes, no doubt shocked by the shamelessness of the ploy. Malakai looks up at his brother.

"Fine," says Ishmael. His hand drops from Malakai's shoulder. "We'll go. But Malakai stays with me. I know he helps you with your projects here, but if we go to the Apiary he stays with me. I need to keep him close."

Dr. Rio nods the smallest of nods and turns away. He moves to the hall by the stairs before pausing and turning back to Tasha, who sits on the couch seething.

"You and Azalea know the route, Ms. Lockett. You may take a car of your choosing, and backpacks, food. I can place you with a pod, or you can continue on to California as a pair if you prefer. Although I recommend the pod. Safety in numbers, you see. Every wolf needs a pack." He takes another step toward the hallway, then turns one more time. "Oh, and your badge, Ms. Lockett. You can give it to Ishmael. I doubt you'll be needing it. Thank you."

Then he's gone, leaving the four of them in the living room staring at one another.

CHAPTER 31

Malakai is at the stove in his mother's house, stirring the contents of the stockpot. It's only broth so far, but soon he will add canned potatoes, corn, carrots and tomatoes, all rinsed. Soup again, and one of the subs, divided. The sandwich doesn't smell as if it's gone bad, but Tasha is a little suspicious of it. She doesn't know why she and Z were silly enough to pack sandwiches with meat and cheese on them. The Perishable Combo, please, with chips. Thanks.

"Should I add the pepper now?" Malakai asks, peering into the pot.

"Some. Not a ton."

He adds the pepper and keeps stirring.

"You don't have to keep stirring it, Kai."

"I don't want it to burn."

"It's broth. It won't burn. Come play spades with us."

Malakai raps the spoon on the edge of the pot and comes to take the seat across from Z, who is studying her hand of cards. They have not discussed the events at Rio's house hours earlier. They gathered their things and walked home, avoiding one another's eyes and watching each other's backs.

"How do you play this again?"

"We want to win the tricks we bid," says Malakai, who is her partner. "We look at what we got dealt and we figure how many tricks we think we can win. You bid at least one trick. Spades are always trumps. It doesn't matter who wins the bid as long as we make the contract."

Z stares at the cards in her hands, then looks suspiciously at Malakai. After a long pause,

"What the hell did you just say to me?"

Malakai sighs patiently and begins to explain again, but Z waves the hand not holding the cards and throws them on the table.

"Look, forget it. Can't we just play Fish? Everybody knows how to play Fish."

"Fish!" cries Malakai, disgusted. "I haven't played Fish since I was like nine."

"Luckily that wasn't too long ago," Z jeers.

"Hey! I turn twelve in, like…how long, Ish? What's today?"

"Um…I don't know off the top of my head. We have the calendar, but I'd have to look, you know…"

This quiets them. Tasha feels a little like a goldfish. She's been swimming and swimming, but who knows how much ocean she's actually traveled through, if any? A fishbowl couldn't contain this amount of swimming, she hopes, yet a date will tell her exactly how many days she's been at sea.

The cheerful calendar, its bright, adorable pictures of kittens in antique watering cans with hats on their fuzzy heads—all of it makes her painfully aware of everything, everything close and heavy, a feeling like the sudden worry that she has forgotten to pay the light bill, or that she left the oven on. The house could be burned to the ground in the midst of such neglect. She clutches her empty finger whenever possible, the realization that she'd left the photograph of her parents on Foster rekindling her grief. And now she'll be separated from Ishmael and Malakai. From somewhere in her brain she hears her father's voice reciting a practically ancient poem he'd known well: *The art of losing isn't hard to master...*

Tasha shakes her head and leans forward and sweeps all the cards on the table toward her like poker chips. An eight of spades flips over. It irritates her. She flips it back over quickly, piling all the cards together and shuffling them awkwardly. The crisp *flap, flap* of them riffling together reminds her of a wheel spinning, the eternal ancestors of Vanna White flipping letters, their thighs carefully exposed.

"Who taught you to shuffle?" Ishmael is watching her.

"No one," she says, looking down at her hands. She flips over a card. Eight of spades again. Cheeky fucking thing.

"Well, that's obvious." He takes the cards from her, grinning.

"Oh, *thanks*," she laughs, relinquishing the deck. "Show us how it's done."

He shuffles the deck, placing the cards on the table and using his thumbs to riffle them together. It could be better. Impressive, but no expert.

"Oh, Christ, give me those," Z sighs.

She snatches the cards and does a fast, flourishy Hindu shuffle, followed by a snazzy display of hand-to-hand riffling. The sound of the cards is like the beating of birds' wings—small, hurrying birds.

"You don't even know how to play spades, but you can do that?" Malakai teases her.

"Fancy," says Ishmael, "trying to make me look bad."

"It wasn't hard," Z sniffs.

Ishmael shoots his hand out and smacks the bottom of the deck as she does a pass, the cards rippling, and they all go fluttering to the floor, the faces of queens and kings littering her feet. Z cries out, surprised, then laughs. Ishmael jumps up and goes to the stove.

"Oops, somebody better pick those up. I've got broth to stir."

"I'm not picking them up!" Z declares, crossing her arms. "You did it!"

In the end, Malakai picks up the strewn cards, handing sections of them to Tasha to stack neatly as he gathers them. Tasha turns over the top card in her stack, ready to fling the whole deck if it's the eight of spades. It's not. It's the Queen of Spades, smiling serenely off into the distance, clutching her flower, unaware of her crown.

Or is she? Maybe she's just as smug as that kiss-ass eight of spades. Maybe they're best friends and they chat it up all day in the box, pissing off all the other suits. Maybe the other queens are jealous bitches; maybe the Queen of Spades is lonely, and she can't talk to the jacks or kings because the other queens will spread rumors that she's a slut, so she has no choice but to talk to the eight, her own suit, someone who might understand. Probably the eight just listens. It doesn't have a mouth. Well, unless it has two mouths; two circular mouths. Tasha studies the eight.

"You're doing it again."

Tasha looks up. Z is looking at her, smiling.

"What are you thinking about?"

"Oh, just...nothing. I don't know."

"You're sure you didn't have a boyfriend before all this? You're always somewhere else."

Malakai's head pops up above the table from where he is rising with a last stray card to add to the deck.

"You have a boyfriend?" he asks, handing the card to Tasha. Jack of Diamonds. Let the rumors begin, Tasha thinks, as she puts the jack on top of the queen. Now they'll call her a gold-digger *and* a whore.

"No, I don't have a boyfriend. I wasn't even thinking about anything real. I just...my mind just wanders."

Ishmael is opening cans at the stove. There's a clang that makes them all jump.

"Are you okay? What happened?" Tasha asks him, half rising.

"I'm good. Can opener isn't."

He holds it up. One handle has broken off from the rest of it, leaving it useless.

"We can use mine," Tasha says. "Malakai, can you go up

and get it from my backpack upstairs?"

As Malakai disappears up the stairs, Ishmael drops the broken opener into the trash with a sigh.

"That was my grandma's," he says, closing the trashcan's lid. "I remember using it at her house when I was a kid. It's been around this whole time."

"You don't wanna keep it?" Z asks, looking pained.

"Nah, it's just a can opener. If I need that to remember her, then what kind of grandson am I?" he laughs.

Malakai appears, extending Tasha's backpack to her.

"You could have just brought the can opener," she says, taking the bag and opening its flap.

"My mom said to never go into a woman's purse," he says solemnly, looking almost fearful.

"What do you think you're going to find?" she laughs, fishing out the can opener. "A bomb? Or worse…tampons?"

Malakai laughs nervously, as if she's said some awful curse word. He takes the can opener from her and hands it to Ishmael, who's laughing freely.

"I'll try not to break it," Ishmael says, holding it up.

"You're no better at opening cans than you are shuffling cards," Z calls as she heads for the bathroom.

Tasha sets the backpack on the table; Malakai sits across from her, still wary. This is the dark spreading ring for him, she thinks, amused. The kid can be chased by crazy cannibals and be an apprentice to a borderline sinister doctor and not bat an eye, but tampons send him scurrying. Boys.

"So. I like your backpack," he ventures. "I meant to tell

you before."

"Oh yeah?"

"Yeah. It's nice. Where'd you get it?"

He reaches for the bag and pulls it closer to him. He does this quickly, like someone with cynophobia confronting their fear by petting the closest spaniel.

"From the Apiary when I worked there." she says, "I got an employee discount."

"Cool," he says, rubbing his thumbs over the Prada label. "Prada? That's like really nice or something, right?"

Tasha feels a little embarrassed. It was an obscenely expensive bag.

"Um…yeah. Yeah, it's pretty expensive. But the discount, you know, it helped."

Ishmael dumps a can of tomatoes into the broth and stirs.

"You could've paid your rent with that purse," he says over his shoulder.

"It's a *bag*," she corrects. "Not a purse."

Malakai looks skeptical.

"But you put stuff in it like a purse."

"Yeah, but it's a bag. I wear it on my back. It's a backpack."

"Aren't there cheaper backpacks?"

"I mean, yeah…but they're not Prada."

"What's so special about Prada?" Ishmael dumps in the diced potatoes.

She doesn't have an answer. In some lifetime far away she had a reason, an excuse, a justification. She had traveled in circles that needed no explanation. Now the words are like the mysterious fuzzy shapes floating in her eyeballs—the moment she flicks her eyes toward them they swim away, always out of sight.

"I don't know," she says slowly, "it was something to love, I guess."

Ishmael turns from the soup and regards her for a moment. She looks back. After a few seconds he turns back to the stove and resumes his stirring, saying nothing.

Malakai has opened the front pocket of the backpack and fishes out Tasha's Apiary ID, his effort to appear unaffected by the potential presence of the mystical tampon now bordering on trespassing.

"You looked so different before." He's holding the ID with both hands, studying it.

Tasha snatches it from him, cupping it against her chest.

"Yeah, well, it's not a recent picture."

"Dr. Rio didn't seem like he cared." Z has reentered the room and dries her hands on an embroidered towel hanging from the oven door.

"No, he didn't." Ishmael is adding corn now.

"He probably doesn't even need the badge for his little project," Z teases, sitting back down at the table and twirling the re-boxed pack of cards with her thumb. "He just thinks you're hot and wants a picture of you to carry around with him."

"I think he was married or something," Ishmael says irrelevantly.

They're dancing around the subject. It's a campfire they all want to sit by but are afraid of the flames.

"His little project," Tasha says, approaching the heat. "I wonder what the hell he wants in the Apiary."

"He's talked about it before," says Malakai. "I've heard him talk about the Apiary."

"You know a lot," Z says, no longer spinning the pack of cards. "What has he said?"

"Well, I've heard him say a couple things. He starts mumbling when he's looking over his papers and maps and stuff. And when he's had some of his whiskey."

"He has whiskey?" Ishmael says with interest.

"A little bit."

Tasha thinks that the whiskey probably explains a lot: the long speeches and the rolling gait. Sometimes he reminds her of Jack Sparrow. Captain Jack Sparrow.

"Okay, well, what have you heard him mumbling, smarty pants?"

Malakai smiles at Z. She has a way of speaking sometimes that has the effect of hands on one's ribcage. She talks with a tickle.

"He just talks about Cybranu mostly."

"He does that all the time," says Tasha. She's serious, shielding her funny bone from Z.

"Yeah. But when he's looking through his files and doing calculations, he kinda forgets I'm there. He says...stuff."

"Say it, Malakai," Ishmael commands, brandishing a ladle. "seriously. No games. Why does he want us to go to the Apiary? If I'm going in there with him—with you—I want to know what the hell we're doing."

"He says there's a cure."

It's the moment when the audience gasps and exclaims, the echo of "A cure?" rippling around the room; ladies fainting; the lonely dirge of a werewolf leaking in through a door everyone thought was locked but is actually swinging open. But no one says anything. Silence. Ishmael's ladle is dripping and Z's mind is turning so busily Tasha can see the thought-gears grinding and grinding. Malakai waits, a magician waiting for the onlookers to acknowledge the fantastically white dove he's just drawn from empty air. Tasha doesn't like to be the ganderer, tossing breadcrumbs to an obviously eager pup, but she can't help but feel her blood quicken. What if Dinah had been right? What if the guys in the soccer stadium had been right? Z? What if there is a massive off switch, hidden in the Apiary of all places, that needs to be flipped and everything would be fixed?

"A cure." She tries to stay calm, her heartbeat in her ears.

"Yeah." Malakai knows he has them. Z's eyes are strobe-like in the ferocity with which they flicker over his face, and Tasha knows her thoughts are the same as Z's. Ishmael's ladle is still dripping, the tomato base creating a red puddle on the old linoleum.

"A cure at the Apiary. Why the hell would a cure be at a shopping mall?"

"I don't know." Malakai shrugs. "I don't know everything. I just know he wants to go to the Apiary. He says he can finish it there."

"Finish it," repeats Tasha.

Finish what? Everything?

"It's a central location," Z says quietly, to herself. "I can't believe he waited 'til today to tell us," says Ishmael, shaking his head. "We were supposed to go to California tomorrow. My mom is already on her way."

"He didn't want to give you enough time to think about it to say no," Tasha says, not even trying to keep the edge out of her voice.

Ishmael looks a little sheepish.

"I have to help him, Tash," he says, and she flushes a little, hearing the shortened version of her name. No one calls her that. "He helped my mom, and Marcus. He took care of Malakai. I owe him."

"Yeah, yeah, I know," says Tasha, looking at the floor. Cure or not, the idea of going on to California without him, and Malakai too, pains her in a familiar way. It feels like spreading ash. She wonders what it's like to be ash, fluttering across a field. "And so does he."

"Even if there's a cure..." Ishmael begins, and then stops himself. "I mean, we had this plan. There's no Chips in California. Even with a cure, we can't really stay here. My mom."

"We're still going to go," says Z, speaking for Tasha. "No point in sticking around. Plus Tasha's sister is out there. West."

"But we were supposed to go together. The whole Apiary thing throws a wrench in the plan."

The "we" had crept into reality by the absence of

contradiction. Tasha has had her private moment of decision, and she suspects the others had done the same at some point. It had never been much of a question for Malakai and Ishmael, going: their mom was already on the road and they had to follow. Z had needed only the smallest bit of coaxing, plus a solid plan. The red lines she has seen drawn on maps, the ration plan she's been told about, might as well have been signatures on a dotted line. After being pried from the Web, Z didn't cling the way Tasha clung. Tasha had been a sloth on the bough, each of her three slothy toes coming away from the bark in the slowest possible motion. But once she'd dropped from the branch, she felt as if she'd hit the ground as something infinitely quicker.

"We're going with you," Tasha says suddenly.

Everyone looks at her and her face feels hot. She nods, affirming her own words. She decides to repeat them.

"We're coming with you. Right, Z?"

Z looks at her and smiles, and Tasha thinks of the way she had come to sit beside her on the couch when Rio was looming above. Wing-woman.

"Yeah, we're coming," says Z. "I didn't really fancy more quality time with the good doctor, but it is what it is. I hope he has a car with some room because he's not sitting on my lap."

Malakai is smiling but Ishmael frowns and rubs his cheek.

"Guys…," he starts.

"Nah," says Tasha, shaking her head. "It's like Rio said. Every wolf needs a pack. And I don't really consider myself a wolf—you know, maybe, like, a cat or something, or a panther.

But I have my pack."

Ishmael stares at her, still holding the ladle. Malakai looks from Tasha to his brother and back. The air in the kitchen is bread waiting to be cut. Z obliges them.

"Well," she says brightly, clapping her hands together and rubbing them. "That settles it. We're going to. If there's a cure, yay. We'll send a carrier pigeon to Ishmael's mom. If not, and Rio is a fucking walnut, then on to the West coast. Who's up for a shopping trip tomorrow? More Prada, Tasha? Hmm? Perhaps some for you, Ish? There's no shame in a man-purse."

Ishmael stares at Tasha a second longer, a smile forming, and then pretends to look stricken at Z's words.

"It's not a purse, *Azalea*. It's a *bag*."

Later, after the soup is eaten and the house is still, Tasha lies in bed with Z. She can't see the ceiling, but she knows it's there and her eyes grope for it.

"Are you awake?" Z's whisper is ragged like a cornhusk, a ghost's murmur, and Tasha's nape prickles. Z clears her throat and says again,

"Sorry. Are you awake?" Her voice is her own again, sweet like always. Like some kind of fruit.

"Yeah." Tasha wonders what her voice would be if it were a fruit. A kiwi? A pineapple perhaps, a sweet thing wrapped in rough.

"Thinking your weird secret thoughts?" It's Z's tickling voice and Tasha smiles in the dark.

"Something like that."

Z shifts a little in the bed, causing Tasha to shift. She thinks of the mattress as the earth, the depressions caused by their bodies sinking into tectonic plates, dragging trees and wildlife into the crack. The crack. Tasha thinks of Dr. Rio's face, the wild universe that opens up in it when he forgets himself.

"Do you really think there's a cure?" Tasha whispers the words. She hasn't whispered in a long time, not in the dark. She'd whispered to Ishmael on the front porch of Dr. Rio's house, but it was a voice made soft by necessity. Whispering now, in this dark room, the covers up to her neck, reminds her of being eight years old, Leona ten, sharing a room when relatives had come to visit and Tasha had to give up her bed. She had crossed ankles with her sister then, their hair combining on the pillow to make soft brown coils of moss. Whispering to Z isn't so different. The only thing that seems changed is the shade of the secret she whispers now versus the things she told her sister in the dark then.

Z breathes out in the stillness. Tasha thinks she must be emptying her lungs of lies.

"I don't know. I mean, there can't be, right? Why would he send us all to California if he knew there was a cure right here in Chicago?"

Tasha has considered this already.

"Yeah. But maybe the cure takes awhile to kick in or something. Maybe it doesn't happen right away. California is still the safest place to be. No Chips. No Cybranu. No MINK." She never thought she'd hear herself say these things.

"Yeah, maybe. Anything is possible. Obvi."

They lie quietly, letting this sink in. If anything is possible—and it all became possible, everything, the moment an eight-year-old boy in a Spongebob shirt got up with a crater stitching itself together on the back of his skull—then Tasha can walk to California, and take Z, and Malakai, and Ishmael, and find her sister and Morris and baby Amani—who must be walking by now, and Christ, probably talking—and keep them all in one room and never lose anyone again. If it's possible for a girl in a yellow dress to wilt while the roots of Chicago break up the earth and send everything in its garden spinning, then it's possible to cross an ocean of grass and arrive on the other side, gasping at oxygen cleaner than that which had darkened her parents' lungs.

"I guess we'll see." Z's voice comes like an echo called across a canyon. "The Apiary would be a good place to hide a back-up plan if something went wrong." She's half asleep, slipping into dreams while still imagining what the next day will reveal to her. Tasha can make out the arch of her nose in the dark, and below it her lips, parted to make way for deep, easy breaths. Tasha stares at her until her face blends with the mist of dreams, her breath joining a breeze over hilltops dotted with smiling dogs, and somewhere, her sister laughing.

CHAPTER 32

The smell is back, the unpleasant stench of cabbage and tar. Tasha wonders if it's Dr. Rio himself, but his goatee is neater than ever, and why would a man bother trimming his beard but not washing his body? It must be his car, which they all are crowded into; one of the first models of electric cars, a Chevrolet, modeled after the Nova. Ishmael is in the backseat with Z and Tasha, his legs bent like a grasshopper's. Malakai had offered to let him sit up front where there is more legroom, but Ishmael refused. Tasha has the feeling that he's pissed at Rio. She is too, of course. Sneaky, guilt-tripping bastard.

Tasha and her friends had shown up for the final caravan, helping pods pack last-minute items the way they had before. But when the cars had pulled off, the four of them—Tasha, Z, Ishmael and Malakai—remained on Rio's front lawn. He looked at the group of them and nodded once, but his hand had gone from claw to fist. He was angry, Tasha is sure, but she doesn't care. They'd all piled into the Chevy without speaking, their bags in the trunk, Ishmael in the backseat beside her, as far from Rio as possible.

Or maybe Ishmael just wanted to sit next to her. If so, mission accomplished. The backseat is too confined to allow much space, and she's acutely aware of the meeting of their shoulders and thighs. Do men have "thighs" the same way as women, she wonders. Men have legs. Women and chickens have thighs, or so men's tablets would have her believe. She makes a mental note to comment on a man's thighs the next chance she gets. She looks down at Ishmael's, so near in their denim. She could comment on his thighs. But it doesn't seem like good timing. Instead she looks at the axe that he holds on his lap— it's not the same one she had seen him use on the Minkers the first night. It's a bit shorter, but not quite a hatchet.

"What's with the smaller axe?" she says, nodding at it.

"Travel-sized," he says.

They've been driving down Lafayette and are now turning right onto Marquette, which will take them to State, Dr. Rio steering the Chevy easily around debris and the dead. The radio is on but turned down, and obviously there's no music or broadcasts to pick up, so the sound in the car is the muted buzz of static. Z had passed the iPod she took from the red Ferrari into the front seat, and Malakai had plugged it in, but somehow the play button was never pressed, so they ride in silence. The static sets Tasha's teeth on edge, but she's already asked for someone to crack a window to air out the stink of tar, so she doesn't want to be needy. Z drums her fingers on her knee and blows her hair out of her face.

"So…anybody wanna play I Spy?" she offers.

Dr. Rio smiles at her in the rearview mirror but it's not an encouraging smile. Tasha gets the feeling he has not even heard her. She looks at the compass sitting on Z's lap, which Rio had handed back to her when they pulled out of the garage. Apparently he had also noticed Z's intense study of the maps in his living room. He did not assign anyone the role of captain in their little pod; Tasha assumes this means he is the captain. Naturally.

Malakai doesn't bite at Z's suggestion either—perhaps they all know she wasn't serious. Everyone is anxious. The car's tires hum. They pass a church just before 58th Street—Greater Prayer Garden, it says—outside of which a group of eight or nine Minkers wearing violet choir robes gapes at the passing car. One of them shambles toward the road. Tasha cocks her finger gun—thumb and forefinger—at him and fires. Ishmael looks at her, surprised, then laughs. He blows on the barrel for her. Z nudges her almost imperceptibly.

"Why did some of them go downtown," she asks, referring to the march of the penguins she and Ishmael had witnessed the day before, "and some of them stay here?"

She doesn't really expect an answer.

"Different Chips received different programming," Rio says simply. And then, "You have your Apiary badge, I trust?" He's looking at Tasha through the rearview now. Tasha is tempted to tell him no, she'd left it, lost it, fed it to a Minker. Instead she just nods.

"Good."

"Why the Apiary? What makes it so special?"

He looks up at her in the rearview mirror, regarding her coldly.

"Cybranu's headquarters," he says coolly, returning his eyes to the road. "Cybranu's headquarters are on the 103rd floor of the Apiary. The restricted elevators are the only ones that will take us to the upper floors, and your badge will get us into those elevators."

Tasha absorbs this. On some level she had known that the Cybranu headquarters are in the Apiary—she remembers seeing the information on the plaque at the implantation center. It makes sense: the Batcave wasn't in the Wayne mansion. It was nearby, but separate and hidden.

It occurs to Tasha that no one, not even Malakai, had responded to Rio's revelation of their destination. They'd known they were going to the Apiary, but this adds a layer of intrigue to the mood inside the Chevrolet. Tasha wonders what their combination of thoughts would sound like if their heads were opened like the doors of a music hall: the ticking of many clocks, she thinks, or the rustling of snakes' coils against glass. They are all thinking along the same narrow trail, she knows: combining previous conversations about the possibility of a cure with this new information about headquarters and the 103rd floor. For all her skepticism and fragile hope, Tasha wonders if perhaps there is a cure after all, a vault concealed by a picture frame, or stowed behind a wall disguised as a bookshelf. They'll have to follow Sherlockian clues to reveal it, deciphering ancient texts or breaking codes. Or maybe it will be sitting on a table in an empty room, or behind easily-smashed glass in a sanitized laboratory. What does a cure look like, Tasha wonders. At first she imagines a vial filled with iridescent green fluid, but this hardly fits the kind of malady they're faced with curing, so she replaces the image in her mind with a simple metal briefcase. It could contain anything, be capable of anything.

They're passing the Harold Washington Library, deemed an historic site. It's dwarfed by the surrounding buildings, the green gargoyle owls perched on its rooftop peering down at the Chevy's progress. The owls seem very near, with the tops of the other buildings so much higher. The blue car could be a prehistoric mouse, scuttling along a jungle floor, in constant danger of being snapped up. Tasha looks out the window as they pass the empire of Columbia College, which takes up most of the Loop. She and Z had just driven through here a few days earlier, but she expects things to be changed somehow. Entering the Loop is like leaving the prairie for the redwood forest: the canopy stretches vastly above, the predators thicken.

"Two o'clock," says Malakai from the front seat, pointing.

He's played way too much Halo, Tasha thinks, and looks.

A squad of Minkers has emerged from the shadows of what used to be the Loop precinct of the Chicago Police Department. They swarm out onto the street and stumble toward the Chevrolet, which Tasha assumes they perceive as large blue prey. Like most Minkers, they're not quick, but they're not slow either. They amble gamely after the car, their hollow barks echoing in the vast emptiness of the city.

"Better step on it, Dr. Rio," says Malakai, only a little

nervous.

But Dr. Rio doesn't step on it. If anything, he slows down, the Minkers gaining on the Chevy's bumper. Tasha cranes her neck and peers up into the rearview mirror—she can see the distorted faces of the creatures as clear as day. One or two have pulled even with the back tires, and more are following. Their badges—CPD glowing gold—gleam through the windows.

"Um…Rio?"

The car moves ever slower. There are Minkers on all sides, some even at the front end of the Chevy, their leaden hands slapping against its steel. Tasha is in the middle of the backseat, Z and Ishmael both cringing inwards away from the windows as glaring predators snarl in at them. It's how the President must have felt, being driven through crowds of protestors—they're on all sides like dead-eyed fish crowding a submarine. Dr. Rio drives calmly onward, his hands at ten and two on the wheel, his back straight as a chauffeur's. This is his way of punishing us, Tasha thinks, for coming, for complicating his little plan.

The crowd of Minkers is around them. If the car stops, they'll find a way in, and there's no way the five of them will survive.

"Rio, what the *fuck*!" Tasha says. It's more like a shriek. The time for manners has well passed.

His eyes flicker up at her in the rearview as the window on Z's side of the car smashes, glass exploding inward as two pairs of hands grope inside, searching for anything. Z screams as one of the hands knots itself into her hair, the snatching fingers tightening into a fist and yanking her head out the window.

Tasha sees teeth, teeth, teeth, Dinah, Vette, the girl in the yellow dress...

Her knife is in her hand and she's slicing out the window, screaming curse words, some of them aimed at Dr. Rio. The tip of the knife skewers one of the Minkers' eyeballs like a shish-kabob before she begins using the blade like a saw on the wrist that holds Z's hair in its grip.

She must have severed a tendon, for the hand suddenly slackens and Z jerks her head back in the window, banging her skull on the edge in the process. Tasha is still cursing, Ishmael is shouting, Malakai hyperventilating—the noise is such that it takes a moment before Tasha realizes that the car is moving quickly again, speeding up State, leaving the group of Minker cops staggering around the street in their wake. Tasha is whimpering her curses now, her knife on the floor of the backseat as she holds Z's head with both hands.

"Are you okay? Are you okay?" she says it over and over. There's blood.

"I'm fine. I'm fine." Z is also on repeat. She says it twenty times.

And she is fine. She has a few cuts on her face and head from the broken glass of the window, and her hair needs a brush, but she hasn't been bitten or otherwise broken. Her eyes are wide and her hands are like spiders flitting over her body, checking to make sure she's in one piece. She is.

Malakai has fished a long cloth bandage from his backpack and passes it into the backseat, his face lined with tears that he struggles to dam up. Tasha starts to wrap it around Z's entire forehead, but it's kind of pointless, so instead she dabs at her friend's small wounds with edges of the white fabric. She sniffs. The car is silent.

"No need to rush," Dr. Rio says, a snake's voice, and no one responds. You don't scold a rabid Rottweiler with no leash.

Rio turns left onto Jackson, ignoring the one-way sign, and drives under the L tracks, which add to the feeling of a forest. The deeper one goes into the city, the less of the sky one can see. The Chevrolet passes the occasional Minker that moans after them if it sees the car in time, but the car doesn't slow again until they turn onto Dearborn, where Dr. Rio murmurs,

"We're near the Financial District. There'll be a lot of them over here, I think."

Them has changed irreversibly. *Them* will always mean *them*, now: Minkers. The rest have been transformed into "us." Tasha thinks of "us," of the running man on Broadway on the day she'd gone to the Post for Leona's letter. She doesn't think there are too many runners left this late in the game. There are hiders, and refugees. And then, of course, there are the dead. There are lots of the dead here, downtown where everyone was either on their way to work or already on the clock. Had the Change happened all at once, like a light switch turning on or off? She's never thought of this before. Perhaps it was more like a flood of water barreling down an alley, enveloping some before drowning others, bystanders watching in horror as block by block the waterless flood overtook the city. She shudders, looks straight ahead out the windshield in order to see less of the dead on the sidewalks around her.

Ahead, on Madison and Dearborn, a fire hydrant that had been burst by the collision of a Jeep somehow still gushes water. They're a block from the Apiary.

"We'll park here," Dr. Rio says, and stops the car very near the hydrant. "If any of our little friends come around while we're inside, they'll be less likely to notice our return if they've already grown accustomed to the movement and noise of the water." No one argues. They'd defied him by coming along on this mission—he'd only wanted Ishmael and Malakai—but in general, they obey. Somewhere between the last flash of the sickle and the most recent incident in the car with the police, Tasha and her friends had slipped on the inky puddle of fearful subservience and fallen into the role of voiceless minions: Muppets. Chess pieces, Dr. Rio pulls their strings, slides them along the alternating colors of squares. Tasha slips back into the groove of obedience that she'd moved beyond since the Change. Perhaps this is why they called him the Shepherd, she thinks with a trace of resentment. *Baaa.* She starts to put her backpack on, but Ishmael stops her.

"Leave that, just bring your knife. If we have to run, you want to be as light as possible. Don't forget your badge."

Tasha reluctantly removes the strap she had slipped over her shoulder. She's used to having the backpack, especially during times like this. She's run many blocks—hell, miles—with the green canvas bumping against her butt. To leave it now feels somehow ungrateful. She takes her Apiary badge out, then props the backpack up in the seat and slips out of the car after Ishmael onto the street.

Z has come around from the other side of the Chevy, her battered face drawn, and stands with them as Dr. Rio quietly opens the trunk. He motions to Malakai, who approaches him slowly, like a terrier who'd received a slap a moment before and is reluctant to put himself in the line of fire again so quickly. Together they hoist out three backpacks. Ishmael takes one.

"What's this?" Tasha points at the bags.

"Necessities, Ms. Lockett," Dr. Rio replies. "Now, the idea is getting in as quietly as possible. Move slowly if we're seen. No sudden movements. They're not too bright, but if one of them decides to come after us, they all will."

He's as animated as Tasha has ever seen him. He shoulders the backpack easily despite its obvious weight and looks at them, from face to face.

"Does everyone have what they need?"

He means weapons. Tasha carries the Wusthof, of course, Z her box cutter. Malakai has his trusty shovel, and Ishmael carries his axe—the huntsman. Dr. Rio carries nothing but the backpack—the sickle hasn't been seen since the garage—but Tasha assumes he has a trick or two up his sleeve if they run into trouble.

Rio nods, satisfied, and steps up onto the sidewalk, staying close to the buildings. They pass a Starbucks, which is predictably packed with bodies, both living and dead. Rio motions Malakai against the wall, and the whole group follows suit. Tasha cranes her neck, trying to be small. She can see the baristas, still behind the counters; one chewing on a customer who Tasha hopes has been dead for some time. Although they could be fresh—she can easily imagine some of the caffeine-addicts from Before sneaking out into the jungle, braving the hordes for a frappuccino. The Minkers don't notice Tasha and her group—they go on munching and swaying. Tasha still isn't sure if their noses are any more advanced than her own, but she hopes her fear isn't fragrant. Perhaps the smell of coffee beans will mute her scent. She wishes Dr. Rio had put on some deodorant before they got out of the car—god forbid they pick up his cabbagey, oily smell.

Rio pauses as they reach an alley, he and Malakai stretching their necks around the corner to check for Minkers. They're all dodging and dipping: ducking behind cars, flattening against walls, contorting their bodies to remain behind street signs and fire hydrants. It could be a game. Ishmael hangs back from Rio, staying close to Tasha. So does Z. If they've chosen her for a rock of strength, they've picked the wrong pebble: she feels as if she'll vomit at any moment, faint away like a corseted Southern belle. Tasha has done her share of creeping up and down city streets, but this feels different. There are so many of them: crouching in the Corner Bakery, wandering in circles inside boutiques. They seem preoccupied with the stores they've laid claim to, and none pay much attention to Tasha and the others. She wonders if the noise of the Chevy is what drew the few who had given chase, including the cops—otherwise she doesn't know how to account for the difference in behavior. Although not all of the shops' window-fronts are broken—maybe they can't see through the glass, maybe they can't hear them. She remembers the Minker from the Post. There was no glass to see through, but still she had not even acknowledged Tasha until Tasha had crossed the threshold of the building. She needs a course on the biology of the Minker: what can they see, smell, hear? What do they think? Maybe Rio was right about the different programming for different Chips. They're unpredictable. The stillness and grayness of downtown seeps into her and spreads through her veins like caffeine, leaving her jittery.

"Rio," she whispers, annoyed at having to address him. None of it makes sense, and it pisses her off. "Why aren't they looking at us? Why aren't they chasing us? They're all around; some of them must have seen us." She needs something more than lame references to random Cybranu programming.

"Yeah," says Z, her voice barely above a whisper. She still seems dazed after having her head yanked out the window by the Minkers. Tasha wishes she could have hidden her somewhere safe until after they left the Apiary.

"Programming," Dr. Rio says without looking back at them. "There are pawns and there are knights."

Tasha wants to throttle him—he and his predictable, cryptic bullshit. They pass a combined hair salon and coffee shop. This time, the woman inside—protective cape still around her shoulders, her tresses folded into squares of aluminum foil for dyeing—stares directly at Tasha. Blood wreathes her mouth, staining her skin all the way up to her under-eyes. She has been face-deep in someone's flesh. Tasha freezes, and so do Ishmael and Z, but there's nothing to hide from. The woman's gaze doesn't crinkle with annoyance the way Tasha knows a Minker on the attack's face is apt to do. The woman just stares, dizzy-eyed, her expression cloudy.

"It's like she ate everyone in the salon and then just stopped. I don't think she's even left the shop," Ishmael says, cautiously moving on, somewhat assured by the Minker's lack of reaction that she won't give chase.

But Tasha wants to *know*. Her experience with the Post worker was a trial, but one trial doesn't make a theory.

She steps quickly to the door of the salon, which isn't a door anymore on account of the body that smashed through it, a man who lies half-cannibalized in the frame.

"Tasha, come back—"

She feels Ishmael's fingers snatch at her arm but she's away from him, through the door, stepping into the territory of the woman with the hair foil.

It's as if Tasha pulled a trigger. As soon as she crosses the doorframe, the woman's eyes narrow and come together like two irate caterpillars crawling. A hoarse bark rises from her throat and she stumbles forward, arms outstretched, ready to embrace Tasha and chomp on her organs. But she's slow, and Tasha hops backward, outside the territory of the salon in a single step.

The woman draws up short, reined in by an invisible bridle. She's close enough to touch. She's still snarling. Tasha is sure the woman can see her. The eyes are those of a mongrel in a cage, waiting for curious fingers to wander between the bars. Tasha glances at Ishmael, whose mouth is open, saying nothing. Rio has just noticed Tasha's lag and is hurrying back from the next corner, his forehead furious. Tasha feels bold, defiant. She crosses the threshold of the salon once more, the Minker's snarl only just beginning before Tasha brings back her arm and hacks the neck with full force. The spark of the Chip dying is a pop of a lightbulb, the bark gurgling back down inside the volcanic throat of the Minker woman. There is no one else—the salon is empty except for its rows of mirrors, which Tasha doesn't need.

Then Dr. Rio is there and he has her by the shoulder, the fingers of his always-curling left hand digging into her body.

"That was very, very stupid," he says from between his teeth. "You might have lost your Apiary badge."

Tasha wrenches away.

"We're almost there," she says, going back out onto the street.

Continuing down the block, Tasha keeps Z nearby, who is still wordless. At least she's walking; she hasn't dropped her box cutter yet. Ishmael is on Tasha's other side. All three of them are behind Rio, who stalks ahead with Malakai.

"He's right about the programming," Ishmael murmurs.

Tasha glances at him but doesn't need to respond. She already knows.

"There are sweepers and there are keepers," he says, mostly to himself. "There are the ones that wander the streets and take out their targets, then there are the ones that have a keep to hold down. Un-fucking-believable."

She looks at him longer this time, until he looks back.

"Like soccer. Well, and video games," he says, unembarrassed. "Just saying."

They pass the new Chase building—the tallest tower in the city—and find themselves standing outside twelve revolving doors: the west entrance to the Apiary.

"Ready?" Dr. Rio's eyes are bright behind his dignified spectacles. Tasha's shoulder still glows with a dull pain where he had grabbed her in the salon. Now the crack is beginning to show at the edge of him, the lava starting to glow through his pupils. "Remember…slow. Quiet."

As they push through the revolving doors, Tasha breathes in the familiar, heavily perfumed air of the Apiary, mixed with the smell of marble and money. Its spell is strong, and she remembers the magic well. It's a smell that makes one lazy; it tricks the nose into whispering to the brain that they were never happy until they arrived here, and if the brain is smart, it will never let the body leave.

And the Apiary is busy.

All of Chicago seems to have gathered inside, milling and gaping, moving in and out of stores. The colossal center atrium rises as far as the eye can see, a long shaft with the endless spiral of stores wrapping around it, up and up. Somewhere up there is Level 51, where Tasha had stood so many times, looking down at the levels of ants, people moving from shop to shop, sitting on the REvolve, perched around the fountains, buzzing up and down on escalators. But the people are no longer ants. The buzz is no longer harmless chatter. The people are bees, ready to sting, and Tasha has entered the hive.

CHAPTER 33

"Quiet," Dr. Rio reminds them, his voice a hiss. "Slow."

Quiet. Slow. Quiet. Slow. The words are a chant in Tasha's mind. Her head swims. Through the haze of it she realizes Z is gripping her arm. Tasha winces but says nothing. She doesn't mind the pain: it's like a pointy anchor keeping her from floating up into the atrium. Returning to her old haven, she's forgotten why they've come here. This place can't be survived. She looks incredulously at Dr. Rio, who's holding his hand out to them, his eyes on fire. He's a shepherd on the mountain face, guiding his paralyzed goats over the precipice. Is he a good shepherd? Will he deliver them to a clovered meadow? Or does only the altar await?

To herself she says, *There might be a cure. There might be a cure*, and Tasha takes a step forward, which brings Z as well since she's still pinned to Tasha's arm like a jumper (mind changed) clinging to the window ledge. Across the first floor from them is the gargantuan sculpture of the bumblebee, constructed entirely of glass. From above, Tasha knows, it looks like an angel made of ice, spreading its wings. The Minkers cluster around it now like zealots at worship. Through the transparent wings, Tasha can see the warped shapes of the Minkers. Are they sweepers or keepers? Where does their territory begin? At the doors? Should she hesitate before entering? But then Tasha and her group are within the threshold. All it takes to trigger the swarm is drawing the Minkers' notice.

"Quiet," Tasha whispers to Z, and to herself, "slow."

Ishmael follows her. The hand that holds the axe is trembling.

Looking up, Tasha feels like Mowgli entering Monkey City. The din must have been worse in his jungle, but the silence here has its own clamor. Everywhere is the muted swish of the swarms, their feet wandering along the polished marble in aimless circles. Tasha can see them inside Tiffany's here on the ground floor. One woman slumps against the glass counter, bumping it over and over. From where they stand, it looks like she's humping the diamonds.

"Are they going to come for us?" Malachi wasn't privy to Ishmael and Tasha's conversation; nor had he seen the experiment with the salon Minker. Tasha wants to tell him, but it would require more words than she feels safe uttering in the present circumstances.

"They're at rest," Dr. Rio replies, hushed. "They've come here to be still, not to hunt."

"Home base," Ishmael mutters.

"In a manner of speaking. It *is* the Apiary, my dear boy,"

Rio says with a small smile. He is a secret-keeper. "They've followed the scent their maker left."

Tasha has no idea what this means. How would the Minkers know Cybranu's headquarters were in this building? They *couldn't* know. Unless something in the Chip itself is guiding them here. Tasha thinks of what Ishmael said about military technology, embedded in the implant. The Chip protected the body of the soldier—perhaps it also served to guide them back to base. But wouldn't that mean all the Minkers in the country would be grazing their way toward Chicago at this moment? Perhaps they are. Unless there are other bases. Other malls. The Mall of the America, she thinks suddenly, if it hadn't burned down…

They move in slow motion along the wall, like moon-men, or lazily floating sea urchins adrift on the ocean floor's current. Tasha's body feels anything but lazy: her muscles are loaded rifles. Although at this moment she'd rather be a sloth again, slow and safe in a tree someplace. A sloth with a shotgun.

Dr. Rio seems to know what he's doing. There's a bank of elevators fifty yards ahead by the first-floor fountain, a massive thing that took months to install. Tasha is all too familiar with the elevators: she had slouched into them morning after morning, standing zombie-like as they propelled her up to Level 51, sometimes getting stuck and forcing her to take the stairs—all fifty-one flights—as employees were prohibited from using the public elevators. The doors of the elevators are a mosaic of differently-colored metals, inlaid with retired pennies, thousands of Abrahams staring out accusingly at whoever stands before them.

Z steps on Tasha's heel. She's lagging behind, her nails lacerating Tasha's skin. Tasha is nearly dragging her to the elevators. Z has the look of a rabbit, too afraid to run, too afraid to stamp its feet to warn the warren. She's waiting for the hound to close its jaws around her soft throat. She's done so well after leaving the Web—now the fear is catching up.

"Z," Tasha whispers, "Z."

They're almost to the elevators. All around them and above them the Minkers are swaying. Tasha hasn't heard a single bark—that would mean they're ready to hunt. Still, the sound could come at any moment. Tasha is in the keep. They are all floating on their lily pads, the pond placid. But crocodiles don't doze for long.

"Tasha, if you please." Somewhere it's Dr. Rio's voice.

Tasha is staring at a woman standing by the fountain, gazing into its pool. It glitters with coins. She is fur-clad and middle-aged, no doubt one of Fetch Fetchers' regulars. The luxurious stole around her shoulders is probably the pelt of one or two or six micro lynxes she might have purchased. Perhaps it had been Tasha's sale, Tasha handing the cats over to their doom, her tongue tied. The woman stares at the pool, her mouth opening and closing. *People wish for stupid things*, Z had said in the Web. What did this woman wish for? What does she wish for now? Is there anything human left in her, tossing in coins for a faithful husband, a new car, a cure for cancer? Or is the only desire rattling around in that seething brain the need for blood and flesh?

"Tasha. Your badge." Dr. Rio, echoing.

They are standing in front of the elevators. Ishmael nudges her, accidentally touching her ass. Even in the present circumstances he stutters an apology. She ignores him and reaches into her back pocket for her Apiary ID. She presses her face into the waiting hand of Dr. Rio, his thumb covering her Cresty smile as he takes the badge and holds it in front of the entry pad.

The idea that it might not work sprouts and wilts at the same time. The light above the pad turns green. The doors slide open with a mechanical sigh.

"After you," says Dr. Rio, handing Tasha her badge. Malakai enters first. His face, Tasha sees as he steps into the elevator, is very stiff, his mouth a straight line, his eyebrows high. Her anger at Dr. Rio flares. She hates him for bringing Malakai, for seducing him into this scheme: he's just a kid, not even a teenager. He's afraid, of course, but maybe he doesn't even know enough to be as afraid as he should be. As afraid as Tasha is, and Z, and Ishmael. Dr. Rio is the only one who is cucumber-like in his cool. His lips are even turned up in the smallest of smiles.

Tasha tries to step into the elevator, but Z's weight pulls on her. Tasha turns. Z's feet are planted. She's staring at the woman in the fur stole, only ten yards away. She's close, it's true, but her back is to them. Like the other Minkers, she seems lost in her thoughts, sleepwalking.

"Z," Tasha whispers close to her ear. "Z. Come on. We're going up."

She feels as if she's talking to a child. Maybe Z hit her head harder than Tasha thought.

Ishmael grits his teeth and prods her.

"Z," he urges her, "Z, get in the elevator."

Z doesn't move. Her box cutter hangs limply at her side.

"We're going to die," she whispers, and Tasha prays Malakai doesn't hear.

"Tasha." It's Dr. Rio. He looks at Tasha with his eyebrows raised, his mouth disapproving. It's a father's face. It's the "Don't make me pull this car over" face. Tasha wants to punch him. She's about to snap at him when the elevator, kept too long from closing, verbalizes its displeasure in the form of a long, loud *ding*.

Slowly, the middle-aged woman by the fountain turns her head to look at them. Her gaze is cloudy. Even from this distance, Tasha can see the furrow between her brows deepening in annoyance. Her body turns heavily after her head. She's facing them now, her head cocked brokenly to the side, eyeballing them fiercely like an open-mouthed bird of prey.

"Z...," Tasha whispers, still staring at the woman, who stares back. Z doesn't budge.

Quiet, slow. Quiet, slow.

The Minker barks. It's a yap, a strangled sound. It rises into the fantastic atrium like the first notes of a ghoulish opera. The sound hangs for a moment, vibrating. Then the chorus begins, the calls of the hive pelting Tasha's group like bullets.

"AZALEA."

It's like a slap. Z starts, looks, then throws herself into the elevator, dragging Tasha and Ishmael in with her. She jabs her finger on the Door Close button just as the woman wearing the fur takes a step toward them. Others have rallied with her, a teenage boy wearing a Roosevelt University shirt among them. He is quicker, heading toward the elevators in a limping trot. The door between them closes slowly, not to be rushed after being held open so long. It dings with each inch, the Roosevelt kid barking with each step, quickening his pace.

On his t-shirt, Tasha can see the smaller print—"We Did It!" a graduation celebration—as the door closes in his face. Malakai, who has said nothing, breathes a heavy sigh. Z looks around at them.

"My bad."

Tasha and Ishmael shrug.

"Are you okay?" he asks, raising an eyebrow. Okay to proceed, Tasha assumes he means, but it's not like she has a choice at this point.

"I guess. I don't know, it's just that I saw those cops on State Street and I saw all the Minkers in their stores at their jobs and I felt like…like the world was over."

"Well, it is," says Tasha, trying to sound sarcastic but instead just sounding sad. Dr. Rio has pressed 103, and they're moving now, but here at the Apiary again, Tasha feels like she's standing still.

"I guess I meant I thought I was going to die. *My* world was over," Z insists. "Like this elevator was gonna take me to hell or something."

Tasha just stares at her.

"Or maybe I just hate shopping," Z adds, and they both smile.

The sides of the elevator are glass, like everything else in the Apiary. As they rise higher in the atrium, level by level, they can see each floor's flocks of Minkers swaying around the walkways, loitering inside stores, standing around entrances, gaping. Looking down, Tasha can see a bit of a crowd gathering where Roosevelt and the fur-wearer had sounded the alarm. Tasha thinks they will probably have dispersed by the time Dr. Rio has done whatever he's come to do. Or maybe, with the cure, the crowd will have gone from barking freaks to confused, sleepy Chicagoans, rubbing their heads and wondering where the time had gone and how this blood got in their teeth.

They pass Level 51 and Tasha peers out, hoping to catch a glimpse of Fetch Fetchers. She doesn't really know why—she hated that job. But it's like driving past the scene of a crime, the yard wrapped in yellow tape: one needs to see it, just to know. Her mother's ring is in there: it's like a beacon. She feels it pulling on her, tugging her sleeves.

"You can put your badge away, Tasha." Dr. Rio nods to her. "We don't need it to get in once we get to Cybranu. I have my own badge for that."

"You didn't turn it in?" Tasha can't help but mock.

He smiles, unperturbed.

"No. Although I'm sure they would have liked it back very much."

The elevator smells like cabbage and almonds. It *must* be

him, Tasha concedes. He's too dignified to smell like cabbage. It's really a shame, creepo or not.

The elevator sighs to a stop.

"You've reached the 103rd floor," the benign male voice of the elevator tells them. Its accent is British. If Tasha were alone she would thank it in a British accent.

Malakai steps out first, followed closely by Ishmael. They even look like brothers from behind: something about the shape of their heads. The fact that they both wear backpacks now adds to the similarity. They could be schoolboys waiting for the train on the first day of school.

Z steps out beside them, then Dr. Rio, then Tasha. The 103rd floor, like most of the upper floors, is much dimmer than the shopping floors of the Apiary, with many fewer windows. Wall sconces, painted a deep crimson, decorate the walls. Tasha feels as if she's been swallowed by a tall, long-throated beast; a beast that has also swallowed numerous lit matches to light the way for its prey. The beast has also conveniently posted a directory for directions to its various stomachs.

Dr. Rio approaches the directory. While he studies it, Ishmael turns to Z.

"Really though, are you okay?"

"Yeah, I'm okay now. I'm good. I was freaking out. I don't know. Sorry."

"Oh shit!" Tasha has never heard Malakai curse before, and she almost reprimands him before she sees the cause.

A man in a blue suit is approaching them, his swaying, lurching gait unmistakable. He lunges for Z, who sidesteps nimbly and slashes with her box cutter. It connects with his neck, but she hadn't clicked the blade out, so the neat strike accomplished nothing. Still, Tasha is pleased to see her acting like her old self. Tasha is stepping forward to take the guy out when Ishmael swings the axe. The force of the blow knocks the guy in the suit over, almost severing the head, but Ishmael has struck on the wrong side of the neck, and Tasha can see the light of the Chip flashing against the carpet as it attempts to knit the gaping hole back together.

Z bends down, her box cutter ready this time. She gives the guy a push, rolling him onto his other side and exposing the side of the neck with the Chip.

"Gross." Malakai says what they're all thinking at the sight of the reaching membranes stretching across the wound like tentacles. The guy is snapping his teeth at Z and flopping. She digs the box cutter into the flashing flesh and pops the Chip out like a battery from a remote. It sparks and lies dead. So does the man in the suit.

Dr. Rio turns back to them from the directory.

"It's down the…oh. Well. I'm glad I brought you four along," he chuckles.

Tasha can feel her mouth hanging open. Is he for real? She exchanges a look with Ishmael, who shakes his head once. When all this is over, he seems to say, I'm transferring to a different captain.

They follow Rio down the dim hallway, weapons at the ready. Tasha feels like the Secret Service, escorting the President through a haunted house filled with assassins. She also feels a bit like an assassin herself—Tasha Bourne—though who will be assassinated remains to be seen.

"Here we are," Dr. Rio says, as if they've just arrived at a tea party.

The door of the tea party is a fogged glass entranceway, large windows—equally opaque—on either side. The door bears a plaque, labeled simply "Cybranu" in small white letters. It could be a doctor's office, a therapist's.

Rio reaches into his pocket, withdrawing a wallet; the old-fashioned leather kind. When he opens it, Tasha glimpses several photographs in the little plastic protector most old folks' wallets have, and she cranes her neck to see, but he guards them as carefully as she had guarded her Apiary ID. He pulls a badge from the wallet and swipes it through what looks like a credit card terminal on the wall beside the door. It beeps softly and a female voice—also with a British accent; what's with the British accents—says "Welcome, doctor." A muted click sounds inside the door's steel casing and Dr. Rio gives it a push.

Tasha expects to find more suited guardians inside, but there is only a large, open room containing a long wooden conference table lined with chairs, and a whole wall of bookshelves. It looks more like a study or a library than a lab where billion-dollar schemes were hatched. Tasha blinks in the sudden brightness. The entire back wall of the room is a window, and on the 103rd floor they are above the mottled mammatus clouds that have dappled Chicago's skies for as long as Tasha has lived here. The brightness reminds her of Kentucky. Looking out over the clouds, she could be anywhere. She forgot it could be so bright.

Tasha moves toward the window in wonder, like a cub whose eyes have just opened, seeing the sun for the first time. Malakai joins her, his mouth slack.

"I've never seen it like this," he says, squinting a little. He was probably only two or three when the clouds rolled in, low and quilted. The two of them stand close to the window, peering down. From here the city looks like a collection of pillars rising out of mist. Some buildings aren't tall enough to break the mammatus layer, and Tasha can barely make out their rooftops below the gray surface. The Chase building rears its head brazen and blue a little to the west. Somewhere at its root, deep beneath the surface of the clouds, waits their Chevrolet, their little lifeboat on the titanic deck of Chicago.

Ishmael and Z have come to look too. Tasha hears the gentle *click*, *click* of Z toying with the box cutter. Up here it's easy to pretend nothing has happened. You could pretend you were already in heaven up here, Tasha thinks. An angel with bloody jeans and a kitchen knife, far removed from the horror below.

Tasha turns from the window and looks for Dr. Rio, who is uninterested in the view. He's standing at one of the great oak bookshelves that line the wall, his hands behind his back, gazing fixedly at something on the shelf ahead of him. Tasha's curiosity is more powerful than her dislike, and she moves closer to see.

"Greatest Medical Breakthrough," he says as she approaches. He's reading a large shining plaque, one of many that adorn the shelves in place of books. There are ornamental trophies too. One statue looks like an Oscar, but it's silver and the figure's hands are clasped above its head like a prizefighter.

Malakai has come to stand behind Tasha. The room is quiet except for the vague drone of wind outside the window.

"This is the room where they would sit and congratulate themselves," Dr. Rio says, running his finger over the inscription on the plaque. "Masters of the universe, peacekeepers, money-makers. People called us geniuses..." His voice trails off.

"They didn't know this would happen...," Z says from the window, looking sad and maternal. She has momentarily forgiven him for all his creepiness, not to mention the incident with the car, Tasha guesses.

Dr. Rio looks at her, and his face brims with something hot, something like hate.

"They knew. They knew, I knew. And now we're all dead. They sat in this room with their glasses of champagne and toasted to our destruction. They are rich, and we are dead."

The air in the room seems to be crackling. Tasha feels the hair on her arms rising as if someone has rubbed a balloon over her flesh.

"Where is the cure, Dr. Rio?" Ishmael has joined them by the bookshelves.

Dr. Rio's laugh, a harsh bark, startles Tasha. He does it again, seeming to enjoy the sound.

"It's on your back, dear boy," he says, returning his gaze to the plaques on the shelves.

Ishmael stares at him for a long moment, then slowly removes the backpack, setting it on the floor. Dr. Rio has walked away from them, still talking as he walks to the window. Tasha wonders at his speeches. Maybe he'd been drinking before they'd piled into the Chevy.

"I spent months preparing to leave the facility," he says, hands behind his back once more, "gathering supplies, reading files, mining information from my colleagues. I was worried from the beginning. I had a family. The whole thing didn't sit right with me. I compared some of the notes on the initial model to the schematics of the conclusive model, the one that went to production—the plans were different. Someone had approved tweaks that I'd never heard of. The Expiration Dependence Fuse caused the implant to protect the body, but override the brain. Neuroimaging on the test subjects showed the brain going dark…all except one tiny, obscure part in the center, deep inside the hypothalamus. The body was protected, but only that tiny part of the brain showed any activity. It was lit up like a Christmas tree."

He snaps his fingers several times in a row, staring out at the clouds.

"I tried to tell them. They bought me a car." He laughs. "A Porsche! I drove it all the way to Chicago from Arizona, with all my supplies in the backseat and trunk, all my findings. I hid with them in the church after I shoved the car into Lake Michigan. They found it, of course. But not me."

Ishmael has unzipped the backpack. He's peering inside with his eyebrows low.

"I didn't know *when* it would happen, but I knew it would happen." Rio's voice is rising. Malakai moves closer to his brother. "Certainly not on this scale. Certainly not all at once. I don't know how they managed that. My contacts in Minnesota handled their location, but I wasn't ready. I thought I could get here before it all happened."

Tasha has no idea what he's talking about. She's angry, but she's also afraid. The sane layer of the good doctor is peeling back. His body is trembling, his claw-hand a rock.

"There's an on switch, my dear," he says, still staring out at Chicago. "But no off switch. Not here. I should have been able to reach the base before the switch was flipped."

He's rambling, she thinks. Incoherent. Dr. Rio turns away from the window to face them, spreading his arms wide. His face is open, the magma free-flowing, hot and bright. He chuckles.

"Better late than never!"

"What is this?" Ishmael starts to reach into the backpack.

"Leave it," Dr. Rio snaps. "You don't need the cure."

"Dr. Rio," Malakai's voice is soft, "what are we doing here?"

"I'm here to cure Chicago. I only wish they were here to see it." He gestures at the empty conference table, its fifteen swivel chairs. Dr. Rio, always gesturing at empty chairs.

"Cure it?"

"Did you think there was a cure other than this?" Rio's voice becomes a howl, and they all cringe. "This perfect piece of sabotage? Did you think there was a pill? A button? A magic spell?"

They had. They all had.

"This won't be enough," Rio says. "It will only fry

communication for the Minker population in range of this base's signal. And there are so many other bases…"

"Bases?" Tasha snaps. "What are you talking about?"

"This is only one," Rio says, his eyes drilling into her. "We can't get them all, but if we take out the big ones—"

"Dr. Rio…what is in this fucking bag?" Ishmael interrupts. He has left the pack on the floor and is standing with both fists clenched.

"The same thing that's in mine." His voice is soft again. He unslings the backpack from his left shoulder. "And Malakai's. Put it down, Malakai, thank you."

Malakai does as he is told, staring at Dr. Rio with something between fear and bewilderment. Any reverence has been replaced by the feeling a blind man gets upon realizing that the tabby cat he's been petting is a tiger.

"Dr. Rio…?" Malakai doesn't ask the question, but Tasha knows what it is. *Are you there? Is that you?* The tabby cat is gone.

"Dr. Rio," Tasha says, trying to make her voice sound less like jelly and more like a stone. *I am not a pineapple*, she thinks. Be a stone. A stone fruit. "What…is in…these bags?"

He looks at her and blinks, the magma roiling.

"Why, bombs, of course. Bombs."

CHAPTER 34

Time stretches like taffy across a hot tongue; long, stringy, melting.

"Cyclonite, to be quite specific. I'm sorry for that terrible smell of cabbage. It's the odorizing taggant. They mix it in the explosives so the canines can smell it on bomb sweeps. No dogs here, of course." He chuckles.

"Where did you get it?" Z has moved instinctively toward the door. She is no longer the rabbit from the lobby. Her body is a wire snare, ready to spring.

"I have low friends in high places."

Tasha bets he does. His smile is the stoat, charming baby birds from the branch.

What do people in movies say when a lunatic is threatening to blow them all to hell? She's seen all the movies but the words sound hollow and brittle in her head. *You don't have to do this. There's another way. We can fix this. Step away from the bomb. Think of the children.* These are things people say.

Tasha wonders about the blast radius. How do bombs even work? This wasn't part of her Liberal Arts education. Will it take out the whole block? Just the building? The entire city? Judging by the size and heft of the backpacks there must be close to eighty pounds of—what did he say?—cyclonite, if not more. Even if it blows off only the top floors, will the building collapse? Will everyone in it and under it be crushed by pieces of the Apiary, by its burning, buzzing inhabitants?

"Are you going to do it now?" It's the only question she can think to ask. She's standing right beside one of the backpacks. Malakai, his eyes huge, is standing even nearer. They're toast.

"It's already been done. The detonators for all three packages are on a single timer. I started the timer the moment we entered this room."

Tasha doesn't know how Z crossed the room so quickly, but her claws are already in Tasha's arm and she's dragging her to the door. She's got a hold on Malakai too. She fumbles with the sleek metal door handle, her nails making faint screeching sounds before she finally yanks it open. Ishmael is right behind them.

"This won't fix everything, but it's a start! You have about seventeen minutes," Dr. Rio calls after them. "If you'd be so kind, take care of Arizona for me. Give my best to your sister."

He turns away. As the door shuts, Tasha sees him at the window, looking out onto the tops of the clouds. His shoulders are shaking, whether from sobs or laughter she'll never know.

There's another Minker in the hall, another business suit. Tasha sends him flying with a stunning kick to the stomach. If she isn't blown into a million pulpy pieces when all this is over, she thinks she'll see if any senseis survived the Change and learn a little karate.

Z slams her palm against the down button. Nothing happens.

"Badge! Badge!"

Tasha's fingers are fumbling; they are made of giant slabs of meat. She juggles the badge before finally pressing it against the entry pad. The elevator opens immediately, as it never left their floor. Malakai enters first, then Tasha, then Ishmael, then Z. Tasha drops the badge as she enters the elevator. As the steel doors whisper shut, she sees her make-upped face on the floor of the 103rd story of the Apiary. That's where it will stay.

It was only a short sprint from Cybranu to the elevator, but they're all panting. Their breaths are ragged, clashing with the inappropriately cheerful elevator music. Tasha hadn't noticed it on the way up, but now it's distracting. She thinks she recognizes it as an instrumental of an old Nicki Minaj song she recognizes from a Classics stream online: *Boy you got my heartbeat running away, beating like a drum and it's coming your way.*

The numbers on the panel go down and down: 100, 99, 98. Damn this tall building to hell, Tasha thinks. Her blood is vibrating. Z is hopping up and down.

"Fuckfuckfuckfuckfuckfuck," she chants.

Malakai has dropped his shovel somewhere along the way. Tasha looks at her hand, still clutching the Wusthof. She's so accustomed to carrying it now that it feels like an extension of her arm, much like her Glass used to be. Where is her Glass?

Somewhere in a building on Foster. Is that place even on this planet?

Ishmael is staring hard at the shrinking numbers. 85, 84, 83. His fist is clenched and pressed against his forehead. Malakai just shakes. 80, 79…

"Is he really going to blow us up?" The boy is twelve.

This is the part Tasha is no good at: the comforting, the reassuring. But she opens her mouth, and the words come:

"He's going to blow up the building, yes. And himself. But we're not going to be here when he does it."

It's an answer Leona would have given to her daughter. Amani. Will Amani know about bombs?

65, 64, 63. Tasha thinks of the seconds on Rio's detonator, also counting down, shrinking and shrinking into an enormous, explosive zero. 58. The elevator stops. "You have reached the 58th floor," the inexplicably British voice says.

Z slams her palm on 1.

"We want one, we want one," she begs.

The doors stay open. Minkers mill about everywhere. Only one has stopped to look. Z presses Door Close one too many times—there is the fatal *ding*. It echoes like a siren through the muted mall. Barking follows, the herds alerted and annoyed. Malakai moans.

"Come on," Tasha grabs someone's arm, and rushes out into the atrium. "The employee elevator is always fucking up. We'll take the public. Come on."

Z is beside her. Ishmael has hold of his brother's hand and he's out too, waiting to follow.

Tasha rushes toward the atrium and the bank of twelve public elevators. They pass Hermes. It's filled with staring, swaying shoppers, the slow heads turning to focus on Tasha and the others as they whiz by.

"Go!"

They are running, sometimes sliding on the waxed marble like polar bears on ice. A Minker appears in front of them, his mouth wide. Behind him are two more, two men in fine slacks and jackets. Tasha shoves the man, bowling him over; he knocks down one of the others on his way to the floor. Z shoulders the remaining guy aside, and Tasha thinks she sees Ishmael take out one of the guy's legs with the axe.

They make it to the elevator, Tasha pressing the down buttons on one side, Z pressing the ones on the other side. It's like playing Whack-a-Mole. Where will the first one pop up? Meanwhile, their flurry of activity has attracted the crowds of Level 58, and a herd appears from the east side of the building, at least fifteen deep. Too many for their four. The elevators' buttons are still illuminated; from somewhere in the building they're approaching unhurriedly. An employee of L'Occitane is the first to reach them. She grabs for Malakai's sleeve. Malakai punches her, but with little effect. No elevator.

"Stairs," Tasha yells. "Stairs!"

"Stairs?" Z gapes.

"Not the whole way. Just to an emptier floor. Come on, come *on*!"

The stairway is only a few yards away. They ram into the push door. Ishmael makes sure it shuts behind them before they stampede downward. They plummet down two levels, taking stairs two at a time. They come out on Level 56 and run directly into Apiary security, a muscle-bound guy with a crew cut who begins barking almost immediately. He has a posse, a woman wearing diamonds, plus nine or ten others nearby. Tasha wheels away from them and shoves Z, who was on her heels, back into the stairwell.

"Wrong floor," she says. More stairs. The sound of their feet ricochets around the narrow stairwell like war drums. They fly down a couple more flights, until Tasha sees the familiar Level 51 sign at the door. Why not.

"Come on!" She's breathing hard. How many minutes have passed? Is Dr. Rio still looking out the window? Or has he changed his mind? Or did he leave the detonator and start racing down another staircase in some other part of the building? Or maybe he jumped. She imagines Dr. Rio as a comet falling from the sky. *The* comet. The Big Bang. The end of the dinosaurs.

They burst through the door onto Level 51. There are Minkers, but they're on the other side of the atrium. The REvolve cruises by on its track, carrying a woman and her teenage daughter, disintegrating sandwiches half eaten on the REvolve's counter in front of them. They couldn't figure out how to get off, apparently. They look weak and only emit pale yelping sounds as Tasha and her group pass.

Twenty yards from the elevator bank. There's the Prada store, across from Fetch Fetchers. She feels some red string in her stomach give a tug, like she's being gutted. Something in her is hungry. An invisible hand squeezes her throat. She slows, thinking of her backpack down in the Chevy. When she'd bought the bag, they'd had a canvas clutch to match it, another thousand dollars. She couldn't swing it at the time. But now...

But then there's Fetch Fetchers and thoughts of Prada dissolve into expensive dust. She slows. She looks down at her hand, holding the knife. Her empty finger. Inside the store, so near, is her mother's ring. Tasha had left the photograph of her mother, her parents, on Foster, and if this building blows with her inside, she'll never touch her mother, her family again. She needs that ring. She wheels toward Fetch Fetchers.

"What? What is it?" Z looks around, thinking there must be a swarm of the Minkers blocking their next route.

Tasha doesn't explain. She dashes into the store.

"What the *fuck* are you doing!" Z doesn't raise her voice—it's too risky—but she follows Tasha into the store cursing her. "Is there an elevator in here? *What?*"

Tasha ignores her and runs to the back of the store, hearing Malakai ask Ishmael,

"What are we doing? Where is she going?"

There's the back room. It's where Marla sat while Mrs. Kerry attacked Tasha and took her mother's ring. It's where Cara had carried the ring as Tasha was escorted out, her face burning. If she can just get into that room... She may not know the combination of the safe, but if she can just get into that room, she'll just take the whole goddamn thing.

"Doing a little *shopping* are we, Tasha?" Z tries to grab her but Tasha shakes her off and dashes toward the tall black door of the back room. She almost reaches it, her hand reaching out to turn the handle, when a huge weight slams against her body from the side, sending her sprawling to the floor.

Barking. Two kinds of barking. One is the low, miserable keen of an animal in pain, and one is the high, perturbed yelp of a Minker. The source of the first, Tasha sees as she topples to the floor, is a brown poodle on a grooming table, held in place by the table's leash, miraculously still alive but very thin and barely standing. The source of the second is Cara, who is scrabbling on top of Tasha like a blonde whirlwind, scratching and snapping and snarling. Cara's hair is an electric spur made brighter by the store's glaring fluorescent light. The poodle is crying, it must be nearly dead—dehydrated and starving and now scared witless by the nearness of the beast that is Cara.

Tasha's former supervisor's mouth is wide open, showing her perfectly bleached teeth, her pink tongue lashing out from between them like a serpent's. Tasha has managed to force her palm against the woman's forehead, preventing Cara's jaws from closing on her earlobe. Tasha squirms. She'll be damned if she'll walk around for the rest of her life with a chunk out of her ear because of the likes of this jackass. Tasha struggles but her opponent is heavy—Cara would have hated that.

Tasha can hear Z and Ishmael running to her rescue, but she throws her weight to the side, sending Cara's body crashing to the floor. She scrabbles up, grabbing Cara by the front of her violet blouse. Cara is snapping and spitting. Her eyes are exactly as they were before the Chip—dull, angry, senseless. Only the smirk is gone. Her still-manicured hand swings up for Tasha's throat, slapping against her face. Tasha gasps. This feels a little too much like a catfight. This is not a catfight.

Using all her strength, she grips the ruffle on Cara's blouse and slams the blonde head against the tile floor. She hears the dull crack, but doesn't wait for the black tentacles to weave the hated skull back together. She gropes for the Wusthof—it's too far.

"Tasha!"

Z kicks Tasha's knife, which had spun across the floor when Cara tackled her. The Wusthof skids across the tile, wedging itself under Cara's back. Tasha has to lean closer to Cara to reach it, her former boss's stale breath fogging her oxygen in the brief moment before her fingers clutch the knife's handle. She clenches it, draws it back, then slams its point into Cara's neck. The knife is six inches long and she buries it up to the hilt, through the resistance of ligaments, feeling it catching against bone, skewering the Chip. Bullseye. The tip of the knife is visible under Cara's left ear—the blade has gone straight through her neck.

It's over quickly. Cara jerks and then goes limp, blood pooling around her head, dyeing the platinum hair crimson. Tasha, panting, stands stiffly, stumbling a little. She looks down at Cara, whose arms are outstretched like a fallen magpie, her glimmering hands, fingers covered in rings, the neck still swathed in silver. One ring catches her eye: the simple silver band, the small black stone, a soft-cornered square.

It's her mother's.

In another time, she would have been polite and slipped

it over the knuckle. Not now. The Wusthof comes down one more time on Cara's hand, a clean efficient chop. The ring is freed. Tasha wipes the blood on Cara's shirt and slides the ring back onto her hand, which had missed it.

Back on earth, she hears barking—not the Minkers, but the real, animal sound of the poodle on the table. A flash of the antique gates, the acre of chain link pens, her mother's hands buried in Borzoi. There is living to do. Tasha turns away from Cara's bloody corpse.

"Malakai, grab the dog."

In a moment they're at the elevators on Level 51, all the buttons pressed and illuminated. The waiting isn't as long as on 58—during their flight down the stairs and the brief stop in Fetch Fetchers, the elevators had made it to Level 58, and now only had to move seven floors to reach them.

When the door opens, they crowd on, Malakai clutching the poodle wrapped in the sheet from the grooming table. It makes soft growling sounds, probably from delirium. Its fur is shaved into the classic Continental clip, the gorgeous Afro-esque style on its head and the well-rounded puffs around its chest, feet, and tail. The rest of the coat is shorn close. The dog looks ridiculous, but grand. She's probably a year old, Tasha estimates, brought in by her owner and then left in the store when everything went bad. She'd sat on the table since Day 1, tied in the noose, beautiful but dying.

40, 39, 38. Tasha hopes the seconds on Dr. Rio's detonator are much higher.

CHAPTER 35

One.

"You have reached the first floor," the voice intones, and the door opens to reveal a welcoming party. Twenty or thirty Minkers milling outside the elevator. A hundred on the other side of the ground floor. None of them have seen the group in the elevator yet.

"Out," Tasha whispers, "out before the elevator rings."

They creep out beneath the atrium. The poodle has quieted; perhaps she's dead, Tasha thinks. Malakai clutches the dog like a lifejacket.

"Quiet, slow," she sighs. "Quiet. And slow."

She realizes Ishmael is holding her hand. His other hand grips the axe. Z is clutching her box cutter, poised. Tasha thinks of Vette. *Why do you get the big knife?* Yellow sundresses flutter like butterflies. What was her name? Dinah. No, not Dinah. Dinah is in her tomb on Foster. The faces of the dead flit through her brain like blowing leaves, her parents among them.

The herd is very near, making sounds in their throats, shuffling in their dazed circles. Over by the employee elevators the crowd with the Roosevelt kid has dispersed, as Tasha had thought it might. She'd gone into that elevator with Rio and the others, half-believing she floated upward toward a cure. The people around her are not cured. The way they are is the way they will be, which will be nothing before too long, she thinks. Dr. Rio will scorch the earth, destroy the mother ship, leaving a burning patch of city street. It's a hell of a suicide note, Tasha must admit.

"Slow," Tasha says.

"We can't afford slow," Z says out of the corner of her mouth as they inch across to the exit. "The whole building is gonna blow."

Tasha hears a whimper. Whether it's Malakai or the poodle, she's not sure. She wants to pet them both. The possibility of getting out of the Apiary alive shrivels from grape to raisin. They are surrounded; the first floor of the mall packed with the wasps of Chicago, at ease only until someone sneezes, or trips, or drops a pin. Tasha and her group can pick their way—quiet, slow—through the crowds of them, but at that pace, they will still be in the honeycomb when the bombs blow. Their corpses will mingle with the Chipped—archaeologists will find Tasha's fossilized teeth and assume that her incisors, too, tore at the flesh of her fellow citizens: history will mark her down as one of a million cannibals. She will have died in the Apiary. She looks across the ground floor at the massive crystal bee. Even now it has power: the swarms of the Minkers are drawn to it like a beacon. She can almost hear it buzzing—or maybe that's just her head. *Please don't let me die in the Apiary*, she thinks, her palm sweating against Ishmael's, *I hated it here. At least let me die on the street.* She sees Z. Her face is bright with sweat, her eyes large and wild. Malakai clutches the poodle.

A redheaded man in a suit—suits, always suits; the black and navy and gray of lawyers, stockbrokers, owners of various things—looks straight at them. Tasha sees his brow furrow. Any second he is going to open his mouth and bring the hordes down upon them. There's no way they can make it to the exit in time if he does. His lips begin to part. This is it. The end. Tasha grips her knife. She'll take some of them with her before she's brought down, either by beasts or bomb. Maybe Malakai and the dog can escape. Ishmael has seen the redhead too—he half-raises the axe.

Light from an Apiary sconce catches the edge of the hatchet like the first crescent of the sun over the horizon. It rises before Tasha's eyes, as slow and bright as anything. Her hand reaching out for it might be her hand; she's not sure, she feels only her palm releasing Ishmael's grip and the vague new weight of the axe in her grasp. Across the universe is the Queen bee and in that moment, Tasha wants nothing but to crush it, to pulverize its crystal influence and destroy its drones. She draws back her arm like a catapult, then swings it forward and releases the axe. She is Zeus with a thunderbolt, but with better hair—and better aim. The earth's rotation slows. The axe arcs over the heads of the swarms of Minkers and with a sound like an enormous chandelier shattering, smashes into the glass bumblebee. The statue nearly disintegrates, all the delicate facets and design and craftsmanship exploding into splinters, the sound of infinite mirrors destroyed.

The herds of Minkers immediately flock to the sound, their faces crumpling in irritation. They slouch over to the destroyed bee, bumping against each other, the sound of their feet on the marble like a body bag dragged on ice.

"Go," Ishmael hisses. "Go!"

A few Minkers remain between the refugees and the doors. Ishmael gives two his shoulder, sending them flying. Z is slicing like a madwoman. Malakai runs, still clutching the poodle, holding her head against his chest to keep it from jolting. Z is out front, Tasha bringing up the rear as they enter the revolving doors that turn silently to let them pass.

458 OLIVIA A. COLE

CHAPTER 36

Tasha can see the Chevrolet, parked beside the rushing water of the blood red hydrant on the gray street. The clouds have not changed: dappled sunlight breaks through in places, striping the pavement with gold. Some Minkers on the street turn to watch the group stampede by and eventually give delayed chase. Sweepers. One is a Driver, alike in build to the one Tasha killed on her way to the Post an eternity ago. She screams threats at him, almost laughing, drunk with the adrenaline of escape, drunk with elation. The sound of the bee shattering echoes in her ears.

Z runs alongside Tasha, hair flying like a tail behind her. She scoops up a bottle off the ground as she passes it, and throws it at the Driver. It bounces off his head.

"Did you play softball?" Tasha calls, leaping over a prone form on the sidewalk.

"What?"

"Softball!"

"Baseball!" Z yells back.

Almost to the car.

"Keys!" Tasha cries. "Keys!"

"He left them in the car!" It's Ishmael, close.

"Shotgun!" shouts Z.

There's someone between Tasha and the Chevrolet—yet another man in a suit. So many men in suits: he is nothing. He wants to stop her; he wants to keep her here to die. She has already decided she will not die. Her knife, the knife that she has carried since the beginning of all this, which she still clutches now in the end, is a streak, silver among gray. Her knuckles, clutching the blade, still bear the marks of Dinah's door. Across the car she sees Z, rushing past stumbling wolves, their mouths wide. Tasha will not lose her. This time, she will not be stopped.

Ishmael opens the back door and throws his brother and the poodle into the backseat. Both yelp. So the dog's alive. Well. Tasha leaps behind the wheel and Z clambers in across from her. All doors slam. Tasha feels strangely like a soccer mom—*Everyone buckle up*, she thinks brightly. A guy with broken sunglasses paws at Z's door, barking.

"I believe he wants in," Z says with a country club accent, waving at him through the glass.

Tasha stomps on the gas. The Chevy slams into a Minker whose face Tasha doesn't see. The creature rises and staggers after the car, but the wheels are devouring Clark Street, the gray buildings rushing, blurred like watercolor. The stores have no names, the mannequins have no faces, the advertisements have no power. It's been a long time since Tasha has put her foot on the gas, and gone. She goes.

"Music," she commands.

Z turns on the iPod from the Ferrari and CeeLo's voice comes through the speakers once more as the car screeches left onto Washington. Tasha doesn't brake. Whatever is behind her, she will beat.

When things start splitting at the seams and now...

"Louder!"

She's going west, and west, and west. She's running stop signs and disobeying traffic orders and doesn't use her turn signal; she doesn't yield. The blocks blur past in gales of brick and steel. Wells. Franklin. Red lights are just decoration.

The whole thing's tumbling down...

They go west. Behind them is the rumble of the Apiary ballooning, shaking the street; but she doesn't look back, even as the steering wheel trembles under her palms. The sky turns white, then orange, the mammatus clouds on fire. Somewhere Dr. Rio is sinking into the explosion, already ash. Tasha doesn't wonder what it's like to be ash—she is infinitely hotter. The Chevy hums. Ahead is road, and sky, a far-off coast with a vegetable garden, a sister with answers to questions. In the garden is a little girl kneeling, the half-moons of her fingernails beautifully black with soil from the ground. Tasha reaches for her roots.

"Wind," she orders, and she's rolling down her window again, letting in the titan, its colorless hand finding its way into her curls and turning them into waving grass. She is among the grass, leaping across the prairie toward California in lithe animal bounds. This feels like a cure.

In Kentucky the trees will be in full blossom. Are there dogwoods in California? Rosebuds? Goldenrod? The world is pouring through the window, bringing in the smell of moving air. Tasha puts her arm out into what's rushing past, what she's rushing toward. She drives over the rust-colored Chicago River, an army of eyes watching her: empty eyes above gaping, barking mouths; hesitant, shambling steps trailing, too slow, after the progress of the Chevrolet, before sparking and freezing in place, their programming interrupted by the immense ball of fire that their hive has become. Listless, they glare after the blue machine, oblivious to what it carries. To them, Tasha is just a copper something, a streak of noise: her arm out the window is an extension of a rocket—wildfire, untouchable.

ACKNOWLEDGMENTS

Love, light, and gratitude to my father—the editor and sounding board—and my mother, the reader. Kwame Alexander, for giving me a chance and opening doors. Tracy Chiles McGhee and Danielle Koon for their endless enthusiasm. Cia White, for her belief. Stuart Cipinko, for his love. Victoria Spencer, Sam Gauss and Aaron Mitchell Reese for their eyes and their skills. Dana Lynch and Caralanay Cameron for their devotion. Jane Intrieri, for her glee. Jovan Leslie Monique and Jessica Estelle Huggins for their genius. Sean Carter, for his support. Beverly Bond (and BLACK GIRLS ROCK!) for her work and her spirit. Alexis Garrett Stodghill, and her mother LaBrenda Garrett-Nelson, for being wonderwomen. Band of Horses and CeeLo for drilling "No One's Gonna Love You" into my soul. Nicki Minaj, for "Super Bass." Madonna, for "Material Girl." Octavia Butler, Alice Walker, Toni Morrison, and Margaret Atwood for giving me dreams. My Indiegogo donors and Twitter followers, whose belief has made this book possible.

And finally, for Ms. Hart in eighth grade, who said, "You can't." And for Ms. Thomas, who said, "You can."

CPSIA information can be obtained at www.ICGtesting.com
Printed in the USA
LVOW06s2135160415

434958LV00004B/243/P